Welcome to
New York...
for luxur...
sin... ...crets.

PARK AVENUE
Scandals

Three fabulous high-society stories set in the
heart of Manhattan from Maureen Child,
Laura Wright and Jennifer Lewis!

Park Avenue Collection

March 2012   April 2012

PARK AVENUE
Scandals

MAUREEN   LAURA   JENNIFER
CHILD   WRIGHT   LEWIS

Mills & Boon, an imprint of Harlequin (UK) Limited, Eton House, 18-24 Paradise Road, Richmond, Surrey TW9 1SR

PARK AVENUE SCANDALS
© Harlequin Enterprises II B.V./S.à.r.l. 2012

High-Society Secret Pregnancy © Harlequin Books S.A. 2008
Front Page Engagement © Harlequin Books S.A. 2008
Prince of Midtown © Harlequin Books S.A. 2008

Special thanks and acknowledgement to Maureen Child, Laura Wright and Jennifer Lewis for their contribution to the PARK AVENUE SCANDALS series.

ISBN: 978 0 263 89750 0

010-0312

Harlequin (UK) policy is to use papers that are natural, renewable and recyclable products and made from wood grown in sustainable forests. The logging and manufacturing processes conform to the legal environmental regulations of the country of origin.

Printed and bound in Spain
by Blackprint CPI, Barcelona

HIGH-SOCIETY SECRET PREGNANCY

MAUREEN CHILD

Maureen Child is a California native who loves to travel. Every chance they get, she and her husband are taking off on another research trip. The author of more than sixty books, Maureen loves a happy ending and still swears that she has the best job in the world. She lives in Southern California with her husband, two children and a golden retriever with delusions of grandeur.

Dear Reader,

Whenever I'm invited to take part in a continuity series for Desire™, I'm eager to jump in. This time was no different.

The chance to work with authors such as Laura Wright, Jennifer Lewis, Barbara Dunlop, Emilie Rose and Anna DePalo was not only exciting, but fun. The e-mails fly fast and furiously between the continuity authors as we work out details for our stories. We talk about everything, from the kind of clothing one character wears to the way another one speaks.

Six women, each of us with different writing styles, working together to build a world we hope will tempt you, the reader, into entering the lives of the people who live at 721 Park Avenue.

In my story, you'll meet Max Rolland, a self-made billionaire who can't seem to get Julia Prentice out of his mind. One night of passion has sent these two on a path neither of them expected—but one that neither will turn away from.

So join us on Park Avenue, in the heart of New York, one of the world's most exciting cities. Surround yourself with the passion and lies and deceptions and, finally, surrender to the love.

Happy reading!

Maureen

For Alicia Estrada, as she starts off on the
biggest adventure there is. You've been a joy all
of your life, Alicia, now I wish you that same joy
in the brand-new world you're entering.

One

"Damn it, Julia, answer the phone," the deep voice growled into the answering machine, and Julia Prentice winced when the caller hung up a moment later.

She'd been dodging Max Rolland's phone calls for two months now, and he still hadn't given up and gone away. Not that he was stalker material or anything, Julia reassured herself. No, he was just an angry male looking for an explanation of why she'd been refusing his calls since their one amazingly sexy night together.

The reason was simple, of course. She hadn't been able to think of a way to tell him she was pregnant.

"Whoa." Julia's roommate and best friend, Amanda Crawford, event planner extraordinaire, walked out of her bedroom. "He sounds royally pissed off."

"I know." Julia sighed. And she could even admit that Max had a right to be angry. She would have been, too, if she'd been in his shoes.

Amanda crossed to her, gave her a brief hug, then said, "You've got to tell him about the baby."

Sounded good in theory, Julia thought as she dropped into the closest chair. She looked up at her friend and saw the gleam of sympathy in Amanda's gray eyes. "How'm I supposed to do that?"

"Just say the words." Amanda sat down, making their gazes level, which she pretty much had to do all the time. Julia was short, at five feet two inches, and Amanda was eight inches taller. Built like a model, Amanda had short, choppy blond hair, beautiful gray eyes and a loyal heart.

"Easier said than done," Julia said, smoothing one hand over the sharp crease in her pale green linen slacks.

"You can't wait forever, honey," Amanda told her. "Sooner or later, you're going to show."

"Believe me," Julia said, "I know. But that night I spent with him was an aberration. I mean, things got all hot and heavy so quickly I didn't have time to think and then the deed was done and Max was telling me he wasn't interested in anything more than a mutually satisfying sexual relationship."

"Idiot," Amanda offered.

"Thanks for that." Julia smiled. "Anyway it seemed that that was the end of it, you know? Max wanted uncomplicated sex and I wanted more."

"Of course you did."

She dropped her head against the chair back and stared up at the ceiling. "Now everything's different and I don't know what to do."

"Yeah, you do. You just don't want to do it."

"I suppose." Blowing out a breath, Julia said, "He deserves to know about the baby."

"Yep."

"Fine. I'll tell him tomorrow." Decision made, Julia actually felt a little better about things. After all, it wasn't as if she was going to ask Max to be involved in his child's life or even to pay child support. She could afford to raise her baby on her own. So, all she had to do was break the news of impending fatherhood, then let him off the proverbial hook.

"Why have I been obsessing about this?"

"Because you're you," Amanda said, smiling. She gave her friend's knee a pat. "You overthink everything, honey. You always have."

"Well," Julia said wryly, "don't I sound exciting?"

Amanda laughed. "Hey, don't knock it. You overthink and I act on impulse too often. We've all got our crosses to bear."

"True. And it's time to pick up yet another cross." Julia pushed herself out of the chair, then tugged at the hem of her white linen blouse. "I've got to go to that residents' meeting."

"Lucky you."

"I really wish you could come with me," she said.

"Not me, thanks," Amanda countered. "I'm meeting

a friend for dinner, where I will have a lot more fun than you will tonight. Personally, I'm glad to be only a roommate, with no place at those meetings. I'd be bored to tears in ten minutes."

Sighing, Julia said, "Five."

Julia checked the slim, gold watch on her wrist and just barely managed to stifle a sigh. The residents' meeting in Vivian Vannick-Smythe's apartment hadn't even started, and already she was wishing she could leave.

She felt as though her insides were twisted into taut knots that kept getting tighter. Despite that talk with Amanda, the tension gripping Julia felt as tight as ever. She could hardly remember ever feeling calm.

This whole thing with Max had gone on too long. She was just going to have to face him and tell him the truth. Tomorrow, she promised herself, she would call him, arrange to meet and drop the bombshell in his lap. Then, duty done, she could go back to her life secure in the knowledge that a man so dead set on avoiding any kind of emotional attachment wouldn't be bothering her again.

"You look bored," a soft, female voice said from beside her.

Julia smiled in spite of her thoughts and shifted a glance at Carrie Gray. The woman's green eyes were hidden behind a pair of too-practical glasses, and her long, chestnut hair was pulled into a high ponytail at the back of her head. She wore jeans, a T-shirt and sandals that showed off a dark red pedicure. Carrie was officially a house sitter for Prince Sebastian Stone in 12B, but she was also a talented—though currently unemployed—graphic designer and a good friend.

"Not bored," Julia whispered, leaning toward her, "just preoccupied."

Hard to keep your mind on what was happening in the apartment building when it was already focused on something far more profound. Far more personal.

"Anything I can do to help?" Carrie asked.

"No," Julia said, knowing no one but her could handle the situation she found herself in. Still, she added, "Thanks, anyway. I appreciate it. Anything new with you?"

"Just working. Or trying to," Carrie grumbled.

Julia smiled, instantly understanding. "Still getting Trent's drop-bys?"

Carrie rolled her eyes, pushed her glasses up to rest on top of her head and said, "It's a nightmare, Julia. Trent Tanford must spend every spare minute trolling for women, because they're trooping down my hall night and day."

Trent was a notorious playboy. A favorite of the gossip rags, he had a new woman every other day. And those women continually made their way to 721 Park Avenue.

"I swear," Carrie said in a hiss, "these women are all looks, no brains. They keep ringing my doorbell, thinking it's Trent's place. What? They can't tell the difference between 12B and 12C? Tanford doesn't date women who can read?"

Chuckling, Julia just patted her friend's hand and turned back to listen to the rest of the meeting. At least half listen. Hard to concentrate on resident business when her mind was racing in circles.

Julia glanced around 12A, the Vannick-Smythe apartment, and as always, couldn't find an ounce of taste in the place. Everything was cluttered to the point of chaos. It was so gaudy, Julia's eyes hurt just looking around. So expensively tacky, it was impossible to get comfortable there. Which was probably a good thing. Since no one was at ease in the apartment, these terminally boring meetings never seemed to last long.

Just at that moment, Vivian Vannick-Smythe herself, the de facto leader of the residents' group—since no one else wanted the job—clapped her hands to get everyone's attention. In her early sixties, Vivian had been Botoxed within an inch of her life and as a result, her thin face was nearly expressionless. Only her icy blue eyes snapped with emotion. She was very thin, dressed in stylish, classic lines, had short, elegantly cut silver hair and the bearing of a military officer.

Thankfully, tonight Vivian had corralled her two shih tzus, Louis and Neiman, in her bedroom. But even the heavy door separating the twin terrors from the meeting didn't completely muffle their frantic barks and yips.

"I thought," Vivian said once she had everyone's attention, "that before we actually begin the meeting, we should have a moment or two of silence for Marie Endicott. I didn't know her well myself, but she was, however briefly, one of us."

Obediently, the restive room fell silent as each of them supposedly focused on the death only the week before of a young woman who'd lived in the building. Julia and Marie had been no more than nodding acquaintances, but Marie's death in a fall from the roof had made quite an impact on everyone's lives.

Newspaper and television reporters had been staking out the front of the building for days, harassing residents, scrambling for quotes or, better yet, some hint of scandal.

"Do we have any more information on what exactly happened to her?" Tessa Banks, a slender blonde, was the first to speak after the silence.

"Good question." Elizabeth Wellington spoke up next. "I actually heard a few of the reporters saying that the police think Marie might have been *pushed* off the roof."

"That's just speculation," Vivian assured her.

"Did anyone find a suicide note?" Carrie called out.

"Not that I know of," Vivian said, frowning a little. "The police aren't very forthcoming with information, after all. But I'm sure none of us has anything to worry about and soon enough, this tragedy will be supplanted in the news with something else."

True enough, Julia thought as her fellow residents continued to talk and wonder aloud about Marie Endicott. In a few days, the reporters would give up and go away and life would go back to the ordinary.

Well, not for her.

"I have a couple of other announcements," Vivian proclaimed, her voice easily carrying over the rumble of mixed conversations. "I'm sorry to tell you all that Senator and Mrs. Kendrick, long-time residents of 721, have moved. I'm not sure where, but I believe they're somewhere in the city. Their co-op is officially for sale."

More rumbling, more conversations, and Julia slid her glance across the small crowd gathered there. Gage Lattimer sat off by himself, no surprise there. A tall, gorgeous man, he rarely attended these meetings and when he did, as now, he didn't mingle.

Reed Wellington, Elizabeth's husband, sat beside her, but his scowl made it clear he wasn't happy to be there. Elizabeth, too, was holding herself stiffly, her body language declaring she'd rather be anywhere else.

Tessa was tapping the toe of her shoe against the carpet, and even Carrie, beside Julia, was beginning to fidget. Julia, though, had been trained by enough nannies to know how to sit still when you wanted to move. To know how to keep your emotions from showing on your face. To know how to bottle up everything inside, where no one could see.

"Just one more item now, if you'll all give me your attention," Vivian said. "I have an announcement. It's very exciting and I'm sure you'll all be as pleased as I was to hear." She waited until everyone was focused on her before she gave them all a tight smile and said, "I've recently been informed that our home—721 Park Avenue—is up for Historical Landmark status!" She waited for a buzz of excitement that didn't come, then frowning, said, "I think we should have a party to celebrate!"

As Vivian moved around the room, talking to people, trying to spur enthusiasm for her celebration, Julia edged her way to the door. Carrie had already beaten her to a quick exit, but Julia would be right behind her.

"Julia, dear."

Darn it.

Stopping dead, Julia turned, a practiced smile on her face as she greeted Vivian. "Hello, Vivian. The meeting went well."

"Yes, it did, didn't it?" The older woman tried to smile, but her too-tight skin simply wouldn't allow it. "Forgive me if I'm intruding, my dear, but you look troubled. Is everything all right?"

Surprised, since Vivian wasn't exactly known for her interest in anyone besides herself, Julia took a moment or two to answer. "Thanks for asking, Vivian," she said, forcing a smile she didn't feel, "but I'm fine. Just tired, I think. And this sad situation with Marie Endicott has us all feeling the strain."

"Oh, of course." Vivian nodded and her sleek, silver bob hardly moved. "Poor woman. I can't imagine what must have been on her mind to jump from the roof like that."

"So you do think it was a suicide?" Julia asked.

"Surely you do, too." Vivian looked at her for a long moment. "Why, anything else would be too distressing. Imagine. If she were pushed off the roof, one of *us* might have done it."

Julia hadn't really thought of it in those terms, but now that the seed had been planted, she shivered as she sent another glance at the people who lived in her building. Vivian was right. Julia couldn't imagine any of them being a killer. Marie must have jumped. Which was a sad thought. How horrible to feel so alone, so miserable, that your only solution was to end your life.

"Now I've upset you," Vivian said. "Not my intention at all."

She had, but Julia didn't want to talk about this anymore, so she smiled more brightly and said, "Not at all. But I am tired. So if you'll excuse me…"

"Certainly," Vivian said, already looking past Julia to someone else in the room. "You go on home now."

Julia did just that, hurrying her steps down the hall to the elevator. When the doors opened and she stepped inside, she simply stared at the row of floor numbers. She should go home, she knew, but Amanda was out somewhere and Julia didn't really want to sit by herself and listen to silence. So on impulse, she hit the ground-floor button and leaned back against the elevator wall as the doors swished shut and the motor engaged.

Tugging her small designer bag higher on her shoulder, Julia stepped out of the elevator at the lobby and quickly crossed the ivory marble floor. A scattering of Oriental rugs in bright colors softened the cool sterility of the marble and muted the click of her heeled sandals as she walked.

The muted blue walls of the lobby were dotted with expensive artwork and mirrors with elegantly ornate, gold-rimmed frames. The ceiling was high, and a massive crystal chandelier hung in the center of the lobby almost directly over the doorman's wide, mahogany desk. The front doors of 721 were heavy glass framed in gleaming mahogany, allowing passersby a glimpse into the elite, elegant lifestyle of the residents at 721 Park Avenue. Julia had always felt that somehow she and the others who lived there were something like specimens in a zoo. They stayed in their gilded cage while people could stop and stare in at lifestyles so different from their own.

Lots of happy thoughts tonight, she told herself.

"Hello, Henry," Julia said as the doorman stepped out from behind his desk to hustle to the front door. Around five-foot-seven, Henry Brown had shoulders that stooped a little, brown hair, soft brown eyes and an obsequious manner.

"Hello, Ms. Prentice. Nice to see you, as always."

Julia waited as he opened the door for her and held it. It would have been easier to do it herself, of course, but Henry was very territorial about his duties. "Thanks, Henry."

He was still smiling as she stepped out onto the crowded street. Summer nights in New York were hot and sticky, and tonight was no exception. Traffic hummed, car horns blasted and an angry cabbie shouted at the pedestrians ignoring the light and streaming across the street in front of him. A halfhearted wind blew down Park Avenue and carried the scent of hot dogs from the corner street vendor's wagon.

Julia smiled, tucked her bag more tightly beneath her left arm and moved into the steady flow of foot traffic.

After sitting still for so long, it felt good to be outside, part of the rush and bustle of the city. She was alone and yet part of a crowd. And there was a certain kind of comfort in that. Here, she was only another body hurrying along the sidewalk. Here, no one expected anything of her. No one was watching her. No one paid any attention to her at all, as long as she kept moving and didn't slow down the flow.

She didn't have far to go, just a few steps to the Park Café on the corner. Most of the residents of 721 treated the little coffee bar as if it were an extension of the apartment building.

Tonight, though, Julia was hoping she wouldn't run into anyone she knew. She didn't actually feel up to chitchat, but neither did she want to go back to her own apartment and be by herself. She walked into the café and was greeted by the combined scents of cinnamon, chocolate and coffee. The hiss of the espresso machine played counterpoint to the brisk conversations and bursts of laughter.

There were wide, overstuffed chairs, oversize sofas and low-slung tables. Ferns bristled from copper baskets hanging from the ceiling, and soft jazz drifted through the overhead speakers. Julia placed her order, then carried her iced decaf drink and scone with her to a chair in the far corner. Then she curled up in the shadows and tried to be inconspicuous.

Max Rolland's apartment was just down the street from the Park Café and he usually hit the trendy but convenient coffee spot at least once a day. In fact, it was here he'd first met Julia Prentice, the woman currently making him crazy.

He remembered his first sight of her with absolute clarity. She'd looked so cool and elegant, sitting by herself in a corner chair, watching the comings and goings of the other patrons as if she were in a box seat at a Broadway play. Her shoulder-length white-blond hair had been loose in soft waves around her face and her big blue eyes had fixed on him the moment he'd walked in.

He'd felt her gaze right down to his bones, and when he met it for the first time, he'd experienced a blood-burning heat that had forced him to approach her. Ordinarily, he wouldn't have. He wasn't looking for the kind of relationship a woman like her no doubt wanted and needed. But that night, it was as if all bets had been off.

They'd met, talked, touched and ended up in his bed for a night like nothing he'd ever had before. Just the memory of her body moving beneath his, the soft silk of her skin, had him hard and aching again.

Which only fed the anger that continued to churn just beneath the surface of his steely calm. Damn the woman. Why wasn't she answering his phone calls? And why the *hell* was he acting like some moonstruck teenager with his hormones in overdrive?

He picked up his black coffee—no designer crapola for him—and turned to leave. That's when he felt it. The power of her gaze. Just like that first night two months ago.

Max shifted his gaze to the chair in the far corner and there, in the shadows, he found her.

Again.

And this time, he'd be damned if she'd get away so easily.

Two

Max headed across the crowded room, his gaze locked with Julia's. He could feel the tension building in her body even at a distance. Her studied, cool mask of indifference wavered a little as his gaze bored into hers, and he actually enjoyed knowing that he made her nervous.

What man wouldn't?

"Julia," he said, his voice pitched low enough that no one but her would hear him.

"Hello, Max."

One black eyebrow lifted. "Hello? That's it? You've been avoiding me for two months and all you've got to say is hello?"

She broke off a tiny crumb of her scone, lifted it to

her lips and chewed as though it were a chunk of beef jerky. Stalling. He recognized the signs. Well, she could delay their talk as long as she wanted. But now that he had her cornered, so to speak, she wasn't leaving until she explained why the hell she'd been so studiously avoiding him.

He pulled the chair beside hers even closer, then sat down, perching on the edge of the seat. Cradling his coffee between his palms, he stared at her, drinking in the sight of her. So many nights he'd woken up with her image drifting through his brain. He'd told himself he was remembering her wrong. No woman was that beautiful. No woman could be such a stirring mix of both innocence and sensuality. He'd almost believed his own lies.

Until now.

Now that night with her came roaring back, and he saw that not only was she everything his memory had promised, she was more. The scent of her alone— something light and floral—was enough to tempt him. As if he needed tempting.

"I was going to call you tomorrow," she was saying, and Max jerked himself back to the present. With a woman like Julia Prentice, it only made sense to pay attention.

"Were you." It wasn't a question. More of a statement, letting her know that he didn't believe her for a minute.

She got the message, he told himself, since a slight flush colored her cheeks and had her dropping her gaze from his.

"Look, I know you're angry," she said, and a muscle in his jaw twitched.

"I passed angry a few weeks ago."

Lifting her gaze to his again, she shook her head and said, "We had one night together, Max. And when it was over, you made it perfectly clear you were only interested in a sexual relationship."

He laughed shortly and glanced around, reassuring himself that no one was listening in. No one was. Everyone here was huddled with a group of friends or sitting solitarily behind a computer, the glow of the screen reflecting off their faces. He and Julia might as well have been on an island.

"Didn't seem to bother you that night," he pointed out.

"No, it didn't," she admitted, and licked her dry lips. An action that had his body tightening to the point of actual pain. "We both got carried away that night. We did things that—"

"I've been thinking about ever since," he interrupted her neatly, making sure she was filled with the memories that had been haunting him.

He'd never been with a woman so controlled on the outside and so completely uninhibited in bed. She'd gotten to him despite his efforts to maintain a safe emotional distance. And that infuriated him. Max wasn't stupid. He knew her type.

The society woman. Born into a world he'd only entered through years of hard work and persistence. She carried a pedigree and he was a junkyard dog. Their differences were blatant. But in bed, those differences hadn't mattered. In those hours together, they'd each found something in the other that they hadn't anywhere else.

At least, that was what he'd thought.

"Believe me when I say," she told him, "that I've been thinking about that night, too. A lot."

"Then why are you dodging me? We both enjoyed ourselves."

"Oh, yes…"

"So what's keeping us from having another night— and more—just like it?"

Her gaze drilled into his. "I'm pregnant."

If she'd pulled the chair he was sitting on out from under him, Max couldn't have been more stunned. Her simple statement. Her clear, steady gaze. The grim determination of her mouth. All made it clear she was telling the truth. But if she expected him to believe that it was *his* baby, she was in for a big surprise.

He knew something she didn't and because of that one fact, he had no doubt at all that he wasn't the father of her child.

"Congratulations," he said tightly, pausing for a sip of his coffee. The hot, strong liquid burned his tongue and he hissed in a breath, relishing the sting because it gave him something else to concentrate on besides the unspoken plea in her eyes. "Who's the lucky father?"

She drew her head back, widened her eyes and said, "You are, of course."

He laughed. Loud enough that several heads whipped around to see what was so damn funny. Then Max sent a glare around the room and the interested parties found something else to look at. When he turned his gaze back to Julia's, he sneered at her. "Nice try, but I'm not buying it."

"What?" She looked as stunned as he felt. "Why would I lie?"

"An interesting question," Max said, and set his coffee cup down on a nearby table. He silently congratulated himself on the calm he was maintaining. No one would know by looking at him that anger had spiked—along with a sense of disappointment. Taking her drink from her, he set it down, too, then muttered, "Get your purse. We're leaving."

"I don't want to leave."

"And if I was taking a vote, that would matter to me," he said. Then, standing, he simply stared down at her until she grumbled, grabbed her bag and stood up. Taking her elbow in a firm grip, Max steered her out of the coffee shop and onto Park Avenue.

"Where are we going?" Her much shorter legs were scrambling to keep up with his long strides, but Max didn't slow down.

He was a force of nature that somehow managed to part the throngs crowding New York City's sidewalks. People stepped aside, moved out of his way, as he tugged Julia along in his wake. This was not a conversation he was going to hold in public. If she wanted to play out this game, then she'd damn well do it at his place, where he could tell her exactly what he thought of blue-blooded women trying to run scams.

His apartment building was much newer than hers. Less old money, more nouveau riche billionaire. It suited Max down to the ground. The doorman scurried to open the chrome-and-glass door, then stepped back as Max half dragged Julia across the gleaming tile floor to the bank of elevators.

He stabbed one of the buttons and while he waited, he looked down at her. "Not another word until we're alone."

Stiffly, she nodded, wrenched her elbow from his grasp and quietly smoothed her long, blond hair back from her face. He glanced at her reflection in the elevator door, and in spite of everything else he was feeling, desire reached up and grabbed hold of the base of his throat.

The elevator arrived with quiet speed, and once they were inside, Max entered his key card and punched the button for the building's only penthouse. He lived at the top of the world, with a view that told him every time he walked into the room that he'd made it. He was on top. All of his hard work had paid off big-time, and he'd made his dreams come true.

At the penthouse, the elevator opened into his foyer. Six thousand square feet of living space, and Max, but for the housekeeper who came in daily and then left every evening, lived alone now. He'd tried marriage once.

He'd learned his lesson the hard way.

And part of that lesson was the reason he knew Julia was lying to him.

Stepping aside, he waved a hand, inviting Julia inside. She'd been here before, of course, their one and only night together. But damned if he hadn't been seeing the ghost of her every day since.

"You want a drink?" he asked, walking past her and down two short steps into the living room. "Oh, wait. You're pregnant."

She didn't respond to his goading, merely asking, "Do you have any water?"

He ground his teeth together, poured himself a stiff shot of scotch, then retrieved a bottle of water from the wet-bar fridge. Then he walked to where she stood beside a bank of floor-to-ceiling windows that displayed an incredible view of the city and the harbor beyond.

"I'd forgotten what a nice place this is," she said, taking the water and unscrewing the cap.

He liked it. It was decorated in a clearly masculine style, now that Camille was gone. A few rugs dotted the wide-planked oak floor. Oversize sofas and chairs were gathered in conversational knots that were rarely used. A fireplace hugged one wall and on either side were bookcases, stuffed with everything from fiction to the classics.

"It's a lovely view," she said.

"Yeah. You mentioned that the last time you were here." He sipped at his scotch and let the fiery liquid burn away the cold inside.

She glanced up at him. "I don't know why you insisted on coming here, Max. I've already told you what I had to say."

"Uh-huh. You're pregnant with my baby."

"That's right."

"That's a lie."

Her hand tightened on the water bottle. "Why would I lie to you about this?"

"Just what I want to know," he murmured. "The night we were together, you told me you'd just come off a long-term relationship. So what I'm wondering is, why are you trying to palm off his baby as mine?"

Julia took another drink of her water. "Terry and I hadn't been...together like that in months before we broke up. We were friends."

"Too civilized for hot, sweaty sex, was he? No wonder you came to me for a night of good times."

"That's not how it was," Julia argued, wondering how this had gone so wrong. She hadn't expected him to be happy about a surprise pregnancy, but she also hadn't expected him to deny being the father. "When we met, you and I, there was a connection. I felt it. You must have, too. A sort of—"

"Don't make it into something it wasn't, sweetheart," Max said, reaching out to stroke the side of her face with his fingertips. "We were both needy that night and it was the best damn sex I've ever had. But it wasn't more than that. There was no dulcet choir of angels singing. It was what it was."

Julia felt as though he'd slapped her. *This* was

exactly why she was no good at meaningless relationships. She needed to feel a bond with a man before she climbed into his bed. And that night, as swept away as she was by Max's pure magnetism, she'd convinced herself that that bond was there. Could she possibly have been *that* wrong? Could she have mistaken pure sexual hunger for something else?

God, she was an idiot.

"So whatever you're up to, it won't work," he said softly. Leaning to one side, he set his scotch down on a glass-topped table, then straightened up and moved in closer. "I don't know what you're after, Julia, but I know what we both need. What we both want."

"No, you're wrong," she said as he pulled her into the circle of his arms. He held her tightly to him until there was no mistaking the hard, rigid length of him pressed against her. And just like that, her insides turned to liquid fire.

An ache blossomed between her legs, and the throbbing need she remembered from that one night with him began drumming in her veins.

His hands moved up and down her spine, sending tingling shards of awareness through her body, and suddenly, Julia couldn't breathe. Couldn't concentrate. Couldn't quite remember that she'd planned to say no to him. To tell him that sex without commitment wasn't what she was looking for.

He leaned down, brushed his mouth over hers and then pulled back, his gaze meeting hers, his eyes shining with a raw hunger that shook her to her core.

"Tell me now," he whispered. "If you mean no, say it now and I'll stop."

Say it! her brain ordered.

But just as quickly, her body took over. There was no future with Max. He didn't believe her about their baby. And to prove it to him with a paternity test, she'd have to wait until the child was born. So there was no convincing him. If she had half a brain, she'd walk out of this gloriously appointed apartment, away from this man with his near magical touch and console herself with the fact that she'd done the right thing. She'd told him about the baby. It was his choice to not believe her.

But she didn't want to go.

She wanted another night.

Every square inch of her body was clamoring for it. Every beat of her heart made the need for him more desperate. So she made another decision that would no doubt come back to haunt her.

"I'm not saying no," she said, and lifted her hands to his chest. She ran her palms across his open-collared dress shirt and felt the hard muscles beneath.

He drew in a long, deep breath, then let her go just enough to slide his hands to her breasts. Through the fine linen, he cupped her and ran his thumbs across her hardened nipples. The lacy bra she wore was not enough to keep the heat of his touch from seeping into her skin.

"Then say yes," he demanded, squeezing her breasts a little harder, just enough to make her need him even more.

"Yes, Max. Damn you, *yes.*"

Triumph shone in his eyes briefly, before he took her mouth with his again. The moment his lips touched hers, Julia closed her eyes on a sigh of surrender. Heat spiraled through her, burning through her veins, electrifying every cell. His tongue parted her lips and she took him inside, tangling her tongue with his in an erotic dance of expectation.

While he kissed her, his hands moved quickly, surely, to the buttons of her blouse. In seconds, they were open and her shirt was dropping off her arms to lie on the floor. Her bra came next and then his hands were on her breasts, stroking, rubbing, squeezing. His fingers tugged at her nipples all the while his mouth drove her insane with a need that nearly swamped her.

He broke the kiss abruptly and bent to take first one nipple, then the other into his mouth. His tongue and lips and teeth worked her flesh, playing her body as if she were a finely tuned instrument. Higher and higher she flew, and as she cupped the back of his head, holding his mouth to her, her eyes opened to slits. She stared out at the breadth of Manhattan, sprawled out below them, and the lights of the city blurred into a kaleidoscope of color.

"More," he whispered against her skin.

"Yes, Max, more. Please, more." She'd never felt as she did when she was with him. This one man was to her body what a lit match was to a stick of dynamite. Why was he the only one who could create such incredible sensations?

His fingers deftly undid the button and zipper of her slacks and he slid them down the length of her legs, tugging her lacy thong down at the same time. The cool air of the room kissed her skin and she shivered. She wasn't cold, though. How could she ever be cold while Max's hands were on her flesh?

"Hold on to me." He knelt in front of her and waited until her hands fell to his broad, muscular shoulders. Then he lifted her right leg, laid it across his back and looked up at her.

Desire, passion and more glittered in his eyes and Julia felt caught in that steady, studying gaze of his. She trembled as, keeping his gaze locked with hers, he moved closer and inched his mouth toward the aching center of her. With his fingers, he parted the pale blond curls at the tops of her thighs, and Julia sucked in a gulp of air, capturing it in her lungs as if afraid she might never draw another.

But that stolen breath flew out of her in a rush the moment his tongue touched her most intimate flesh. He closed his eyes, leaned into her and began to gently torture her with clever strokes and long, damp caresses. Julia curled her fingers into his shirt and hung on for all she was worth. Her balance was precarious, but she wouldn't have moved for all the money in the world.

She wanted to be just like this forever. To have the feel of his mouth on her, the warmth of his tongue, the brush of his breath, the slide of his fingers as he pushed first one, then two up and inside her.

"Max!" She swayed and he used his free arm to

steady her. To hold her tightly in position so that he could continue his gentle invasion.

As his fingers moved in and out of her body, his mouth continued its delicious torture. He tasted and teased, built her internal fire into a conflagration, then eased back before she could burst into flame. He kept her on the edge of release, teetering dangerously close, but always just a breath away.

Julia's body was a quivering mass of need and raw passion. She held on to him and rocked her hips against him as best she could. Her eyes opened again and she looked down at him as he took her, drove her, faster and faster until breathing was a memory and the only thing that mattered was the shattering climax that remained just out of reach.

"Max, please," she whispered, her words broken. "Please, now. Now."

His mouth pushed her onward, his fingers dancing in and out of her body, keeping time with the stroke of his tongue. And when she knew she couldn't take another moment, Max gave her that one last stroke that sent her tumbling into oblivion, the only steady point in the universe being his shoulders beneath her hands.

Before the last tremor had coursed through her system, Julia was swung up into his arms. He looked down at her and she saw on his features the rigid control he was maintaining. She lifted one hand, cupped his cheek and said, "More, Max. I want you inside me."

"You'll have me," he promised, already striding across the wide room toward a hall. Down that hall, his footsteps sounded out like a frantic heartbeat against the shining wood floor.

Julia couldn't tear her gaze from him, drinking in the strong line of his jaw. The way his dark hair fell across his forehead. The shine in his grass-green eyes. Her body quickened, already needing him again.

His bedroom was a massive space, lit only by the moon and the city lights below. A bed big enough to comfortably sleep six sat positioned opposite the wall of windows. A red silk duvet was already pulled down and when Max dropped her onto the mattress, she felt as if she was surrounded by softness.

She watched, speechless, as he quickly tore off his clothes. Her gaze dropped to the hard, thick length of him, and everything in her tingled. Lifting her arms to him, she welcomed him to her and when he covered her body with his, Julia luxuriated in the feel of his flesh aligned with hers. Rough to smooth, their bodies moved against each other as if made for this and nothing more.

His touch sent her spinning again, whirling with emotions, sensations too many to identify. She didn't try. Instead, she concentrated solely on being with him, and when he rolled onto his back and drew her atop him, Julia went willingly, eagerly.

How had they come to this? she wondered. That one magical night with him had created life. Life he didn't believe in or care about. Life that she looked forward to nurturing.

Two strangers they'd been and really still were. And yet, here in this room, on this bed, she felt as if she'd known him forever. As if a part of her had always been waiting for him to walk into her life. As if her body recognized his.

His hands clamped her upper thighs as she rose above him. His mouth curved into a lazy smile and Julia couldn't quite resist bending over him to kiss that mouth. Her hair fell on either side of them, a soft, blond curtain, shutting out everything but the two of them.

Mouths met, tongues twisted together and breath mingled, as if they were one. As if this was somehow meant to be. But before she could give that thought any more consideration, he lifted her hips and slowly, expertly, guided her down atop him.

Julia straightened, arched her back and hissed in a breath as he slowly, inexorably filled her. His hard length pushed into her heat and she took him deeply within. She was impaled on him and felt his body claim hers completely.

Staring down into his eyes, Julia sighed and wiggled her hips, grinding her body to his, and her reward was watching his eyes wheel.

"My turn," she whispered, her voice a mere hush as her body began to move on his. She rocked her hips, she twisted and arched her back. She ran her hands up and down his chest, scraping her short, even nails along his skin, across his flat nipples.

He groaned and fixed his gaze on her as if he didn't dare look away. As if nothing in the world was more important to him in that moment than she was. And it was a heady feeling. Julia kept her gaze locked with his as she lifted her hands, sliding them up her own body to cup her breasts.

As he watched, she tweaked her own nipples, and in the flare of excitement in his eyes, she felt her own eagerness build. She'd caught him, trapped him in her web now, and it was he who had to do nothing but to accept. To feel. To take that slippery climb to completion.

Pure, feminine power roared through her as Julia watched Max's fixed gaze. She read his hunger, saw his need, felt his passion. Smiling, she lifted both arms high over her head, arched her back again and rode him harder, faster. Her hips bucked and her soft moans murmured into the darkness. His hands at her hips tightened until she felt the sting of each fingertip burning into her skin.

Then he slid one hand down to the point where their bodies were joined. He touched her. That one incredibly sensitive piece of flesh. He found that one spot and stroked it as she rocked on him, and in seconds, he'd turned the tables. Now it was Julia again, clamoring, breathlessly racing toward the peak awaiting them.

When she screamed his name and shattered in his grasp, she heard his own hoarse cry echo hers an instant later. Then his arms came around her, and holding her tightly, Max cushioned their fall back to earth.

Three

With Julia curled up beside him, Max drew his first easy breath in two months. He finally had her back where he wanted her. He wasn't sure what she was trying to pull with this baby ruse, but whatever it was, he'd find out. Now that she was back in his bed where she belonged.

He wasn't an idiot. He knew damn well she'd enjoyed herself every bit as much as he had. So what was the point of the lies? he wondered. What could she possibly be after?

Going up on one elbow, he looked down into her eyes, gave her a half smile and said smugly, "Now do you want to try to tell me you're not interested in a sexual relationship?"

Her wide blue eyes narrowed perceptibly as she met his gaze. "What I said was, I'm not interested in a *solely* sexual relationship."

"I think you just proved that wrong. In a spectacular way, from my perspective."

Muttering something he didn't quite catch, she shoved herself away from him and scooted off the edge of the bed. Naked, she was enough to make his mouth water. Her build was small, almost fragile, but toned. She had strength in her slightly too-thin frame, and as she stalked around the edge of the bed headed for the living room, Max could freely admit that he wanted her. Again.

Quietly, he slipped out of bed and followed her, his bare feet making no sound on the floor. He watched as she bent down to scoop up her clothing, then he leaned one shoulder against the doorjamb and watched as she quickly got dressed.

"What's your hurry?"

She flashed him a look, sucked in a gulp of air and said, "I didn't come here for *this*."

"Maybe not, but we're damn good at it. Why not do it again?"

"Because," she said, tugging her panties and then her slacks up and over her legs, "there's no point."

"You screamed," he said with a satisfied grin. "I think that's the point."

Scowling at him, she tossed her blond hair behind one shoulder, slipped her bra on and clumsily hooked it into place. "There's no talking to you, is there?"

"If you want to talk, we'll talk." He walked toward her, comfortable with his own nudity. She, however, looked a little nervous at the fact that he was still naked. Good. He was a man who liked knowing he had the advantage of his opponent. And no matter how else he could describe their "relationship," *opponent* was definitely part of the mix.

"You could start with why you're trying to convince me you're pregnant."

She kept her gaze determinedly fixed on his. "I *am* pregnant," she said. "I only told you because it was the right thing to do."

"Oh, concerned about doing the right thing, are you?"

"Honestly?" she countered. "It's becoming less and less important to me with every word you say."

She slipped her white blouse on and before she could button it, Max was there, hands at her shoulders. He pulled her in tightly to him, looked down into her eyes and asked quietly, "What is this really about?"

For one moment, he thought he read disappointment in her eyes, but then that moment passed and her eyes were once again a cool, dispassionate blue. "You don't believe me, so why should I bother trying to convince you?"

A niggling doubt began to chew at the back of his mind, but he set it aside quickly. It didn't matter what she said. He already knew the truth. "I want to know who told you to try this," he said.

"What?"

"Word get out that I wanted an heir, is that it?" His fingers tightened on her shoulders briefly.

"I don't know what you're talking about."

"Please. We both know that salacious gossip is your society's life blood. The rich and spoiled's rumor mills put even Hollywood to shame."

She stepped back out of his grasp and Max let her go. Tidily, she did up the buttons on her shirt, scooped her hair back from her face and finger-combed it until it looked less like she'd just rolled out of bed with her lover. Then she turned away, picked up her bag from where she'd dropped it earlier and stepped into her sandals.

Only when she was ready to leave did she turn back to him again. "Believe what you will, Max. But I told you the truth."

"As you see it, of course."

"Isn't that the only way any of us see it?"

He frowned after her, but he let her go and didn't try to stop her when she stepped into the elevator and left.

"I'm an idiot," Julia groaned to Amanda an hour later as she dropped her head onto the back of the couch. Her body was still humming from Max's touch, and her temper was still simmering with the sting of his distrust. Why would he simply assume she was lying? For heaven's sake, he didn't even ask for a paternity test!

She closed her eyes, opened them again and looked around her apartment. She'd built a little nest here, a place where she felt comfortable. Happy. The walls were a soft mauve, the window treatments sheer white and the overstuffed couch and love seat were covered in ivory spattered with cabbage roses. In this apartment, Julia had finally made a home for herself.

Unlike the places she'd grown up, there was nothing cold or formal or rigid here. She always felt at ease here—until tonight. And that was her fault as much as it was Max's.

Staring up at the ceiling, she said, disbelief coloring her tone, "I went right back to bed with him. It's like he can hypnotize me or something."

"Lucky you," Amanda said.

"Lucky?" Julia shook her head. "It's like an out-of-body experience or something, except I'm right there in my body. I just don't have control over it anymore." She slapped one hand over her eyes. "For pity's sake, we didn't even use a condom. *Again*."

"A little late to be worrying about protection, don't you think?"

"I'm *not* thinking. That's the solid truth. It's like my brain shuts down when he touches me. I don't understand this at all."

"Why try to understand it?" Amanda said on an envious sigh. "Just enjoy it."

"You're not helping." Julia turned her head to glare at her best friend, seated cross-legged on the love seat opposite her.

"What do you want me to say?" Amanda laughed and dipped her spoon into the pint of chocolate-chip ice cream. "Oooh. Bad Julia. Having sex. Shame." She took a bite, smiled and shook her head. "Not gonna happen."

"But he didn't believe me about the baby."

Amanda frowned, leaned forward and picked up the other carton of ice cream, already open, a spoon jutting up from its frozen heart. Handing it to Julia, she said, "Okay, that's terrible. He should have believed you. I've never met anybody as scrupulously honest as you."

Julia took a bite of her strawberry ice cream, let the frozen sugar dissolve on her tongue and then said, "You should tell him that. He didn't even consider what I was saying. Just flat out called me a liar."

"And then to get back at him for that insult, you had sex with him." Amanda laughed. "That'll teach him."

Julia grimaced, picked up a pink, ruffled throw pillow and tossed it at her friend. "I already said I'm an idiot."

Still chuckling, Amanda asked, "The question is, was it worth it?"

"Oh, God," Julia said on a sigh. "The man has magic fingers. And a magic mouth and a magic—"

"I get the picture. And color me jealous." Amanda stabbed at her ice cream, scooped up a huge bite and ate it.

Julia winced. She shouldn't be going on and on about Max and the incredible sex. Wasn't Amanda here, living with her, because her own romance had ended badly? "I'm sorry, sweetie," she said guiltily.

"Oh, don't be," Amanda said, lifting her chin. "Not

on my account, anyway. Yes, I loved a loser, but that's over now. I'm good. Perfectly content with my chocolate-chip ice cream and vicarious thrills through you."

"Humph. Those thrills have come to an end," Julia said, hoping that her firm tone would even convince herself. "I can't do this with Max again, Amanda. Sex isn't enough."

"Hmm. Won't convince me of that at the moment."

"Don't I have enough problems?" Julia countered. "What am I supposed to do?"

Setting her ice cream down on the table in front of her, Amanda looked at her friend and said, "You're the only one who can decide that, Jules. It's your baby. Your life. What do you want to do?"

The answer to that question was easy and complicated in turns. She wanted her baby. But she was terrified of what would happen in the coming months.

Sighing, she said, "You know I always wanted kids."

"True."

"But I'd expected to be married first."

"Naturally, but things don't always go in order, either."

"I want the baby," Julia said. "But what happens when people find out about it?"

"Honey, this isn't the fifties. Times have changed."

"Times maybe," Julia acknowledged. "But my family hasn't. You know my parents."

Amanda shuddered. "Good point. They wouldn't exactly throw a party, would they."

"To say the least." She stopped for a moment and

imagined having this little chat with her parents. She could almost *feel* their disapproval. Their shame. Their complete distaste for what she'd done and who she was.

The elder Prentices' only concern was how things looked. If they found out their only child was pregnant and unmarried, they'd do everything they could to make her life a living hell. True, they couldn't force her to get an abortion, but they'd surgically slice her out of their lives—and as bad as they were, they were her only family. Could she really stand being tossed aside?

Julia shivered and pushed those thoughts aside. "It's not just my parents to consider, either. What about all the old-line charities I raise funds for? You think they're going to appreciate the 'unwed mother' thing?"

"Your family will get over it," Amanda said with more certainty than Julia felt. "As for the rest, you'll deal with it as it comes."

"Easier said than done."

"If you want this baby," Amanda said reasonably, "what choice do you have?"

By morning, Julia was still thinking about her friend's question. All night long, she'd been plagued by nightmares. She could still feel the panic she'd experienced in her sleep as she'd run down long, dark streets, empty of people, but filled with shadows. She'd held her baby in her arms, and the infant's wails had echoed off the buildings on either side of her. Rain stained the streets, and her frantic gaze couldn't find a single person to help her.

To befriend her.

She shivered a little, shoved aside the remnants of the dream and cupped both hands around her mug of hot tea, hoping the heat would seep into her bones. She squinted into the bright spear of sunlight slanting in through the windows and told herself that dreams were not reality.

Besides, this was ridiculous, and she knew it. Here she was, twenty-eight years old, a college graduate, with a steady income, her own home and a select group of good friends. So she was pregnant and not married? What was the big deal? Other women faced this problem all the time. Why was she making such a mountain out of her own personal molehill?

"Are you that big a coward?" she asked herself and was half-afraid of the answer.

"Mail's here." Amanda strode into the breakfast room, dropped a stack of envelopes onto the table and headed for her bedroom. "I've got an appointment with a nervous bride in about an hour. Her prospective mother-in-law is trying to arrange the wedding *her* way. Hello, red flag, blushing bride! Run for the hills!" She shrugged, grinned and said, "Should be interesting."

As an event planner, Amanda was always rushing to and from meetings with clients, suppliers and site committees. She was wearing a dark red business suit that looked amazing on her. As she walked away, she smiled over her shoulder and said, "Let me know if there's anything in that stack for me."

Julia dutifully flipped through the envelopes. Bills,

circulars, party invitations… She stopped when she came to one without a stamp or postmark. It was addressed to Julia Prentice, but there was no street address on the envelope, only her name. Frowning, she broke the seal, took out the single sheet of paper and read the all-too-brief message.

Ms. Prentice—I know about your baby. If you don't want the world to know, wire one million dollars to this Grand Cayman account. You have one week to comply.

There was an account number listed below the message, but obviously, no signature. A blackmail letter? Julia's hands shook, then fisted on the single page of paper. Who was behind this? Someone in the building? Someone she thought of as a friend? Apart from herself, no one but Amanda and Max knew about the baby. Max didn't believe her about it, and Amanda would never betray her.

So how had this…person found out? Had someone been listening at the Park Café? Had she been overheard despite her attempts to keep her conversation quiet? Concentrating, despite the rush of adrenaline inside her, she racked her brain, trying to remember the faces of the other patrons at the café the night before. But she couldn't. She'd been too engrossed in her own thoughts. Too wrapped up in her own world and situation to take note of anyone else around her. And truth to tell, once Max had shown up, the building

could have been on fire and she'd only have seen
Max's eyes.

"Oh, God."

She dropped the letter to the table, slapped one hand
to her mouth and fought for air as she suddenly found
it hard to breathe. What was she going to do? She didn't
have the kind of disposable income that would allow
her to pay out a million dollars in cash. And she
couldn't stand the thought of her private business being
the subject of titillating gossip or speculation.

"Sweetie?" Amanda's voice cut through the clamoring noise in her mind and Julia looked up through
tear-glazed eyes at her friend. "What is it, Jules? What
happened?"

Julia glanced at the letter and Amanda snatched it up
and read it.

"Damn! Who would do something like—" She
broke off and said, "Never mind. What are you going
to do about this?"

"I don't know."

"You should go to the police, Jules."

"What good would that do?" She shook her head and
fought to think clearly, to fight down the panic already
clawing through her. Her stomach was churning, her
heart was pounding and her mouth was dry.

"Blackmail's a crime."

"I know that," Julia said softly. "But what can the
police do about it? Find the blackmailer? Would that
stop whoever it is? They'd still leak my secret."

"It won't be a secret forever, sweetie," Amanda

reminded her gently. "People are going to find out you're pregnant. It's not really something you can hide."

"Yes, but they'll find out when *I'm* ready. Not when some malicious bastard decides to throw me to the gossip wolves. I can't let my parents find out about this from reading it in the papers. And I can't tell them myself yet, either."

"So what *are* you going to do?"

Julia pushed up out of her chair, walked a few steps, then turned around to look at the other woman. "I can't go to my parents with this. And I can't pay the blackmail myself. There's really only one thing I *can* do," she said. "I have to go to Max."

Max sat at his desk, trying to focus on the day's activities. Keeping his finger on Wall Street's pulse was the secret of his success. He had an innate ability to see which way the market would roll. To make his move before others had even considered the situation in front of them.

His reputation was such that his advice was taken as golden, and his rivals kept a close watch on him in hopes of getting the jump on him. Which hadn't happened. Max enjoyed his work. Enjoyed being the best. He relished the swings, the ups and downs, of the market and delighted at defeating it, bending it to his own whims.

But today, he couldn't focus. Couldn't make himself care about oil prices or hog futures or any other damn thing on the screens. Today, all he could think of was Julia.

He hadn't slept because his bed smelled of her. He closed his eyes and he could feel her body on his. His mind continued to dredge up image after image of her. Her blond hair mussed, tangled, her eyes soft and wide, or glittering with passion. Her mouth, full and delectable as she rose over him, took him inside.

The damn woman was haunting him.

He sat back in his office chair, swiveled it around to turn his back on the view of Manhattan and, instead, swept his gaze around his office. The room was big, the furniture was black, chrome and glass, and the atmosphere quietly successful. When he held meetings in here, this room was enough to put his adversaries on the defensive. This room said plainly that Max Rolland was a man to be taken seriously. With a lot of caution.

His world was exactly the way he'd always dreamed it would be. He had money. He had prestige. He had the whole city by the damn tail. What he didn't have was a family. A son. An heir.

Jumping out of the black leather chair, he stalked across the room, poured himself a cup of coffee from the silver urn atop the wet bar and took a long sip while his thoughts raced. He'd married Camille, fully expecting to build the family dynasty he'd always planned on.

She'd had good bloodlines. She would have given his children the pedigree they deserved and he would have given them what they needed to excel in the world he'd wanted to hand down to them.

"Best-laid plans," he muttered darkly, letting himself remember, however briefly, the look on Camille's face the last time he'd seen her.

She'd looked at him with pity. With disgust. And her last words to him still echoed in his mind.

You can't give me what I want, Max. A child. So I'm leaving you for someone who can.

He set his coffee cup down, shoved both hands into his pockets and rocked back on his heels. That was why he was so certain that Julia was lying to him about her pregnancy. He already knew he couldn't have children. He was infertile. He'd let go of his dreams of building a family empire.

There was a brief knock at his office door, then it opened, and his assistant, Tom Doheny, poked his head around the edge of it. "Mr. Rolland? There's a woman here to see you. A Ms. Prentice. She says it's urgent."

Max smiled and it couldn't have been a pleasant one since Tom's features tightened in response.

"Send her in."

Four

Once she'd explained everything, Julia stopped talking, turned around and faced Max. She hadn't been able to look at him while she told him about the blackmail letter. She couldn't force herself to face him and admit that she didn't have enough ready cash to pay the blackmailer what he/she wanted. And she really couldn't bring herself to do exactly what she'd gone to him to do in the first place.

Ask for help.

Now, as she stared across the massive office to where he sat perched on the edge of his desk, long legs stretched out in front of him, feet crossed at the ankles, she took a breath and waited. Seconds ticked past, measured by the hard thump of her heartbeat. Her mouth was dry, her stomach was in knots, and looking into Max's cool green eyes didn't make her feel any better.

When the silence stretched on, Julia broke first. "Well? Aren't you going to say anything?"

He folded his arms over his chest, cocked his head to one side and asked, "Why come to me with this?"

"Because it's *your* baby I'm carrying," she argued, and knew the moment she'd said the words it had been the wrong tack to take.

"Don't start that again," he said, lips so grimly compressed it was a wonder any words at all had escaped his mouth. "Let's stick with the facts, shall we?" He pushed away from the desk and started to prowl the room.

Julia's gaze fixed on him as he moved, his long legs making great strides, his footsteps soundless on the thick carpet. Diffused sunlight speared through the tinted windows, and the sounds of the city were so muted as to be nonexistent. It was as if she and Max were the only two people in the world.

How unfortunate that they weren't friends.

"The way I see it," he said, stalking the perimeter of the room, making her turn to keep him in sight, "you're pregnant and you don't want the world to know it just yet."

"True." Julia took a breath, held it for a second, then blew it out. "If this person makes good on his threat—" She broke off, unwilling to put into words the fears that had chased her since opening that damned envelope.

"You'll be fodder for the gossips for months."

"Years," she corrected darkly. "My child would hear the whispers and I can't let that happen."

"Eventually, you'll be faced with this problem, anyway," he pointed out.

"I'll think of something," she said, hoping to convince herself, as well as Max. "But I can't let this get out now. Not yet."

"And the reason you're not going to the father of this child?"

She glared at him. Did he honestly believe she was the kind of woman who would be pregnant with one man's child while telling another that *he* was the father? His features were twisted into a sardonic smile that let her know it was exactly what he thought. "He won't believe me," she said.

"Ahh. So I'm not the only man in your life with a low tolerance for lies."

She jerked as if he'd slapped her. What had she been thinking, coming to him? She'd deliberately walked into the lion's den, asked him to open his mouth, then set her head inside it so she could allow him to bite it off!

"You know what?" Julia muttered, turning for the door. "This was a mistake. I see that now. Just…never mind. Forget I was here."

He caught her before she could reach out and grab the doorknob. His grip on her upper arm was firm, unshakable. Still, she tried. When she failed, though, she lifted her gaze to his, gave him a glare that should have frozen him solid on the spot and said, "Let me go, Max."

"I don't think so." Instead, he turned her around, steered her to his desk and gave her a gentle shove into one of the leather chairs. "We're not through talking."

She tilted her head back to give him another dirty look. "Oh, I think we've said everything there is to say."

"Well, you're wrong," he told her, and sat down in the chair beside hers. Bracing both elbows on his knees, he locked his gaze with hers and said, "Bottom line it for me, Julia. Why'd you come to me?"

Her posture got even straighter, if possible. Her chin lifted and she gathered up what little dignity she had left and wrapped it around her as if it were an ermine cloak. "I don't have enough readily available cash to pay this person. I thought maybe you could loan it to me." When he didn't say anything to that, she hurriedly added, "I'll pay you whatever interest you think is fair and—"

"No."

She blinked at him. "That's it? Just 'no'?"

"Paying a blackmailer's never a good idea." He sat back in his chair, propped his right foot on his left knee and idly tapped his fingertips against the arm of the chair. "You think a million will satisfy this person? No. Once you pay, you'll be forced to keep paying."

"Oh, God." Perfect posture forgotten, Julia slumped into her own chair. How had this happened? Who was behind this and why? What had she ever done to make someone act so viciously? And what was she going to do?

"The way I see it," Max said softly, as if plotting out a response even as he spoke, "your only choice here is to make your secret not worth telling."

"Excuse me?" Julia looked at him. His green eyes were narrowed, his strong, hard jaw tight and his mouth hardly more than a grim line. This was not a man to take lightly. This was the face of the man who'd taken Wall Street by storm. A modern-day warrior who'd slain his would-be competitors by leaving their financial bodies littered in his wake.

This was Max Rolland.

The unstoppable force behind Rolland Enterprises.

And Julia had the distinct feeling she was about to find out firsthand what it was like to have Max the Marauder going into battle on her behalf.

"All you have to do is marry me."

Did he actually *say* those words?

She couldn't be sure. It was as if the whole world had suddenly stopped and tilted weirdly on its axis. If there was one thing she hadn't expected, it was a proposal.

"Are you— Did you— Why would you—" Not a good sign. She couldn't even string a complete sentence together.

He smiled at her and the smile was cold and calculating and didn't even approach his eyes. "Surprised?"

"Uh…yes," she admitted. "That would be a good way to put it."

"You shouldn't be." Standing up again, Max moved to the wet bar across the room, poured himself a cup of coffee and then asked, "You?"

"No, thanks."

"Right." He nodded to himself and smiled. "No caffeine for you. Don't know how you'll manage."

"I've got bigger things to worry about at the moment. And why should I have expected you to propose marriage to me? You don't even believe that this is your baby."

He took a sip of coffee, then walked back to where he'd left her. Looking down at her, he said, "No, I don't. But that's not the issue anymore."

She choked out a laugh. "What is?"

"You can't pay the blackmail. I *won't* pay it. I'm guessing you don't want your family to know about this pregnancy yet, either, am I right?"

More right than he knew. Julia got a cold chill just imagining breaking the "unwed mother" news to her parents. They'd once stopped speaking to her for six months because she'd dated a musician briefly.

The Prentices weren't exactly your average American family. She and her parents had never been close—which made one question why she cared what they thought of her life choices. But even if Margaret and Donald Prentice were cold and mostly uncaring, they were the only family Julia had. And now, more than ever, she couldn't afford to lose touch with that one fragile thread of connection.

"Yes," she whispered, ducking her head because she couldn't meet his eyes when she said it. "You're right."

"And the actual father of this child is no longer in the picture."

Wryly, she muttered, "You could say that."

"Seems to me, the one option open to you is marrying me. If we're married, then there is no scandal about your pregnancy. The blackmail will go away, end of problem."

"And beginning of another one," she countered, standing up now because tilting her head back to look at him simply put her at too great a disadvantage. "Max, I really appreciate your very unexpected offer of help, but don't you think it's going too far?"

"Why?" He set his coffee cup down on his desk, dropped both hands to her shoulders and held her gently, yet firmly. "We've got plenty of chemistry together, Julia. That's been proven."

"But a marriage?"

"Doesn't have to be forever," he qualified. "We can put a time stamp on it. Call it a marriage for a year. My attorney will draw up some papers and—"

"A year?"

"Less time would look suspicious, wouldn't it?"

"I suppose…" She felt as if she were being swept out to sea on a receding tidal wave. There was no ground beneath her feet. Nothing to grab hold of. Nowhere to turn. Nowhere to look but into his eyes. "But I still don't understand *why* you would do this."

"I want a son. An heir." He let her go, walked around the edge of his desk and stared out at the skyline of the great city sprawled out in front of them. "That's really all you need to know." Turning back to her, his gaze speared hers. "I'll marry you, give your child my name.

He'll be mine, legally and emotionally. You'll sign legal papers asserting that fact."

"And if the baby's a girl?"

He looked startled—as if he hadn't considered that possibility at all. Then he brushed the notion aside. "Doesn't matter. Girl or boy, the baby's mine the minute we get married. Agreed?"

No problem, she thought but didn't say. The baby *was* his, despite what he thought, so she wouldn't have any issues signing whatever documents he required. But there remained another question. "If we get married and want it to look real, we'll have to live together."

"Naturally."

"As husband and wife."

"Absolutely." He came back to her, his gaze never leaving her face.

Julia felt heat start at the top of her head and slide all the way down to the soles of her feet. His gaze swept her up and down as surely as a touch, and just like that, Julia's body slipped into overdrive.

When he touched her, she half expected to burst into flames. But all that happened was more heat, seeping from his hands on her shoulders down deep into her flesh.

"You'll move into my place. My bed. As far as anyone else knows, this is a whirlwind romance."

"Whirlwind…" She smiled in spite of everything. "Sounds appropriate."

"And when we're married," he said softly, "I'll expect you to tell me who the baby's father really is.

I'll want to know who to watch out for. Who to guard against."

"Max—"

He kissed her and Julia's mind simply shut down. There was no room for thinking when sensation was spilling through her like a river of molten lava. Every cell in her body was alive and awake and clamoring for more.

Max's hands swept up and down her spine, molding her body to his, pulling her in so tightly to him that Julia thought wildly for a moment that her body was going to slide right into his. Her arms came up and linked behind his neck, holding his head to hers, his mouth to hers. He parted her lips with his tongue and she lost her breath on a ragged sigh of pleasure so deep, so soul searingly complete, she gave herself up to the wonder of it.

All of this happened even while a small, still-rational corner of her mind explored this new situation. Marrying Max? Was she asking for more trouble? Was she blindly walking into a situation that was only going to lead to misery? Was she setting herself up to be broken and hurt?

Did she have a choice?

Max broke the kiss. He didn't let her go, just lifted his head and looked down at her. "Well? What's it going to be, Julia? Do we get married?"

Her head still reeling, her body whimpering, Julia looked up into those grass-green eyes. She saw the future stretching out unknown in front of them and knew that he was the best choice for her and her child. She didn't really *want* to marry a man who thought her capable of lying to him about something so personal, so important. But if she didn't marry Max and the blackmailer made good on his/her threat, then she and her child would be the subject of vicious gossip for years. Besides, it wasn't as if she was marrying a stranger. He was the father of her child.

This was her best…her *only* real choice. So she would marry Max. And somehow, she would find a way to convince him that the child she carried was his. With that thought firmly in mind, she heard herself say, "Yes, Max. We get married."

"Excellent."

Then he kissed her again and the deal was sealed.

"A prenup? You're getting married? When did this happen?"

Max looked across the table at his attorney and friend, Alexander Harper. Tall, with dark hair and dark eyes, Alex looked dangerous, which Max appreciated in an attorney.

"It's a sudden decision," Max allowed, taking a sip of the fifty-year-old scotch in front of him.

"Damn sudden if you ask me," Alex said, lifting a hand to signal the waitress for a scotch like his friend. He'd arrived a little late for their business lunch and had some catching up to do. "Aren't you the guy who swore he'd never get married again after what happened with Camille?"

Frowning a little, Max nodded. "This is different." In a few short sentences, he laid it all out for his friend, who shook his head and thanked their waitress for his drink when it arrived. Lifting the heavy crystal tumbler, he took a sip, set the glass down again and said, "That's a hell of a thing, Max. And Julia Prentice is quite the catch."

Max knew that. Hell, Julia's bloodlines were better than Camille's. The Prentice family was old money. They'd been around forever and guarded their name with the tenacity of a pen of pit bulls. Wryly, he admitted silently that he'd love to see the faces of Julia's parents when she broke it to them that she'd be marrying him. A self-made billionaire, son of a truck driver and a housewife.

His gaze swept the interior of the small, upscale restaurant. Only a dozen or so tables filled the wood-paneled room, and those tables were covered in snowy-white linen. Waiters wearing black slacks and crisp white shirts moved through the room with silent efficiency. The darkly tinted windows looked out on Fifth Avenue, and for a moment, Max distracted himself by staring at the crowds of people streaming along the sidewalks.

"So," Alex said, drawing his attention back to the conversation at hand, "you don't believe her about the baby, but you're marrying her, anyway."

"That's about the size of it. I need you to draw up a prenup and also a document stating I'm the father of her child." The more he'd thought about this situation in the hour or so since Julia had left his office, the more Max liked the situation. He was getting a bed partner who lit his sheets on fire, and he was getting the child he so badly wanted. It was a win-win as far as he could see. And knowing going in that the woman he was about to marry was a beautiful liar gave him the advantage. Again. "I want it signed, notarized…hell, I want it bronzed, before the ceremony."

"All doable," Alex said, then pinned his friend with a hard look. "But tell me something. Why are you so fast to discount the possibility that you are the baby's father?"

Frowning again, Max said, "You know why."

"Yeah, Camille told you the tests came back saying you were infertile."

Max scowled at him. Alex had never been a fan of Camille's. Even knowing that his friend had been right didn't change things. "I *saw* the damn test results."

"You saw what Camille wanted you to see."

They'd been over this before and Max was tired of the trip. So he cut his friend off at the pass. "Look, I don't want to talk about ancient history. I just need you to take care of these details, all right?"

"Sure, Max," Alex said with a shrug. "I'll take care of it. How soon do you need it done?"

"The wedding's in two weeks."

Alex whistled, low and long. "I'll have to hustle to get it all set up."

"Well, my friend," Max said with a self-satisfied smile, "that's why you make the big bucks, isn't it?

Now, let's eat. I'm picking Julia up in an hour to go see the police."

"At least that much makes sense to me," Alex said, picking up his leather-bound menu to peruse it. "Who're you going to be talking to? Do you have a name?"

"A Detective McGray," Max said, sliding his gaze over the restaurant's offerings. "He's in charge of the investigation into the death of the woman who lived in Julia's building. I figured, the blackmail's in the building, too. Might as well see the man who's already investigating what's happening at 721."

Detective Arnold McGray looked tired.

His salt-and-pepper hair stood on end and his eyes had dark shadows beneath them. A five-o'clock shadow stubbled his jaws, and his dark blue tie had been loosened at his undone collar.

"Let me see if I have this straight," he said, glancing down at the notepad he'd been writing on since Julia had started talking. "You're being blackmailed and you have no idea who might be behind this?"

"That's right." Julia stiffened, instinctively uncomfortable in the bustling detective area of the local NYPD precinct building.

Around her, overworked and underpaid police officers were hunkered down over desks littered with manila file folders, towering stacks of papers and ringing phones. The cacophony was deafening. A drunken homeless man was singing to himself, a hooker in a bright red dress was trying to proposition her way out of an arrest, and a bearded younger man rattled the handcuffs that kept him locked in his chair.

This was so far out of Julia's everyday world, she didn't know where to look.

"And you think this might have something to do with the death of Marie Endicott?" McGray's voice was pitched just loud enough to carry over the noise.

"What?" Julia shook herself and frowned. "No, I mean, I don't know. It's possible, I suppose…" She glanced at Max, sitting beside her.

Even in this setting, his personal stamp of power was easy to read. He didn't look intimidated or threatened by the surroundings. Clearly, he was a man completely at home and confident of himself wherever he was.

As if picking up on her uncertainty, Max took the thread of her conversation and finished it himself. "Detective McGray," he said, "the truth is, my fiancée and I have no idea who might be behind this blackmail attempt. My feeling was that we should bring the matter to you, as it could very well be part of what's happened at my fiancée's building."

Julia had to force herself not to jerk in reaction to the word *fiancée*. He'd used it twice, as if making a point either to her or the detective. Which? she wondered, and then asked herself if it mattered.

She'd already agreed to marry him. And though a part of her was worried about what would happen, another, more cowardly part was grateful for the reprieve Max had offered her. The fact that the child she carried actually *was* his, was, she thought, ironic.

"I appreciate you bringing the matter to my attention," McGray said, slumping back in his tattered chair. "Frankly, I wouldn't be surprised if there was a connection."

"Really?" Julia asked.

"Seems unlikely that two such unrelated events would happen in the span of a couple of weeks—in a place that's seen no trouble at all in more than ten years."

"My thoughts exactly," Max said, reaching out to give Julia's cold hand a squeeze.

"Well, I've got all I need for the moment," the detective said, standing up behind his desk. "I'll look into this and if I find anything, I'll be in touch."

Max stood up, too, and held out one hand. When the older man shook it, Max thanked him. Then almost before she knew what was happening, Julia found herself being steered out of the police precinct and led outside.

"Do you really think the blackmailer has something to do with what happened to Marie Endicott?" Julia asked when they were alone.

He glanced over her head at the teeming streets, then led her down the steps to the sidewalk. Lifting one hand to hail a cab, Max glanced down at her. "My gut says yeah. They're related."

"Then that means…"

"We're not sure what it means," he cautioned, his

green eyes going cold and hard. "But yes, your blackmailer could have been involved in that woman's death."

"Oh, God." Julia hadn't wanted to think of Marie committing suicide. But the thought of a murderer walking free through 721 Park Avenue was even more disquieting.

A chill swept over her, making her shiver despite the cloying heat and humidity pounding down on the city.

Five

Max stared up at the edifice of 721 Park Avenue, craning his neck to take in the entire fourteen-story brick facade. A prewar structure, 721 was a classic in the old style. The building settled into the corner of Park and Seventieth like an old woman in a comfortable chair.

The city itself had grown and changed over the years, but the old building remained the same, sitting in the heart of the most expensive slice of real estate in the United States. Politicians, celebrities, old money and new, all gravitated to the Upper East Side of New York. And this place was one of the crown jewels of the neighborhood.

All around him, the city pulsed with life and

energy. People streamed past him on the sidewalk, and on the streets car horns blasted out a cacophony of sound.

Max ignored it all, though, as his gaze fixed on the roof and his thoughts turned to the woman who'd fallen to her death from that very roof. Then he thought about the blackmail attempt on Julia and asked himself, just what the hell was going on at 721? He agreed with the police detective they'd spoken to the day before. It seemed highly unlikely that two such-out-of-the-normal events could happen within a couple of weeks of each other and not be related somehow.

Lowering his gaze to the glass door that opened into the quietly elegant lobby of the building, Max spied the doorman wandering over to his desk. Smiling to himself, Max stepped up, pulled open the front door and stepped into the cool quiet of the lobby. Vastly different from his own building's entry, 721 reeked of old-world elegance and a time long past.

Instantly the doorman's gaze snapped up to meet Max's. "Good afternoon," he said. "May I help you?"

Max walked up to the impressive mahogany desk behind which the much smaller man stood. Taking a quick look around the lobby area, Max spotted the mailboxes for the tenants and smiled to himself. Just as he'd thought. The doorman would have had a good view of whoever might have slipped a blackmail letter into Julia's mail slot.

Rather than answering the man's question, Max gave him a tight smile and said, "You're Henry, right?"

The doorman looked surprised. "Yes, sir. Henry Brown."

"My fiancée lives in this building," Max said, and realized that it was getting easier to say the word fiancée. "Ms. Prentice."

There was a flicker of surprise in Henry's dark brown eyes, which disappeared a moment later. "Are you here to see her, then? She's not at home at the moment, but I'd be happy to deliver a message for you."

Trying to get rid of him? Max wondered. "No," he said, "actually, I came to talk to you."

"Me?"

Max had made it a point over the years to learn how to read people. It came in handy in negotiations and was invaluable when meeting new clients or prospective business partners. And every instinct Max had told him that Henry was nervous. It didn't show clearly, of course, and if he hadn't been looking for the signals, he might have missed them himself.

But Henry's gaze was furtive, darting around the lobby as if looking for help that wasn't going to come. His right hand was fisted on his desk and the fingers of his left hand tapped restlessly against a pad of paper with 721 in elegant script across the top.

Interesting, Max thought and smiled inwardly. "Yes, Henry. I want you to think back on the last few days."

"About what?"

"Have you seen anyone in here who didn't belong?" Max leaned one arm on the desktop. "Anyone who might have dropped an envelope into one of the mailboxes?"

Henry blinked as if he was stepping out of the shadows and into the light. His mouth opened and closed a couple of times, then he swallowed hard and shook his head. "No, sir, I haven't. And nothing like that would happen without me seeing it. I'm on duty right here. No one would get in who didn't belong."

"I did," Max pointed out.

Henry licked his upper lip, blew out a breath and said, "What I meant was, no one could stay inside who didn't talk to me first. And no one but the mailman and the residents go near the mailboxes."

"You're sure about that?"

Henry lifted his narrow chin, met Max's gaze with the direct stare of an honest man and said, "Absolutely."

Max was sure about something, too.

Henry was lying.

Max couldn't prove it, but he knew it down to his bones. And that made him wonder what exactly was going on at 721. The old place looked quiet, dignified. But there were undercurrents here and Max didn't like it. He didn't want to think about Julia staying here. One woman was dead and Julia herself was being blackmailed.

Something was very wrong in this building.

"You're pregnant?"

Julia winced as her mother's voice hit a particularly high note. She'd known this was going to be an ugly meeting. She had to face her parents not only with the news of her pregnancy, but her upcoming marriage, as well.

She sighed a little as her mother stood up from her silk-brocade chair and stared down at Julia as though she were a particularly appalling bug. *Just imagine,* she thought, *what this scene would have been like if you hadn't been able to tell them you're getting married.*

The sting of their only daughter being an unwed mother was something her parents might never have recovered from. All her life, Julia had been a disappointment. She knew that. Her parents had made sure of it. And all of her life, a part of Julia had tried to make them proud. To make them love her. Despite her efforts, nothing had changed.

She looked up at her mother and felt…nothing. No connection. No bond. No threads of affection or familial loyalty. Just…nothing. As sad as that made her, Julia realized that accepting this was the first step in finding her own kind of peace. The first step in building her own family. Her own world, separate and apart from the people who'd made her.

"Yes," Julia said, smiling into her mother's disapproving gaze, "I am. And my baby's father and I will be getting married in just a couple of weeks."

"That's something, I suppose," her father muttered from the chair where he sat glaring at her. "As long as you're married quickly, no one will have to know the reason."

Julia glanced at him and noticed that his bushy gray eyebrows were drawn together in a too-familiar frown of disgust. She couldn't remember a single time in her life when her father had held her, hugged her, told her that she was pretty or that he loved her. How strange it was to sit here in this place and realize the sad truth of her life.

She didn't have a family. She had biological parents. That was all.

And because she knew that they would never approve of her or give her the kind of love she'd once longed for, Julia was free. Free to speak her mind. To tell them what she'd feared telling them only days before.

Straightening in her chair, she clasped her fingers together tightly in her lap and said, "People will know I'm going to have a baby, Father."

"Eventually," he conceded with a shake of his head.

"Donald, you're missing the point here," Margaret Prentice snapped. "This will make us *grandparents*. For heaven's sake, I don't want people thinking I'm old enough to be a grandmother. This is a disaster."

"Thank you," Julia muttered.

"You will not speak to us in such a fashion, Julia," her mother said as her cold blue gaze fixed on her daughter. "At the very least, you owe us civility and respect."

"Respect is a two-way street, Mother."

Margaret laughed shortly. "Respect? You expect us to respect you for being stupid enough to get pregnant? You ask too much."

"Having a baby isn't stupid," Julia argued.

"You're not even married," her father said.

"I will be soon," she responded, feeling a fire begin

to build inside her. For years, when there were "discussions" like this one, she'd kept her mouth shut, done what was expected of her. But not anymore. She owed her child more than that. She owed *herself* more than that.

"How could you do this to me?" Margaret's voice shrieked a little.

"I didn't *do* anything to you, Mother…"

"None of my friends are grandmothers," her mother said hotly. "How will this look to people? How can I face my friends?" She crossed her too-thin arms over her narrow chest, but not tightly enough to wrinkle the cream-colored silk blouse she wore tucked into the waistband of linen pants the color of wheat. Margaret's elegantly styled hair was short and dyed honey-blond every four weeks. Her manicure was perfect, her makeup expertly applied, and her unlined face was a billboard for the best cosmetic surgeons in the city.

"Mother—"

"Don't speak to me."

"If we keep the ceremony quiet," Donald Prentice mused more to himself than anyone else, "it's possible—"

"What?" Margaret turned on her husband like a cobra. "That no one will notice when Julia's body begins to swell? People will notice, I assure you. And my friends will never let me forget that I'm a *grandmother,* for pity's sake."

It was as if Julia wasn't even present. They talked around her, over her, about her, as if she wasn't their daughter at all, but some annoying distant relative who'd made a claim on them they didn't care to acknowledge.

This she was used to. She'd grown accustomed to being nothing more than an annoyance to the people who should have loved her the most. Her succession of nannies had given her the only affection she'd known in her childhood, and as she grew older, Julia had realized that her parents had never wanted children in the first place.

At fifteen, she'd actually heard her mother telling a friend one day about "accidentally" getting pregnant and what a horror it had been. Julia glanced around the living room of the home where she'd grown up and realized that she'd never once felt comfortable there. Never once had she felt as though she belonged.

And that still held true. The walls were a glaring white with only a few abstract paintings lending garish splotches of color to the cold room. The floors were white tile and the chairs and couches, upholstered in subtle, differing shades of beige, were designed more for appearance than comfort. Even the smell of the house was sterile, as if the air in the place had long since died and was only being recycled by the people who continued to breathe it.

Rubbing at her temples, Margaret glared at Julia. "Who, may I inquire, is the father of this unfortunate child?"

Julia squirmed in her chair and cupped one hand over her still-flat abdomen as if she could prevent her baby from hearing its grandparents' dismissal of its very existence. "His name is Max. Max Rolland."

Margaret frowned, though her too-tight forehead prevented it from showing. "Rolland. Hmm. No, I don't believe I know any Rollands. Donald?"

Julia waited, knowing that this news would completely wipe away her parents' fury at hearing about the baby. Discovering that their only child was about to marry a man with no pedigree would put everything else they'd heard into perspective for them.

Strangely enough, Julia was almost looking forward to their reaction.

"Max Rolland…" Her father repeated the name thoughtfully.

"Who are his people?" Margaret demanded.

"His parents have passed away," Julia told her.

"I didn't ask *where* they were," Margaret reminded her, "I said *who* are they?"

"I know the name Rolland," her father said from his chair. "I just can't place it."

"Max is from upstate," Julia told her mother. Then, smiling, she took a breath and added, "His father was, I believe, a truck driver and his mother was a housewife."

Margaret slapped one hand to her chest and staggered backward as if someone had shoved a sword through her body.

"Rolland!" Donald Prentice shouted the name and pounded one fist against the arm of his chair. "That's how I know the name. That upstart running roughshod over Wall Street. He's made something of a name for himself, but—"

"A *truck driver?*" Margaret moaned softly, dropped back into her chair and lifted one hand to cover her eyes. "Oh, dear God, how did this happen?"

Julia paid no attention to the drama. "Max is very successful," she said. "He's a…good man." That might have been a bit of a stretch, she told herself, but at the same time, she realized that only a good man would have proposed to help her out. Whether he saw it that way or not, if he'd been a different sort of man, he'd have left her to solve her own problem or drown in her own misery.

"A *housewife?*" Margaret whispered the word as if afraid someone might hear her.

"People say he's cold and ruthless," Donald was saying, though his wife wasn't listening and Julia didn't want to hear him. "Could be quite a force in the city if he had a family name behind him."

"He's doing just fine without a 'name,'" Julia argued.

"No doubt," Donald said with a frown. "But there are limits to what a man like him can accomplish."

"Because his blood isn't blue?" Julia stood up and looked at her parents each in turn. "That's ridiculous. Max Rolland is a good, hardworking man who made his own fortune rather than inherited it."

"Exactly," Donald said with a slow shake of his head.

Sunlight streamed through the windows, glancing off the white walls and floors until Julia's eyes stung with the cold, hard brilliance of it all. Why had she been so concerned with telling her parents about her baby? Why had she been so terrified that she might lose this one slender thread of family?

The truth was, she'd never had a family to lose. She'd always been alone.

Until now, anyway.

Now she had her baby.

And she had Max.

"You can't possibly be serious about marrying this person." Her mother posed it as a sentence, not a question.

"I'm more serious about it with every passing second," Julia assured her, picking up her purse and slipping the slim leather strap over her shoulder.

"Julia, don't do something you'll regret," her father warned.

"I've already done that, Father," Julia told him as she turned to leave. "I came here expecting support. I'm not sure why, exactly, but this visit is definitely something I regret."

She walked briskly across the room, through the doorway and down the stairs where a maid in uniform waited to open the front door for her. Julia reached the bottom of the steps and turned when her mother called her name sharply.

Margaret Prentice stood at the head of the stairs, looking as cool and unapproachable as a queen. "What is it, Mother?"

"Don't think for one moment, young woman, that your father and I will acknowledge your marriage to this man. If you do this, you turn your back on your family."

A small twist of fear became a knot in the pit of her stomach, but then, as she drew one long breath, that knot dissolved. Strange, Julia thought, that it was at the moment her life was most in turmoil that she should find such an incredible sense of peace.

"I understand, Mother. Goodbye."

The door closed firmly behind her.

By the following day, Julia was too busy to spend much time worrying about her parents. She had a wedding to plan and a move to organize.

"It's going to be great," Amanda said as they settled into a couple of armchairs at the Park Café. Reaching into her leather briefcase, Amanda pulled out a thick day planner and quickly scanned her notes. "I know Max wants a fast wedding," she said with a wink for Julia, "but that doesn't mean it can't be fabulous. I've got the names of some caterers and I'd like you to look at some samples from the florist I've been working with."

Julia had notes of her own to check and they didn't have anything to do with her upcoming wedding. She was in the middle of a fund-raiser for a Manhattan shelter, and there were still one or two things that had to be nailed down. "Why don't you pick the caterer, Amanda? I swear I haven't had enough of an appetite to even *think* about food lately."

Her friend frowned a bit, reached for her ice blended

mocha and took a sip. Her gaze fixed on Julia until she squirmed uncomfortably.

"You haven't been feeling well ever since you went to see your folks," Amanda said.

"Can you blame me?" Julia forced a smile and told herself she'd be fine. She'd be *great*. She had her work, she had her baby and soon she'd have her very own husband, complete with prenup, baby contract and suspicion.

"No," Amanda said, "who can blame you? I'm just saying, the wedding's coming and you really should pay attention."

Julia closed her folder, sighed and leaned back into her chair. The café was crowded at lunchtime, and the noise level was such that Julia felt safe enough talking about what was really bothering her. "It's not the wedding or my parents," she said, leaning in a bit closer. "It's the fact that I'm moving in with Max in a few days."

Amanda laughed. "Honey, you're marrying him."

"I know, I know." Julia frowned and told herself she was being foolish. "But living with him is a little…"

"Exciting?"

"I was going to go with 'unnerving.'"

"Why?"

"Because of the way we're getting married," she said. "And the fact that he still doesn't believe me about the baby."

"Well, he's an idiot. We already decided that." Amanda went back to her lists.

"I know, but how'm I supposed to convince him that he is the father?"

"You may not be able to until the baby's born. Then you can do a paternity test."

"So that leaves me with seven months of my husband thinking I'm a liar."

Amanda closed her folder, picked up her mocha and idly twirled the straw through the thick, pale brown liquid. "You know I'm with you, no matter what, right?"

"Of course."

She smiled. "And you know I'm completely excited that you're letting me take over your apartment when you move in with Max..."

"I know."

"But," Amanda said, leaning forward to pat Julia's hand, "if you're really worried about this, don't do it."

"What?" Julia glanced across the room when someone laughed too loudly. Then, looking back at Amanda, she said, "I have to."

"No, you don't. You've already faced the worst part. You've told your parents."

"And the blackmail?" Julia shook her head slowly, despite being grateful for what Amanda was trying to tell her. God knew, after the afternoon with her parents, Julia was even more thankful to have Amanda's unswerving support. But the simple truth was, she had to marry Max. Otherwise, her child would be the subject of vicious gossip before it was even born. And she wouldn't allow that. "I appreciate it, sweetie," Julia said. "But I have to marry Max."

"Getting married for the wrong reasons is so not a good idea," Amanda said softly.

"Marriage for *any* reason isn't usually a good idea." A deep voice resonated from just behind Julia and she swiveled to look up at the man staring down at her.

"Hello, Max."

Six

"Okay," Amanda said, grabbing her drink and standing up in one smooth move. "That's my cue to hit the road."

"You don't have to go on my account," Max said, already dropping onto the couch beside Julia.

"No, it's okay. I've got lots of calls to make," Amanda told him, then shifted her gaze to Julia's. "We'll talk later at home, okay?"

"Sure, see you later." Julia watched her friend leave, then turned her head to look at Max, who was studying her carefully.

"Your friend trying to talk you out of this?"

"She's worried about me."

"Should she be?" He ran the tips of his fingers down

the length of her arm, and even through her linen shirt Julia felt heat, a heat that began to slide through her veins.

"Good question," she said, and shifted slightly, drawing her arm back and away from him. How could she think when he was touching her?

"Is there an answer?" He eased back, the sides of his black suit jacket falling to either side of him, displaying what she knew to be a rock-solid chest and abdomen hidden beneath the custom-made dress shirt.

She lifted her gaze to his and blew out a breath. "I don't know. Max, Amanda's my friend. She's trying to be supportive, letting me know she's on my side no matter what."

"She knows what's going on?" he asked. "The baby? The blackmail?"

"Yes." Julia glanced around the coffee shop, checking to see who was watching them. Who might be listening. She knew darn well that whoever was behind the blackmail had to have overheard her and Max talking about the baby in here. When she looked back to him, though, she let the worry go. The blackmail had already happened. What more could this person do to her? "I told her everything."

"Including the name of the father of your baby?" he wondered aloud, his gaze narrowing slightly.

"Max…" Irritation spiked inside her and Julia fought the distinct urge to kick him in the shins. Honestly. She'd lived her whole life by the rules. She'd maintained the sophisticated facade that life in society demanded. She'd never stepped out of line, always done just what she should.

And the minute she met Max, all that had disappeared. Not only had she slept with him right away, she'd gotten pregnant. Not only was she being blackmailed, she was marrying a man she hardly knew. Not only was he the father of her child, but she couldn't make him believe she wasn't a liar. And now, the well-behaved, always discreet Julia Prentice wanted to kick a man and scream at him in public, and the only thing keeping her from doing just that was what was left of her self-control.

"Wow," he mused aloud, a barely concealed chuckle in his tone, "you just had quite the talk with yourself, didn't you?"

"What?"

He sat up, braced his elbows on his knees and locked his gaze with hers. "Your face. It's so easy to read, it's ridiculous. You don't keep secrets well, do you."

"No, I really don't," she muttered, disturbed a little at how easily he could read her. But then she told herself it didn't matter, since even reading her face so expertly, he didn't believe what he saw. "I'm not a good liar, Max. That's why I don't lie."

"Uh-huh." Max would have liked to believe her, but how could he? Those big blue eyes of hers seemed to look right through him, and he wondered what she saw in him. What she'd seen from the beginning that had sent her to him for help when her world had crashed down around her.

He glanced around the café and reassured himself no one was paying the slightest attention to the two of them. Turning back to Julia, he watched her squirm uncomfortably on the couch and read her body language easily enough. She was uneasy in his presence and he thought he knew why.

"You went to see your parents yesterday, didn't you?"

Her eyes darkened a bit in memory, and Max knew he'd guessed right. He was willing to bet that the elder Prentices hadn't been happy with their daughter's news.

"Yes."

"Told them about the baby?"

"Yes." She shifted, tugged the hem of her pale blue skirt closer to her knees and crossed her feet daintily at the ankle. As neatly as a nun, she folded her hands together in her lap. "They were…unhappy."

He laughed shortly. "I'm guessing that's an understatement."

She winced. "Pretty much."

Max didn't need her to explain what that conversation had been like. He'd met her parents briefly at some social function in the city and hadn't exactly been impressed with their warmth. In fact, he found it amazing that a woman with the fire Julia had could have come from people so inherently cold.

Oddly enough, looking at her now, seeing the distress that still clouded her eyes at the mention of her parents, Max realized that he'd like nothing better than to go see them. Tell them what he thought of parents who couldn't bring themselves to support their own child.

"My mother," Julia said, capturing his attention, "is appalled at the idea of being labeled a grandmother."

"Her loss," he said tightly, and was rewarded by a flash of light in her eyes. Wanting to see that spark again, he said, "My mother would have been on cloud nine."

"Really?"

Max smiled. He didn't often think of his parents, because memories only made him miss them more. But now he allowed his mother's smiling image to fill his mind. "Oh, yeah. She used to harp on me all the time about making her a grandmother. She'd have been excited at the prospect."

Julia's mouth curved gently, sadly. "I'm sorry she's not here to know you're going to be a father."

Instantly his insides tightened. "We both know that's not true, though, don't we?"

"Max, please believe me," she said, reaching out one hand to him. Her fingers closed around his and in response, he felt heat shoot up the length of his arm and slam into his chest.

And because that sensation was so strong, he battled it back, refusing to be swayed by it. Instead, he squeezed her fingers briefly, then let go. "What'd your folks have to say about the wedding?"

She sighed, clearly understanding that he wanted a change in subject. "Well, that news took their minds off the baby."

This time, Max's laugh boomed out into the café and several heads turned to look. Ignoring them, he straightened, leaned in closer to her and said, "Not surprising, is it? The fact that I could buy and sell your father three times over isn't enough to make up for the lack of a pedigree?"

"Not to them."

"But you don't care?" He watched her. He'd know if she lied in her response, and suddenly, he really wanted to know what she thought. He knew she was only marrying him because she felt she had no choice. But he needed to know what she thought of him. What she really felt.

"Of course I don't," she said, and he knew instinctively that it was the truth. A glint of anger shone briefly in her eyes as she fixed her gaze on him. "Do you really think I'm that shallow? Do I strike you as someone who cares more about a person's background than the person himself?"

He studied her for a long moment, taking in the heightened color in her cheeks and the light of battle in her eyes. "No," he said finally, his voice low and soft, "you don't."

"Well, that's something, anyway," Julia muttered. "You still think I'm a liar, but at least you don't believe I'm elitist about it."

He gave her a quick grin. "See? We're already getting along great."

Julia frowned at him.

"They really gave you a bad time, didn't they?" he asked, his smile fading.

"No more than I was expecting."

"I'm sorry it was hard on you," he said, reacting more to the glimmer of pain in her eyes than to anything else.

"Are you?" she asked.

"Of course I am. I'd feel sorry for anyone who'd had to grow up with those two polar bears."

She stiffened a little and Max admired her instinctive defensive posture. Even though she and her parents weren't close, it was apparent she wasn't going to let anyone else speak badly of them.

"They're not bad people," she said, and he wondered if she was trying to convince him or herself. "They just never should have had children."

Again he studied her for a long minute, then said quietly, "I'm glad they did."

"Really?" She shook her head and gave him a wry smile. "Why would you be glad? You're marrying a woman you don't love and agreeing to be the father of a child you don't believe you created."

"I'm marrying my lover," he said, lowering his voice until it was nothing more than a low rumble of sound pitched so only she could hear him. "A woman who sets my body on fire with a glance. And I'm getting the heir I want. Like I said before, a win-win for me."

"I don't understand you," she said, tipping her head to one side as if trying to get a better picture of the man. "You're taking this so lightly."

"No, I'm not," Max assured her, leaning in so close that he felt her breath on his face. "Trust me when I say I'm taking this very seriously."

"What if we're miserable together?"

"We won't be."

"How do you know?" Her gaze locked with his.

"I'll just keep you in bed as much as I can. We've already proven we get along just fine there."

"There's more to a marriage than sex."

"Sure," he quipped. "There's children, too. And we've already got that taken care of."

"Max—"

"Stop trying to make this harder than it has to be," Max said firmly. He wasn't going to let her change her mind. Wasn't going to allow her nerves to stretch to the point where she simply snapped and called everything off.

He'd gone into this with his eyes open, knowing he could help her and himself. And now that they'd reached an agreement, Max could admit that he wanted this marriage. He wanted her in his house. In his bed. There was no way he would let her wriggle out of their bargain.

"I'm not," she argued. "I guess I just need to know that we're doing the right thing."

"Do you have the money for the blackmailer?" he asked flatly.

"No."

"Do you want to tell your parents that the wedding's off, but the baby's still on?"

"No," she said and slumped back into her seat.

"Then we're doing the right thing."

"I wonder," she said, "is the *only* thing necessarily the *right* thing?"

"You're thinking too much," he said. "Decision's been made. Let it go."

Her gaze locked on his and her expression was even easier to read than usual. Stubborn resignation. Good. At least she was accepting that this wedding *was* going to happen.

"Look," Max said abruptly. "I was on my way to a meeting when I walked past the café and saw you sitting in here with Amanda. I only came in to tell you something." He wasn't going to let her know that it had been a spur-of-the-moment decision. That seeing her had hit him so hard he hadn't been able to resist coming in to talk to her.

"Fine, then. What is it?"

"My lawyer says he'll have the papers ready for us to sign tomorrow morning."

"So soon?" She looked a little nervous, and a part of Max was glad to see it. Those few nerves told him that she wasn't a cold, calculating woman—as if he needed to be convinced. She might be lying to him, but he was willing to bet she hadn't set any of this in motion on purpose.

Max checked his watch again, then met her gaze. "I'll pick you up at nine. We can take care of the paperwork and be finished before the movers show up at your place."

"Oh, I didn't hire movers yet."

"It's already arranged," Max said. "They'll be at your place to pack by eleven tomorrow."

"Tomorrow?" Julia stared at him. "That's too soon.

I'm not ready, and besides, don't you think I can handle this myself? I don't need you to step in and—"

He leaned in and kissed her hard and quick, instantly cutting off her arguments. "No need to thank me," he said, giving her a grin that let her know he was completely aware of her frustration.

"Max…"

"I've got that meeting. I'll see you in the morning." Then he stood up and walked out, never looking back. Not that he had to. He felt her gaze boring a hole in his back.

Impatient, Julia tapped the toe of her shoe against the cold, marble floor of her lobby while she waited for the ancient elevator to arrive. Irritation with Max's high-handedness still stung.

"I can take care of myself," she muttered darkly. "Been doing it for years without any help, thanks very much."

Then she winced and glanced over her shoulder to make sure the doorman hadn't heard her. But Henry was oblivious to her presence, chatting away on the telephone at his desk. Good. She didn't need one more male sticking his nose into her business.

Honestly, did Max really think he could simply arrange her life to suit him? If he did, this temporary marriage was going to get off to a rocky start. She glanced up at the old-fashioned dial on the elevator and saw that it was going up, not coming down. Apparently someone in one of the penthouses had called for it.

Sighing, Julia turned, crossed the lobby and headed for the residents' mailboxes. Might as well pick up the mail now since she had a few minutes.

"Ms. Prentice!" Henry called.

Inserting the key into her box, Julia opened it, took out the stack of envelopes and mailers, then closed and relocked it before answering. "Yes?"

Sunlight slanted through the glass door and lay in a wide swath on the marble. Henry walked right through the light and stopped a couple of feet from her. "I wanted to tell you, like I told your fiancé..."

Fiancé, she thought, and wondered if she would be used to the sound of that word before she had to become accustomed to the word *husband*.

"Max? You talked to Max?"

"Yes, ma'am," Henry said, and bobbed his head nervously. But then, Henry always looked nervous and a little too cowed by the residents of the building. "He asked if I'd seen anyone hanging around the mailboxes and I told him I hadn't."

Julia glanced at the mailboxes and tightened her grip on the envelopes she held. Max had thought to question Henry. She hadn't and she should have, darn it. But in her own defense, she'd been a little too upset by the whole blackmail thing to sit down and rationally investigate it. Still, now that the thought was in her mind...

"Are you sure, Henry?" she asked, staring directly into his eyes until he shifted his gaze from hers. "It wouldn't have taken long for someone to drop a letter into one of the boxes."

He shrugged and when the phone at his desk rang, he jumped as if he'd been shot. "I'm sure. It's my job to watch over this lobby."

"Yes," she was saying, but Henry had already turned away, headed back for the phone like a drowning man reaching for a life preserver. "But—"

"721 Park Avenue," Henry said, cutting her off neatly and devoting himself entirely to whoever was calling.

He kept his back to her and it was obvious to Julia that he had no intention of getting off the phone until she was on the elevator. For whatever reason, Henry didn't want to talk anymore about what had happened. That didn't necessarily make him guilty of anything, though, she reminded herself. All it did was underscore just what a nervous type the poor guy really was, and increase the tiny seed of suspicion about him that Max had planted.

Shaking her head, Julia headed back across the lobby, the sound of her heels clicking musically against the floor. The elevator dinged as she approached, the doors slid open and Elizabeth Wellington stepped out and stopped dead.

"Julia," she said, flashing a smile that wasn't deep enough to display the dimples in her cheeks.

Instantly, Julia felt a wash of sympathy for her friend. Up until a year or so ago, Elizabeth had been happy and bubbly. Now her green eyes looked sad and her red hair was mussed as if she'd been distractedly running her fingers through it.

"The grapevine in the building works incredibly well," Elizabeth was saying as she gave Julia another wan smile. "I hear congratulations are in order. Both for your engagement and your baby."

Julia nearly winced. Now she felt not only sympathy but almost a twinge of guilt, too. She'd been so worried about her unplanned pregnancy, and poor Elizabeth was miserable, dealing with her infertility issues.

"Thank you," Julia said, and meant it sincerely. She guessed what it cost Elizabeth to be happy for someone else when she so badly wanted a child of her own. Reaching out, she hugged her friend tightly and bit her bottom lip when Elizabeth briefly squeezed her back.

"You must be excited," the other woman said, forcing happiness into her tone.

"I am," Julia replied, wishing there was something she could say, something she could do, to make this less painful for Elizabeth. "And a little overwhelmed. It's all happening so quickly."

The pretty redhead gave her another wistful smile, then seemed to gather her inner strength while squaring her shoulders. "Enjoy it, Julia. Seriously. Make sure you take the time to enjoy every minute."

There it was again, that pang of sympathy, and everything in Julia yearned to ease the pain flickering in her friend's eyes. Some things, though, simply couldn't be helped by a warm hug or a heartfelt wish. "Elizabeth…would you like to come up for tea?"

"No. No, thanks." Elizabeth lifted her chin and forced a bright, yet brittle smile. "I've got to run. I'm meeting a friend for an early dinner and I don't want to keep her waiting."

"Sure," Julia said, realizing that Elizabeth was trying to make a hasty getaway. And who could blame her? "But if you ever need someone to talk to…"

"Thanks. I appreciate it, really. But I'm fine. We're fine. Reed and I, I mean." She took a breath, blew it out and said, "Now I'm babbling, so I'm gonna go." She took a few steps away, then stopped, looked back and said, "Just remember what I said and make sure you relish every minute of this, okay?"

Then, as if she'd said too much, Elizabeth hurried across the lobby and nearly beat Henry to the door in her haste to get outside.

Julia stepped into the elevator and noticed the faint scent of Elizabeth's perfume still hanging in the air. As the doors swept shut, Julia closed her eyes briefly and wondered where the justice in life was. Elizabeth wanted a child so badly, and the absence of a pregnancy was slowly destroying her happiness. And Julia was marrying a man who didn't love her because of a surprise pregnancy.

As the elevator lifted, she dropped one hand to her stomach and whispered, "Don't take it personally, though, little one. I *like* surprises."

Smiling to herself, Julia leaned back against the elevator wall and idly listened to the hum of the motor as she glanced through the mail she still held in one hand. She thumbed through the envelopes until she came to one that looked chillingly familiar.

Tearing open the flap on the plain white envelope with only her name scrawled across the front, Julia ripped the single sheet of paper from it and quickly scanned the words written there.

Congratulations on your so sudden marriage. You've escaped me. This time.

Seven

They left the lawyer's office and Max steered Julia out onto a crowded sidewalk. Pedestrians hustled past them, a few of them clearly irritated at being forced to walk around the couple, who only stood there and stared at each other.

"I want my own lawyers to look over the papers before I sign," Julia said for the third time since leaving Alex's office. "It's only reasonable."

"We don't have a lot of time," Max told her, taking her hand and dragging her out of the flow of foot traffic. He shifted until her back was against the dappled marble of the office building and his own body shielded hers from passersby. Then he looked down into the big blue eyes that had been haunting him for weeks.

He tried to read her thoughts, but for whatever reason, today she seemed able to disguise what she was thinking. Which only troubled him more than usual.

"You looked at the papers yourself. They're perfectly straightforward. What's the problem?"

"You're rushing me," she said, glancing to either side of her as if to assure herself that no one was paying them the slightest amount of attention. "I don't like to be rushed."

He laughed shortly. "You're the one with the tight schedule here." He shot a quick look at her flat belly and then lifted his gaze to meet hers again. "We want this marriage sewn up tight before you start showing, remember?"

She glowered at him and her eyes danced with sparks of anger. "I'm not going to sprout overnight, Max. Another day or two can't possibly make that much difference."

It did, though. To him. Since setting out on this path, Max had become more determined with every passing day to have her be his. Legally. He wasn't willing to look at why; all he knew was that he wanted her. In his bed. In his home. In his life. And he wasn't willing to give her a chance to change her mind and waltz out of his world as breezily as she'd waltzed into it.

"Who's your lawyer?" he asked. When she gave him the name of one of the city's top firms, Max nodded. "We'll go there right now."

"Max, I can take care of this myself."

"No reason you should have to," he said. "Besides,

you'll want to be at your apartment when the movers show up."

"That's another thing!" she snapped, lifting her chin and narrowing her eyes. "I didn't ask you to arrange for movers."

"You didn't have to. I saw what needed doing, so I did it. End of story."

"To you, maybe."

Max moved in closer as the crowds thickened behind him. Julia shot a nervous glance around her as if trying to find an escape route. As if he would allow that to happen. He bent his head to hers, and her eyes looked huge in her face. Her breath quickened and the pulse point at the base of her throat began to throb in time with her heartbeat.

Max smiled, enjoying the effect he had on her even while having to deal with how his own body responded to her nearness. Walking wasn't going to be comfortable for a while, but damned if he could force himself to back up any. The scent of her reached him and clawed at his self-control.

Lifting both hands to his chest, Julia gave him a shove that didn't move him an inch, then, disgusted, huffed out a breath. "Honestly, Max, you can't just take over my life."

One corner of his mouth lifted as he skimmed his fingertips along the side of her jaw. "You think that's what I'm trying to do?"

She batted his hand away. "Aren't you?"

"No," he said, and meant it. Hell, he liked her just

the way she was. Opinionated, stubborn, with a barely contained wild streak—which was the very reason she'd allowed herself to fall into bed with him the night they'd met.

He'd known from the moment he saw her that he wanted her. And the sparks between them had flown fast and furious that night. Still, he'd been surprised that Julia Prentice, society princess, had stepped out of her entrenched-in-rules life long enough to lose herself to passion.

That night had been a revelation to him. He'd seen beyond the facade she showed society to the woman she was beneath her well-tailored clothes and appropriate behaviors. And that was the woman who continued to haunt him. She was an intriguing blend of buttoned-down conventionality and uninhibited siren—and just standing this close to her made him hard and eager to have her again.

He wouldn't risk losing her now. Even if the marriage they were about to enter was a temporary one, he intended to get everything he could out of their time together. He wanted her. He wanted her child. He wanted it all.

And Max Rolland always got what he wanted.

"If you're not trying to steamroll me, then back off a little, Max."

He slapped one hand to the marble wall at her side. The cool stone was just beginning to warm up due to the wash of morning sunlight. From down the street came the mingled scents of car exhaust, coffee and hot dogs cooking on a cart. It was morning in New York City and the sights, scents and sounds surrounding him were like old friends.

Max smiled, stared into her eyes and said, "I'll back off as soon as we're married."

She frowned at him. "How do I know that?"

He shrugged. "Because I'm telling you I will."

"Oh," she said with a roll of her eyes, "well, that changes everything."

He smiled, enjoying the sarcasm, even enjoying the sparks still shooting from her eyes as she looked at him. Whatever else their businesslike marriage would be, it wouldn't be boring.

"Let's get this settled, all right? Get married. Get rid of the blackmailer and—" He stopped as her eyes widened and she inhaled sharply. "What is it?"

"The blackmailer," she said, opening up the long, narrow black leather bag she carried tucked beneath her arm. "I meant to tell you as soon as you arrived this morning, but you were so full of directives and commands, I forgot all about it."

He ignored that and demanded, "About what?"

She pulled an envelope from her purse and handed it to him. "This was in my mailbox yesterday."

Max pushed away from the wall, glared at the envelope and cursed viciously once he'd read the brief note. "So at the very least, this proves that whoever's behind this is privy to what goes on at 721."

"Apparently," she said, and this time when she looked at him, her eyes weren't shooting angry daggers at him, but were, instead, soft, confused and just a little worried. "How else would this person have known that I was getting married? And that they wouldn't be able to blackmail me now that I won't be pregnant and single?"

Scowling, Max took care to refold the letter and slide it back into its envelope. Then he tucked the missive into the inside pocket of his suit jacket and said, "You're right. Somehow this person is getting information about you. We haven't announced the wedding, so the only way they could have known is if they were somehow connected to 721. Either this person lives here, or knows someone who does."

"It could be anyone," she murmured.

"It could," he agreed, and sent a seeking glance out over the passing pedestrians as if he half expected to see a familiar face watching them. When he saw nothing, he drew Julia away from the building, dropped one arm around her shoulders and pulled her into his side. Then steering her into the moving, jostling throng, he bent his head to say, "Once we're married, the threat to you is over. I'll get this latest letter to Detective McGray, and you…"

"Yes?" She tipped her face up to look at him.

He gave her a half smile and said, "You can get the papers to your lawyer with orders to look them over quickly, then you can direct the movers. The quicker we get you settled at my place, the sooner you can put this behind you."

She frowned again, but nodded in agreement. "Fine.

I really hate to admit that you're right. But you are. At least about this."

Max raised one dark eyebrow as he looked down at her. "I think I just won the war."

"Not the war," she said, giving him a grudging smile that tugged at something inside him, "just this battle."

"For right now," he said, relishing the sweet tang of victory, "I'll settle for that."

"I can't believe all of your stuff is gone," Amanda said, turning in a slow circle in the middle of the living room. "It looks so…empty in here."

"I know." Julia sighed and dropped into one of the two remaining chairs. The movers Max had hired had, of course, been extremely diligent. They'd swept into the apartment, packed up everything she'd pointed at, then left to deliver it all to Max's penthouse. Julia had supervised, but her presence hadn't really been necessary. Within a few short hours, it was all handled and she was officially no longer a resident of 721 Park Avenue.

Which left her feeling a little odd. She'd loved her apartment. She had a lot of good memories wrapped up in this place. Now she was moving on, marrying the father of her child, preparing to be a mother and walking away from everything familiar and into a brand-new world.

Plus, she was leaving Amanda here in the very building where a blackmailer was running rampant. She was a little worried about her friend, though when she said so, Amanda pooh-poohed her.

"Oh, please," she said, pulling on a pair of short black boots. "What do I have going on in my poor, pitiful, loveless life that could interest a self-respecting blackmailer?"

"Fine, maybe you're right," Julia said, scooting forward until she was perched on the edge of the chair, arms braced on her knees, staring into her friend's guileless eyes. "But what if *Max* is right? What if this blackmailer had something to do with Marie Endicott's death?"

Amanda stilled for a minute, then reached up and ruffled her short blond hair with both hands until it looked stylishly tousled. "Okay, you had me there for a minute, but there's no proof that that poor woman was murdered. It's just as likely she either fell or jumped."

"I know but—"

"You may have a point," Amanda announced as she stood up, then pulled Julia to her feet, too. "But I'm not going to worry about something I can't change. I'll be careful, I swear, so don't worry. But I'm not going to spoil the pleasure of having this great apartment all to myself by scaring myself silly over what's probably nothing."

Julia smiled reluctantly. If Amanda wasn't too worried, then there was no reason for Julia to try to make her so. She settled for teasing her friend. "Fine. I can see that you're going to miss me horribly. You're already rubbing your hands together gleefully at the thought of living alone!"

"Oh, honey!" Amanda grinned, swept in and gave

Julia a quick, fierce hug. "That's not what I meant at all! Of course I'll miss you. Who will I have to join me in a midnight splurge on hot-fudge sundaes? Who will be here to listen to me moan and complain about my irritating clients? Who can I steal…er, borrow purses from?"

Julia shook her head and laughed. "Okay, I'm convinced I'm loved."

"You are, you know," Amanda said, her smile fading into seriousness. "And not just for your great purses and shoes, either, though they are a consideration. I'm really going to miss you now that you're moving in with Mad Max."

Julia laughed even harder. "Mad Max?"

Amanda shrugged. "It's how I think of him. I mean, come on. He's rough and rugged—so not one of the usual society types all cool and icy—and he's a little arrogant, which is just so sexy, don't you think?"

Julia did think so. The man oozed sex. All he had to do was walk into a room and she was ready to find the nearest flat surface. Although, even as that thought rolled through her mind, she remembered that only that morning, when he'd braced her against the office building, a part of her had wanted him to lean in and take her right there. Crowds or not. Busy city street or not. She didn't need a flat surface at all. She only needed him.

Not that she'd admit this to anyone else, of course.

"Humph," she said, with a wicked look at Amanda. "A week ago, you were warning me not to marry him."

"Well, as a best friend, that's my job. But since you *are* going to marry him and he *is* the father of your baby, let's at least admit that the man is a treat for the eyes."

"He is that," Julia said on a sigh. "And for other things, as well."

Amanda groaned and slapped one hand to her heart. "You're killing me here. Remember me? The not-by-choice celibate roommate?"

"Vaguely," Julia said, grinning, since she heard the self-deprecating tone in Amanda's voice quite plainly. After all, Amanda herself had chosen to steer clear of relationships after her last one had ended so badly.

"Fine, fine, make light of my pain." Amanda grabbed her purse, tossed Julia's black bag to her and said, "And now, to make up for showing so little sympathy for my lack of a sex life, you get to go shopping with me."

Julia tried to pull away and looked longingly at the chair she'd just left. "Amanda, I'm exhausted…"

"Nothing that a latte and a doughnut won't cure. My treat."

"Seriously, I've got to get to Max's. The movers have unloaded everything, but I've got to finish organizing my stuff and—"

"You can do that anytime," Amanda protested, already dragging Julia toward the door. "How many times will you get to help me buy a new couch? Oh, and tables. And maybe a couple of lamps. And what do you think about new drapes?"

Groaning, Julia followed in her friend's wake,

knowing there was no escape until Amanda's shopping bug had been fed.

As they stepped out of the elevator into the lobby, Amanda was promising her that latte before they got busy shopping. Both women stopped and smiled at Carrie Gray, waiting for the elevator.

At twenty-six, Carrie had gorgeous chestnut hair she forever tied back in a ponytail, big green eyes hidden behind a pair of glasses and a figure most women would kill for, nearly always disguised beneath oversize shirts and baggy jeans. A friendly woman, Carrie lived in apartment 12B but was officially a house sitter for Prince Sebastian Stone of Caspia. Carrie spent most of her time in the apartment, working on her sketches and trying to find a job doing what she loved.

Today, though, she looked exhausted. Even as Julia noticed the shadows under her friend's eyes, Carrie yawned and laughed at the same time.

"Sorry, sorry," she said, then blinked her eyes rapidly as if trying to wake herself up.

"Late night?" Amanda teased.

"Not the way you mean, unfortunately," Carrie admitted.

Behind them, the elevator closed with a quiet swish of sound and in the center of the lobby, Henry stood at his station, sparing the three of them only the barest glance.

Amanda was grinning. "You still having trouble with Trent's Troops?"

Julia groaned. The three of them had come up with

the title "Trent's Troops" for the mind-boggling string of women who came and went from Trent Tanford's apartment on a daily basis.

And, by the way Carrie's green eyes lit with fury, Julia guessed Amanda had been on target. Trent Tanford, heir to a huge entertainment empire, was a classic playboy. The man was far too handsome for his own good and regularly had women dropping at his feet. Unfortunately for Carrie, Trent's women wandered in and out of the building all night long, and apparently, most of them were confused enough to ring Carrie's bell in apartment 12B, instead of Trent's in 12C.

"Honestly, you guys," Carrie said, then checked her voice and lowered it so that Henry wouldn't overhear. Leaning forward, she said, "It's completely out of hand. That guy's got hot- and cold-running women all night long. What is he, a rabbit?"

Amanda laughed and even Julia had to smile, despite the fact that Carrie looked fit to kick something.

"Last night?" Carrie shook her head and her long ponytail whipped from side to side behind her. "The doorbell rings at 3:00 a.m. and there's this barely legal blonde standing there smiling at me like I'm the maid ready to usher her into the sex god's presence. Mind you, two other women have already gotten me up during the night. Apparently Trent can't find women who can read, since none of them can tell the difference between a *B* and a *C*. So I'm running on no sleep and zero patience by this time."

"Uh-oh," Julia muttered.

"Exactly," Carrie said, then continued with her story. "The blonde says, 'Hello, I'm Lauren Hunter,' as if I care who she is." Fisting her hands at her sides, Carrie took a deep breath as if just remembering the night before was churning her temper again. "So I'd had it. I just lost it with this woman. I yelled at her, told her she was at the wrong apartment and that if she was going to go get a quickie with Trent, then the least she could do was make sure she got his address right. For God's sake, is it really so hard to check before ringing somebody's doorbell in the middle of the night?"

"Good for you," Amanda said.

"Felt good, but she looked shocked," Carrie said. "The next time one of his bimbos knocks on my door looking for him, though, I'm not going to take it out on her. I swear I'm going straight to Trent and let *him* have it."

"Maybe you should," Julia said. "Maybe he doesn't know his women are disturbing you."

Carrie slid her a long look. "You really think Trent Tanford is worried about disturbing me? I don't think so. The man is interested in one thing only…"

She left the rest unsaid and, really, why not? They all knew the only thing Trent wanted from women.

Amanda reached out and gave Carrie a brief hug. "You want to come to Park Café with us and get a latte? I'll buy you a doughnut!"

Carrie chuckled, half turned and punched the up button on the elevator. "Thanks, but all I want right now is several uninterrupted hours of sleep."

As she and Amanda left the lobby of 721, Julia thought wistfully that now that she'd be living with Max full-time, she wouldn't have any more of these spur-of-the-moment conversations with her friends again. No more meeting in the elevator. No more chitchatting in the lobby. No more laughing with Amanda over late-night cookie binges.

Of course, there were compensations to living with Max that she didn't have now, too.

Say, for example, living with the man she loved. Although she knew he didn't love her back.

Eight
<u></u>

Julia pushed at the heavy, mahogany dresser and managed to move it a couple of inches along the gleaming wood floor. Then she stopped, huffed out an impatient breath and glared at the blasted thing as if it were being deliberately stubborn. You'd think the thing would slide a little more easily. It wasn't as if she was trying to push it into the next room, after all.

She stopped and looked around the master bedroom. Hers and Max's bedroom now. She wondered how it would be to fall asleep beside him every night and wake up next to him every morning. She smiled to herself as she silently acknowledged that in a bed that wide, they might not even notice each other's presence.

But as soon as that thought sped through her mind,

she discounted it. She was always hyper aware of Max, no matter where they were. Lying beside him in that big bed, she knew, was going to be both glorious and miserable. Julia never would have agreed to marry him, even for the rescue he offered her, if she didn't care for him. If she didn't love him.

How she'd managed to fall in love with Max Rolland so quickly, so irrevocably, was beyond her, but that step had been taken and there was no going back. Julia sighed a little as she stared at the bed covered in a dark red silk duvet, and she wondered if living with Max without his love was going to be a little like dying just a bit every day.

Her only recourse was not to let him see what she felt for him. To behave no differently than she ever had around him. And to hope that sometime during the year of their temporary marriage, he might come to love her, too.

"What're you doing?"

She jumped, startled, and spun around, one hand at her throat as she stared at her soon-to-be husband standing in the doorway. Her heart jolted a little and her insides began their now familiar twist into expectant knots. But with her latest resolution to keep what she felt for him to herself in mind, she blurted, "You scared me!"

"Same to you," Max snarled, glaring at her. He stalked into the master bedroom, marched directly up to her and grabbed hold of her right arm. He paid no attention at all to the electricity that zipped through his veins at the merest touch of her skin to his. He wasn't about to be sidetracked by desire. "I said, what're you doing?"

She pulled her arm free, gave him the same disgusted look she'd just directed at the dresser and quipped, "What am I doing? Brain surgery. You?"

"Funny," he said, not smiling in the least.

He'd arrived at the penthouse loft only a minute or so ago and had noticed the difference in his home the moment he walked in. There were bright, colorful throw pillows on the sofas and chairs in the living room. There were fashion magazines spread across the coffee table and a pair of high heels apparently kicked off in front of one of the couches.

But he hadn't even needed to see those physical hints of Julia's presence. Standing in the foyer, he'd *felt* the difference in the atmosphere instantly. Until today, every night when he walked into his empty home, he told himself it was as he wanted it. Privacy. Space. Time to think with no one making demands on him.

But with the simple act of moving into the penthouse, Julia had changed that. There was life here now. Even the air was faintly scented with her perfume. The rooms seemed warmer, the apartment itself more welcoming somehow. And he found he relished it. So naturally, he'd gone in search of his almost wife only to locate her in the bedroom, pushing a huge piece of furniture.

"Are you nuts?" he demanded, waving one hand at the dresser. "That thing's got to weigh a couple hundred pounds. What're you doing trying to move it by yourself?"

Both of her eyebrows lifted, she gave him a tight smile and, ignoring his bluster, turned to shove at the thing again as if he hadn't said a word. Max could hardly believe it. He wasn't accustomed to people disregarding what he said. And he didn't much care for it.

Max pulled her away, turned her around and held on to her shoulders with a viselike grip. "You're pregnant, Julia. You shouldn't be trying to move heavy furniture."

She sighed. "I'm not an invalid and the baby is perfectly safe."

"You're not doing this," he said and to avoid further argument, bent down, scooped her up into his arms and carted her over to the wide bed, where he dropped her on the mattress. She bounced a little and then looked up at him through narrowed blue eyes.

"Max, I'm perfectly capable of—"

"Where were you trying to move it to?" He cut her off as he walked quickly to the dresser.

She sighed again, shook her head and pointed. "There. Just a foot or two to your left."

Muttering darkly about women being unable to leave things as they were, he put his back to it and in moments had the dresser exactly where she wanted it. "There. Happy?"

"Deliriously."

He brushed back the edges of his jacket and planted both hands on his hips. "Why didn't you have the movers do that for you when they were here this morning?"

"Because I didn't think of it then." She scooted toward the edge of the bed, dragging the sumptuous duvet with her.

When she was on her feet again, Max walked toward her, looked down into her eyes and said, "I don't want you doing any heavy lifting or pushing. Understood?"

She tipped her head to one side and he tried not to notice how her blond hair looked lying against her throat. "Are you really worried, Max?"

Frowning, he studied her a long moment before saying, "Of course I am. You're going to be my wife. You're carrying the child who will be my heir."

"Wow," she said softly, wistfully. "That's just so special and touching."

His scowl deepened. Was that disappointment in her voice? What had she expected him to say? More importantly, what had she wanted him to say?

Then she was speaking again and Max reined in his thoughts. He'd already learned that it made good sense to pay attention when she was talking.

"I won't be coddled, Max," she said quietly. "I'm a big girl and I can take care of myself."

"You're pregnant."

"Yes," she said, smiling, "I know."

"I won't have you risking yourself or the baby with ridiculous stunts."

"Ridiculous?"

"That's right," he snapped, wondering where this

overprotective streak was coming from. All he knew was that when he'd seen her shoving a piece of furniture that weighed more than twice what she did, he'd felt something inside him break.

"If we're getting married, Max—"

"*If?*"

She ignored that and continued, "If we're getting married, then you might as well get used to the idea that I don't like being ordered around."

"That's a shame." Why was he still practically vibrating with a jumble of emotions he didn't really want to acknowledge? And why the hell was he issuing a deliberate challenge to a woman he knew damn well would fight him tooth and nail over it?

"Yes, it is. For *you.*" She took a step closer to him, shook her hair back from her face and lifted her chin so that her gaze could spear his more easily.

He knew she was trying to look steely, immovable. But damned if he didn't find those glints in her eyes so sexy he wanted to tumble her backward onto the bed.

"I'm perfectly capable of taking care of myself."

"You're marrying me," he told her, his voice low and hard. "That makes taking care of you *my* responsibility."

She actually smiled briefly, but the expression didn't have a trace of amusement in it. "You sound like a medieval prince or something."

"I can live with medieval," he said, nodding at the image.

"Well, I can't."

"Is it so hard for you to accept help?"

She blew out a breath that ruffled a strand of hair falling across her eyes. "I don't mind *help,* Max," she said, keeping her gaze locked on his as if trying to will him to understand what she meant. "I came to you in the first place because I needed help, and somehow, I knew instinctively that you would be there for me."

Something in Max's chest tightened at those soft words, so simply spoken. In business, Max knew his allies and even his competitors respected him. Knew that once given, his word could be trusted. But in his personal life, he'd been stung badly and so had pulled back from making the kinds of commitments women wanted.

He'd considered himself cold, withdrawn and had thought himself at peace with himself. Yet, those few words from Julia meant more to him than he wanted to admit. The wall of ice around his heart seemed to splinter, jagged shards of the damn thing slicing at his insides. But as the pain tugged at him, a corner of Max's mind, still logical, still fighting the sexual pull dragging at him, whispered, *She came to you because she knew you'd help her even though she's pregnant with another man's baby. She came to you for help, but lied to you to get it. Why? Because she knew you'd come through for her, or because she thought a society princess was doing the common man a favor?*

But did it matter?

He'd gotten what he wanted.

Her. And the heir he'd craved. A part of him still

wondered about the father of her baby. If he'd come back. Change his mind and demand rights to the child Max was already thinking of as his own. And if this nameless sperm donor changed his mind about his baby, wouldn't he also want Julia? Who the hell *wouldn't* want Julia?

His brain raced as he walked to her, every step measured. His gaze locked on her as he told himself he'd never give her up. Never let her go back to the man who'd left her pregnant and alone. She was his now. As was the child.

The closer he came to her, the more he felt that territorial surge pumping through him. *His.* One word, it echoed over and over again in his mind. Julia Prentice would be his wife. Her baby would be his heir. And he'd ruin *anyone* who tried to change that.

His body was hard, his blood was thick and hot in his veins, and the racing thoughts in his mind scattered like autumn leaves in a high wind. She was too close for him to be thinking about anything but having her. Drowning in her eyes, losing himself in her body, surrendering to the incredible rush of heat and longing that sprang into being whenever he saw her.

"I will be there for you and the baby," he finally said, fighting the urge to grab her, hold her, take her mouth with all the hunger pumping inside him. "And since I'm now that baby's father, I'm not going to stand back and watch you endanger the baby without saying something."

"I wouldn't endanger my child," she argued, her gaze caught in his, her body leaning toward him.

"I know," he allowed. Silently he asked himself where this was coming from. Why just looking at her made him alternately want to wrap her up and make sure she was safe and at the same time strip her down and lose himself in the glory that was her body. But any answer he might come up with would only jangle his nerves more than the question, so he let it go.

"Are you going to be giving me orders for the next seven months?" Her eyes glittered, reflecting the soft lamplight in the room, and Max felt as though he couldn't breathe when he looked at the deep blue of those eyes shining at him.

He blew out a breath. "Probably," he admitted, then added, "Look, I know you wouldn't do anything deliberately to hurt yourself or the baby. But you can't do everything you used to do without stopping to think of the possible consequences."

A minute of silence hummed between them, fraught with emotions neither of them were willing to admit to. Seconds ticked past and Max had to fight the urge to pull her close to him. To bend his head, taste her lips, strip her down and lose himself in the feel of her beneath his hands.

Finally she said, "You're right."

"Now, there's something I never thought I'd hear you say again." One corner of Max's mouth turned up. "I think we're having a moment here."

She laughed a little, shook her head and warned, "Don't get used to it."

Max lifted one hand, cupped her cheek and stared

directly into her eyes. Then he spoke, a soft warning for both of them. "Maybe neither one of us should get too used to this."

"This?"

"Being together."

"We will be, though," she reminded him. "For a year, anyway."

He smiled again and stroked the tips of his fingers over her cheekbone. A year of Julia in his life. In his home. In his bed. Did it matter that she'd lied to him to bring them to this point? No, it didn't. Not to him. She'd lied, but she'd done it for her child. That he could understand. Hell, admire. And it had brought her here. To him.

"So you've decided to sign the papers, then?"

"Yes." Her gaze shifted to one side briefly before coming back to meet his again. He felt that powerful blue gaze punch into him, and the hunger inside roared with a need that nearly brought him to his knees.

"My lawyer went over them this afternoon," she said. "I signed them. Left them on the dining-room table."

A knot of tension he hadn't been aware he was carrying dissolved inside him, and Max threaded his fingers through her hair at her temple. The silken strands slid against his skin, warming him, tempting him—as if he needed further tempting.

"Good," he said, and heard the husky note of need in his own voice. "That's good. So it's official. We're a couple."

"A trio, actually," she said, her smile fading into an expression of desire as his fingers continued to slide through her hair.

"I stand corrected," he whispered, lowering his head to hers. "I also stand hungry."

"Dinner's in the fridge," she murmured, twisting her head into his hand, so that she could feel more of him. "Your housekeeper left it and—"

"That's not what I'm hungry for," Max said, and took her mouth with his. It began as a gentle brush of his lips on hers, then quickly became something much more. Something he found he desperately needed.

She leaned into him and Max caught her up, pulling her close, molding her body to his, feeling the need inside him clawing for release. He groaned as the taste of her filled him, swamping him, drowning him in sensation that only grew more complex, more overpowering. Her scent wafted around him, teasing his every breath with another layer of *her*.

His hands swept up and down her spine, feeling every curve, defining every line. The taste of her swam through him in a rush of something so powerful his mind quieted, his thoughts faded, and he gave himself up to the moment.

She sighed and his heartbeat quickened. She leaned into him, wrapped her arms around his neck, and everything in him roared. He broke their kiss, tearing his mouth from hers, only to move to her jaw and trail hot, damp kisses down the length of her slender throat. When he reached that pulse-pounding point at the base of her neck, he tasted the evidence of *her* need. The frantic beating of her heart, the staggering sighs of her breathing.

Julia groaned, allowing that one small sound to slide from her throat into the stillness of the room. The touch of his hands was like fire. Her head dropped back and she stared blankly at the ceiling as Max's mouth moved up and down her throat, trailing hot, urgent kisses. His hands swept over her, sliding beneath the hem of her shirt, tugging it up and over her head. Once he had the silky garment in his hands, he tossed it over his shoulder to land on the floor. Then he flipped the catch on her bra, slid it off and down her shoulders and filled his hands with her breasts. His thumbs smoothed across her hardened nipples until Julia was nearly whimpering with the sensations coursing through her.

He walked her backward until the backs of her thighs hit the edge of the massive bed. His gaze locked with hers, she couldn't look away. Couldn't seem to see anything but the green eyes watching her, devouring her.

Ribbons of need unwound inside her, and Julia surrendered to the inevitable. When he laid her back on the bed, she felt the cool slide of silk against her bare skin. She lifted her hips as Max unhooked her slacks, slid the zipper down and then pulled them down her legs. All she wore now was a scrap of pale pink lace underwear that was gone in the next second. Naked, hungry for the sight of him, the feel of him, she scooted farther back on the bed and watched as he quickly stripped off his own clothes, his gaze never leaving hers.

"I want you," he whispered as he joined her on the bed, sliding his big hands up her calves, her thighs, her hips. "I always want you. It's like fire in the blood. Never quenched, never satisfied, always burning."

"I know," she said, reaching for him, tugging his mouth down to hers. "I know just what that feeling is like. It's never been like this for me before. Only with you."

"Only me," he repeated, and dipped his head for a quick kiss. But when she tried to hold him there, hungry for the taste of him, he escaped her grasping hands and moved, trailing hot, damp kisses along her body. He gave each of her tender, sensitive nipples attention, then moved on, sliding lower and lower over her body until Julia was twisting and writhing beneath him, eager for what she knew was coming, what she wanted desperately.

He knelt between her thighs, scooped his hands beneath her bottom and lifted her until her legs dangled free and she was helpless in his grasp. "Max..." She swallowed hard, took a breath and held it.

"I want the taste of you in my mouth. I want all of you," he whispered. Then he bent his head to the core of her and flicked his tongue over that one small, too-sensitive spot.

Sparks shot through her bloodstream and exploded behind her eyes in a dazzling shower of light and heat. Again and again, he used his tongue to lick and stroke and gently torture her. She rocked her hips, grabbed fistfuls of the silken duvet beneath her and held on with an iron grip. The world seemed to teeter around her, spinning wildly out of control, and it was all due to the man so intimately loving her.

He pushed her higher, higher, and Julia fought for air. Fought to reach that peak he kept her climbing for. Tension coiled, tightening until she couldn't think, couldn't breathe, could only feel. When release came, her climax slammed into her, and Julia rocked helplessly in his grasp, riding the wave of completion that seemed to roll on forever.

"Max—"

"Not finished yet," he promised, and laid her down on the bed. Her body was still humming, still trembling with the force of her orgasm when Max turned her over and she lay facedown on the cover. She turned her head to one side and watched him as he stroked his hands up and down her spine until finally bringing them to rest at her hips.

He lifted her until she was on her knees and Julia felt a brand-new surge of want filling her. Amazing. She hadn't even stopped trembling from her last climax, and already, her body hungered for another. For the feel of his body pushing into hers, for the sensation of being filled by him.

"Take me, Max," she whispered, arching her back, offering herself to him. "I want you inside me."

He braced his thighs on either side of her and she felt the hard, warm strength of him surrounding her, claiming her. Then he leaned his body over hers and pushed himself into her depths.

Julia called out his name and pushed backward, meeting his thrusts, taking him deeper and more fully into her body than she ever had before. Again and again, he withdrew and entered, claiming more of her heart and soul with every slow thrust.

He moved one hand around her body and cupped her breast as he took her higher and higher. She moved with him, loving the feel of his hard, strong body covering hers, filling hers. She gave herself up to the wonder of it, and when her body exploded into glittering shards of pleasure, her breath shattered and she didn't breathe again until she felt him join her on that blissful slide into nothingness.

<u>Nine</u>

They settled into a routine of sorts over the next few days. With the wedding getting closer with every passing day, there were details to be dealt with and Max was astonished by how easily Julia managed everything.

On Monday she had a fitting for her wedding dress.

On Tuesday she dragged Max to the caterer Amanda had recommended.

On Wednesday they visited three florists with Amanda until a decision had been made.

On Thursday the judge who would perform the ceremony met with them to discuss what would be a brief, civil service.

And on Friday they had to attend a charity ball for the Midtown Shelter, one of the organizations Julia raised funds for.

Max hated wearing a tuxedo.

Somehow, they always made him feel like a fraud. Glancing around the room at the glittering stars of society, gathered together to be admired for the money they were donating, he felt like just what he was. A blue-collar kid from upstate New York.

It didn't seem to matter that he had more money than most of the attendees. Didn't matter that he'd worked for more than a decade, building his company into one of the fastest-growing financial institutions in the country. Didn't even matter that he was soon to be marrying into one of the oldest families in New York.

Because at gatherings like these, there were always the sidelong glances directed at him. The barely concealed snubs. These people might need his financial advice, but they didn't consider him one of them. And they never would.

Normally at one of these functions Max made the rounds, spoke to a few people, handled his donation and left, usually with some sparkling, empty-headed beauty on his arm. Tonight, though, everything was different.

His gaze focused on the reason.

Even from across the room, one glance at Julia and Max's body went hard and hot. She wore an off-the-shoulder, sapphire-blue gown with a low-cut bodice and a back that dipped so low, you could almost see the top of her behind. Her hair was done up on top of her head into a mass of curls, and her blue eyes shone with excitement and satisfaction.

She'd worked hard to pull this night off and Max felt a stir of admiration for her. His gaze followed her as she worked the crowd. A smile here, a brief touch on the shoulder there, a quick word and a laugh with an older man and she was moving again, sifting through the crowd, the rich hue of her gown soaking up the overhead lights and making her shine in a roomful of crows.

All around him, the hum of conversations rose and fell like the ocean's waves. The air smelled of expensive perfume and the banks of roses that studded the walls. At one end of the massive ballroom, an orchestra was tuning up and at the other end, an incredible buffet was laid out to tempt appetites. Caterers moved through the crowd offering trays laden with crystal glasses of champagne, yet Max hardly noticed any of it.

His gaze was solely for Julia. She was a part of this crowd as he never would be. She belonged to it. But, he thought with an inner smile as he took a sip of champagne, she also belonged to him.

"Don't look now," a deep voice said from right beside him, "but you're drooling."

Max laughed shortly, shot his friend a quick look, then turned his gaze back to Julia as she continued her parade through the milling throng. "Alex," he said. "Didn't know you'd be here."

"Oh," Alex Harper said, "I show up at these things occasionally."

"Surprised you were willing to take time from work." Max knew only too well that his friend's devotion to work rivaled his own.

"Believe me," Alex told him, "this is work." He accepted a glass of champagne from a passing waiter, took a sip and said, "Do you have any idea how boring it is listening to some of these people?"

"Yeah, I do." Max's eyes narrowed. Julia had stopped alongside a tall, blond guy who looked as if he'd just stepped off the cover of *GQ*.

"Still," his friend went on, "you've got to take the time to see clients in social settings once in a while."

"Uh-huh." Did she have to lay her hand on the guy's arm?

"Clients expect some personal treatment outside the office, too."

"Sure." She was smiling now, leaning into the blond guy so he could kiss her cheek. What the hell was that about?

"And then sometimes the clients want me to train their camels to do a high-wire act for the circus."

"Yeah, I know." Kissing *both* cheeks? Who was this guy?

Beside him Alex laughed and clapped a hand to Max's shoulder. "You've got it bad, don't you."

"Huh? What?" Tearing his gaze from Julia and her new "friend," Max glared at Alex. "What did you say about camels?"

"Nothing." Alex shook his head, reached out and took Max's champagne glass, then said, "The music is starting. Why don't you go get that gorgeous woman before you pop a blood vessel or something."

Scowling, Max shoved both hands into his pants pockets. "I don't know what you're talking about."

"Sure, you don't." Alex laughed a little. "For God's sake, Max, if looks could kill, that guy would be six feet under and stone-cold."

"Who the hell is he?"

"Who cares? She's not engaged to him. She's going to marry *you*. So go ask her to dance."

"Since when did you start giving advice on women?"

Alex laughed again. "I'm always ready to *give* advice. It's the taking of it where I draw the line."

When Alex walked away, Max shifted his gaze back to the woman currently driving him insane. The blond guy was still standing too close, and Julia still appeared to enjoy talking to him. So maybe Alex was right. Maybe it was time to remind both Julia and her friend just who she'd come here with tonight.

Making his way through the crowd, Max stopped alongside Julia and felt a flicker of pleasure when she grinned up at him and immediately linked her arm through his. "Max, hi. I was just telling Trevor about you."

Trevor.

"Is that right?" His voice came out a little harsher, stiffer, than he'd planned, and the quick flash of worry in Julia's eyes forced Max to lighten up as he held out one hand to Trevor. "Max Rolland."

The other man shook his hand and said, "Trevor Swift. I hear congratulations are in order." He beamed at Julia. "You're getting a hell of a woman."

Max drew Julia closer to his side. "I think so. How do you two know each other?"

"Oh, our families have been friends for years," Julia said quickly.

"Yes," Trevor admitted. "Julia and I used to go off together to avoid our parents whenever we could."

"Is that right?" Looking into the eyes of the man smiling at him, Max felt a sharp stab of something unexpected. Something unfamiliar. Jealousy. Trevor and Julia had grown up together, in the same social circle. A part of Max resented the fact that this guy knew the woman he would be marrying far better than he himself did.

"Having Julia around was the one thing that kept me sane when dealing with my parents," Trevor was saying, clearly unaware of Max's slow burn.

"I'm sure," he said, fighting the urge to plant a fist into the man's smiling face, just to let him know that Julia was taken now.

"Um, Max?" Julia tugged at his arm until she had his attention.

He shifted his gaze to hers and saw uneasiness flickering in her eyes. Was he so easy for her to read, then? Forcing a smile, he bent, kissed her quickly, then straightened and said, "You'll have to excuse us, Trevor. I want to dance with my fiancée."

"Of course, of course."

But Max wasn't listening. He'd already turned to steer Julia through the mass of people toward the dance floor. He swung her into his arms as the music swelled. It was an old tune from the forties, soft, dreamy.

She slid her left hand up his arm to lie on his shoulder and followed his lead smoothly as other couples joined them in a swirl of color and motion. His right hand lay at the small of her back, and the feel of her skin against his palm sent bolts of desire shooting through him.

Holding her right hand in his left, he gave her fingers a squeeze, looked down into her eyes and said, "So you and Trevor are close?"

"Yes," she said, her voice pitched just high enough to be heard over the swell of the orchestra but not loud enough to be overheard. "Since we were kids. His parents and mine have been friends for years, so Trev and I spent a lot of time together growing up."

"He loves you." The signs had been unmistakable. The warmth in the other man's eyes. The timbre of his voice when he spoke about her.

"I love him, too," she said, and sent a sharp knife through Max's chest. The pain was only alleviated a little when she added, "He's like my brother, Max."

He moved her into a tight turn that sent the skirt of her gown swirling about her legs. She moved closer to him, pressing her breasts to his chest, and Max could have sworn he felt her heart pounding against his.

"Are you jealous?"

He scowled down at her. "Apparently."

She smiled, damn it.

"If the two of you are so tight," he asked because he had to know, "why didn't you go to him when you needed a husband? Why come to me?"

A dizzying array of emotions darted across her features in a moment's time. Frustration, disappointment and anger merged together to set off a glint in her eyes that signaled her own temper beginning to build.

"A couple of reasons," she told him. "First, being that it's *your* baby I'm carrying…"

He rolled his eyes and shook his head. "And?"

"And," she repeated, bending her head closer to his, lowering her voice dramatically, "Trev's gay, Max. His parents don't know, but he lives with a lovely man named Arthur. Somehow I didn't think Arthur would be pleased to have me marry the man he considers to be *his* husband."

Relief swept through Max in such a rush it nearly stole his breath. Then in the next instant, he felt a tug of sympathy for the other man. If Max felt like an outsider at one of these things, how much more did a man like Trevor feel? Max at least could be himself and those who didn't like it were free to move on.

But Trevor couldn't even be himself with his family.

Staring down into Julia's eyes, Max frowned a little and said, "I thought—"

"I know what you thought," she said softly, shaking her head slightly and sending her mass of blond curls into a dance of their own. "Max, you have to trust me or we have nothing. This marriage won't even last out the year if you can't believe in me."

"Trust isn't something I give lightly."

"What have I done that makes you think you *can't* trust me?"

The music ended and he drew them to a stop. Looking down into her glimmering blue eyes, he said, "You won't tell me the truth about your baby."

"I have—"

"Don't keep trying to tell me it's mine," he whispered, the words scraping his throat as he spoke them. "I know different."

She let her hand fall from his shoulder and Max felt the absence of her touch as clearly as he'd felt the touch itself. "How can I make you believe me?"

"You can't."

"Then why are you going to marry me? If you won't trust me, can't believe in me, why do you want me?"

When the music rose again in another ballad designed to lure couples onto the dance floor, Max pulled her into his arms again. Holding her tightly to him, he allowed her to feel the hard eagerness in his body. When her eyes widened, he said gruffly, "Because you do that to me with a look. Because you walk into a room and everything but you disappears. Because you're *mine*."

The next hour or so flew by in a whirl. Julia felt Max's gaze on her wherever she went. As she talked to the caterers, schmoozed with patrons, dealt with any number of minor problems, Max's gaze filled her with heat.

And while she did everything that was expected of her, Julia's mind raced with the implications of her last conversation with Max. He didn't trust her. And that fact stung. All her life, Julia had been the kind of woman people could depend on. She prided herself on giving her word and keeping it. Now, knowing that the one man who *should* have believed her didn't, she felt more hurt than she wanted to admit.

"Good evening, Julia."

She stiffened, plastered a hard, tight smile on her face and turned to greet the woman behind that icy voice. "Hello, Mother. I didn't expect to see you here tonight."

Actually, that wasn't true. She'd been hoping not to see her parents. But the way her luck was running lately, their presence wasn't really a surprise.

"Of course we came," her mother said, sniffing delicately, then turning her head to observe the crowd. "Our friends would have missed us if we'd stayed away. And that would have led to questions we prefer not to answer."

So her parents hadn't resigned themselves yet to her upcoming wedding, Julia thought.

"I suppose your paramour is here," her mother said.

"If you mean my fiancé, then yes, Max is here tonight."

Margaret Prentice shuddered and the column of gold silk she wore wrapped about her too-thin frame rippled with the motion. "Your fiancé."

"Mother—"

"I won't discuss this with you, Julia. Not until you've come to your senses and called off this travesty of a marriage with a completely unsuitable man."

"Present," Max said suddenly from directly behind Julia.

She felt the heat of his body, the hard, solid strength of him behind her, and silently thanked him for coming to her aid.

"I beg your pardon?" Margaret asked, lifting her gaze to meet his.

"You were speaking about Julia's completely unsuitable fiancé. That would be me." He reached around Julia with his right hand while dropping his left hand onto her shoulder in an unmistakable claim. "Max Rolland, Mrs. Prentice."

Margaret briefly lowered her gaze to his outstretched hand, then pointedly ignored it. "I have nothing to say to you, Mr. Rolland. This is a private conversation between my daughter and myself."

Julia felt embarrassed. For her mother. For Max. For herself. This situation could only disintegrate and she wondered how to avoid what was bound to be more unpleasantness. All her life, she'd been alone against her parents' rigorous expectations and cold disapproval. She'd faced them both countless times and had always come away from the encounters feeling as though she would never measure up.

Now, she stiffened her shoulders, lifted her chin and prepared herself for what she knew was coming. Her mother's icy displeasure.

Then Max let his hand drop to wind about Julia's waist, pulling her back tightly against him. Margaret Prentice winced at the unseemly public display, but

Julia was grateful for the arm he kept wrapped around her. His broad, muscular chest was at her back and the solid thump of his heartbeat was a reminder that she wasn't alone. She didn't have to put up with her parents' dissatisfaction anymore. It was as if silently, Max was reminding her that times had changed. She wasn't a young girl desperately seeking support. She was a grown woman now, more than able to think and choose for herself. And the man she'd chosen stood behind her in a blatant display of solidarity she was more than grateful for.

"Anything you have to say to Julia, you can say in front of me."

"Julia, please tell this individual to leave."

"No."

Margaret's eyes widened and she couldn't have looked more stunned if Julia had reached out and slapped her.

"Excuse me?"

"I said no, Mother," Julia repeated, enjoying herself even more the second time. "I'm here with Max and we're busy right now."

Margaret's small, pinched mouth tightened even further, until her lips nearly disappeared from her face entirely. "This is unacceptable, Julia."

Around them, several heads began to turn their way, as if sensing gossip-worthy news.

Max must have noticed because just then, he smiled and said, "You're right, Mrs. Prentice. This is unacceptable. This is neither the time nor the place for this kind of conversation. So, if you'll excuse us, I think I'll just steal Julia away for another dance."

"My daughter and I are—"

"Finished talking," Max interrupted, leaving the older woman's mouth opening and closing like a landed trout gasping for air.

Before Julia could really enjoy the image, though, Max swept her away, pulled her into his arms and led her into a slow, romantic dance. Soon enough, Julia's mother was the furthest thing from her mind.

"Thank you," Julia said hours later as he entered their bedroom.

"For what?" He tore off his elegantly tied bow tie and tossed it negligently onto the nearest chair.

"For coming to my rescue," Julia said, stepping out of her high heels and nearly groaning with the pleasure of being barefoot. "With my mother."

Max shrugged out of his jacket, then unbuttoned his vest and shirt. "Not a problem. Felt good to leave her standing there staring after us."

When she didn't say anything, he looked at her. "Was she always like that?"

"Like what?"

"Cold."

"Yes." Julia couldn't remember a single moment in her life when either of her parents had offered her affection or even warmth. There had always been a careful distance between the Prentices and the child they hadn't really wanted.

Julia reached behind her for the zipper at the back of her dress, and when she couldn't quite get it, she walked to Max and turned so he could do it. She sucked in a breath as the backs of his fingers came into contact with her skin. With the zipper undone, the sapphire gown dropped to the floor between them and Max bent to pick it up for her.

"Can't imagine growing up like that," he muttered, sliding one hand across her behind, then around to the front, to dip his fingers beneath the slim band of elastic at the top of her black thong.

"It wasn't easy," she admitted, sighing a little as he stroked her skin.

"You did it, though," he whispered, bending to kiss the curve of her shoulder. "You survived them. And became an amazing woman."

Warmth settled in her chest and tears stung the backs of her eyes. "Thank you for that, too."

"I had family," he said, still moving his hand up and down the column of her spine. "Parents who loved me. Pushed me. Supported me."

"You were lucky."

"I know. Which is why I admire you even more than I did before. Everything you are," he said softly, his breath dusting across her neck and shoulder, "is your own doing. You owe them nothing."

His words filled her heart, his touch filled her soul, and Julia leaned back into him, suddenly needing him more than she ever had before.

"You're beautiful," he murmured.

"Max," she said, arching into his touch.

"I want you again."

"I know," she whispered, feeling the heat of his skin seep into her own. She hissed in a breath as his fingertips slid lower, lower, until he found that already heated bud of flesh at the heart of her.

"I wanted you at the party, too," he said softly, dipping his head to the curve of her neck. "I wanted to hold you like this."

"Max…" Julia's mind splintered as he began to move his fingers in and out of her heat. She parted her thighs for him and leaned back against him, counting on him to support her even as he tormented her.

"Don't talk for a minute, okay?" His words were muffled against her skin as he slowly moved, turning her in his arms until they were facing the mirror over the dresser.

Only one dim light burned in the room, and the glow of it wasn't bright enough to dispel the shadows crouched in the corners. Outside the expanse of windows, Manhattan lay covered in night, with the lights of the city sparkling like jewels. A nearly full moon shone in the distance, sending pearly silver light streaming into the bedroom, and in its glow, Julia looked at Max and her reflected in the mirror.

He was so much bigger than she. Broad in the shoulders, arms muscled and tanned against her white skin. He was dark where she was fair and the differences between them lay starkly revealed as he met her gaze in the mirror.

"Watch," he whispered, and with a quick twist of his wrist, tore her thong free and let it float to the floor. "Watch what I can do to you. What you do to me."

She couldn't look away. Couldn't tear her gaze from the couple in the mirror. He moved his left arm over her shoulder and cupped her breast in his palm. His right hand slid over her abdomen, caressing, stroking. His strong, tanned hands looked erotic sliding across her so-white skin, and Julia rubbed herself against him in response to the image they made.

"I want to touch you. And I want you to watch me pleasure you."

"Max…" She licked dry lips and watched with an avid gaze as his right hand slid lower and lower until he was once more stroking that tight bud of sensation between her thighs.

Again and again, his big hand dipped into her heat and she widened her stance, went up on her toes as he touched her. His left hand tweaked and tugged at her nipple while his right hand did amazing things to her core. She was hot all over. Her skin felt as if it were on fire. She rocked against him, teetering on her toes. Reaching back, she hooked one arm around his neck and closed her eyes.

"Open them," he demanded, and when she did, she met his heated gaze in the glass. She read hunger there and knew an answering hunger was in her own eyes. What he did to her was magic. What he made her want was more than she'd ever thought possible.

Tingles of expectation awoke inside her and she

knew she was poised on the very lip of a climax that would shatter her. While she watched, unable, unwilling, to look away now, he slid first one finger and then two inside her while his thumb continued to stroke and rub that one spot that ached for completion.

She watched herself writhe in his grasp and felt wild for the first time in her life. She wasn't controlled, wasn't thinking about anything but the effect Max had on her body. Every cell was alive and singing. Every nerve in her body jangled with bright anticipation. Her breath strained as she focused on the spiraling tension inside her, giving herself up to the frantic, driving need.

When the first shattering wave struck her, she screamed his name, looked into Max's reflected gaze and let him see everything he was doing to her. And when her body stilled, the last of the tremors fading into memory, he swept her into his arms and carried her to the wide, silk-covered mattress.

Much later, when she lay in his arms, both she and Max absolutely spent and cocooned in their bed, Julia traced his broad chest with the tips of her fingers, tangling them in the thatch of dark curls. Her body was sated, but her mind couldn't rest. Now that the fiery passion between them had been eased for the moment, there was something she had to know.

He'd stood alongside her tonight, allying himself with her against her mother. He'd given her his support, played the part of the loving fiancé in public and was the lover she'd always dreamed of in private. Still, he held back from her. Distanced himself. Refused to believe in the possibility that the child she carried was his. She had to find out his reasons for shutting her out.

"Max," she whispered, "I need you to tell me why you won't believe me about the baby."

He sighed, came up on one elbow and looked down at her. In the wash of moonlight, his green eyes shone like emeralds under a spotlight. His dark hair tumbled across his forehead and his mouth was tight and hard. "You're not going to let this go, are you?"

She shook her head on the pillow and met his gaze squarely. Reaching up, she cupped his cheek in her palm and brushed her thumb across his skin. "I can't, Max."

"Fine." Staring directly into her eyes, he said, "I've known from the beginning that you're lying to me. I can't be the baby's father, Julia. See, when she couldn't get pregnant, my ex-wife and I had all the tests done. I found out then that I'm infertile. I'm *nobody's* father."

Ten

"You're wrong." She looked confused. "There was a mistake. You have to go back to the doctor. Take the test again."

"What would be the point?" Max shook his head and blew out a frustrated breath. Finding out that he would never be able to father a child had cut at the very heart of him.

Even now, he remembered the sense of failure that had filled him when he was faced with the indisputable facts. That Julia could cling to her lies even when she knew the truth was astonishing. Looking into her eyes now, Max said, "Let it go, Julia. You don't need the lies. We're getting married. I'm going to adopt your child. At least let's have truth between us."

"I *am* telling you the truth."

Her eyes didn't flicker. She didn't look away. She didn't bite her lip or show any other sign that what he'd said had changed anything for her. So what the hell was she after? Why was she clinging to this ridiculous story?

Wasn't it enough that they were getting married? He was going to give her and her baby his name. Why couldn't she at least treat him with some respect? Give him the courtesy of some damn honesty?

"I've got some work I should be doing," he said, and pulled away from her, edging off the bed.

"Max, stay with me."

He glanced at her and saw she was sitting up, the silk duvet pooled in her lap, her breasts brushed by moonlight. Her pale hair was tumbled across her shoulders and she looked the image of every man's dream lover. There was nothing he wanted more than to get back into bed with her. To have her beneath him, his body locked with hers.

Because he wanted it so much, he ignored the urge and stalked naked across the room to the walk-in closet. There, he grabbed a thick, black cashmere robe and shrugged into it. When he stepped back into the bedroom, she hadn't moved. She was still sitting there, bathed in moonlight, watching him, a wordless plea in her eyes.

"Go to sleep," he said tightly, already headed for the door, since he didn't trust himself to stay too long. "I'll see you in the morning."

He closed the bedroom door behind him, and alone in the darkened hallway, he walked to his office, trying to put that last image of her out of his mind.

A part of Julia wanted to give up. To throw in the towel and just admit that Max would never be the husband she wanted him to be. How could they have *anything* together if he didn't believe her about something as big, as basic, as their child?

Her mind had been whirling for days. Ever since their late-night conversation when Max had told her what he believed to be the truth. She couldn't find a way past the wall he'd erected around himself and she was half-afraid she never would. And if she couldn't, what did that signify? Maybe she should rethink this marriage. Walk away and take her chances with the blackmailer.

Everything inside her cringed away from that idea. Yes, times had changed and single mothers were no longer the social pariahs they once had been. But Julia didn't want to do that to her baby. She wanted her child to have *two* parents. To be loved. To grow up surrounded by support and safety.

Besides, she thought, as she glanced around what was now Amanda's apartment, she couldn't move back in here. Her friend was so happy with the place and had already turned it into her own private nest.

"Did I tell you?" Amanda called from the kitchen, interrupting Julia's thoughts. "Elizabeth Wellington hired me to plan her and her husband's five-year anniversary party."

"That's great," Julia said, hoping she'd forced enough enthusiasm into her voice.

"I know! Although," Amanda added as she walked back into the living room, carrying two tall glasses of soda over ice, "between you and me, Elizabeth didn't look happy."

"What's wrong?"

"I don't think she meant to let this slip, so keep it between us, okay?"

"Of course."

Amanda handed her one of the glasses and said, "Elizabeth is worried that she shouldn't be celebrating a marriage she's afraid won't last another year."

"Oh, God. Poor Elizabeth. This has all been so hard on her." Julia took a sip of her soda and let the icy bubbles slide down her throat.

"She looked so sad for a minute, then she plastered on a smile and went back to talking about the party. Almost makes me feel guilty for taking the job."

"No," Julia said softly. "Just make it a great party. For her sake. I so know what Elizabeth is feeling. Sometimes we simply have to go through with something even when we've got doubts."

"That has the ring of personal experience."

Julia looked at her friend's concerned gaze and couldn't hide her feelings. Amanda knew her too well and wouldn't be fooled even if Julia tried. But the truth was, she needed to talk to someone about all this, and who better than her best friend?

"Max won't listen to me," Julia said, curling up on

one of the new chairs Amanda had purchased for the apartment. Her fingertips idly traced the outline of a pink cabbage rose on the arm of the overstuffed chair, but she wasn't really seeing it. Her mind was filled with the image of Max's face as he'd called her a liar. Again.

"This surprises you?" Amanda took a seat in the chair opposite her. "You knew going into this that he was stubborn. Heck, the man's made his name on Wall Street by being the hardest-headed man in the country. Everyone says that once he makes up his mind about something, nothing can change it."

"That's a comforting thought." Julia took a drink of the soda, then set the glass down on the table in front of her. "I don't know what to do, Amanda. What he's doing now goes beyond stubborn. He won't even discuss the possibility that the fertility tests he had done a few years ago were wrong."

Julia had come to Amanda the morning after Max's big announcement, so her friend had already been sworn to secrecy.

"I still don't know what to tell you about this." Amanda tucked her long legs up under her and shook her head. "You can't *make* him believe you."

"But he should. I mean, if I were lying," Julia said, jumping up out of her chair to pace, "wouldn't that have been the time for me to confess all? I mean, seriously, why would I keep insisting he's the father of the baby if he's not and I knew he wasn't? Does that make sense?" She stopped, shook her head, then rubbed at her temples. "I swear, sometimes I think I'm just going around and around in circles."

"Honey, you guys hardly know each other. It's no big surprise that he won't take your word for something as important as this."

"That's the point, though! I told him to go get retested, but he won't even discuss it. Says there's no reason for it."

"Stubborn, as already stated," Amanda said, giving her a supportive smile. "But I don't see what you can do about it."

"I can't, either." Julia huffed out a frustrated breath and shrugged. "I guess I just needed to rant."

"Nothing wrong with a good rant," Amanda told her. "And I'm always happy to listen. But—" she reached for a manila folder on the tabletop "—if you're finished for the moment, we could go over the last-minute details of the wedding."

The wedding. In a few days, she'd be marrying a man who was convinced she was a liar. How could that possibly be a good thing?

"Uh-oh," Amanda said softly. "I'm seeing hesitation in your eyes. Changing your mind about getting married? 'Cause if you are, tell me now so I can start the cancellations."

"No." Julia's head snapped up and her gaze fixed on her friend. "I'm not backing out." She laid one hand on her belly, as if she could comfort the child within. "No matter what he thinks, Max *is* the father of my baby. And my child deserves to have his father's name."

"True." Amanda tipped her head to one side and stared at her. "But what about *you?* Don't you deserve better than what Max is offering, Jules? Don't you deserve a man who trusts you? Loves you?"

Yes, she did. Julia's heart gave a little ping of pain. She wasn't foolish enough to think that Max loved her. But she knew he cared for her. He couldn't be as protective and supportive if he didn't feel *something* for her. And if he felt something, then he could eventually love her, right? After all, once the baby was born, she could insist on a paternity test. Then he'd know. Then he'd believe. But, God, she wished he could trust her without proof. Wished he could look into her eyes and see that she wouldn't lie to him about this.

Shaking her head, she walked back to her chair, dropped into it and said, "I deserve to marry the man *I* love. And I do love him—not that he'd believe me if I told him so," she added ruefully. Then her eyes narrowed, her chin lifted and her spine stiffened with determination. "But somehow, someday, I'm going to get through to the big jerk. And when that day comes, he's going to have to do some serious groveling to convince me to forgive him."

"Attagirl," Amanda said with a wide grin. "If anyone can do it, you can. Besides, there's nothing better than a good grovel."

"Any news on the blackmail front?"

Max lifted his head and shot a look at Alex. His friend had brought over some legal documents concerning the apartment building Max had just purchased. But now that their business was complete, Alex seemed in no hurry to leave.

"No, nothing. I spoke with Detective McGray yesterday and he says they have no leads. The blackmailer could have been anyone. But whoever it was is smart enough to leave no fingerprints on the notes left in Julia's mailbox."

Alex snorted a laugh. "That could be anyone who watches a crime show on television."

"True." Max leaned back in his leather chair and folded his hands across his middle. "According to the detective, they don't have anything new on that woman who died at 721, either."

Frowning, Alex said, "Seems unbelievable that a woman could die and leave no clues as to why."

"I know," Max said, glad that Julia had moved out of 721. He much preferred her living at his place, where he knew she was safe. There was definitely something not right going on at 721 and until the police discovered just what it was, Max thought no one would really be safe there.

"Poor woman," Alex said.

Max nodded. "McGray says that without more information, the police simply have nothing to go on."

"Must make you feel more relaxed having Julia out of there."

His words were so close to Max's thoughts it was a little disconcerting. His friend really knew him well.

"Got the invite to your wedding in the mail," Alex

said abruptly, as if deliberately steering them away from the troubling conversation.

"Yeah?"

"Still can't believe you're going to do this. I seem to remember that after Camille left, you vowed to never again step into the marriage 'bear trap,' I believe you called it."

"Things change."

"Uh-huh," Alex said wryly. "Though I've got to say I've seen happier bridegrooms. Hell, I've seen happier death-row inmates."

One of Max's eyebrows lifted and he sat forward, leaning his forearms on the pristine desktop. "What's to be happy about? This is a business deal, pure and simple."

"Sure it is."

"What's that supposed to mean?"

Alex laughed shortly. "You can try to fool yourself, man. But you're not fooling me."

"Is that right?"

"You forget, I've seen you two together."

"So?" Max shifted uncomfortably in his seat.

"So I've seen the way you look at her." Alex grinned and it was clearly the smile of an unattached man enjoying the sight of his friend being tied up in knots.

Irritated and just a little disgusted, Max stared at his friend. What the hell was going on lately? Was he losing his famous poker face? "I don't know what you're talking about."

"You don't want to know, you mean." Alex smiled and said, "You care about her."

"Don't be ridiculous." Despite the tension slowly coiling inside him, Max scoffed at his friend's statement. "You drew up the papers. You know damn well this is an arranged marriage. A convenience for both Julia and me."

"I know that's how it started."

Max stood up, turned his back on Alex and stared out the window at the sprawl of Manhattan beyond. Everything in him felt so tight it was a wonder he could breathe. Hearing Alex say he'd noticed Max's feelings only made this harder all the way around. He was a man who prided himself on keeping what he was thinking, feeling, to himself. The fact that his mask was slipping bothered him more than he could say.

"Hey, I don't blame you. Julia's great."

Yes, she was, Max thought, as unwillingly, his mind drew up an image of her, big blue eyes shining, delectable mouth curved in a smile, arms open to welcome him. Something inside him stirred and he had to fight for the control that had once been so easy to manage. But he'd noticed lately that control was a slippery thing for him. One thought of her and his body took over.

Julia had wormed herself into his life, his heart, and now he wasn't at all sure that he could manage to keep the careful distance between them he believed was so necessary.

He wouldn't allow himself to feel more for her than he already did. She was lying to him about something so elemental, it couldn't be overlooked. And despite being faced with facts, she refused to surrender the lie.

What did that say about her?

And what did it say about *him* that he was willing to put up with it?

"She's still lying to me," he muttered, more to himself than to Alex.

"Maybe she's not."

Max fixed him with a glare. His friend knew the truth. Knew why and how his marriage to Camille had ended. "We both know she is."

"We've talked about this before, Max."

"Yeah, we have, so let's skip it today, all right?"

"Fine." Alex held up both hands in mock surrender. "You've always been a stubborn son of a bitch."

Now Max laughed. "What's the old saying? Takes one to know one?"

Alex nodded. "Point taken," he said, then changed the subject. "Anyway, now that we've taken care of business and done the small-talk thing, how about we go get lunch?"

"Good idea." Pushing thoughts of Julia to the back of his mind where they'd simmer and burn, Max followed Alex out of the office.

Max found her in what would be the baby's room, painting the plain, beige walls a soft, restful green. She had earphones on and her hips were swaying to whatever music she was listening to. Her long, blond hair was tied back in a ponytail, her worn, faded jeans clung to her legs like a lover's hands and the hem of the T-shirt she wore stopped a couple of inches above the waistband of her jeans, displaying a ribbon of pale flesh.

He bit back a groan, leaned one shoulder against the doorjamb and folded his arms across his chest. With her back to him, she was completely unselfconscious. Her bare feet did intricate dance steps on the plastic covering the wood floor, and as she reached high to push the paint roller to the top of the wall, Max had to take a deep breath and hold it in an effort to steady himself.

He should go to her, he told himself. Take the roller out of her hands and tell her he'd hire someone to paint the damn room. She didn't have to do this herself. But as he listened to her soft voice singing, he realized she was enjoying herself and didn't want to take that from her.

When she turned to dip the roller into the paint tray behind her, she saw him, pulled off her earphones and shrieked. "Max! Why didn't you say something? Let me know you were there?"

"I was enjoying the show."

Her face flushed and she dipped her head before saying, "I, um…"

"You're a good dancer." He was enjoying her embarrassment. Hell, usually, she was so put together, so in control, it was a nice change to catch her unawares.

She smiled at him and said, "Yeah, I'm going to try out for the Rockettes next year."

"You've got my vote." She had paint drops speckling her cheeks and a streak of green across her forehead. Max reached out and rubbed at that streak with his thumb. "You've also got paint on your face."

"Great." She laughed, rolled her eyes and said, "But the room looks good, doesn't it?"

"Yeah," he said, his gaze locked with hers. "It does. But you should have told me you wanted to do this, Julia. I could have gotten a team of painters in here to—"

"I wanted to do it myself," she said quickly. "It's important to me, Max. I want our baby to feel welcome from the very beginning."

Our baby, he thought, as something twisted around his heart. He'd give a lot for that to be reality. To actually *be* this baby's father in more than name. Startling himself with the force of that wayward thought, Max put it aside. "He can be welcome without you wielding a paint roller yourself."

She set the roller down on the tray and peeled off the plastic gloves she'd been wearing to protect her hands. Smoothing her hair at the sides of her head, she said only, "I wanted to do it."

"Okay," he said, then asked, "you planning on painting the connecting room for a nanny?"

She shot him a quick look. "No nannies. No helpers. I don't want strangers raising my child."

"Good," he said, nodding as he pulled her up close. "I don't want that, either."

"Max." She tried to pull back. "I'll get paint on your suit."

"Doesn't matter," he said, his gaze moving over her,

his hands lifting to cup her face. Heat rushed through him with an intensity he was becoming all too used to. "I've got lots of suits." His fingers moved over the frecklelike specks of paint on her cheeks. "Green looks good on you."

"I bet you say that to all your fiancées."

"Only the pregnant ones."

And then he kissed her, pushing his doubts and worries out of his mind to be drowned in the rising tide of passion.

Eleven

A week later the wedding went off without a hitch.

Julia wore a floor-length, strapless ivory gown, and felt like a princess standing beside her very handsome groom in a three-piece black suit. The dozen or so guests were all close friends and thankfully, there'd been no last-minute crises.

Her parents didn't attend the wedding, for which Julia was extremely grateful. She didn't want or need anything to distract her from the jumble of feelings already charging through her system.

The judge, a friend of Max's, conducted the brief civil ceremony in Max's penthouse with an easy friendliness that should have eased Julia's nerves. But standing there beside Max as the judge talked about cherishing and loving and till death did them part, all Julia could think was, *What if I'm making the biggest mistake of my life?*

Stupid, no doubt, to be thinking about that now. But she couldn't help herself. She loved Max, but she was beginning to doubt that he would ever allow himself to love her in return. Even now, as they stood together thanking their guests for coming, she felt a distance between them. Felt him holding himself apart.

She'd hoped somehow that actually getting married would dissolve some of Max's detachment. That once they'd made the legal commitment to each other he would permit himself to form at least a tenuous connection with her. But so far, anyway, she'd seen no sign of that and her heart ached a little—for herself and her child.

She wanted a family. She'd always wanted to build the kind of family she'd dreamed of as a child. And she knew that if Max would just let her in, they could have everything she'd ever dreamed of and more.

"Where are you?"

Max's whisper came against her ear, startling her out of her thoughts. Julia turned her face up to his and gave him a smile. "Just thinking."

"From your expression, not very happy thoughts," he said, keeping his voice low enough that only she could hear him.

"Sorry," she said, and meant it. She didn't want Max or anyone else thinking that she was having second thoughts. "I guess it's all just a little overwhelming."

He nodded and stepped in front of her, turning his back to the crowd, cutting her off from anyone who might be interested enough to watch them. "I know this was fast, but we're both getting what we want, right?"

Some of what we want, anyway, she told herself as she looked up into his green eyes.

"So let's just get through the reception and then we can relax."

"You're right," she said, and smiled more brightly, forcing a cheerfulness she didn't feel.

"Hey," Alex said as he came up behind Max and tapped him on the shoulder, "no hogging the bride. According to tradition, I get to claim a kiss."

Max swiveled his head to give his friend a dirty look. "Since when are you traditional?"

"Since I want to kiss a beautiful woman without her new husband decking me for it."

Julia laughed at the look of consternation on Max's face and took some heart in the fact that he clearly didn't want to share her. That was something, right? Stepping around her new husband, she smiled at Alex. "Far be it from us to defy tradition."

Almost as handsome as Max, Alex gave her a smile that let her know he understood that she must be having mixed feelings about the ceremony. Then he stepped in close, leaned down and kissed her hard and fast.

There was no *zip* in the contact, just a feeling of warmth and support. Especially when Alex paused long enough to whisper, "Be patient. He'll come around."

Before she could say anything to that, though, Max was tugging his friend away and saying, "One kiss per customer. Move it."

Alex only laughed and tucked his hands into the pockets of his slacks. "Fine, fine. Be greedy. Guess I'll just have to go and find a different girl." He swept the small crowd with a keen eye, then suddenly narrowed his gaze. "Like that one, for instance," he said softly.

He was gone before Julia could see who he was talking about, and then Max was turning her into his arms and she forgot all about their guests. "I didn't get a kiss from the bride yet."

"Yes, you did," she said, smiling up at him. "At the end of the ceremony."

"That one was for everyone else," he told her, already dipping his head down to hers. "This one's for me."

His mouth took hers and the world fell away. Julia's heartbeat quickened and every cell in her body lit up in celebration. Would it always be like this? she wondered.

She leaned into him, giving him everything she had, willing him to read the truth in her kiss. Willing him to sense that she was offering him her love. Willing him to *want* it.

When he lifted his head finally and she saw the dark gleam in his eyes, she knew desire was thrumming through him.

He lifted one hand, touched her cheek, then smoothed his thumb across her bottom lip. "Did I tell you today that you make a beautiful bride?"

"No, but thank you."

"I want you to know…" Max stopped, caught in the onslaught of feelings that were crashing together inside him. From the moment she'd stepped out of the master bedroom to walk to him down a short, makeshift aisle, he hadn't been able to see anything but her. It was as if no one else in the room existed. She was everything.

Her eyes were the color of a summer sky. Her mouth was curved in a soft smile. Her hands were cupped around a bouquet of pale pink peonies, and fragile sandals were strapped to her small, delicate feet. She was the picture of what every bride should look like and all Max could think was *She's mine*.

He knew the taste of her, the feel of her beneath him, the satin of her skin under his palms. He knew how she danced when she thought no one was looking, and he'd seen the hurt in her eyes when her own mother had turned on her. Her laughter warmed him and her tears cut him off at the knees.

She'd become…important to him. She'd become a part of his days, his nights, his life. And that realization staggered him. He hadn't planned for this. Hadn't expected to care. Hadn't *wanted* to care.

He had to find a way to stop.

"What, Max?" Julia reached for him, the sapphire-and-diamond ring he'd just given her flashing on her left hand. "What did you want me to know?"

He shook himself, as if he'd just stumbled in out of a summer storm. Deliberately, he sent those tender feelings he was experiencing flying from him like unwanted raindrops. His brain struggled to keep up and he tried to remember what he'd been about to say to her. Damned if he could. Which was probably just as well, since a moment or two ago, he'd been in the grips of an emotional whirlwind he wanted no part of.

"Nothing," he said, retreating into the cool, dispassionate world he felt so much more comfortable in. He gave her a smile that never reached his eyes and said, "It was nothing at all."

Julia didn't spend another moment alone with Max for the rest of the afternoon. It seemed that every time she came near him, he found someone else to speak to—usually on the other side of the room.

Several of their guests had already left and as the reception wound down, Julia noticed Amanda and Alex standing in a corner. They looked striking together, and judging by the animated way Amanda's hands moved as she spoke, they were finding plenty to talk about. Was Amanda the woman Alex had seemed so interested in before? Julia hoped so. Her best friend was due some good luck with men after having had such a worm for her ex-boyfriend.

"It was a great party," someone said from close by, and Julia turned to smile at Carrie Gray. "And you make a gorgeous bride, which I'm trying not to hold against you."

Julia laughed, hugged her friend and said, "Thanks for coming, Carrie. I really appreciate it."

"Are you kidding? Wouldn't have missed it." Carrie

stepped back, slung her purse strap over her shoulder and asked, "So where are you going on your honeymoon, or is that a state secret?"

"No honeymoon," Julia said. "We're both so busy right now…" She let her voice trail off, hoping Carrie wouldn't hear the disappointment.

"Well, that's a shame," Carrie said, pouting. "Doesn't seem fair, does it? Well, maybe you two can sneak off in a month or so."

"Maybe," Julia said, and waved as Carrie left. Max hadn't wanted a honeymoon. He said that there would be no point since this wasn't exactly a conventional marriage.

One by one, the other guests trickled from the penthouse, until only she, Max, Amanda and Alex were left.

"It was a great wedding if I do say so myself," Amanda said, smiling as she gave Julia a big hug.

"You outdid yourself and on really short notice, too," Julia told her. "I don't know what I would have done if you hadn't planned all of this with me."

Amanda looked great in a dark red sundress with short sleeves and a full skirt. Her short blond hair was ruffled, as always, since Amanda tended to run her hands through it a lot. But her big gray eyes were shining as she said, "What do you think of Max's friend Alex?"

"I like him. He's nice. Ambitious. Funny."

"Hmm." Amanda sent a quick look to where Max and Alex were talking together.

"You interested?" Julia asked.

"I'm not *not* interested," Amanda said. Then she shrugged and grinned. "Anyway, I'm heading out. I just wanted to say be happy, honey. And if you ever need anything, you know where to find me."

"I do."

"Hey, you're getting really good at that phrase."

Julia laughed, hugged her best friend again, then wistfully watched her stride across the room with a wave for Max before heading out to the elevator. Alex left right on her heels and Julia silently wished Amanda luck.

"So," Max said as he walked toward her, "the deed is done."

"It certainly is." She rubbed her thumb across her shiny new wedding ring.

The sunlight coming through the bank of windows was diffused slightly by the tinted glass, but still the light hit Max like gold, making his green eyes shine as if lit from within. When he came closer and reached for her, Julia went willingly. He was her husband. She loved him. And for just today, anyway, she was going to let go of the niggling doubts and worries gnawing at her mind and do what every other bride was entitled to do.

Make love with her groom.

A few days later Max sat in on a meeting with investors and found his mind wandering. Until Julia, that had never happened to him. Now, though, instead of concentrating on spreadsheets and financial predictions, his mind insisted on turning to images of his wife.

His *wife.*

While one of his employees ran through a presentation, Max's gaze dropped to the plain gold band on his left hand. He'd never thought to wear one of those again. Had never wanted to.

Now, like it or not, he was a husband.

The past few days hadn't been easy. Julia was already so firmly entrenched in his life, Max had to wonder how he would let her go at the end of the year. That worried him. He couldn't trust her, damn it, and how the hell could he stay married to a woman he didn't trust?

But could he stand watching her walk away? His thoughts idly drifted to that morning, gathering Julia's warm, naked, pliant body against his, filling his hands with her breasts, burying himself deep inside her. And as he remembered, so did his body, until he was uncomfortably hard in the middle of a damned meeting.

Scowling, he tapped a pencil atop the long, walnut table and only stopped when he saw a flicker of unease in one of his vice president's eyes. Tossing the pencil down, he forced himself to pay attention and couldn't figure out how it had come to this. He'd *always* been on top of his business. Always had his fingertips on the pulse of Wall Street. Always ran the meetings at his company with an iron fist and a steely eye. He'd never zoned out, even when he was married before.

But then, Camille hadn't haunted him morning and night as Julia did. Julia and her lies. His back teeth ground together and when the lights in the conference room clicked off for a slide show, he was grateful for the darkness.

In the shadows, Max could silently admit that he actually wanted to believe in Julia. Wanted to trust her. But how the hell could he? He'd seen the results of the fertility tests his ex-wife had insisted on.

As his employees' voices droned around him, Max frowned again, thinking of his ex. Camille had made him pay through the nose in their divorce settlement *because* he was infertile and she couldn't have the child she'd wanted.

That old sense of failure settled in his chest like an cold rock and he rubbed at the spot as if he could make it disappear. But the icy sensation remained. There was only one thing he could do. He had to pull back from Julia, from what he was feeling. It was better that way.

For both of them.

Several hours later Julia was still waiting dinner for Max. He was supposed to have been home two hours ago, but hadn't shown up. Or called. She walked to the bank of windows overlooking the city and stared down at the tiny cars and the sea of tiny people hurtling along the crowded streets. *Where is he?*

A glance at the table behind her sent pain jolting through her. The white tapers were burned halfway down and the breathing red wine had inhaled so much air it probably wasn't any good anymore. She blew out a sigh and decided to be annoyed rather than sad.

"Why didn't he at least call?" she muttered aloud, then another thought hit. "What if he *can't* call? What if he was in an accident? What if he was run down in the street by a careening cab? What if…" She stopped talking and moved to the phone in the living room.

Dropping onto the nearby couch, she lifted the wireless receiver, punched in Max's work number and waited. Three rings later, his familiar, deep voice said, "Rolland."

"Max?" Relief swept her first. He wasn't dead in the street. But he could be dead, anyway, in a minute or two! "You're still at work?"

"Obviously."

That single word was clipped and cool and about as friendly as a kiss from a polar bear. She curled her legs under her and wrapped one arm around her middle. "Is there something wrong?"

"No," he said. "What're you calling for? Did you need something?"

Julia sucked in air and held it for a second. Over the past few days, she'd almost convinced herself that she and Max were going to be able to make something of this marriage. She'd pretended that he was warming to her. That he eagerly reached for her every night because he was coming to care for her.

Clearly, she'd been fooling herself.

"I was worried," she admitted a moment later, her voice soft. "Dinner was ready a couple of hours ago and when I didn't hear from you I—"

His impatient huff came through the phone loud and clear and hit her like a slap.

"Julia, don't do this."

"Do what?"

"Act the part of the aggrieved wife," he said, voice clipped and dispassionate. "We're married, yes, and we have to keep up a good front for our friends. But you and I know the truth."

"Which is?" Her hand on the receiver tightened as her gaze fixed on a tall porcelain vase across the room that only that morning she'd filled with summer flowers.

"That all we've got between us is a carefully worded business deal and some great sex."

"Max—"

"You needed help," he said. "I needed an heir, so I'm accepting another man's child as my own. Period."

Pain lanced her, but as quickly as it appeared, it tangled with a quiet fury.

"You'll never believe me, will you," she said, speaking more to herself than to him.

"No."

"Not even when the baby is born and I can provide you with a paternity test, you still won't believe. You'll still doubt me. You'll probably accuse me of falsifying the test."

"Don't do this, Julia."

"I'm not the one doing this, Max." She unfolded her legs, stood up and scooped one hand through her oh-so-carefully arranged hair. She glanced down at the slinky, dark green dress she'd worn just for him and told herself she was all kinds of fool.

"Julia…"

She desperately pulled in air because she felt as though she'd never be able to breathe easily again. Her lungs were tight, her heart was aching and her hands were shaking with repressed anger.

"I'm leaving, Max."

"What?"

How strange, she thought, to be doing this over the phone. But even as she thought it, she realized that it was a very appropriate goodbye to a marriage that had never promised more than distance between the very people it should have joined.

"I'm leaving. I can't do this," she said, already walking toward their bedroom, the phone clutched tightly in one hand. She paused at the dining-room table long enough to blow out the candles, then idly watched as spirals of gray smoke rose and twisted in the chill of the air-conditioned room.

She thought about breaking the wine bottle, pulling the Irish-linen tablecloth off the table and scattering the Limoges china across the wood floor, but didn't. And points for her. Continuing on to the bedroom, she listened to Max, still speaking calmly.

"We have a signed agreement between us," he said.

"Sue me."

"Damn it, Julia…"

"I thought I could do it," she said, assuring herself that she was making the right decision. "I really thought

I could. I thought *we* could make this marriage work. But as long as you continue to believe the worst of me, we don't stand a chance."

"You can't leave."

"Oh, yes I can." She should hang up. Hang up, pack and get out. But for some damn reason, she couldn't bring herself to hit the end button on the phone. She didn't want to shut his voice off. "I'm sorry, Max," she said softly. "For both of us. But I can't remain married to a man who thinks so little of me, and I will not allow my child to grow up feeling his father's innate rejection every day. I was forced to do that myself and the pain is something that's still with me."

Max had eased it a little, she remembered, but now that was done, too, and she wouldn't have him in her corner when dealing with her parents anymore.

"I told you I would love your child."

"He's *ours,* Max." Julia yanked at her hair in frustration, then muttered, "I should have known this was a bad idea. My fault. Entirely my fault."

"And the blackmailer?"

"I'll be a divorced woman. Nothing to blackmail me with."

"Damn it, Julia. I can be home in twenty minutes. We can talk about this in person."

"No," she said, gathering up handfuls of underwear, bras and whatever else she could grab quickly. Not caring about neatness, she tossed it all into the suitcase, she wasn't worried about neatness, she headed for the closet again. Yanking down a few shirts and pairs of slacks, she carried them one-handed to the suitcase and tossed them in, too. She could come back for the rest. Or not. Maybe she'd just buy all new stuff.

As she zipped the case closed, she dropped onto the edge of the bed and said, "You know what the saddest part of this is, Max? I actually love you."

"What?"

A short, sharp laugh shot from her throat. Julia turned her head to the view outside the bedroom window and concentrated on the sea of city lights spreading out into the distance. "Yeah, it surprised me, too. After all, how could any rational, logical woman love a man who's too stubborn to change? Too filled with anger to see that sometimes things aren't what they seem?" She stood up, grabbed the suitcase and pulled it off the bed. "How can I possibly love a man who's too arrogant to acknowledge that maybe, just maybe, he isn't right about everything?"

"Julia—"

"Goodbye, Max." She punched end, tossed the phone onto the bed and walked out of the apartment, out of Max's life, forever.

Twelve

The next few days crawled past.

Max didn't race home after Julia's phone call. Mainly because he'd assured himself she was bluffing. When he finally strolled in hours later, he was alone in the suddenly too-big loft penthouse. Even then, though, he had told himself that it was for the best. He'd begun to care too much for her. Having her leave was the best thing that could have happened.

Besides, because of the legal papers she'd signed, he still had a claim on her and her child, which meant she wouldn't be getting rid of him as easily as she'd supposed.

He left the apartment at dawn every day and stayed late at the office every night. He told himself it was because he was free to devote as much of his time to his work as he wanted. But the truth was, he hated the silence in his apartment. He hated that he could still hear the echoes of her laughter, her sighs, her soft whispers in the night. He hated that her clothes were still in the closet and just the act of his choosing a suit every morning meant he was assailed by her scent. He hated that he'd left the high heels she'd kicked off on her last day in the apartment right where they'd landed on the floor at her side of the bed.

And he really hated that he hated all of that.

He shouldn't care.

Should be glad to have his own life back the way he wanted it.

He wasn't, though, but he'd be damned if he'd go racing after her. He'd done the right thing by her. He'd married her, offered to take her child as his own. He'd protected her from a blackmailer, gotten her out of an apartment building that might not be safe, and all he'd asked in return was the truth.

She'd refused to give it to him, instead, clinging to her lie. It was a *lie,* wasn't it?

"You're thinking about her again."

Max jolted out of his thoughts and shifted a hard look to Alex, sitting across the linen-draped table from him. Their weekly lunch was over, the servers had cleared the dishes, leaving only two steaming cups of black coffee behind. Max didn't answer, just picked up his coffee and took a swallow, the hot liquid searing his esophagus.

"I did some checking," Alex was saying, idly turning his coffee cup in its saucer, the china making a low singing scrape as it moved on itself.

"Into what?" Max set his cup down with a click of sound.

"Into Julia's ex-boyfriend. You know he's an attorney at my firm."

Max scowled at him.

Alex ignored it. "Turns out, Julia and he were nothing more than good friends the last few months they were together. No sex. No chance that he's the father of her baby." Alex lifted his coffee cup to take a sip, but paused long enough to say, "Seems the only man she slept with was you."

The tension in Max's body tightened perceptibly, but he shrugged off Alex's words. "Doesn't matter what that guy says. Camille showed me the fertility reports."

"Right." Alex set his cup down, braced his forearms on the table and glared at Max. "In case you've forgotten, let me be the first to remind you that Camille was a bitch."

Max sighed. "Agreed."

"So why is it you're willing to take Camille's word over Julia's for anything?"

"Good point." Max took a breath, gritted his teeth and asked himself if he'd been a complete ass. He'd turned away from Julia, refusing to listen to her, believe her, because Camille had turned him inside out. What if his ex was the one lying to him? What if Julia was right and Camille had somehow forged the results of that test? What if he'd had everything he'd ever really wanted and let it slip through his fingers because he'd been too arrogant to admit he might have been wrong?

"Judging by the look in your eyes," Alex mused, "I think you've just had an epiphany."

"Maybe I have," Max admitted, lifting one hand to signal the waiter.

"Never mind," Alex told him. "I'll get lunch."

"Thanks." He slid out of the leather booth. "I've got to check something out."

"'Bout time."

"Yeah, yeah." Max shot his friend a tight smile as he felt the first stirrings of hope.

"Hey, before you go…"

Max looked at him.

"How about giving me Julia's friend Amanda's phone number?"

Max grinned. "Get your own girl. I've got problems of my own to worry about."

"You've got to get out of the apartment," Amanda said.

"I know, don't worry." Julia snuggled deeper into the armchair in Amanda's living room. She hadn't wanted to crash back at her old apartment with her best friend, but she'd had nowhere else to go when she left Max's place. She certainly couldn't go to her parents'. And she hadn't wanted to be alone in an impersonal hotel room.

Amanda had been great, welcoming her back, staying up late every night to listen to Julia, torn between misery and fury, ramble on about Max. But she was right. Julia had to move out. She couldn't stay here. She'd have to find her own place.

"I'll see a Realtor tomorrow," she said. "Promise. I'll move out as soon as I can."

"You dope," Amanda said, dropping down onto the arm of the chair. "I didn't mean you had to *move* out. I meant you had to *get* out. Walk outside. Get some air."

"Oh." Feeling like an idiot, Julia smiled up at her friend. "You've been so nice, Amanda. Letting me stay. Letting me rant."

"What's a best friend for?" The tall, pretty blonde smiled. "But, Jules, honey, you've been locked away inside the apartment for four days. That's not healthy. Your skin's already pale. Much more sunlight deprivation, you're going to fade away completely."

"I just don't feel like seeing anybody," Julia said quietly, looking around the familiar and yet different apartment. Amanda had put her own stamp on the place in just a week or so. There were feminine touches everywhere. "I feel like I want to crawl into a hole and pull the hole in after me."

"Shame on you."

"What?" She looked up into Amanda's steady gray eyes.

"You're hiding, honey. And you didn't do anything wrong." She paused to scowl a little. "Well, except for falling in love with a man who clearly doesn't deserve you."

"I'm not hiding, I'm…regrouping." Just until she

got over Max. Shouldn't take her more than ten or twenty years.

Reaching out, Amanda patted her hand. "You know you're welcome to stay here however long you want."

"Thanks."

"But…"

"What?"

Amanda gave her a sad smile. "The truth is, you'll never be happy without Max. You're a one-man woman, sweetie, and he's yours."

When Amanda got up and walked to the kitchen, Julia sighed and fought the sting of tears in her eyes. Amanda was wrong. She had to be. Because Max didn't want her and Julia really didn't want to spend the rest of her life miserable.

"I need to see my test results," Max demanded, leaning against the edge of the doctor's desk. The office was cluttered, the air was cool and the older man smiling up at him seemed completely unperturbed by Max's presence.

"Of course, Mr. Rolland. There was really no need to bully my secretary."

"I'm in a hurry." God, was he in a hurry. If he was right and Camille had lied to him, he had a hell of a lot to make up for.

The doctor walked to a bank of file cabinets, opened one and flipped through the files until he found the one he wanted. Pulling it free, he handed it over. "As you'll see, the results are just as I told you two years ago."

Max stopped listening. There was a roaring in his ears as his blood rushed and pumped in a fury. He stared down at the test results and felt rage and relief tangle so tightly in his chest he could hardly draw a breath.

He wasn't infertile.

Camille had lied.

Julia was telling the truth.

And he was the biggest damn fool in the city.

Lifting his gaze to the doctor, he handed the file back, muttered, "Thank you," and left.

He hit the crowded Manhattan street and came to a dead stop as his brain raced. The summer sun beat down on the city and the humidity was so high a man could sweat to death standing still. But Max felt cold to the bone.

He'd had a chance at something real. Something lasting, with Julia and his child.

His child.

He closed his eyes, shook his head and cursed himself for being so stubborn, so arrogant. As pedestrians bumped into him as they passed, he remembered every moment he'd had with Julia. The ups, the downs, the lovemaking, the laughter and arguments, and he knew, with a certainty that reverberated in his soul, that she was the only woman in the world for him.

Now he had to find a way to convince her that he was a changed man. That he loved her. Opening his eyes, he stalked down the sidewalk like a man possessed and people scrambled to get out of his way.

* * *

When the doorbell rang, Amanda went to answer it. Max wasn't sure what her response to him would be, but it only took a second for her to grin at him. Well, why wouldn't she? He was standing in the hallway, holding a bouquet of flowers as big as a small child and no doubt had a haunted expression on his face.

"Who is it?" Julia shouted in the distance and Max's gaze shot in that direction.

"It's for you," Amanda called back, reaching out to grab her purse and sling it over her shoulder. "I'm running out for a latte. Be back in a bit." When she stepped past Max, she paused long enough to whisper, "Good luck."

He'd need it. Max closed the door after her and stood where he was until Julia walked into the room. One look at her and everything in him shifted, eased, as if an unseen chain around his heart and lungs had been released. She was more beautiful than ever, though her eyes looked wounded and wary. If he could have, he would have kicked his own ass for putting those emotions in her beautiful eyes, and he wondered if it was too late for him to fix this. But she hadn't turned away from him. Hadn't left the room. Surely that meant something.

"Julia…" He took a step and she moved backward.

"What do you want, Max?" She twisted her hands in front of her waist.

"You," he said simply. "I want you. Tell me I'm not too late. Tell me you still love me."

Her blue eyes widened and surprise flickered in their

depths, overshadowing the pain. When she didn't speak, didn't back farther away, Max walked closer, moving slowly, cautiously. He'd made his fortune by knowing which move to make when. What to say and who to say it to. Now, though, when he needed that instinctive sense of rightness, it had deserted him.

This was too important to screw up.

This conversation would set the course of his life. So he started at the top.

"I was wrong, Julia. So wrong about so many things. I should have believed you. Believed *in* you." In the reflected sunlight, he saw a sheen of tears on her eyes and it nearly killed him. "I'm so sorry, Julia. For everything."

Still she didn't speak and a panic like he'd never known before jolted him so hard he almost hit his knees. God, what he'd come to! He laughed shortly and the sound was a raw scrape of pain. "I never apologize. Ask anyone. So I'm not very good at it, but I'm trying, because you're too important to me."

"Since when?" she asked, her voice a hush of sound almost lost in the silent room. "Since when am I important to you, Max?"

"You always have been," he said, glancing at the flowers in his hands and wondering why he'd been stupid enough to think they would sway her. Tossing them onto the closest chair, he took another step toward her. Toward salvation. "From that first night. The first time I saw you. Touched you. I knew it. On a bone-deep level, I knew that you were the one for me. I just couldn't bring myself to admit it, I guess."

"Until now?" She shook her head and her soft blond hair moved over her shoulders like a caress. "Why now, Max?"

He told her everything. About Camille's lies. About the truth in the fertility reports. "You're carrying my baby, Julia, and I should have believed you. I'll never be able to make that up to you, I know. But I want to be with you. Want to love you. *And* our baby."

She moved to the side, inching a bit farther out of his reach and shook her head again. Her eyes gleamed at him like shards of broken turquoise. "I'd like to believe you, Max, you don't know how much. But I know now I'll never be satisfied being with you just because of our baby. I want your heart, Max. I want it all. Or I want nothing."

"You have it," he said, moving so fast, it surprised even him. He took hold of her shoulders, pulled her close to him and looked down into the blue eyes that had haunted him from the moment he'd first seen them. "You have my love. You have *me*. I'm no damn prize, Julia. I know that. But I guarantee you no man will ever love you as much as I do."

A single tear escaped her right eye and disappeared into the soft blond hair at her temple. "Max…"

"Julia," he said softly, stroking her face, her hair, "there's only one person in the world who could bring Max Rolland to his knees. The woman I love."

"What?"

Keeping his gaze locked with hers, Max dropped to

one knee in front of her. Picking up her left hand, he kissed the wedding ring he'd placed on her finger only days before, then looked up into her shining eyes.

"Give me another chance, Julia. Let me love you as you should be loved. Let me be a part of your life. Let me help you raise our children." His thumb smoothed over her knuckles. "Let me inside you, Julia. And never let me go."

She bit her bottom lip as tears began to rain down her face. Then she laughed a little and Max took his first easy breath in days. She hadn't turned her back on him. She was smiling at him.

"Get up, Max."

He did, and taking those tears and her smile to heart, he pulled her against him again, relishing the warm softness of her. The strength in her. She was everything he'd always wanted and so much more.

She was, quite simply, everything.

"Will you come home with me?" he asked, kissing her forehead, her cheeks. "Now?"

"Answer one question first," she said, pulling back to look up at him.

Uneasiness whipped through him, then dissolved as he saw the gleam of happiness in her eyes. "Anything."

Her hand cupped his cheek. "You said you wanted me to let you help raise our *children*. How many did you have in mind?"

He laughed for the first time in what felt like forever and peace showered down on him like a warm summer rain. Holding on to her as if it meant his life, he whispered, "As many as we want, my love. As many as we want."

Then he kissed her and felt his life, his world, come right again.

* * * * *

FRONT PAGE ENGAGEMENT

LAURA WRIGHT

Laura Wright has spent most of her life immersed in the world of acting, singing and competitive ballroom dancing. But when she started writing romance, she knew she'd found her true calling! Born and raised in Minneapolis, Laura has also lived in New York City, Milwaukee and Columbus, Ohio. Currently she is happy to have set down her bags and made Los Angeles her home. And a blissful home it is—one that she shares with her theatrical production manager husband, Daniel, and three spoiled dogs. During those few hours of downtime from her beloved writing, Laura enjoys going to art galleries and movies, cooking for her hubby, walking in the woods, lazing around lakes, pottering in the kitchen and frolicking with her animals. Laura would love to hear from you. You can write to her at PO Box 5811, Sherman Oaks, CA 91413, USA, or e-mail her at laurawright@ laurawright.com.

Dear Reader,

You must be hungry for more New York! I know
I am.

This series has been such a pleasure to work on.
With "killer" story lines and five wonderful authors,
I was in writer heaven.

My story in particular turned out to be one of my
favourite books of all time. It's funny—when I first
looked at the characters of Trent and Carrie, I saw
them as merely the playboy jerk and the girl next
door, but as time went on and as I started writing
them, creating their dialogue, they developed in
ways I hadn't imagined they would. They actually
started fighting me, fighting how I wanted to write
them. They pushed me to write their way, where
their characters should go and who they really were.

This was a new experience for me and just a little
bit intimidating. But after a while, I learned to let
go and allow them to be who they wanted to be...
good or bad, wrong or right. And I'm thrilled with
the results.

I love hearing from you all, so don't be shy. Let
me know what you think of Trent and Carrie. Of
course, if you don't approve of them, I'm afraid they
have only themselves to blame :-)

All the best, friends!

Laura

What a wonderful opportunity to work with five amazing women. Barbara, Maureen, Jennifer, Emilie and Anna—you are the apples of my eye! (pun intended)

One

...wire one million dollars into an untraceable offshore bank account...or else your past indiscretions will be exposed...

In the center of his steel-and-suede office, Trent Tanford leaned forward in his chair and tossed the letter into the trash. He felt no anger, no concern, just a desire to get back to work. He was no stranger to threats—e-mailed, snail-mailed or otherwise. He'd received them from his father; from recently fired and subsequently pissed-off employees of his family's media empire, AMS; from women, past lovers who had refused to accept the end of a relationship.

The threats were irritating, yes. But impactful?
No.

The thirty-one-year-old media mogul knew who he was and what he wanted—in business and in life—and no amount of outside influence was going to change that.

Trent signed a stack of contracts as outside the floor-to-ceiling windows to his left, the sun crept up the horizon bringing with it a hot new August day and an office building buzzing with activity.

"Good morning, Mr. Tanford."

Trent's door was open, as it usually was before 7:00 a.m. He nodded at one of his new young executives as she passed by, a pretty and brilliant redhead who had just graduated New York University the previous year. He glanced at the clock on his monitor. "Six-thirty. Good for you."

"Yes, sir." She smiled an ultraprofessional smile and moved on.

Trent went back to work. She was pretty, but he never dipped his pen into the company ink pot, not to mention the fact that she was way too young. But he did like redheads. In fact, he had a date with one tonight. A woman who was just as pretty, but not nearly as brilliant. Which was fine. Trent sniffed as he recalled their date the previous evening. The woman had spent twenty minutes assuring him that Mitt Romney was no politician, but was in fact a famous baseball player.

Trent grinned. He loved women. He loved the way they laughed, smelled, moved—each so different, yet so similar in their belief that she was going to be the one to change him, the one to bag him, the one to make him so deliriously happy he'd forget all about that ultrastrict dating code he'd followed for the past ten years: four weeks maximum then all ties cut.

Why didn't they get it? Why couldn't they understand that he'd never come to heel? He'd never be bagged. In his past experience, Trent had learned the hard way that in four weeks a woman could become more than a casual distraction, and going there again was unacceptable at this point in his life.

Trent moved on to his computer and the must-see lineup for the following year. He was no insensitive ass when it came to his view of relationships. He was always up-front about the four weeks, and what *not* to expect from him. It wasn't a personal attack on anyone; it had nothing to do with a woman's beauty or her personality. It was simply a fact, a rule of order…and, maybe, if Trent was forced to admit it, a way for him to have his cake and his ice cream and his steak and his candy and eat it, too—without getting a raging headache afterward. A relationship headache that would keep him from his one and only desire—his ascent to president of AMS when his father retired.

Now, much to Trent's chagrin, his father subscribed to a very different view on the matter of relationships. According to James Tanford, a wife and children stabilized a man, made him stronger. A family made a man more open to power and in turn made him respected by his peers and competitors. In the man's 1950s view of things, a wife took care of the details and let the husband focus on the real issues.

Unfortunately, the senior Tanford believed this so completely that after several failed attempts to coax his son into settling down, the older man had resorted to memos referencing the subject. This last one Trent held in his hand. The memo had been placed—by one of his father's faithful minions, no doubt—under one of Trent's computer monitors, a warning that James might decide not to step down as head of AMS until Trent was settled into matrimonial bliss.

Or matrimonial hell, Trent mused darkly.

Yes, threats came to Trent's office in all shapes, sizes and media.

All in a day's work.

Trent tossed the note from his father into the trash, watching as it settled beside another crumpled ball of BS on the bottom of the trash bin—the one that demanded he wire a million dollars into an untraceable, offshore bank account on Grand Cayman Island if he didn't want certain unsavory actions from his past revealed.

Something as likely to happen, he mused, as über-bachelor Trent Tanford taking a bride anytime soon.

It was Sunday brunch in the Big Apple. A sacred event for most Manhattanites, who worked sixty-hour work-weeks and used Sunday midmornings to continue to de-compress before they started it all over again on Monday.

Normally Carrie Gray celebrated brunch with pastries, eggs, bagels, schmear and, if it were appropriate, booze. Unfortunately, she'd been too tired to set up such a feast for her friends that morning. Hell, she'd barely had enough time to stick her long, brown hair up in a ponytail. And forget about contacts. It was glasses all the way today.

After a late night working on a few sketches of a logo concept for a graphic design job she was trying to land, she'd been woken up by another member of "Trent's Troops."

Trent being Trent Tanford, the dark-haired, blue-eyed, dimple-cheeked tall drink of water who lived in the apartment next door, a man who had constant guests of the female variety coming and going at all hours of the night. These were his "Troops." The name had been invented by Carrie and her two girlfriends, Amanda Crawford and Julia Prentice, who were good enough friends of Carrie's to allow her to bitch about her annoying neighbor.

The problem was that some of Trent's lady friends hadn't learned how to read yet and were mixing up Carrie's pad, 12B—the Upper East Side apartment she house-sat for European businessman and prince, Sebastian Stone—with 12C, Trent's apartment at 721 Park Avenue. And last night around 1:00 a.m., another of Trent's size-zero glamazons, complete with red hair and plump lips, had come knocking.

"Again, I'm sorry about the spread," Carrie told her

two beautiful blond friends as they sat around the glass-and-wrought-iron coffee table in Sebastian Stone's uncluttered but artfully furnished three-bedroom apartment.

Amanda's gray eyes flashed in a friendly, teasing way as she crossed her long, thin legs. "No worries. Coffee and doughnuts are classic."

Julia touched her growing belly and added, "And these glazed ones are my baby's favorite." Four months pregnant, Julia had occupied apartment 9B in Carrie's building, until she moved in with her fiancé, Max Rolland, last month. Now her previous roommate, Amanda, had 9B all to herself.

Relieved at her friends' forgiving words, Carrie watched the pair as they downed their doughnuts in ten seconds flat, then reached for another. It was so funny. Julia and Amanda couldn't have been more different from herself. Both blue bloods, both graduates of the chichi Ivy League school Vassar, both impeccable dressers.

And then there was plain old Carrie with her green eyes and mop of dark hair, her big breasts, curvy hips and a very anti-high-fashion tie-dye hippie dress. She was okay, cute maybe, but nothing like her stunning, fabulous friends. And she was fine with that. Carrie had no insecurities about her looks or background. She was who she was. And Julia and Amanda couldn't agree more. The socialite and the event planner didn't care about Carrie's lack of looks and breeding or her lack of funds. They just wanted her friendship.

"Besides a chicken sausage quiche and an arugula salad I really wanted to make cinnamon rolls," Carrie told the two women in between sips of coffee. "But the dough's rising time and mine didn't mesh well today."

"It's no big deal, Carrie, really," Amanda assured her. "Did you have a late night?" She grinned, her makeup-free face model perfect. "A date, maybe?"

"No," Carrie answered with a laugh, as if that was the silliest question in the world. And then she stopped and wondered why that would be so silly, and how long it had been since she'd had a date. Had it been in this millennium? Sure. A year, maybe, before her mom was diagnosed…

Her blue eyes narrowed, Julia broke into Carrie's thoughts. "Let me guess. Another late-night visitor?"

"She said she didn't have a date, Jules," Amanda said, reaching for another doughnut.

"I didn't mean a male visitor," Julia clarified. "I was talking about a member of the 'troops.'"

Amanda nearly choked on her doughnut. "Oh, no. One of Trent's ladies came by?"

"Yes," Carrie said, falling back into the beautiful oak Glastonbury chair.

"The blonde again?"

"Redhead."

Amanda shrugged. "At least the guy's versatile."

But Julia wasn't about to be so relaxed about the whole thing. The woman may have been petite in stature, but she had the temper of a protective tigress when she saw injustice. "Carrie, this is total insanity. You need to confront him."

"I know," Carrie said evenly. And she did know; it was just that—

"Or at least put a sign on your door," Amanda joked, pouring herself another cup of coffee, her short blond hair falling about her face.

Julia shook her head. "You swore if another woman came looking for Trent, you'd—"

"I know, I know," Carrie said quickly. She was just embarrassed at her own lack of fortitude in the situation. "I've never had a problem with confrontation before, but this guy…Trent Tanford…he's like…I don't know, too good-looking. Those cute dimples on such a fierce face…it's off-putting. He's like the boy in high school you had a massive crush on and made sure you wore your blue eye shadow and Love's Baby Soft perfume for every day in case by some miracle he noticed you."

Julia lifted a brow. "The boy you had a crush on? Trent is like the boy you had a crush on, Car?"

"I just mean that he's that good-looking, that charismatic, that crush inducing if one was to talk to him or get to know—"

"Do you want Trent to notice you?"

"No." Carrie released a weighty breath. She was doing some major backpedaling here. "I mean, only for the purpose of telling him off."

"Because if you do want to meet him, talk to him, whatever, all you have to do is knock on his door."

"Yes, Jules, I know," Carrie said drily.

Clearly ensconced in her own world, not hearing much of Carrie and Julia's exchange, Amanda sipped her coffee and looked dreamy. "I remember that boy. But it wasn't Love's Baby Soft. It was Patchouli oil."

Carrie and Julia both turned to stare at Amanda, then burst out laughing. When Carrie got hold of herself she said, "Incidentally, that boy never did notice me except to point out when I had a fresh pimple."

"Honey," Julia interjected, "no doubt that boy is now the Fry King at your local burger shack."

"Actually I heard he plays football for the Indianapolis Colts."

"Well, I'm sure he's been rejected by many a cheerleader, then."

Carrie sighed. "I doubt it. Guys like Mr. Touchdown and like Trent, they go their whole lives never hearing the word *no*." She shrugged. "I just don't get it. What makes a woman get all nuts for a man like that? A guy who's arrogant, who's basically just after sex?"

"The tall, dark, rich thing is pretty powerful," Julia said drily.

Amanda nodded. "For some women it's the dating trifecta."

Carrie rolled her eyes. "I'm being serious, you guys."

"So are we," Julia said tightly. "To some women, some people, looks and money are everything."

Sipping her lukewarm coffee, Carrie thought about what her friends had just said, and how naive she was to even argue the point. She understood the realities of the world. It's just that she had a hard time believing that most women, at their core, wouldn't want more substance from their men. Money and looks were great, but they didn't last. They didn't rub your feet when you had a hard day's work. They didn't care when you got a small, but substantial new job. They didn't sit by your side and help you remember your past when you were going through the first stages of Alzheimer's.

Carrie brushed off that last thought. She wasn't going to bring her own baggage into the conversation. Instead, she got up and went into the kitchen, made more coffee.

An hour later, the women were standing at the front door, satiated and thinking about what was next on the Sunday to-do list, what they needed for their Monday morning and the week ahead. They thanked Carrie for the brunch, made some tentative plans for a drink later in the week, and were about to walk down the hall when Julia stepped on something outside Carrie's door.

She bent and picked it up. "Here you go." She held out a copy of the *New York Post*.

Carrie shook her head, but took the paper anyway. "It's not mine. I'm a *Times* girl." She glanced at the name on the sticker above the paper's headline.

Amanda grinned widely. "Mr. Tanford, I presume."

Carrie shook her head. "Unbelievable. Not only do I have to redirect his women, but I have to deliver his paper. I'm so ready to rumble."

"Hey, I think she's fired up, Jules," Amanda said, grinning.

"Finally." Julia squeezed Carrie's arm and whispered, "Go get him, tiger."

"Grrrr," Carrie called as the two women walked down the hall toward the elevator.

Trent had just laced up a new pair of running shoes and was checking out the high octane playlist he'd downloaded on his iPod yesterday when there was a knock at his door.

"Just a sec," he called, walking into the hall, distracted by the strange and unwelcome addition of Yani to his iTunes playlist.

When he swung the door wide, he saw a petite woman in her midtwenties standing there. She was wearing a tie-dyed dress with the same color grass-green as her eyes, which incidentally were veiled behind a pair of tortoiseshell glasses. Her long, brown hair was pulled back into a ponytail and her full lips were set in a pissed-off line. She was cute, curvy and he had seen her in the building before. "Hello."

"Hi," she said, without even a hint of a smile.

"I know you," he said, cocking his head to one side as if that would help him place her. It didn't. "How do I know you?"

She rolled her eyes, shook her head, then thrust the *New York Post* at him. "Here you go."

"Mine?"

"Yep."

She didn't say much, but there was something about her. Maybe it was the way her lips moved. He could watch that for a while.

He took the paper from her. "Are you the paperboy?"

"No."

"Good because it's two o'clock in the afternoon, and if you were the paperboy I'd have to fire you for being so late."

"That's not very nice."

"No. But I'm not very nice."

"Good to know."

"You live in the building?"

This question made her smile. Not a happy smile, but a knowing, almost irritated one. "Down the hall actually."

Oh, yeah. "Right." He grinned. "So, why was my paper delivered to you?"

"Habit, most likely," she said drily, those pink, plump lips remaining parted as if she were going to say something more.

When she didn't, he repeated, "Habit?"

"Your paper isn't the only thing that gets lost by way of my door, Mr. Tanford."

Mr. Tanford. That wasn't good. No women, except the ones who worked for him, called him Mr. Tanford. He racked his brain trying to recall a reason this particular woman might have for disliking him. It took him a moment, but then it dawned on him. His female guests, late nights…wrong apartments. He leaned against the doorjamb, arms crossed over his chest. "Twelve B, right?"

She nodded. "In the flesh."

Heat stirred inside him at her words. Hell, he was male after all. "So, you and Sebastian Stone are…"

"I'm his house sitter," she clarified, her green eyes flashing.

Women with fire, women who didn't like him, women who were totally and completely unaffected by him were few and far between.

Not his type, but he'd definitely have to see her again.

"Thank you for the paper," he said. "And I apologize for the frequent late-night intrusions. I meant to come by and apologize in person."

"Sure you did."

"I've just been busy."

"We're all busy, Mr. Tanford."

"Of course. And again, I apologize. I'll make sure my guests know exactly where to go from now on. But if not, please don't hesitate to stop by again and give me another kick in the—"

"You think this is funny," she said curtly.

He dropped the easy, lighthearted air. "No."

"Yes, you do."

"I assure you that I do not think being woken up in the middle of the night is funny," he said in all seriousness.

She lifted her chin. "Good."

"Unless it's for a very, very good reason."

Her eyes narrowed and she looked ready to pop him

in the stomach. "I expect you to take care of this problem immediately, tonight."

"I don't have a date tonight."

She exhaled loudly. "Maybe you could supply your guests with a map." She paused, then said with light sarcasm, "Or maybe not. They always seem a little flustered with directions."

He liked this woman. Liked her a lot. Maybe he needed to broaden his scope of women. "Do they?"

She nodded. "I actually had to walk one of them to your door."

He grinned. "What can I say? Smart girls don't go for guys like me."

She sniffed, looked away. "Yeah, right," she muttered under her breath.

"Excuse me?" he said, even though he'd heard her. Hell, any excuse to watch those lips move.

"Nothing. I've got to go." She gave him a wave, which sort of resembled a military salute, before taking off down the hall.

"Thanks again," he called after her.

She glanced back. "I'd say anytime, but I'd be lying."

He chuckled. "Hey. Wait a second."

"What?"

"If I see you in the hall or the elevator…"

"Yes?" She arched her brows.

"Can I call you 12B?"

This time she smiled, a real smile, a playful smile. "Not if you expect me to answer."

His mouth turned up at the corners. "What is your name?"

"Carrie Gray."

"You a smart girl, Carrie Gray?"

Again, the smile. "I'm afraid so."

Trent watched her walk back to her door, her round, firm backside swaying from side to side as she moved. Part girl, part woman. Very nice. She was pretty, sexy in her way—but definitely not his usual fare. He hadn't been lying when he'd said that smart girls didn't go for him. It wasn't that he didn't love smart women or love to be challenged by them, but right now he had all the challenge he could handle at work.

For now, he wanted uncomplicated and simple.

He walked back into the apartment, dropped onto the couch and opened the paper, completely forgetting about the run he had just been amping up for before Little Miss Next Door had shown up.

He flipped through the paper. News first, then sports. *Damn Yankees and hiding injuries. Loses credibility, loses respect.*

Disgusted and pissed off at his favorite baseball team, Trent turned the page—and got an eyeful.

"Shi—" he muttered.

Large and loud photographs of himself and Marie Endicott, the woman Trent had dated a handful of times—the woman who had jumped off the roof of his apartment building over a month ago—stared out at him from the Entertainment section of the paper.

The headline read: Suicide Victim Canoodling With AMS Playboy Right Before Her Death?

Trent tossed the paper aside and grabbed his Black-Berry off the glass coffee table. As expected, his e-mail box was flooded with requests for interviews, statements and several more pictures of him and Marie.

"Dammit."

Ten minutes later, the phone rang. It was the police with a request for an altogether different kind of interview.

"Mr. Tanford, we'd like you to come down to the station to answer a few questions."

Two

From age fourteen to age seventeen, Trent Tanford had run with a questionable crowd. Perhaps it was the sheltered, yet pampered life he'd lived with two absent parents, a pressure cooker of a prep school, and one overly protective nanny, but when puberty set in, he found himself battling a magnetlike attraction to trouble.

Under the guise of retiring to his room for homework and a good night's sleep, he would stuff pillows under his blanket and sneak out of the window. He hung out with the boys from town, proving his antimoney, anti-establishment claims by drinking too much, knocking down mailboxes and hot-wiring cars.

It wasn't long before he found his way to the cold, unfriendly walls of the police station.

Needless to say, having to pick his criminal son up from jail was not a proud moment for James Tanford. Before Trent had given up on a relationship with his father, he had actually looked at those car rides home from the station as a way to spend some time with the man, even if it consisted of a stern lecture and a slap or two.

But those years were barely recognizable to Trent now. These days, he was all about the earned dollar, and when he walked into the police station that Sunday afternoon, he sported no fear and had nothing to hide. He had, however, brought his attorney.

Trent was confident, not stupid.

"Thank you for coming, Mr. Tanford."

"Of course." True, it was a pain in the ass to be in the police station on a Sunday afternoon, but he'd liked Marie Endicott. While there had been no chemistry between them, she was a decent person, and he felt bad about what had happened to her. And if he could help, he would.

In a boxy room with overbearing fluorescent lighting and scuffed, faded walls that had once been painted yellow, Trent and his attorney, Evan Wallace, sat at an unsteady card table across from the tired-looking cop in his forties.

Detective Arnold McGray's anemic green eyes flicked over Trent with curiosity and what Trent easily recognized as a premature disbelief in whatever it was that Trent might have to say.

The questions came at him, emotion-free and quick.

Detective McGray held up a copy of the *New York Post,* which Trent had been reading earlier. "Did you post these pictures yourself?"

"No."

"Did you date Marie Endicott?"

"Yes."

"How long?"

"A few times."

"Could you be more specific?"

Trent paused. "Twice."

"Why did it end?"

"It never started."

"Why? She wasn't into you?"

"We weren't into each other."

"It's not easy to be rejected. That must've pissed you off."

Wallace interjected quickly. "This is ridiculous. Mr. Tanford dated the woman twice. Move on, Detective."

Trent silenced the attorney. "It's fine, Wallace."

McGray stared at Trent. "You're used to getting any girl you want, Mr. Tanford."

"Is that a question or a statement?"

"Men like yourself don't take kindly to being rejected."

Trent tried to make it simple. "We had nothing in common. There were no hurt feelings on either side."

"How do you know that?"

"We talked about it on our second and last date, laughed about it in fact. She said she preferred a regular working man to a careeraholic."

The questions continued along the same lines after that—Trent's feelings about Marie and hers for him, where they had gone on their dates, et cetera. As expected, Wallace continued to interrupt with his concerns and the detective continued to push.

Finally, when Detective McGray wasn't getting the answers he was looking for, he moved on to a question that had Trent sitting up straight like a riveted schoolboy.

"Have you received any threats lately? E-mail? Phone calls? Letters?"

"Yes."

Wallace looked up from his BlackBerry. "What? I was never informed—"

Trent continued quickly. "I got a letter."

Detective McGray sniffed. "What did it say?"

"The sender wanted me to wire one million dollars into an account in the Caymans or they'd expose something unseemly from my past."

"And what could that be?"

Wallace gave Trent a sharp, stop-talking-now look. But Trent had nothing to hide, and nothing to do with Marie's death.

"Not a clue. That's why I threw the letter away. I thought it was a joke."

"What do you think now?"

"I think someone wants me here talking to you about Marie's death."

The detective got up, excused himself for a moment and left the room. Trent narrowed his eyes at the door. What the hell had the letter said?

While he was waiting for the detective to return, his cell phone rang.

"What a fine position you've put us in, Trent."

His father. Trent turned around and glared at Wallace, who just lifted his brows before returning his attention to his BlackBerry. Clearly Trent needed to hire his own counsel from here on out. The company attorney had an allegiance to James Tanford first and last.

Trent released a breath. "Hello, James." Trent hadn't called him Father in over fifteen years. And he hadn't used the word *dad* ever.

"I had assumed the days of phone calls to jail were over," the man muttered.

"I'm not in custody. I'm answering a few questions."

"About the woman you were seeing."

"The woman I dated a few times," Trent clarified with mild irritation.

"A woman who died last month in a very shady way. And now there are pictures of the two of you all over the media."

Trent refused to defend the fact that he had been caught up in a coincidence. "What is it you want, James?"

"I want to know how you could be so careless?"

"I dated someone, and she just happened to be suicidal. I hardly call that careless."

Facts wouldn't override the scandal of it for James

Tanford, though. "I want an end to all the speculation and gossip. Now."

Through gritted teeth, Trent muttered a terse, "As do I. Anything else?" He and Marie had only dated a few times, but her death had affected him, and his father's cold way of making her life, her death, into a pain in the ass for himself disgusted Trent.

James sighed. "I'm not going to try and reason with you anymore, Trent. Talking doesn't seem to work with you."

"You're right about that."

"You have a choice to make, and twenty-four hours to make it in."

When was the damn detective coming back? Trent wondered darkly. He didn't have time for this. "Ultimatums and threats don't interest me."

"This one might. With AMS at stake."

Trent chuckled bitterly. So his father was going here again, was he? Damn threats. What the hell? He was practically swimming in them lately.

The older man's words came slowly, like arsenic-laced honey from a bottle. "There is one thing that might salvage our family's good name and business reputation."

"What? Firing me?"

"No. A wedding."

Trent cursed. "This is hardly that big of a scandal."

"A very white wedding."

"We're not here again." As if a really stellar wife could clean up Trent's bad-boy image.

"This is my company," James continued, "my life's

blood, and I will not allow this situation to spin out of control. Advertisers will be all over this, and I won't have any of them walking because of your foolish actions. If you are as devoted to this company as you claim, then you would do anything it takes to keep AMS on top and scandal-free."

Trent said nothing.

"You can be as cavalier as you want to, my boy, but this is a onetime offer. I will secure your future position as head of my company in writing, today, but you must be married by the end of this week."

Trent said tightly, "I will be head of this company because I am damn good at what I do. No one can touch me and you know it."

"Right now I don't care how good you are. Damn you, Trent. Do you care anything for your family's name?"

"You won't like the answer I give you."

James paused, then said tightly, "Announce your engagement by midnight tomorrow night and I will announce your new position to the company executives and to the media. Ignore my desires and I'll take that as your verbal resignation."

Fury coursed through Trent's veins, making him almost unable to see through the fogging glass pane and out into the hallway where the detective was on his way back into the room. "I'm hanging up now."

"One more thing. This woman you choose cannot be your usual fare. Permanently tanned bottoms and jiggly implants are fine for play, but this is a life partner, a

Tanford. She doesn't have to come from money, Lord knows I didn't, but she must have brains and class. Choose wisely."

"Goodbye, James."

"Do you need me to contact Wallace?"

Trent's jaw was as tight as a 7:00 a.m. subway ride. "I think he's already contacted you."

Just as Trent pressed the end button, Detective McGray walked in. Both he and Wallace took their previous seats at the table. The detective lifted his brows.

"You had an expungement as a juvenile."

"Is that a question?"

Wallace jumped in quickly. "Mr. Tanford's records are sealed and not for—"

Trent stopped him, then asked the detective, "What do you want to know?"

The man stared at him without blinking. "How bad a kid were you, Mr. Tanford?"

"Not that bad. But I gave it my best effort."

Trent's easy comeback garnered a half-ass smile from the detective and a nod. Again, he stared at Trent for several seconds, as if he were trying to decide whether to continue down that road or not.

Then he dropped his gaze and leaned back in his chair.

"You're not the only one who's gotten a letter."

That fact surprise Trent. "Who?"

"Someone else in your building."

"You're not going to tell me who?"

"It's not important. What is important is that you tell me everything you can remember about the content of that letter."

It was close to five that evening when Carrie stood on the corner of Seventy-seventh and Second Avenue and hailed a cab. She couldn't really afford the fare, but it was a muggy ninety-eight degrees out and she just couldn't deal with the subway. Plus, she was running late and needed to get to her mom's house and relieve the health-care worker before she had to pay the woman overtime.

Carrie jumped into the cab and tossed out her mother's TriBeCa address. She had tried a hundred times to get her mother to move in with her, as Sebastian Stone had graciously offered, but Rachel Gray would have none of it. Her rent-controlled TriBeCa one-bedroom was the love of her life. It had been their first apartment when she and Carrie had moved from Upstate New York almost twenty years ago. Rachel would get highly agitated if she was away from her space and her things for too long. Carrie wasn't about to force the issue of moving.

The solution was to make her mother as comfortable as possible as she battled through her disease.

Carrie let herself into her mother's apartment with her key. As always the first thing she saw was her mother's artwork on the walls. It ranged from bold to simple, and covered nearly every inch of space. Art was the reason they had moved to the city. Well, one of the reasons…

For fifteen years, Rachel Gray had enjoyed a pretty amazing career. But like any artist, when she stopped producing, the influx of money stopped, as well. She still received payment for any newly sold pieces, and had been smart with her savings. But in Manhattan, that was hardly enough.

Carrie gave the health-care worker, Wanda, who was in the kitchen preparing dinner before she left, a friendly wave, then she walked into her mother's room. It was just as it had been for as long as Carrie could remember: antique lamps, barn-wood armoire that Rachel had brought with her from Albany, photographs and knick-knacks, books on a crowded bookshelf, several original abstract paintings on the walls, some her own and several of her artist friends' work, as well. In the middle of the room was a queen-size iron sleigh bed with garish red bedding and purple throw pillows.

Carrie went to sit beside her on the bed. Tucked under the bright red comforter, Rachel had her dark brown hair piled on top of her head. Her pale face looked drawn. She had always been thin, but now she looked unhealthy. After so many years of coming through the front door after school to hear the blaring sounds of Depeche Mode as her mother hovered over a canvas, brush in hand, Carrie always needed a moment to secure herself in this reality.

Rachel stared at her, her bright hazel eyes searching. "You look like my daughter."

"I am your daughter."

"What's your name?"

"Carrie."

Rachel smiled softly. "Just like the girl on *Little House on the Prairie*."

"That's right. That's who I was named for."

"How nice."

"I think so."

Clearing her throat, Rachel sat up a little. "I'm thirsty."

"I'll get you something to drink. Be right back."

Carrie left the room, immediately missing the soft scent of herbs and mint that had always seemed to emanate from her mother's milky-white skin. Hell, she missed a lot of things. The first time Rachel had said, "You look like my daughter," Carrie had escaped into the bathroom and after several quick breaths had vomited into the sink. It was something a daughter was never supposed to hear from her mother.

Fortunately, not every day was a bad day. Some days were great. Some days Rachel knew exactly who Carrie was. Those days were gold star, blue-ribbon days.

When Carrie returned, she smiled at her mom and handed her the tea. "Here you go."

Rachel looked as though Carrie were trying to hand her a lit bomb. "I don't want that."

"You love iced tea."

Her brows knitted together. "Do I?"

Carrie nodded.

"All right then." She drank the entire glass, then began chewing on the ice cubes. She glanced up and frowned at Carrie. "Who are you?"

Carrie took her mother's hand. "I'm Carrie, your daughter."

"Good." She chewed her ice, then said, "Read to me?"

Yes, some days were worse than others.

Carrie took the book from the bedside table and began to read. She read while her mother ate dinner, then as she dozed off to sleep. But when she left a few hours later, she couldn't remember one word of it.

It was close to nine when Trent stepped into the elevator, his coat slick with rain. He'd left the police station a few hours ago, but instead of heading straight home he'd caught a quick dinner.

As the elevator was about to close, someone stuck the handle of an umbrella between the metal doors, causing them to stutter, stop, then reopen.

Trent nodded at the woman who walked into the elevator. "Hey, 12B."

When the pretty brunette lifted her head, saw who was addressing her, she rolled her lips under her teeth, giving him a really half-assed smile in return. "Hey."

As the doors closed, he took in her dejected expression and wet, moplike hair, the ends beading with rainwater. "Get caught in the storm?"

"Definitely," was the sharp reply.

"You okay?"

"Fine."

Trent watched her as she tried to dry her long dark hair with a tissue from her purse. She was no flashy, in-your-face beauty, but with her pouty lips, small, curvaceous body and don't-mess-with-me attitude she had this thing, this quality about her that made Trent want to pull her into his arms, drop his head and kiss her. Kiss her until she relaxed and forgot about whatever was making her act so pissed off.

Maybe a good, solid kiss would make him forget about his afternoon, too.

He leaned back against the elevator wall, and attempted to curb some of the irritation he felt coming from her. "Sorry."

She looked over at him, confused. "For what?"

"The 12B thing, when you got in the elevator. I was just playing around."

She looked away, then looked back at him and shook her head. "It's fine. I'm just having a hard time with people forgetting my name today."

"Work thing?"

"No. Personal."

"Guy thing?"

A small smile touched her lips. "No. Just personal."

Personal, huh? He shifted against the wall. But not a guy… Why did that fact interest him at all? "Well, I didn't mean to compound the problem. I was just trying to inject some humor into a pretty humorless day."

"Bad day for you, too?"

"Yup."

Carrie felt like a limp, wet dishrag standing there in the pristine enclosure of the elevator, and the fact that she probably also looked like one at that moment made her want to get away from this beautiful man ASAP. She tried not to stare at him in an obvious way, but it wasn't an easy trick. Trent had also been caught in the rain, his hair and face wet, but he looked amazing, even better than he had earlier in the day when she'd dropped off his paper. How was that possible? How was it possible that she looked like something the cat threw up and he looked like the cover of *Men's Health?*

She fought the urge to ask him about his crappy afternoon, swap sad stories. After all, she hardly knew the guy, and she really didn't want anyone else's burdens on her right now. Odds were that Trent's issues were about as deep as some hot blonde who stood him up because she'd managed to score an interview with Karl Lagerfeld.

When the stainless-steel doors finally opened, Carrie gave Trent a small wave, then walked out of the elevator and toward her apartment. She knew he was behind her, close behind her; she could feel him.

"How about a drink? A glass of wine?"

She didn't turn around. She did, however, shiver. "No, thanks."

"You look like you could use something."

She could. But she feared that the thing she needed wasn't alcohol. She was in her lonely phase—a phase she went through a few times a year when her life wasn't going as planned. Tonight she was going to get the pound cake out of the freezer and as she ate through its unthawed buttery goodness she would try to forget how she didn't have a job yet, how her mother was never going to get better and how she, Carrie, might have to get used to being alone permanently. Then later she would move on to the salty snacks and the memory of how good the weight of a man had felt on her once upon a time, how his hands had moved over her skin with a light touch, how his lips had felt on her temple, her ear, her navel.

She was finally at her door. Thank God.

Again she gave Trent a wave. "'Night."

"Wait a sec."

Stupidly, she turned around. The doorknob pressed into the small of her back. "What?"

"I don't know." He stood there, all a hundred and eighty pounds of him, tall as a man should be, his blue eyes unsure of what he was doing at her door. "Maybe we could talk or something."

"I'm not in the mood to talk."

"We could go out. What are you in the mood for?"

"Nothing."

"Come on."

She sighed. "Listen, I don't mean to be rude, but I have a night planned—a lava-hot shower, then an entire loaf of pound cake. And if I don't feel ill by then, a bag of those fire-hot Cheetos that turn your fingers red."

He smiled, and his dimples showed. "Wow."

"Yeah. I am wow. I'm also very tired and wet and…"

"And what?"

She sighed. "And nothing." She shook her head, then turned and opened her door. "I'll see you, Trent."

He caught her hand. Carrie stopped, stilled, listened to the sound of her heartbeat as it pounded against the walls of her chest. If his hand felt good, then…

She never got to finish the thought. Trent turned her around and pulled her against him. His arms went around her, crushing her breasts into the solid wall of his chest. She held her breath as she watched his head drop, felt his hair brush the side of her face, the stubble on his chin against her cheek.

She didn't move. She wanted to know what he had planned, what he was going to do next. He brushed her wet hair aside with his face and kissed that spot between her shoulder and neck. A soft, tame kiss, but for Carrie it was as though that spot were a dam, holding back every ounce of passion she'd been storing up. And when his mouth connected with that spot, the dam broke and the flood of feeling was unstoppable.

Her legs shook, and between them a hot, wet ache circled and teased her senses. She closed her eyes and tipped her chin up, welcomed his mouth on hers. His kiss was warm, soft and unhurried, and she melted into him, let him hold her up, care for her heavy limbs as he cared for her hungry mouth. It had been a long time since she felt cared for, a long time since anyone had carried her.

No one led the kiss. Each had their own style and each gave in to what the other wanted. Trent liked to nip at her lower lip, then suckle it before kissing her deeply. Carrie loved the feeling of his tongue in her mouth, just those soft playful swipes against her lips, teeth, tongue, as her hands played in his hair.

Then she felt Trent's hand on her naked belly, felt his fingers moving upward. She put her hand over his on the outside of her shirt, but instead of stopping him, she led him up to the spot where her heart pounded wildly in her chest.

She said quickly and without thought, "Do you want to come inside?"

He nodded. "Yes."

She smiled.

Then he said, "But I can't."

His words made her freeze, her heart drop into her throat. She swallowed painfully and looked up at him.

His jaw looked tight, as if he was really pissed but trying to hold it in. He eased his hand from her. "I have to go."

"What?"

"I have to go. Now."

She just stared at him, calling herself an idiot. A total masochistic idiot. What the hell had she expected from this guy? "Then please go," she said caustically. She turned around and muttered the word *jerk* as she stalked into her apartment.

Carrie was no drama queen, but on this night, she actually slammed the door. Then she proceeded to bolt it, turn her back on it and lean against it.

Okay.

Yes, she'd been a fool.

But she wasn't going to dwell.

She wasn't about to give in to an all-night chastise-fest. So, she'd kissed a cute guy. Big deal. It happened all the time—maybe not to her, but whatever. It had felt good, and now that she knew what she'd been missing, maybe she'd open herself up, ask someone out, go out on a date or two.

Trent Tanford—forgotten!

Then came a knock on her door, and her gut clenched and twisted.

Releasing the weighty breath she'd been holding, she turned around and opened the door, prepared herself to be civil.

Carrie stared expectantly at the man on the other side of the threshold.

"Please tell me you're not actually back for more?" she said, her tone dripping with sarcasm as she tried not to think about the horrific realization that if her body had a brain of its own it would walk straight for Trent Tanford and lock lips with him right now.

He leaned against the doorjamb, his blue eyes heavy with concern. "I'm such an ass."

For one brief second she thought of slamming the door in his face, but she was a New Yorker. Arguing and sarcastic potshots that masked sexual attraction were much more her style. She sighed. "Add a 'hole' onto that word and you got it just about right."

He laughed, shook his head. "Listen, I had a really bad day today."

"Yeah, I know about those."

He inclined his head. "I apologize."

Her anger slipped just a touch, and she nodded. "Apology accepted."

"Can I make it up to you?"

"Thanks, but I have everything I need."

"Pound cake and hot Cheetos?"

She paused, rewound what he'd just said in her mind and let her shoulders droop. "That sounded really pathetic when you said it."

He laughed. "I insist on making it up to you, Miss Gray."

"There's nothing to make up for. You don't have to do any—"

"Stop, please." He pushed away from the wall. He was just too good-looking. So tall, muscular, dimples and eyes blazing sex. He was breathtaking. He said softly, "I think you know enough about me, or my reputation, to know that I don't do anything because I have to."

"That's probably true, but—"

He took her hand then, and her legs threatened to buckle. His eyes were serious as he said, "I like you. Enough to stop things from going too far in the hallway of our apartment building." When she grinned, he followed. "There's something about you that fires me up, Carrie Gray, and not just in the sex department. I want to see you again."

Awareness moved through her, snaking through her belly, circling her breasts. "What do you have in mind?"

"Go out with me."

"When?"

"Friday night."

Her brows lifted. "A date?"

He nodded. "Seven-thirty." It wasn't a question.

Carrie attempted to toss in a little cold-water sanity. "I hate to say it, but I'm not your type, Trent."

He stared at her, then shook his head, grinned. "Maybe you are. Maybe it's about time that smart *and* beautiful was my type."

Well, then, Carrie mused. Sanity could go take a hike.

She smiled. "All right." Then she remembered that she would be coming from her mom's place. "Can we meet somewhere?"

"Sure. How about The Lexington Church?"

Her brows lifted. "A church?"

He paused a moment, looking just slightly sheepish. "There's something I need to tell you."

Oh God. What now? "You're a priest."

He grinned. "No."

"No," she muttered. "I didn't think so."

"It's actually something I need to ask you."

All of a sudden it felt as though a bag of bugs had been released under her shirt—a sensation that usually indicated that it would be a good time to run the other way.

"Carrie 12B Gray?"

"Yes…"

"This is going to sound completely insane."

"Not the best way to begin a question."

He dropped to one knee in front of her. "I've only known you for a day."

"Not much better, Trent."

"But I think you're the one."

The one? *Twilight Zone* music started to play in her head.

He grinned, flashing those damn dimples. "Will you marry me?"

Three

Stunned wasn't the word for it.

Freaked-out didn't quite cut it, either.

Maybe massively pissed off...?

It was like eighth grade all over again and Mr. Popular Hunk, Stuart Kaplan, had just brought an excited Carrie to the homecoming football game, where he proceeded to hold her hand, kiss her with too much tongue and parade her in front of all his friends. But not because he actually liked her. He was looking to mess with her, which he did by digging out the chewing tobacco from inside his lower lip and smashing it in her hair.

The feeling of that moment would live inside of her forever. Total foolishness, totally duped.

She tried to keep her voice even when she spoke to Trent. "I've been out of junior high for a long time now and I'm not into jock games."

He stood up. "What?"

She raised a brow at him. "You need to go home now."

"I know this sounds—"

"I'm going inside." She turned around and tried to close the door, but Trent stopped her.

"Carrie, wait a second."

"No."

"I'm the ass. Again. I was trying to make light of a really odd position that I find myself in. I really do like you. If you'd just let me explain—"

She shot him a venomous look. "Don't ever knock on my door again." Then she closed the door in his face.

This time she didn't lean against it feeling sad. She walked straight into the kitchen and to the freezer where her pound cake awaited.

She loved New York, but honest to God there were some serious nut jobs running free. And to think she'd been so attracted to him, had actually felt a connection to him, had seen a glimpse of what it would be like to have someone to share a bad day with....

That was, until his cruel side had surfaced.

"Rumors are buzzing around this place like flies in the horse stalls over in Riverdale where my sister goes for her riding lessons."

Trent looked up. Danny, the sandwich guy, stood in

the doorway, a lopsided grin on his round, freckled face. He was bold and unapologetic in the way he addressed the second in command of AMS, always was. And Trent allowed it, though he would never allow anyone else to speak to him that way. To Trent, the young man was entertaining, like a kid brother who was finding his way. A brother Trent had always wished he'd had.

No one in the office knew it, but Trent had been paying for Danny's college tuition for the past two years. The kid was really sharp and would make a killer attorney someday.

"I don't have time for gossip, Dan. You know that."

Danny closed the door and walked into the room. "Even when it's about you?"

"Especially when it's about me."

"All right, but if you do get married you're going to invite me, right?"

Trent frowned. "Don't you have class?"

"Not until two."

"Don't you have sandwiches to deliver?"

Danny grinned. "So, who is she?"

Trent was silent.

"Supermodel or actress?"

"You should get to class early. It shows commitment."

"It shows that I'm a serious nerd. But speaking of commitment…I can't believe you're getting married."

"Have a nice day, Dan."

Danny pointed to work on Trent's desk. "What are you doing there? Writing your vows?"

The look Trent shot Danny had him backing up toward the door with his hands up. "All right, all right."

When Danny was gone, Trent leaned back in his chair and looked over the information his P.I. had procured for him. Carrie Claudette Gray, aspiring graphic designer, house sitter for a prince, had attended public school and had been a great student. Got a job at an art gallery at the age of fourteen, was a candy striper and ESL instructor. Mom was an artist, Dad not in the picture. After high school, attended The School of Visual Arts in Manhattan. Boyfriends, marriages—none to speak of.

Interesting, Trent thought.

She was a good girl, that was for sure—an everywoman—but the best part of all was that she needed financial help. Massive school loans, a temporary position as a house sitter, and no graphic design job yet.

He turned around in his chair and stared out the window at the skyline. Could he actually do this? Be a married man? He'd gotten close once before, back in the idiot years between eighteen and twenty.

During college, he'd met a woman he'd thought was the love of his life. She was a gorgeous socialite, older, twenty-five, and had wanted to get married and have kids right away. A barely legal Trent had been so in love, he'd agreed. One week before the wedding, she'd called to say that she'd married someone else, and was at that exact moment on her honeymoon with him. She'd given no apology, just a quick explanation that the man she'd married had offered her a better life, a better deal.

Trent had been broken for a good year after that. Then he'd come to understand something: that maybe marriage was just a deal to be made and agreed upon when you were ready.

So, he mused, turning back to his desk, was he ready now? Could he make the deal for a short time to appease his father and take control of AMS?

Yes. Being head of AMS was worth a year in jail— especially if the jailer kissed like that.

He grabbed the phone, pushed a few buttons and when he had his father on the line, informed him that they had a deal.

Now all that was left to do was persuade the lady.

The Park Café was located on the corner of Seventy-first and Park and was attached to Trent's building. The spacious wi-fi hotspot was a popular place, especially during the two biggest lulls in brain activity: early morning and between four and five.

When Trent walked in during the latter, he spotted Carrie right away, sitting at a table with Elizabeth Wellington. Elizabeth lived in the penthouse with her husband, Reed, whom Trent had played ball with a few times. He didn't know them all that well, but they seemed happy enough.

As Trent approached the table, he noticed that the pretty redhead was crying as she talked animatedly to Carrie. He couldn't help but overhear a small part of the conversation.

"I've told him a hundred times, but you know Reed isn't the kind of man who'll take—"

Elizabeth spotted him then and immediately stopped talking. When she saw that he was coming over to the table, she leaned in and whispered something to Carrie then grabbed her purse and left the table. She didn't meet Trent's gaze as she pushed past him.

Carrie sat back in her chair, arms folded over her chest. "Trent Tanford, making women run away all over Manhattan."

He nodded. "Yes, I suppose I deserve that."

She took a sip of her coffee. "Are you here for coffee or just to eavesdrop?"

He sat down in the chair Elizabeth had vacated moments before. "I'm here to apologize."

"Already forgotten."

"Doesn't sound like it."

"No?"

He shook his head.

"Fine." She took a breath and said, "Apology heard and begrudgingly accepted then."

The corners of his mouth twitched with amusement. Damn, he really liked this woman. He'd never met anyone like her, anyone who made him smile this much.

"Listen," he began, "the marriage proposal—"

"Okay *that* one is forgotten. Seriously."

"The thing is, I'm not looking for you to forget the proposal—just the way it was delivered."

Before she could say another word or get up and

leave, he moved on. "I have a problem and I need your help. I'm *this* close to having everything I've ever wanted—the position at my company that I was meant to have, that I've worked my ass off to have. But to get it I need to—" he lifted a brow "—be married."

She stared at him for a second, then muttered a terse "Jeez." She stood up and grabbed her coffee. "I'm out of here."

"Carrie, wait." He went after her.

"You need mental help."

"Maybe so, but not for this."

She walked past him and headed for the elevator.

"Where are you going? I need to talk to you."

When he followed her into the elevator and pressed the button for their floor, Carrie whirled on him with her best "I'm-an-ass-kicker" face, her finger jabbing him in the chest. "Look, I get that you're mister high-profile-make-a-lot-of-money-so-I-can-impress-the-women-then-play-mind-games-with-them-stud-wannabe."

"Wow," he muttered, "that was a mouthful."

"And I'm sure there are a boatload of women in this city who are totally into that, but I'm not one of them."

Trent decided to ease up on the back and forth, tit-for-tat play. No matter how fun it was to watch his soon-to-be bride get all fired up, he didn't have a lot of time. He leaned forward and stopped the elevator.

They both jerked forward. Carrie sucked in a breath. "What the hell do you think you're doing?"

"You talk a lot."

"So do you."

"That wasn't an insult. I like it. I love watching your mouth move, and I look forward to watching it in the future, but right now I need you to listen."

Her jaw tightened and her tone was menacing. "You need to move and let me start this elevator back up or I'm going to scream."

"I know your situation."

"What situation?"

"Your financial situation."

She grew still. She swallowed and said with a lack of confidence he'd never seen before, "What?"

"Listen, I had to do what I had to do."

"You had me checked out?"

He shrugged nonchalantly. "Purely professional. If you're going to become a Tanford I had to know about your background."

She threw her hands in the air. "I'm not becoming a Tanford! In fact, right now, the idea of punching a Tanford sounds way more satisfying than marrying one."

"I think we're going to be good together. I need someone who will push me."

"You're delusional." She punched the emergency button and they went sailing upward.

He turned serious. "Marry me, Carrie. Stay married to me for one year and in return I will right all of your debt and kick in five hundred grand."

The doors opened.

He continued, "I'm sure there is something important you could do with that money."

"Goodbye, Trent."

"An apartment of your own."

She ignored him.

"Someone you could help," he called after her.

She paused, halfway down the hall. Didn't move for one whole minute. Then she shook her head and kept walking until she disappeared inside her apartment.

Four

Rachel Gray had been an amazing single mother. Yes, she'd worked night and day and all the hours in between on her artwork. But even so, Carrie had never felt unloved or neglected. Quite the opposite, in fact. Rachel had always found a way to involve her daughter in her work, setting up a canvas beside her own for Carrie or having her mix paints or letting her go nuts with color on one wall of the living room. And when Rachel wasn't working, life was boldly interesting and fun—a dark kind of fun, like waking Carrie up in the middle of the night with several rolls of toilet paper stuffed under her flannel pajama top, and a sly grin on her face.

"Let's go up to the roof deck, give the trees a little white. Pretend it's Christmas."

Carrie closed the prince's high-tech stainless-steel refrigerator door and smiled as she remembered that night. Yesterday and today, she was proud to have such a mother, and she knew that Rachel was proud of her, as well.

She took a breath. Would her mother be proud of a daughter who sold herself for money?

Carrie poured herself a glass of orange juice. Times had changed since those days when Rachel was a full-time painter, free to live life the way she wanted, in control of her thoughts and memories. These days Rachel needed her rent covered, her meals paid for and full-time care, and her daughter was barely making it.

Carrie drank the entire glass of juice, then headed into her room to change out of her best business suit. She needed to keep it in perfect condition for the next interview, because the meeting she'd had this morning was a no-go. Not enough experience. She'd heard it five times in the past month.

The problem was, she kept trying for high-level positions in graphic design, ones that paid high-level salaries. Unfortunately, she didn't have the experience they required. She was just hoping that someone might look past the experience and see her talent and drive, and give her a chance, because an entry-level job was not going to pay her enough.

The bed dipped with her weight. She slipped off her

shoes. She wouldn't go there, not a chance. This insane idea of Trent's.

She took off her stockings.

How could someone even suggest being married for a year? Basically, a business arrangement.

No sex, just for show.

Well. She paused. She was assuming there'd be no sex. But she should never assume—especially when it came to Trent Tanford.

A shiver of awareness moved through her at the unbidden image of lying in Trent's bed as he took off his clothes and stood before her, hovered over her, every inch of him lean and hard and ready to please. Trent Tanford taking off her shoes, her stockings…

Carrie leaned forward, put her head between her knees and tried to breathe.

Her school loans would be a thing of the past. She could actually afford to take an entry-level position at a graphic design house, really work her way up, take the time to learn without worrying about her mother's financial situation. And in the future be able to afford to care for Rachel long term.

The phone rang and Carrie leaped for it, hoping it was Trent calling to beg her to reconsider.

But it wasn't.

"Hey, Tessa." Carrie kept her voice light as she spoke to Prince Sebastian's personal assistant. "How are things?"

"Good, good." Tessa paused for a second and Carrie could just imagine the pretty green-eyed blonde sitting at her desk, which was, as usual, dutifully organized. "I have some news. Prince Sebastian is going to be returning soon."

"Is everything all right?"

"Nothing major." Tessa Banks was never one to gossip, but Carrie sensed something in her tone, a concern for her boss that had never been there before. Of course, Carrie could've been misreading the situation.

"Tessa?"

The woman didn't say anything for a moment, then she sighed. "There's a little trouble with the company."

"Is Sebastian okay?"

"You know the prince. He's not happy if things aren't going according to plan."

"Yes, I do know." Sebastian Stone was a good man, but he was also a demanding boss who showed his dark moods from time to time.

"I'll call you a few days before his flight," Tessa continued, "and I'll make sure your standard room at the Mercer is booked."

While Carrie appreciated Sebastian Stone's thoughtfulness in making sure she had a place to stay while he was in town, living in a hotel was a lonely existence. She wondered again if she should stay with her mother. But there was really no room, and she didn't want to take any space away from Wanda, who was there a good deal of the time. "Do you know how long the prince will be in town?"

"I don't, sorry."

"No problem. Thanks, Tessa."

Carrie hung up the phone and for a good sixty seconds just sat there on the bed, still and silent. Then without another thought, she grabbed a pen and paper off the bedside table. In a calm hand she wrote a brief note, then she snatched up her house keys and left the apartment.

She couldn't do this face-to-face. If she did, she'd probably choke and back out.

Her heart slammed against her chest as she bent down in front of his door and slipped the note underneath.

At precisely 7:00 a.m. the following morning, Trent walked into the Park Café, his gaze raking every table in an almost predatory way. Then he spotted her. She was sitting by herself at a table near the bathroom, staring into her coffee and biting her lip. She was nervous. Trent wondered why. What did she have to say to him? After all, she hadn't given him a definitive answer in her note, just a request to meet her at the café.

Trent maneuvered past the tables; fat, comfortable couches; and a long line of thirsty patrons. He had been only partly surprised to hear from her again. Was she going to accept his offer?

A flash of heat moved through him, not sexual heat, but something altogether unfamiliar to him, something akin to possessiveness. Like an animal, beating its chest and howling. *She was his.* The fierceness of his reaction startled the hell out of him, and as he approached her table, he told himself that it was due to his desperate need to get this done, make this match happen, procure the position as head of AMS, and not a desperate need to have her.

He didn't sit down. "Do I have time to order an espresso, or is this going to be half a cup of the house blend kind of conversation?"

Carrie took a deep breath, then said matter-of-factly, "I'm going to take the deal."

"The deal?" He knew exactly what she meant.

She looked down her lovely nose at him and said tightly, "Marrying you, for the one year."

He nodded. "Good."

She nodded. "Good."

He turned then and waved to the barista, who knew him well and would slip his espresso order in right away despite the line.

Trent knew he appeared calm as he sat down beside her, but inside him a fierceness raged, a satisfaction at getting what he most desired. She was his. She was his for one year. And so was AMS.

He watched her drink her coffee, which was no doubt cold at this point. Though she was without her glasses, she looked the same as she always did: cute, petite and casually dressed in jeans and a black peasant shirt. But as his gaze moved from the top of her head downward, he realized that every inch of her seemed to glow. Her long, dark hair, which was pulled back off her face to reveal those intense, probing, green eyes. And the full, pouty lips that he could still taste. And the curves.

Every damn inch of her glowed under his gaze.

The barista came over and set a double espresso before him, then flashed him her sexiest smile.

He hardly noticed. "Thanks," he muttered.

The woman in front of him was still glowing.

Completely fixed on Carrie, Trent couldn't help the words that tumbled out of his mouth then, like crude stones into a polisher. "I know I suggested that this marriage be a business arrangement, but you should know that I find you incredibly attractive. I don't know how easy it will be for me not to touch you, kiss you again, but if you don't want to go there—"

"I don't."

Her quick rebuff wounded Trent's healthy ego, but he didn't show it. He shrugged. "All right. I can respect that."

"Good." She was quick to add, "But I'll understand if you want to find…that—"

"That?"

"Sex." She whispered the word as though they were in church and not a coffeehouse brimming with groups of people talking and laughing and using their cell phones.

He couldn't help grinning. "Right."

"If you want to find it elsewhere."

His grin remained. "Thank you."

She nodded succinctly. "You're welcome."

Trent watched her expression, her pink cheeks and the unmasked sexual curiosity in her eyes. He was no fool. Carrie Gray liked him, quite a lot if he wasn't mistaken. And whatever her reasons were that day for sticking up the No Trespassing sign, Trent was pretty confident he could get her to remove it in short order.

"You know," he began evenly, "it's been my experience that women don't appreciate sharing their husbands."

"I'm sure that's true." Her green eyes flashed as she stared over her coffee cup at him. "But you won't be my husband—not in any real sense."

Again, that uncontrolled pull of possession moved over him. He lifted his cup and sipped his espresso, the hot liquid doing its best to calm this new, unchecked beast within. "Listen, Carrie, even though you're cool with me getting my pleasure on the side, I'm afraid I can't allow you the same privilege."

He'd never seen anyone sit up in their seat that quickly before. "Allow me?" She repeated his words with slow gall.

"That's right."

"I don't follow orders, Trent."

"Just think of it as part of the deal."

"You can't just add anything you want to this deal anytime you want."

"We are going to be married for one year. Looking for sex outside of our marriage would be humiliating and damaging to both our reputations." He put down his cup and leveled a serious gaze at her. "I swear right here and right now that I will not break my marriage vow to you."

She stared at him, disbelieving. "No other women?"

"That's right. For one year no other woman but my wife."

She swallowed as she registered what he'd said. Then she smiled just a hint of a smile. "So, you're going to be celibate for one year, huh? Do you really think you can do that?"

No. He didn't think so. Especially with her walking around his apartment night and day, bathing in his tub, sitting beside him on the couch, glowing the whole damn time.

Trent took a swallow of his coffee and hissed through his teeth.

"What?" she asked, her concern not lost on him. "Too hot?"

He stared at her. "Could be. Could very well be."

They got married the following Saturday in a rushed affair by elite caterer, Abigail Kirsch, at The Lighthouse at Chelsea Piers. A wonderful location, but far too large a space for their small party, and only managed because of who the Tanfords were in New York society, and who they knew.

No rings and a nontraditional ceremony had been Carrie's two major requests from Trent. Since girlhood, she'd dreamed of the perfect ring and being married in a church. But since this was not the "real" wedding she'd always imagined, she had insisted that she and Trent exchange vows without the platinum and in a location that was totally untraditional—yet public and fabulous enough so that Trent's father would be assured the affair would wind up in the papers.

Which it had, along with James Tanford's imminent retirement from AMS.

Carrie wore a sweet, insanely expensive Amsale dress that had been selected for her by the wedding coordinator working for the Tanfords. She even wore her hair the way the woman had suggested. She felt that, after all, this wasn't "her" wedding, so what did it matter?

All the guests were Tanford guests, of course, as Carrie hadn't invited her mother or any of her friends. She had planned to tell them that her and Trent's wedding had been a whirlwind decision and quickly executed, much like an elopement. But she knew there would be questions, uncomfortable questions, coming her way.

At 4:00 p.m. Saturday afternoon, she stood with Trent, who looked unbearably handsome in a black tuxedo, in front of floor-to-ceiling windows that overlooked the Hudson River. With his guests and stoic family behind them, Carrie and Trent agreed to be married. Afterward, Carrie spoke to his mother and father, who were poised and tall, and seemed genuinely pleased by the match. But they were also as affectionally retarded as most of the extremely wealthy couples she'd met in Manhattan, and quickly opted out of hugging either Carrie or their son.

There was music and an amazing spread, but Carrie ate little. As she walked around the party with Trent, she felt uneasy, lonely. The only thing familiar—the only thing that had warmed her on that incredibly warm late afternoon in August—was Trent's kiss, and the fact that his hand had never left hers since the ceremony had ended.

And then it was over. At seven o'clock they drove home, and with that kiss still lingering in her mind, Carrie wondered what was next, what about tomorrow—and how was she going to face being Mrs. Trent Tanford in name only?

Five

Carrie spent her wedding night in the most romantic of ways—packing up her belongings and moving out of Prince Sebastian's European-style apartment. As Sebastian was coming back to Manhattan soon anyway, she had called him earlier in the week to put in her resignation. He was sorry to lose her, he'd said, but understood her need to move on. Carrie hadn't told him what she was moving on to, but had assured him she would look after his place until his arrival, as promised.

"Ready?"

Trent stood in the bedroom doorway, looking ready to work. He had abandoned his tux for a much more casual ensemble of faded jeans and a funky black argyle

T-shirt with sleeves. When Carrie nodded, the two of them left the Old World of Europe and walked down the hall to a modern two-bedroom ultramasculine bachelor pad.

Trent's place had a very similar layout to the prince's apartment, but the paint choices, decor and "toys" were totally different. There was modern art and framed photographs on the gray walls, most of which were shot in and around New York City in a photojournalistic style. A flat-screen TV sat above the white brick fireplace in the living area, and around the metal-and-glass coffee table were modern black leather and metal couches. Behind that, near one of the windows, was an area that seemed to be designated for relaxation with a high-tech massage chair, surround sound stereo and DVD player, and some other male-oriented gadgets she didn't recognize.

On the way to her new room, they passed by his kitchen, which was open and airy, and looked brand-new, with granite countertops, electric-blue tile backsplash and expensive stainless steel appliances. Carrie grinned and shook her head when she saw dishes piled up in the sink.

He might be a rich guy, but Trent Tanford was a guy nonetheless.

Trent carried her bags into a good-size room that was painted the color of sand and boasted a white oak dresser with stainless steel legs and a metallic gray ceiling fan with wide leaves. Below the fan sat a modern queen-size bed with a creamy-colored upholstered headboard, metal legs and lots of plump white bedding. Two metal side tables held up two modern white lamps. Carrie noticed the short, wide vases on each table that were filled with red roses, cut short and packed closely together.

It was a beautiful room.

Trent set down her bags. "This used to be my office, but I think it'll be much better with you in it."

Her heart moved with the compliment. Very sweet. She looked over her shoulder at him. "That's a nice thing to say."

He raised a brow. "I have more nice things."

She smiled. "I'm sorry about taking your office away from you."

"No problem. But if you feel really bad about it, you can always move into my room and I'll put the desk and computers back in here."

"How about I just say thanks and leave it at that?" He was damn charming, she'd give him that. Resisting him would be difficult, but she had to. If she didn't, what would that make her? His for a year, and then done, out of his life—paid in full.

The idea made her cringe.

Perhaps sensing her discomfort, Trent continued with the tour. He moved beside her and pointed to the door at his right, which was bracketed by two framed photographs of old, paint-crackled window frames. "This room has its own bathroom. There are fresh towels in there, and I had Hannah, my housekeeper, get you a robe and a few…girl things."

"Girl things?" she repeated.

He looked at her and laughed. It was an infectious sound. "I don't know. Come on, give me a break. You are my first true houseguest, Carrie."

"Yeah, right."

"Believe it or not."

"You know which one I'm going with. I used to guide the poor lost lambs over here, remember?"

He walked over to her, his gaze serious. "I had women here, true. But no one stayed past 7:00 a.m."

She was appalled by his honesty. "That's horrible."

"Maybe so, but it was understood."

She raised her brows, unable to speak.

"I am who I am, Carrie. I set up my life the way I wanted it, and whoever decided to come into that life had a choice."

She nodded. "Okay. Fine, I get that. But why nothing after 7:00 a.m.?"

He shrugged. "It sends the wrong message."

"And what is that exactly? I don't like people who sleep late or eat breakfast?"

"No. More like, I don't want you thinking that this is anything more than a few hours of fun."

Her brow lifted. "Breakfast is too intimate?"

"Exactly."

"Talking about what could be next over pancakes and eggs…"

"I'm an honest man. No one came into this house without that knowledge."

"Gotcha."

"Yes, you do." It happened in a flash. He took her hand and brought it to his mouth. "For one year." Then he turned her hand over and kissed the palm.

Carrie's knees nearly gave out as heat traveled up her wrist, into her arm, shoulders…. He had an amazing mouth, gentle and full, teasing her with his slow, deliberate movements.

And then she remembered herself and eased her hand away from him. "I'm going to unpack now."

"And I'm going to let you," he said evenly, though his gaze was heavy with heat.

He was halfway out the door when Carrie called to him, "This is a crazy thing we're doing here."

In the doorway, he stopped and turned. "What? The marriage or the attraction thing?"

Her eyes went wide. "Yes."

He laughed. "You don't do too many crazy things, do you, Carrie?"

She shook her head. "No. Not really."

"Well, just so you know, the level of crazy is entirely up to you."

Perfect, she thought darkly. Leave the decision of how much water to drink to a chick who was dying of thirst. Smart move, Park Avenue Boy!

"I'm going to make some dinner," he said, "After you unpack, you're welcome to join me."

She wanted to say yes. She really did. But she needed some time to think, figure out her next move, the plan for this year-long "marriage." So she shook her head.

"I'm really tired. It's been a long day."

He looked disappointed, but he didn't push. He said, "Well, good night," then closed the door.

And she was alone again.

Releasing a heavy breath, Carrie sat on the bed in her black "wedding night" sweats and stared out the window at her new view, ignoring the grumble in her belly and the heat that still smoldered just inches below it.

It was a dream.

She knew it was a dream. She just didn't want to wake up and have it end. Her body felt like liquid metal, cool, smooth, pliable, the way it moved under his. But her insides, in contrast, her muscles, bones and blood all erupted in a blaze of heat.

"Carrie?"

The soft sound of her name wasn't coming from his mouth, the mouth poised above hers. Although the voice was his.

"Carrie?"

And then he was gone in a flash of white and she could feel the sheets against her back and her hair on her face. She opened her eyes. Trent was standing over her looking like the cover of a magazine. Suit, tie, clean shaven, eyes as blue as faded denim.

Yummy, was all she could think.

"What time is it?"

"Seven," he told her. "I'm sorry about coming in here and waking you up, but I didn't want to leave without saying goodbye. I thought it would be strange for you to wake up and… Well, a note seemed…"

"Right." It was thoughtful of him and she gave him a smile. "Thanks."

From her spot, deep within the white swell of covers, she caught a trace of his aftershave, and the clean, ocean scent made her already shaky, swollen, desire-filled body respond.

If she reached up and grabbed the lapels of his fancy, custom-made suit, pulled him down on top of her and kissed him, what would he do? What would he think of her? What would she think of herself? She'd just married the man yesterday, just stuffed her boxed wedding dress into his "office" closet, just made a pact with herself not to get physical with him.

Then another scent caught her attention, something earthier. Nuts or coffee? She looked to her right and saw coffee, toast and some fruit on her bedside table.

She looked at him, her eyebrows lifted. "That looks like breakfast, Trent."

He grinned. "Yes, I suppose it does."

"What happened to your rule?"

"Those rules we discussed last night don't apply to you or to us."

She felt the wave of happiness move through her, and wished it would never go away. "You're trying really hard, aren't you?" she said.

"What do you mean?"

"To be a good husband."

He grinned. "I've always been an overachiever."

"Well, you've definitely made me feel welcome here." She sat up, knowing full well that her hair was all over the place but not caring at that moment. "So, do you have to go right this second?"

Beside her, she felt Trent's body tense. "Why?"

She took a sip of coffee. "That comment you made last night about me and my lack of craziness…"

"Yes?"

"I think it's time to get a little crazy."

"And how exactly do you plan to do that?"

With a grin, she pointed to the plate beside the bed. "You made this for me, so how about you can feed it to me."

Trent laughed, his whole body relaxing. "I like you, you know that? I like you a lot." He reached over and picked up the white plate. "Here you go." He slipped a lovely blackberry into her open mouth.

When she closed her mouth and smiled at him, he shook his head and muttered, "Damn you."

They both laughed, and Trent continued feeding her until every blackberry was gone.

"Thank you for this," she said sipping her coffee. "Seriously. It's really nice."

"I meant what I said in the Park Café, Carrie. You're the only one."

As her heart expanded at his words, Carrie couldn't help but wonder why this major player in the dating world was so focused on her, why he was being such a kind, considerate husband-type. Was it simply because he honored the vow they'd taken? Or was it something else?

But then he leaned in close to her mouth and whispered, "You're the only one…okay?" She forgot everything she'd just been thinking and she closed her eyes and whispered back, "Okay."

And then he kissed her. And she let him.

First he kissed her mouth, so softly, then her chin, both cheeks, her eyes, her earlobes, then her mouth once more.

It was nothing charged or intensely sexual, but everything south of Carrie's belly ached, pulsed, begged for him to continue.

Where were his hands? His fingers?

But when she opened her eyes, he had backed up, his own gaze looking strained.

"I have to go," he said.

"I know," she said.

"Dinner tonight?"

"I'll cook," she said, then smiled at him. "And I'll feed."

He inhaled sharply and looked away. "You are a devious, torturous woman, Carrie Tanford."

It was as if someone had wrapped a hot towel around her and squeezed. Carrie Tanford. It sounded too strange, wrong, yet she wanted to hear him say it again.

He saw her reaction and he smiled, stopped her before she could say anything. "I'll be home around eight."

When he was gone, Carrie leaned back in her bed and groaned. She was frustrated and unfulfilled, her appetite raging desperately for the man she had married—the man she had vowed not to touch.

Trent was on top of the world.

At one-thirty that afternoon, in conference room C, with every top AMS executive seated around the oval mahogany table, James Tanford had announced his retirement, effective immediately. Taking over as chairman and CEO would be his son, Trent Tanford. No one seemed shocked by this news; they had known it would happen eventually. But for Trent, hearing his father say the words had made his life infinitely sweeter.

After his father's announcement, Trent announced who would be stepping into his previous position and subsequent other positions down the line, before unveiling his plan to rocket AMS into first place in the everpresent media wars before the year's end.

By seven-thirty that evening, he was happily exhausted and ready to head home, to his wife.

With a confident grin on his face, he walked out of the AMS building into the hot August night. His company car sat outside waiting for him, the black paint gleaming in the fading sunset.

His driver, Michael, stood sentry at the door and nodded as Trent approached. "Good evening, sir."

Trent agreed jovially, "Very good."

"Yes, sir."

Michael opened the door and Trent climbed into the

backseat, where the surprise of a lifetime sat directly across from him.

"Carrie. What the—"

"Hi."

She smiled at him in a warm, soft way that made his insides twist with desire. "Hey."

She looked different, though very much like herself in manner and realness. But there had been a definite change. Gone were the jeans, the peasant tops and dresses—all very good things, he mused, but nothing like what was before him. He'd known she had amazing curves, but he'd never seen them before, not like this.

His mouth watered as his gaze moved over her, starting with her feet and the metallic high-heeled sandals that showed off ten beautifully painted toes. Her legs were bare, but mostly covered by a long scarlet-colored strapless dress that hugged her curves and displayed her large full breasts to his hungry gaze.

Trent's only thought in that moment was to flip up the privacy partition and feast on her.

He was so turned-on he could barely talk, barely hear anything going on outside the car or in. But through the buzzing sound of his body in heat, he heard her say, "Do you want to know why I'm here?"

"Yes," he uttered.

"I thought I'd take you to dinner."

"You did?"

"To celebrate."

He stared at her, at her beautiful face that required

so little makeup, at her long dark hair that hung loose about her shoulders.

She laughed at him. "Your big day, Trent."

"What?"

"Weren't you promoted today? The job you've been working for all your life. Any of this ringing a bell?"

He found his way back to reality and nodded. "Right. Of course. I'm just…"

"Just what?"

Yes, what was he? Desperate? Overwhelmed by her? What was he exactly?

In the end, he came up with, "Surprised."

"Well, good." She looked past him. "To Babbo please, Michael."

"Very good, ma'am."

Carrie turned back to Trent. "And just a few short days ago, I was a 'miss.'"

"You look stunning."

She blushed, full on. She looked down, then back up at him. "Thank you."

How he was ever going to go home with her and not touch her was beyond him. What an asinine promise he'd given her—going at her pace or not at all! What a jerk! He leaned back against the black leather. "What if I said to hell with dinner?"

"Then I think we'd be having our first big fight."

"I don't want that."

"Me, either."

He smiled at her. "This is really nice of you."

She smiled back. "I, too, am an overachiever. And a good friend to have."

His smile fell at the friend comment, but he caught himself quickly, and when they pulled up to the restaurant a few minutes later, he had forced himself back into a good mood.

Before she got out, Trent said, "You know that once we step foot in that restaurant you're going to be scrutinized."

"Head to toe?"

"Soup to nuts."

"They'll want to know everything about Trent Tanford's new bride?"

"Yes," he said, stepping out of the car and offering her his hand. "And honestly, who could blame them?"

She smiled at him, took his hand and let him help her out onto the stained, garbage-scented, but ever-magical New York City sidewalk.

They walked hand in hand into one of Manhattan's finest Italian restaurants.

Six

"Stop! Thief!"

Seated at the dining room table, Carrie glanced up from her work. It was ten o'clock and they'd returned from the restaurant about thirty minutes ago. Trent had jumped in the shower and Carrie had jumped into her job search.

Wearing a navy blue robe, Trent walked into the kitchen, his dark hair still wet. "Is that *my* takeaway bag from the restaurant?"

She looked down at her work again, because avoiding the beautiful man in the robe and bare feet sounded like a smart idea. "When did they start calling it that?" she said. "Takeaway bag? What happened to doggie bag?"

"I have no idea. Are you avoiding my question?"

"What question is that?"

Beer in hand, he came to sit beside her at the table. "Where is *your* doggie bag?"

"It's still in the fridge. Didn't you see it there?"

He chuckled, shook his head.

"Look, Trent," she began with mock seriousness, "let's be real here. You are way too cultured, way too chichi to eat leftovers, and you know it."

"That is so not true."

"Which part?"

"I am not chichi." He tipped his beer at her. "Want some?"

"Sure, why not." After a healthy swallow with Trent watching her the entire time, Carrie handed the bottle back to him and returned to her work.

"So, what are you doing here?" he asked.

"Rewriting my résumé."

"Need any help?"

"No. Thanks." He smelled so good, like man soap, musky and off-limits. She tried to breathe through her mouth instead of her nose, which was no easy feat. It sure would've helped to have a clothespin or something. "It's just a matter of making my few qualifications in the graphic design world sound more substantial than they really are."

"Let me see."

He took the paper.

Carrie sat up tall at the table, as though she were

interviewing for a position right then and there. "I am determined to get a real design job by the fall," she said as he studied it. "Entry level is fine, but I really want it to be with a top company. I want to learn from the best of the best."

He gave the résumé back to her and declared, "I know what you need to do to fix this."

"What?" she said, seizing his beer from him and taking a sip.

"You need to change your last name."

"What?"

"Change your last name to Tanford and you won't have a problem finding a job."

She looked shocked. "I can't do that."

"Why the hell not?"

She sat back in her chair and folded her arms over her chest protectively. "I want to get this job on my own merits."

"An employer won't take the time to look at your merits, Carrie." He leaned back in his chair, too, and drank his beer. "Do you know how many people are vying for graphic design jobs in Manhattan? And not the gofer type of job where in between shuffling papers, you're getting coffee and sandwiches for the partners."

She played with her nails. "I'm sure it's a lot."

"Thousands." He put down his beer and took her hand, the one she was playing with, and she looked up at him. "A headhunter will never even read your résumé unless something on it attracts their attention."

"Like the Tanford name."

He nodded. "Exactly."

"But there is more than one Tanford in this city."

"Not Carrie Tanford. Everyone in this city knows I got married, and who I married."

She sighed. "I don't know."

"It's not a bad name."

He looked like a proud little boy just then and she smiled at him. "No, it isn't." What was stopping her? What was it that made her cringe? The fact that she'd only have the name for a year? That it didn't really belong to her?

She was becoming a confused person. She didn't like being confused, not knowing her own feelings, what choice felt right.

The truth was, the more she was around this man, the more confused she became.

"Get the job, Carrie, then show them those merits of yours."

"They're good merits," she insisted, more to herself than to him.

"Very good," he agreed. "Very attractive merits that no company, no one, could turn down."

They were becoming fast friends, she and Trent. She could feel the warmth and familiarity of a growing bond between them. And that was fine, lovely. What concerned her was the undeniable attraction that circled that friendship. And it wasn't just the proximity, though that surely helped the attraction along. No, she'd felt this pull to him on the very first day they'd talked, at his door when she'd reamed him out about his misdirected newspaper and assorted girlfriends.

She took another swig of his beer and looked over her résumé again. She was, after all, Carrie Tanford, Mrs. Trent Tanford. What was the harm? She was a hard worker, a fast learner. She'd be an asset to any company that had the good sense to hire her.

She dropped the résumé on the table and declared, "All right, then. I'll do it."

"Good."

Trent leaned in and kissed her. It was a warm, possessive kiss, one that spoke volumes about what he wanted to do next.

When he pulled back, their mouths were just an inch or two apart. Carrie's heart pounded in her throat and she waited to see what he was going to do.

She wet her upper lip with her tongue.

Then he reached for her, lifted her onto his lap, his mouth searching for hers. Her arms went around his neck, and as she kissed him back she felt his erection press into her backside. She sighed into his mouth. Her body was not her own, or maybe it was just disconnected from her brain. Whatever it was, this was a lost cause. She couldn't resist her own desires anymore. She would just have to deal with the aftereffects when they came.

For now she was going to enjoy herself.

Sick of sitting sideways, she eased one leg over his lap so she was straddling him. His robe opened at the waist, revealing no underwear, just hot, hard, ready flesh, and she dropped down on top of him. His hands raked up her back as his mouth teased hers, changing angles, tongues gently and seductively teasing each other.

Then his hand was at the top of her scarlet dress, easing down one side, exposing her heavy breast to the coolness of the air-conditioned room. Carrie's breath hitched in her throat as Trent lowered his head and lapped hungrily at her nipple. He cupped her breast from underneath, pulled her gently into his mouth, suckled hard as she muttered, "Yes, right there. Stay there."

It was no shock that her panties were wet, and her core ached with a desire she couldn't recall ever knowing before. She wanted Trent in an almost painful way, wanted that rock-hard erection that pulsed against her to be pulsing inside her body.

Neither heard the knock at the door. Not right away anyway. But whoever was there was insistent, and their knock grew louder and more obnoxious with every heavy breath that Carrie and Trent expelled.

Trent cursed and eased back, his eyes unfocused like a drunken man.

"It's eleven o'clock at night," Carrie uttered.

Out in the hallway, they heard the sounds of their very eccentric neighbor's dogs barking, and a high-pitched female voice.

Carrie sighed. "That better not be Vivian Vannick-Smythe."

Trent cupped Carrie's face. "I'll be right back." Then he righted his robe and went to the door.

Carrie sat at the table, groggy and turned-on to the point of wanting to cry if she didn't get to have Trent in her bed tonight. But through her haze, she heard a disturbing sound—a woman's voice, high and persistent, and then Trent's low voice, impatient and annoyed.

Like a possessed animal, a very female animal, she got up, made sure her dress wasn't exposing any of her female bits and walked into the hallway. Trent was just closing the door.

"The past has come calling," he managed to say to her before there was another knock on the door, followed by a female whine. "Trent, please."

Trent shook his head at Carrie. "I'm so sorry. I don't know how she got in here. She saw us at Babbo tonight and is having some issues."

He turned, opened the door again. This time his voice was calm, sympathetic when he addressed her. "Madeline, go home."

The tall, thin, spectacular-looking redhead shook her head and pouted. "No."

"I'll call you a cab."

"I don't want a cab. What I want is for you to tell me why you would drag that little nothing through Babbo and call her your wife."

Okay, Carrie thought. *Little thing coming through.*

She pushed past Trent.

"Carrie, wait," he began.

"It's okay. It's a woman thing." Carrie faced the stunning, yet slightly wasted model at the door and thought that maybe she was indeed a little thing because she actually had to look up the woman, who had to be a good six inches taller than herself. "Hi, Madeline."

The woman looked stunned to see Carrie there, but she recovered quickly. "So you're the one who claims to have married him?"

"Yes, I am," Carrie said calmly. "And you're the very tall, very beautiful person who has had too much to drink and is knocking on a man's door at eleven o'clock at night. Think about that."

Madeline's perfectly arched eyebrows knit together.

Carrie continued in a soft, gentle way, "Doesn't that seem a little too desperate for a woman like you? I mean, look at you."

Madeline swallowed, her pale brown eyes wide. "Yeah. Yeah, it does."

"Go home, take a bath, wake up tomorrow and begin again." Carrie reached out and touched her shoulder. "This is Manhattan, honey, there are moderately handsome, emotionally unavailable millionaires around every corner."

She smiled and nodded vigorously. "You're right. You're right. Thank you…?"

"Carrie," she supplied quickly.

"Thanks, Carrie."

"Can we call you a cab?"

She shook her head. "The doorman will do that. He adores me. Too bad he's only a doorman."

Carrie nodded sympathetically. "I know. Good night."

When Carrie closed the door, she turned to find Trent staring at her, his mouth open, utter astonishment on his face.

She shook her head at him. "I cannot believe it."

"I know. Again, I'm so sorry—"

"I cannot believe that one of your former bimbos actually found her way to your door without help."

He stared at her, then a wide grin broke out on his face, exposing those killer dimples. She smiled, too, and before long they were both laughing.

After a minute, after her laughing eased, Carrie walked past Trent and gave him a pat on the shoulder. "'Night, husband."

"Wait."

She turned. "What?"

It passed between them, the question of should they go there again, finish what they'd started before the Calvin Klein model had knocked on the door and sobered them both with her drunken ramblings.

Carrie answered for both of them with a tight smile and a slow shake of her head.

He nodded, clearly disappointed. "Okay."

"'Night."

"Carrie?"

"Yeah?"

He lifted a brow. "When you said, 'moderately handsome millionaire,' were you talking about me?"

"'Night, Trent." She grinned, then turned and headed

into her room, hearing him toss back a gruff and highly insecure, "You were just saying that to get rid of her, right?"

"I got a job!" Carrie announced a few days later as she sashayed into the apartment with the air of a person who had finally been accepted into an ultraexclusive sorority. "I just picked up the message on my cell phone. I'm so jazzed."

Trent was in the kitchen making dinner. When she rounded the corner and spied him at the island rolling sushi, he looked up and grinned. "Congratulations."

She inclined her head regally. "Thank you."

He looked good. He'd abandoned his suit for the day and was dressed casually in a pair of faded jeans and a pale blue T-shirt that accentuated his lightly tanned skin and fell just perfectly over his toned stomach, chest and shoulders.

"So, who's the lucky company?" he asked, handing her a glass of white wine.

"Ebett and Gregg."

His brows lifted. "Nice. Very nice." He tipped his own glass at her. "Cheers."

"Back atcha." As she sipped the dry Chardonnay, she studied him. "Wait a second."

"What?"

She walked over to him. "Why don't you seem surprised about this?"

"Did you put Tanford on the résumé?"

"Yes."

He lifted his eyebrows and gestured with his hands, as if to say, "That's why."

She slugged him playfully on the shoulder. "Smarty-pants."

He slipped his hands around her waist and pulled her against him. "That's what they call me."

"Really?" she said, her heart thudding in her chest. "They call you that? Around the office and everything?"

"Mmm-hmm."

"So, when your assistant ushers all the top execs into your office, she says, 'Here they are for your two o'clock meeting, Smarty-Pants.'"

With a grin, Trent leaned in and whispered in her ear, "Maybe I should be calling you smarty-pants."

She laughed, then sighed as he kissed her neck. "Smarty-Ass may be more appropriate here."

He growled against her skin, then pushed her away gently. "Go in and check out your closet."

"Why?" She liked being close to him, the weight of him, the warmth of his skin against hers.

"Just do it," he ordered.

She rolled her eyes, then turned on her heel and left the kitchen. Trent followed her into the guest bedroom, then pointed to the closet and stood back.

Confused and wondering what might pop out at her, Carrie opened the closet door gingerly.

"Holy crap!"

Trent chuckled. "Interesting reaction. Not exactly what I was hoping for."

Every inch of her spacious closet was taken up with clothes, shoes, purses and unmentionables. Her size, and perfect color choices. She reached out, fingering a finely tailored gray Chanel suit. "Is this the entire women's section of Barneys?"

"Not the entire section, no," he said with absolute seriousness.

She turned and eyeballed him. "Okay, you knew about this job before I even—"

"They left a message here a few hours ago," he confessed without an ounce of remorse.

"You did this in a few hours?"

"It was nothing."

Carrie sat down on her bed and exhaled. She just couldn't fathom how something like this was accomplished in such a short time. But to Trent it really did look effortless. Maybe some calls and a good deal of money was all it took.

Even so, she mused, the gesture was… She looked up at him. "Trent this is great, lovely, thoughtful—"

He stopped her. "Before you say anything further, you should know that this was a purely selfish move on my part."

"Really?"

"With my new position, we have functions to attend, and well, your—"

Her mouth twitched with humor. "My clothes don't cut the mustard. Yes, I'm aware."

"Besides, you do need clothes for work."

She stood up, walked over to him and gave him a hug. With zero hesitation, as though it were meant to be that way, Trent put his arms around her and pulled her in close. His muscles, his scent, the way her breasts always met with his ribs when they were like this—it was all becoming familiar to her.

Her gaze settled on him. "I'm not one of those girls who will act coy and refuse a lovely gift when she really wants to keep it."

"No?"

She shook her head. "I love clothes, dude."

"Did you just call me dude?"

She broke away from him, laughed. "Thank you."

"You're welcome. And now I'm going to finish making dinner before you drink too much wine and get light-headed and attack me."

"I never get light-headed," she called after him.

He frowned at her before leaving the room, muttering to himself like a cranky teenager, "Well, a guy can dream, can't he?"

"Mr. Tanford, there's a Mrs. Davis on the phone for you."

Trent didn't even look up from his work. He didn't recognize the name, and he had a meeting in ten minutes.

"Take a message."

His assistant didn't leave. He heard her clear her throat. "She says it's very important, sir."

"It's always important," Trent uttered. "Take a message."

"She says it's about your mother-in-law."

"I don't have—" He stopped midsentence and processed what his assistant had just said. Yes, he did indeed have a mother-in-law now. He grabbed the phone, "Put her through."

"Yes, sir."

"This is Trent Tanford," he said, curious as to what Carrie's mother might be calling him about. Carrie had mentioned very little about her—just that she lived in town and was an artist, the same information that Trent had gleaned through the investigator.

"Mr. Tanford," came a crackly older voice. "This is Wanda Davis, I'm Mrs. Gray's caretaker."

"Caretaker?" Caretaker for what?

"We have a situation here."

"What kind of situation?"

The woman hesitated. "Do you know where Carrie is, Mr. Tanford?"

"At work." A shot of alarm went through him. He wasn't sure why. "What's this about?"

"I tried to reach her on her cell phone, and at the home number, but it just goes to voice mail. Mrs. Gray is in such a state. Carrie is usually able to calm Mrs. Gray's agitation so we don't have to resort to the trauma of calling an ambulance."

"What? Mrs. Gray is sick?"

"Well, you know, she has…" Wanda paused. "Oh, my. I thought you would know…."

For one brief second Trent thought about his day, his new position and the back-to-back meetings he had scheduled after lunch.

Then he told Wanda in a calm voice, "Don't call an ambulance. I'll be right there." He grabbed a pen. "I just need the address."

Seven

When Carrie arrived at her mother's apartment, she was close to having a heart attack. She'd been in a meeting with the partners and a new client, and everyone had been asked to turn off their cell phones.

She was never doing that again. Vibrate was going to have to suffice.

She'd listened to the five messages from an increasingly worried Wanda as she'd walked back to her office. Immediately she'd grabbed her purse and left for an early lunch, making sure the assistants knew it was an emergency situation.

The first thing Carrie saw when she walked into the apartment was her mother's frazzled caretaker, pacing in the sunless, shadow-filled kitchen, stopping every few moments to cross herself.

Carrie went to her. "Wanda? What happened?"

Sudden relief flickered across Wanda's pale features when she saw Carrie. The older woman rushed to her, shook her head. "I don't know. She was talking about your father."

"Oh God," Carrie uttered, grief circling her heart.

"She's done that before and…nothing happened. So, this time, I thought she was fine. I was going to make her some soup, then, a moment later she became very agitated, crying, saying she had to find your father, make him listen, bring him back for you."

"No."

"She tried to get up and leave the apartment! She tried to get out the door, Carrie."

"Oh God," Carrie whispered, her stomach clenching in knots. Her mother hadn't tried getting out of the house for six months now.

"I've never seen her so upset. I didn't know what to do. So I called your husband."

Carrie's stomach dipped. "Oh." Trent had no idea about her mother's illness. She hadn't wanted to go there with him until she felt she could trust him with something so personal, not to mention something so scary and painful.

"He's been in there with her for the past thirty minutes," Wanda explained.

"What?" *He was here?*

Carrie's mind went blank. She couldn't imagine the two of them together.

"The moment he got here, he calmed her right down." Carrie barely heard Wanda as she rushed down the hall. "I don't know how he did it."

The door was slightly ajar, and when Carrie entered she found her mother asleep on the bed, looking like a young girl, her pale face relaxed. Trent sat on a chair beside her, a book in his hands. He turned when he heard Carrie come in, put his finger to his lips.

"She just fell asleep," he whispered.

Carrie went to him, put her hands on his shoulders and looked down at her mother's calm, sweet face. "Is she okay?"

"Yeah." He kept his voice low. "She was determined to get out of the house, find your dad."

Tears welled in Carrie's eyes and she shook her head, wishing she could make her mother understand that her father had left a long time ago, and that they were so much better off without him now. But Rachel was falling back into the past more and more these days. Those tangled, painful emotions that were just a whisper of a memory to Carrie were real and vivid in her mother's head.

"How did you get her to calm down?"

"I told her I'd find him for her, and for you."

"No…Trent…"

"I had to, Carrie."

Carrie just nodded, understanding completely.

"She asked me who I was," Trent said, looking up at her. "I told her I was your husband."

"What did she say?"

"At first she wasn't sure who you were, but before she fell asleep she looked at me and pointed at my face and said, 'You're Carrie's husband.'"

Carrie squeezed his shoulders. She couldn't believe he was here, doing this for her. "What book do you have there?"

"Pride and Prejudice."

"A romance?"

"Your mother said it was one of her favorites, so… Anyway, it calmed her down." He shrugged. "And for a romance, it wasn't half-bad."

"Good to know that a literary genius like Jane Austen meets with your approval," Carrie whispered drily.

He cocked his head to one side, studied her.

"What?"

"You remind me of Elizabeth Bennet. She's a smart-ass, too."

Carrie laughed softly. "Yes, she is." Then she took a breath and said, "Listen, why don't you go back to work. I'll take over here."

He shook his head. "No."

"What do you mean no?"

"It's your first week at the company…"

"They'll have to understand."

"They won't. What they will do is fire you."

Carrie stilled. She knew Trent was right. But she

couldn't leave her mother alone. If something happened again, set her mother off again, Wanda would need the extra support.

Trent looked at her with such a serious gaze, she almost stepped back. "I'm staying."

Carrie shook her head. "You can't."

"Why not?"

"You have a job, too."

He gave her an arrogant smile. "I'm the head of a company. I can do anything I want. I've missed three days of work in my entire career. Today I'm spending the fourth with your mother."

"Trent—"

"I'll see you later."

She didn't move. Her mind raced with more questions for this man who was acting like…well, like a husband.

"If she gets worse…" she began.

He assured her, "I'll call you."

This job was her future, her mother's security. She gave his shoulder one last squeeze before releasing him. It was a cold feeling. "I'll be back at five-thirty to take over."

"Sure. Go. Go." He waved her away and went back to his book. "I want to see what this Mr. Darcy character is going to do next."

Carrie smiled at his back, gave one last look to her mother and left the room.

Trent was in bed, reading over a few résumés for the position of senior advertising sales exec when he heard the front door open. It was just after eleven, and he'd been home for several hours after leaving Carrie with her mother around dinnertime. He'd offered to stay with her, but she'd insisted that he go home.

He heard her go into her room, heard her close the door, and after a few minutes believed her to be in bed for the night. Why wouldn't she be? She'd had a long, difficult day.

He went back to his résumés, attempting to defeat his disappointment. But then his door opened and she walked in. His mouth dropped an inch. She was wearing nothing but a silk chemise, one of the creamy white ones he'd ordered for her from La Perla.

As she walked toward him, stood at the foot of his bed, he stared at her in awe. Her face was rosy and scrubbed free of all makeup. Her long dark hair was loose, falling over her shoulders in soft waves, and her full, heavy breasts were barely hidden behind the thin, embroidered silk bodice.

He inhaled, his nostrils flaring.

"Trent," she said softly.

"Stop!"

Startled by the anger and heat in his voice, she froze. "What? What's wrong?"

"Don't come in here dressed like that."

"Why?"

"You know why, Carrie."

Her mouth curved into an understanding smile and

she brazenly lifted the hem of her chemise an inch or two, exposing the white silk panties underneath.

"I'm serious, Carrie," he practically growled, his skin raging with need, his erection clearly visible under the thin sheet that covered him from the waist down. "Now, I'm going to give you five seconds to turn around and leave the room. If you don't, expect to feel my hands on your body and my sheets against your back."

Her green eyes glittered with awareness.

She didn't move.

"One," he began, sitting up, "two…"

She didn't move, but he saw a flicker of a smile on her face.

"Three…"

She took a step toward him.

"…four…"

He didn't say five. What was the point? He was off the bed and had her in his arms in a matter of seconds.

His mouth crushed hers as he pulled her back on the bed. For one brief moment, she was on top of him, looking down into his eyes, and something passed between them that hit Trent deep in his gut. This woman was his. For as long as he wanted her.

Then she pressed her hips into his erection and his mind abandoned him. All he wanted was to taste her, suckle her, crawl inside of her and never come out until they were both breathless and ready for sleep. He flipped her onto her back and devoured her with kisses, starting at the base of her neck.

Carrie released a soft moan and let her head drift to the side, giving him better access. He suckled at the thin cord of muscle that housed her rapid pulse and the blood that flowed through her, giving her life. She moved beneath him, her hips pumping up and down, meeting him, telling him she was ready whenever he was, had been for weeks now.

But Trent was determined to go slow. He was going to claim every inch of her as his own.

Carrie felt a shivering madness in her mind and skin, as if she was on the verge of climax, but was afraid her body wouldn't be able to contain the intensity of what was ahead.

A totally naked Trent had her earlobe between his teeth, nibbling, then suckling and she raked her hands over his shoulders, up until her fingers threaded his hair. "Kiss me, please…" she uttered, coaxing him away from her ear over to her mouth.

"Carrie," he whispered before he captured her mouth with his, his hands slipping behind her back, down until he cupped her buttocks, rocked her against his erection.

She reacted quickly, wrapping her legs around his waist, her hands going to his face in the most intimate, loving of touches. Sex hadn't been a part of her reality for a good two years now, and even then it had been pretty ordinary—nothing at all like this—nothing like Trent and how he touched her, moved her, made her mind whisper with thoughts and dreams she'd never known she'd wanted. But she wanted them now, and she wanted them all with him. And best of all, she knew he'd go there with her. He was so desperate for her and it showed in every kiss, every ragged breath he took.

She was so lucky.

He left her mouth then, blazed kisses down her neck and over her collarbone until he stopped at the thin, silk bodice. With gentle, yet anxious fingers, Trent pulled the straps of her chemise down over her arms, elbows and hands, and as he did, the top of her chemise followed suit, peeling away from her skin, down, down over her belly until it rested on her hips.

Trent's gaze burned with heat as he took in her naked chest, the two heavy globes that begged for his touch, his kiss. Carrie let her head drop back against his pillow, let her nostrils fill with the scent of him as he, too, dropped his head and took one hard nipple into his mouth.

Her breasts had always been sensitive, even wearing a sweater without a bra had at times made her feel restless below the waist. But that little ache was nothing compared to what was happening to her now. As Trent suckled one aching nipple, he used his thumb and forefinger to tease the other, flicking, rolling the hot bud between his fingers until Carrie thought she'd lose her mind.

She pumped her hips, writhed in the tangled sheets, her fingers digging into Trent's scalp. She felt a drop of Trent's seed on her inner thigh, and she lost it. She came quick and hard, crying out like a wounded, desperate animal as her hips thrust as though he was inside her.

"Carrie," Trent whispered, nuzzling her breast as his hand moved between her legs. "Oh, sweetheart. Carrie, you're so wet. Tell me what you need."

As Carrie's orgasm eased, her desire for Trent intensified. "You. Inside me. So deep. My legs…so wide, you—"

Trent was reaching for the drawer in his bedside table before she could say anything more. He ripped open the condom and quickly sheathed himself. After peeling off her chemise and tossing it on the floor, he hovered above her. He opened her legs with his thigh, the hair on his legs tickling her skin, making her body weak, wet and hot with desire.

His erection was poised at the entrance to her body, and Carrie lifted her hips, took him inside her just an inch, just to feel the thickness of him invading her.

They were going to fit perfectly.

Doing this changed everything. She knew it. But her need was too great to examine the irrevocable consequences.

Trent's nostrils flared as he breathed, as he stared down at her like a bull ready to charge.

With a boldness she'd always known she possessed, Carrie put her hands to her breasts, teased her nipples into hard peaks as Trent watched in the light of the bedside lamp.

"You," was all he said before he entered her. One straight, hard thrust into her body.

Carrie cried out, spread her legs wider, wrapped her arms around him and filled her hands with his muscled buttocks. She pressed him deeper inside of her, deeper, until he was against her womb. Then he began to move, every stroke hitting the spot that made her throat tighten, made her breasts tingle, made her desperate and aching and ready to explode.

She wrapped her legs around him and followed his rhythm, pumping with him. Desperate to feel him, not only in her body and on top of her, but in her hands, as well, she slid one hand between them and captured the twin weights at the base of his erection.

He groaned at her actions, and as she played him gently, cupped him, she felt him thicken inside of her, felt his whole body shudder. And then he was moving, quickly, his strokes turning into desperate thrusts, hard, frenzied thrusts that had her gripping the bedsheets for support.

His hands found her breasts and he cupped them as he pumped into her, bucking like an animal, harder and harder until they were both completely out of control.

Then Carrie cried out, climax gripping her, claiming her. Unable to stop himself, Trent followed with one desperate thrust deep into her body before collapsing on top of her, shuddering against her wet, hot skin.

Several minutes passed before either one of them could speak. They lay on their sides, under the sheet,

Trent holding Carrie close against him, her back to his belly, her buttocks against his sated groin.

Carrie felt so calm, more relaxed and peaceful than she had in a long time. Was it the sex, she wondered, or was it lying in her husband's arms? Or was it both, wrapped up in a pink cloud of happiness?

She turned to face him, desperate to see his eyes, see if she could read his reaction to what had just happened between them.

But his eyes were closed, his face peaceful.

Like any persistent, just-mated woman, she did her best to wake him up in a loving, sweet way. She kissed the lids of his eyes, the tip of his nose, then his mouth. It took only a moment for him to respond.

"What is it, woman?" he growled. "Ready for me again, are you?" He reached around her waist and gently spanked her naked bottom.

She laughed, and he opened his eyes and grinned at her. "Like that, do you? I'll have to remember that."

She touched his face. "I like you."

She realized the moment the words were out of her mouth that she was wrong. She didn't like him at all, not anymore. She was over the moon, she was falling for him.

Trent stared at her, his brows coming together in a frown. "What's wrong? Are you okay?"

She nodded.

"Are you sure?" He gathered her in his arms and held her impossibly close. "You look sad. Is it about today?"

She kissed him for his concern. "No. But since you

brought it up, I wanted to thank you for what you did today. For my mom."

"It was for you."

"Thank you."

He didn't say anything for a moment, but continued to hold her tightly against him. When he finally spoke, his tone was soft, cautious. "Why didn't you tell me, Car?"

"I told you about her."

"You told me she was a busy artist."

Carrie rubbed her lips back and forth against his arm. "I don't know."

"Alzheimer's, Carrie. It's a big deal."

"I know that. Believe me, Trent—"

"I'm not scolding you, honey," he said gently. "I care about you, and if I would've known, I could've helped earlier."

She looked at him, slipped her hand behind his neck and pulled him in for a kiss. She had truly misjudged this man. He may have been a playboy, but in his guts, his bones, he was a devoted friend.

"Hey," he whispered against her mouth.

"Hmm."

"Can I ask you one more thing?"

"Of course."

"What about your father?"

She stiffened in his arms, and she knew he'd felt it. But he didn't let go. "What about him?"

"Why didn't you tell me he walked out on you?"

So, her mother had experienced a few lucid moments when Trent was there last night.

She tried to disentangle herself from his grasp. But he wouldn't allow it. He held her firmly. She stopped fighting and said quickly, "Same reason I didn't tell you about my mother. It was all too personal."

"Too personal?"

"Our marriage was supposed to be a business arrangement, Trent. It wasn't supposed to get personal, or sexual, for that matter."

"But it has." He released her then, and she sat up. "I want it to stay that way, Carrie." She turned to stare at him, not sure she'd heard him correctly. He nodded. "You need to tell me everything."

Her gaze flickered. "I don't know if I can agree to that, Trent."

"Why not?"

"One year. That's all we promised each other." She felt a strong need to protect herself at that moment. "We're not like a real married couple, sharing pasts and hopes for the future. This is amazing, you are amazing, but it hasn't been long enough…. No matter how I feel about you—"

"And how is that?"

She shook her head. She couldn't. There was no way she was going to tell this man that she was falling in love with him. Not until he said it first. If he ever said it.

She started again. "No matter how I feel about you, I honestly don't know if I can trust you."

"Carrie—"

The cell phone beside the bed rang. Carrie and Trent stared at each other as it continued. Then Carrie gestured to the BlackBerry and said, "Go ahead."

Trent reached for the phone.

Carrie pulled the covers over her body as she listened to him answer, then say, "Yes. What? Okay, fine."

He slipped off the bed. "I have to go."

"It's close to midnight," Carrie said, feeling cold suddenly.

"I know."

"Everything okay?"

He grabbed clothes from his closet and dressed quickly. "Yes. Nothing to worry about."

Carrie watched him. "Don't exactly trust me, either, do you?"

His jaw was tight as he walked back to the bed. He leaned down and kissed her on the mouth. "Be here when I get back?"

She sighed. They had a long way to go. She and her husband. They both wanted the one thing the other didn't seem willing to give—trust. But after tonight, as she'd predicted earlier when Trent's arms were around her and his shaft was buried inside of her, nothing was ever going to be the same. Everything would change. It had to.

But perhaps trusting each other would be a part of that change.

Her past, her father.

Trent's present, where he was running off to in the middle of the night.

She nodded, said, "I'll be here," and he left the room.

Eight

"There better be a damn good reason why you've asked me to come down here."

In a drab, worn office, across a cluttered desk, Detective McGray took the toothpick out of his mouth and addressed Trent and the new lawyer who sat behind him. "I'm not here to waste your time, Mr. Tanford, or to take you away from that pretty new wife of yours."

Trent's jaw tightened with annoyance. "What is it you want, then?"

"I wanted to show you this."

The detective slid a piece of paper across his desk. And both Trent and his new lawyer, Jerry Devlin, leaned forward and took a look.

"The threatening letter you received," McGray began, "did it look something like this?"

Trent scanned the page.

One million.
Grand Cayman island account.
One week to comply.

The next part, however, was blocked out with black tape, presumably by the police, so Trent couldn't see what the letter writer had threatened the receiver with.

He looked up. "Yes. Looks exactly the same."

McGray nodded. "Okay. Good. Thank you. That's all."

"That's all?"

"We needed to know if the letter matched this one, the first one."

Trent lost it. "Why didn't you have me look at this the last time I was here? In the middle of the damned day?"

"At that time we didn't think it was appropriate."

"But midnight on a weeknight is?"

Devlin put a hand on Trent's shoulder. "Mr. Tanford, please."

"Yes, easy, Mr. Tanford. An agitated witness in a police station can be…" Detective McGray stopped talking as he caught sight of something in the window behind Trent and stood up. "Excuse me a minute."

"Sure, why not," Trent muttered darkly as the man walked out. "This is ridiculous."

"True," Devlin admitted, "but it seems to be over

and done. Let's just keep things relaxed. We don't want the word on the street to be that the head of AMS won't cooperate with the police."

"Fine," Trent ground out.

The lawyer frowned. "I'm going to have a talk with the detective, see if we can move things along, all right?"

"Good idea."

A few minutes later, a man in his midfifties with a stocky frame and a full head of dark hair stuck his very familiar face into the detective's office.

"Trent? Hey, how are you?"

The police captain, who was a longtime friend of the Tanford family, offered his hand.

Trent stood and shook the man's hand. "Good, Mike. A little tired, though."

"Yeah, sorry about that. I'm afraid it had to be done."

"If you say so."

"Case isn't moving forward, and we're getting a lot of pressure from the city." He leaned in. "Between you and me?"

Trent nodded.

Mike's voice dropped to a whisper. "We believe Marie Endicott's death may not be a suicide after all."

Trent frowned. "What? Why not?"

The man's brows lifted. "That I can't tell you. But I appreciate you coming in tonight. Say hello to your mother and father for me."

"Sure."

"And congratulations on your marriage. Never

thought I'd see the day." He winked. "She must be something else."

"She is." Trent had never been the kind of man who talked trash or shared anything personal about the women he was seeing, and he wasn't about to start now.

The two men shook hands and the captain left the room, just as the detective and Trent's attorney returned.

McGray didn't sit down. Instead he gestured for Trent and the lawyer to follow him. They walked out of his office, down the hall and to the door of the precinct. "Thanks for coming in. I'll let you know if I need you or Mrs. Tanford for anything else."

Trent bristled. What the hell was the detective doing? Offering up a threat? Making sure Trent stayed in line and jumped to attention anytime the man called?

"You need to leave my wife out of this," Trent said.

Devlin jumped in quickly. "What Mr. Tanford is trying to say—"

"No, Jerry," Trent interrupted caustically. "What I'm saying to the detective is very simple. My wife has nothing to do with any of this."

McGray's face was a mask of composure. "I'm sure you're right, but you never know."

"I know," Trent insisted, his tone as sharp as a blade. "And I don't want her dragged through a worthless question-and-answer session."

With a shrug, McGray said casually, "If I don't have to, I promise I won't. But I'll expect you to bring forward anything new that comes your way."

Two minutes later, Trent walked out of the police station, stepped into his waiting town car and slammed the door. He couldn't believe he'd actually left his wife curled up in his sheets, naked and warm for thirty-five minutes of total BS.

But as the car sped away, as he leaned back against the leather seat and released a weighty breath or two, he realized that for the first time in his life he actually had someone to go home to. That reality had the power to change his humor into something altogether new to him, something resembling contentment.

When Trent crawled into his warm bed twenty minutes later, he caught the scent of lovemaking in his nostrils and inhaled deeply. It was everywhere, that addictive scent: on the sheets, pillows, and on Carrie's soft, sleeping frame.

He tried to will his erection away as he pulled her to him, but it was impossible, especially when she arched her back and moved her buttocks against him.

"Hey," she whispered.

"Hey." He kissed the back of her neck, suddenly relieved to be home, in his bed, holding her.

"Everything okay?" she asked.

"Fine."

"Do you want to tell me about it?"

"Not tonight."

"Okay. But you're—"

"I'm fine. I promise."

"Okay."

Again, she pressed back against his erection, and his hands went around her waist to her stomach, then moved upward until he cupped her breasts. Her breathing changed as he rolled her nipples between his fingers, and against his pulsing shaft he felt the warm heat of her body.

Ready and willing.

They made love into the early-morning hours, welcoming the crimson dawn with cries of pleasure and need and release.

"I have something to tell you and I don't want you to freak out."

A few days later, Carrie sat on a plump pedicure spa chair, her feet dangling in a hot, soapy whirlpool tub, her two friends bracketing her. Since Amanda had been in New York working diligently on next month's party for 721 Park Avenue's historical landmark status, the tall blonde knew exactly what Carrie was about to say. Julia, on the other hand, had been in Bermuda with her new husband and had no clue as to the goings-on in Carrie's life over the past couple of weeks.

The pregnant blonde eyed Carrie curiously. "Does this have something to do with why you never e-mailed me back during my trip?"

"Sort of."

"By the way, Jules, I can't believe you took the time to e-mail anyone," Amanda quipped, holding up two bottles of nail polish, trying to decide which shade of pink would work best with her skin tone. "You were on your honeymoon, for God's sake."

"So?"

Amanda looked nonplussed. "You should have been doing honeymoon-type things."

Patting her round stomach, Jules said, "The belly's starting to get in the way, okay?"

"Really?"

"Really."

"Can't you just try it from be—"

"Oh my lord, Amanda!" Julia cried, feigning shock and horror at her friend's dirty little mind.

Carrie couldn't stand it anymore. She inhaled deeply, then blurted out her secret. "I married Trent Tanford."

Both women forgot what they had been talking about and turned to stare at her. Amanda just grinned and shook her head, while Jules looked at Carrie as if she'd just grown a second head.

"Excuse me? What?"

"I married Trent. Tanford. My neighbor."

"Oh, I know who he is, Carrie." Julia stared at her for a good minute, perhaps trying to read on her forehead the answer of why Carrie had done what she'd done. Finally she said, "Why?"

Carrie's gaze dropped. "I fell in love with him."

But Jules wasn't about to let it go at that. "When did you fall in love with him?"

Carrie exhaled. She'd expected this, especially from Julia, but she knew it was only because the woman cared about her. The problem was that Carrie didn't want to share the details of her marriage and how it came about with anyone. Firstly, because the reasons were embarrassing. And secondly, because she would have to admit that she didn't marry a man for love—and that was a painful thing to admit.

No one needed to know how her marriage had begun, only how it was now.

"Listen," she said to Jules, "I know this is crazy and sudden and crazy again, but it is what it is. I love the guy."

Now. She loved him now. And that was all that mattered.

A sweet, gentle feeling moved through Carrie at the admission. Yes, she really did love him.

She looked from Julia to Amanda and back to Julia again. "Now, I was hoping for warm wishes and heart-felt congratulations." Carrie held up a hand. "Not because we're friends, mind you, but because I'm treating the two of you to this mani-pedi."

Julia looked as though she wanted to continue with the questions, but instead she smiled, sighed and leaned back in her chair. "And you think you can just bribe your way out of a friendly interrogation with a sugar-and-chocolate foot massage?"

"That was the hope, yes."

Beside Carrie, Amanda let out a sigh of ecstasy. "I think I can forgive you, Car."

Julia snorted. "Traitor."

The three sat in silence for a few minutes, enjoying the hot, swirling water, but soon a woman's need to discuss, chat and interrogate once again became overwhelming.

"So, how *is* married life?" Julia asked.

"You would know, Jules," Amanda pointed out.

"I wouldn't know how it is to be married to Trent." Carrie smiled. "Surprising, actually."

Julia lifted her perfectly manicured brows. "Interesting choice of verbiage."

"Surprising how?" Amanda asked, handing her choice of polish to the technician with a gracious smile. "Little notes under your pillow when you wake up surprising? Or a closet full of whips and chains kind of surprising?"

Julia laughed as Carrie answered, "The first. He's amazing, really thoughtful and caring. He treats me like a queen. It's not at all what I had expected." Especially after the deal he'd offered way back when—that straight-up business deal that he'd offered. That one she'd agreed to.

For a moment, Carrie wondered what Trent thought of her and their marriage now. Did he care for her as much as she cared for him? Was he sitting in a sports bar, talking to his friends about her?

She guessed, probably not.

"Well, you knew some of that, right?" Jules asked. "Before you married him? I mean, that's what made you marry him so quickly, right? Finding out he was this amazing guy and falling in love with that guy?"

"Right," Carrie said quickly. "Of course. I'm just

saying that even though I saw his sweet side before I married him, he was such a player when we met that I was worried, a bit, that maybe he'd never come to heel, so to speak." Carrie stopped herself before her ramblings sounded any more incoherent.

"I get it," Julia said, acting as though she did indeed understand.

Amanda looked at Carrie, worry behind her steely gray eyes. "Just be careful, Carrie."

"Why?"

"Don't make the mistake of thinking you can change a man."

"I don't," Carrie assured her. "I'm not."

"I'm not trying to be a downer, I swear, it's just in my experience…"

"What experience is that?" Carrie asked, suddenly curious. Despite being such an outgoing personality, Amanda had never been all that open about her past.

But Amanda didn't share anything of worth. She shrugged, her gaze on the tub of swirling water before her, her lovely face blank all of a sudden, as though she were trying to hide her emotions from the two of them.

Without missing a beat, Julia stepped in and returned to her favorite topic of the day. Although this time she brought along a brand-new perspective. "Maybe Trent was a player who was waiting for the real thing to come along."

Carrie liked that assessment, and grinned. "I think so." *I hope so.*

Julia held up a hand. "By the way, I want it on the record that it was my idea to have Carrie knock on his door and rip him a new one, which has clearly led to her happiness and a lifelong love."

Amanda looked up, shook her head. "We both encouraged her."

"I don't remember it that way."

"Stop right there, ladies." Grinning at her friends, Carrie attempted to make peace. "Since it is my happiness you are both trying to take credit for, I will just say thank you to you, Julia, and you, Amanda—because honestly, without that little push, I wouldn't be where I am today…very happy and in love."

"You're welcome, Car," Amanda said quickly.

"Yes, congrats, girl." And with that, Julia leaned back in her chair and sighed as the technician began massaging her feet.

Carrie eyed her hopefully. "So, you do forgive me for not e-mailing you back, right, Jules?"

The woman was so lost to the sweet scent of rose oil and the killer hands of Jeanne Marie that she barely registered the question. Her eyes closed, she muttered a clipped, "Huh? Oh, yeah, sure. Whatever."

Carrie turned and looked at Amanda. The two women laughed at their friend, then leaned back in their chairs, closed their eyes and followed her lead.

Nine

Schmoozing with important clients was standard fare in Trent's business. Normally, he did it solo, and had never felt as though a client's respect for him diminished because of his singleton status. But tonight, he saw his world through very different eyes—married eyes—and he was a little shocked to realize that his father may have been right in his belief that persons in high levels of business gain more respect when a wedding ring is attached to their finger and a wife is attached to their side.

Now, his wife had left his side about an hour ago, but only to work the room—something Trent had neither asked her to do, nor even thought about her doing when they'd stepped out of the black limousine and into Nanni on East Forty-sixth.

AMS had rented out the entire restaurant for this event. Hosting the brass from the top AMS affiliate stations on the West Coast was a big deal, particularly for Trent, as this was his first major event as head of the network. His father was out of the country, so Trent and Carrie were the only Tanfords in attendance.

Trent watched Carrie tuck into the center of a group of females—some execs, some wives—with the grace and ease of a practiced socialite. She looked amazing in a pale pink strapless dress that hugged her breasts and fell in a gentle wave down the rest of her body. Her hair was back in a simple, chic bun at the nape of her neck and her makeup was natural and young—just like her.

A waiter silently offered him a risotto puff, which he declined.

He had realized only a few days ago that he was completely over the edge for Carrie. Understanding this fact had put his past relationship into perspective, ending his moratorium on marriage for good. His fiancée had been a young man's crush, unsustainable lust masquerading as something far stronger.

He knew this because he felt that "something stronger" for his wife.

Every time he looked at her he wanted to wrap his hands around her and take her away with him. Every time another man looked at her, he wanted to put his fist through a wall. And there had been several of those

West Coast playboy bachelor types asking if she was taken, and by whom.

She made him feel like a freaking caveman.

"I've never felt envy, Tanford."

Trent looked at the man who had just given him a thumping pat on the back, then followed his line of vision. Alan Dowd was the President and General Manager of one of AMS's largest affiliates in Los Angeles, and was also a longtime friend of Trent's father.

Alan had his gaze trained on Carrie, as she conversed easily with a group of affiliates from Oregon and Washington State. "No. Never felt envious of a man until tonight, that is."

Trent nodded, said pleasantly, professionally, "I am a lucky man."

"Damn right. Don't let that one get away."

"Not possible, Alan. She married me."

The man raised his brows. "Never a guarantee. My ex-wife is living with her new lover in our house in Tahiti and I go to sleep with a folder full of absurd complaints from the Human Resources Department."

While the easy response to a comment like that would've been to laugh, joke around and commiserate, Trent was a seasoned pro. To act like just another "guy" would've deemed him totally unprofessional when Alan reflected on the matter later on. And when Alan was back in his hotel room sobering up, he would've reflected.

So, Trent didn't take the conversation further, but he

did smile broadly, tell the man it was good to see him and that continued success in Los Angeles was expected, and then he walked away, moved on to the GM of his Utah affiliate.

As the night was drawing to a close, Trent made his way over to Carrie, who smiled with her mouth and with her eyes as if she were very glad to see him.

He put his arm around her waist and whispered in her ear, "Ready?"

"Absolutely."

They said their goodbyes to a few remaining guests before heading out of the restaurant and onto East Forty-sixth. They waited only a moment for the limousine to navigate through the heavy midtown traffic and pull up to the restaurant. Trent waved at the driver to remain in the car and he opened the door for Carrie.

When he slid in beside her and shut the door, she dropped back against the seat and exhaled. "Okay, I hate to say this, Trent, because I know you do business with these people, but tonight was—"

"Tedious?"

She grimaced. "I told you I hated to say it."

"My work can be that way at times."

"No, it's not your work."

He grinned. "All right, the people can be tedious at times."

"Actually most of the people were fine. It was just a few of the executives."

"Daniel Embry?"

She pointed at him. "Yes. He was killer dull. Fly fishing and marble collecting…"

"How about Megan Frost?"

"Well, she was just plain nuts."

"And that boyfriend of hers—"

"No," Carrie interrupted, "I think he was an escort. The hired type. And an actor. The guy wouldn't stop talking about himself and asking anyone around him if they knew Andrew Lloyd Webber." She rolled her eyes. "I just wanted to say, 'Step out of the eighties, buddy!'"

Trent laughed and said, "Yeah, but his tattoo was cool."

Carrie laughed with him, and the pretty sound reverberated off the walls of the car and through Trent's chest. He pulled her to him and gave her a kiss. He couldn't help himself. "You were amazing tonight."

She cuddled in close to him. "Thank you."

"A natural."

She shrugged in his arms. "Just doing my duty."

His mouth twitched with amusement. "Well, then it's my duty to give you a proper thank-you."

She grinned. "Oh, my."

Trent's gaze never left hers as he called, "Excuse me?"

The chauffeur answered quickly. "Yes, sir?"

"Circle the park, say…three times before you take us home."

"Yes, sir."

"Three times?" Carrie repeated, her brows drifting up. "What are you planning, Tanford?"

Trent depressed a black button to his right and the

privacy partition went up. Every window was tinted and soundproof, but Trent switched on some music just to be safe.

The smooth and sexy sounds of Ne-Yo moved through the speakers as Trent left Carrie's side and planted himself at her feet.

"What are you doing?" she asked him, her green eyes glittering with playful intent.

He took off her shoes, one at a time. "You spent quite a few hours on your feet tonight. They must be sore." His gaze remained on hers as he massaged her feet.

She sighed, relaxed back against the black leather seat. Trent watched her hungrily. Married life surprised the hell out of him. He was happy, satisfied and completely unconcerned that his four-week rule was fast approaching. Carrie was different. She was his, his wife, his heart.

Carrie had cured him of all of it.

When her feet relaxed against his palms, he moved on to her ankles, her calves. He felt his body go rigid, his breath quicken as his hands lifted her skirt. Carrie opened her eyes, watched him as he eased the pink silk all the way up to her hips.

Her chest lifted and lowered in quick succession as her breathing changed. She watched his hands move to her inner thigh, upward, then disappear beneath the short hem of her dress as he found the warm, wet center of her.

She moaned and arched her back.

Trent thought he was going to climax right then and

there, but he bit his lip and curled his fingers around the pale pink strip of lace that covered the sweet heaven he wanted so badly to taste.

In seconds, her panties were down her thighs, around her ankles and in Trent's suit coat pocket.

Trent could barely breathe. He was really badly off. Hell-bent on giving her pleasure, tasting her, having her scent mark him, having her scent on him all night long.

He reached out, gently splayed her legs, then ran his finger down the center of her, so softly and slowly she lifted her hips to follow his hand as it moved.

He groaned at her reaction.

"What's wrong?" she whispered.

"Nothing. You're so wet."

Her eyes were glassy with desire as she smiled at him. "It's you. The way you touch me."

Her honesty, the way she stared at him, as though she totally trusted him with her body, did something to him and he spoke recklessly, like a tyrant, but he didn't care. "You're mine, Carrie. No one touches you but me. Ever. Do you understand?"

Carrie heard his words, but she could hardly register them. Trent had placed himself between her thighs, and his fingers were pressing the soft folds of her core open. Then his tongue was on her, on the sensitive peak inside, and she moaned and let her head fall back. She was limp and high and wanted to press his head closer.

His tongue lapped at the hard bud deep in her cleft, sending her flying as her hips lifted and lowered. Carrie had no control of her body; it moved and undulated and begged Trent to continue to lick her. He did, and as he did, he slipped one hand underneath her buttocks while his fingers played her, flicking, circling the wet opening to her body.

Then when her breath was coming quick and ragged, he plunged two fingers inside of her.

Carrie cried out, gulped air as white-hot stars imprinted on her closed eyelids.

She was on the edge of climax. Trent must've felt it, too, because he didn't stay still for long. He thrust his fingers in and out of her in quick, hard movements, simulating his sex as his tongue continued to lap at her swollen cleft.

She writhed against him, pumped her hips, dug her nails into the leather seat, and then it hit—climax, wave after wave of rioting spasms inside her.

She lifted her hips, held there. She couldn't breathe, she couldn't think.

And then the fog lifted and her hips lowered and she continued to pump against his mouth, but in slower and slower movements until she finally stilled.

After a moment, Trent took his mouth from her, but kept his fingers inside of her, still thrusting gently as her climax eased.

He watched her face, smiled when she smiled at him, and as they rounded the park for the third time, Carrie managed to find her voice enough to utter the words, "You are so welcome, honey."

* * *

When they pulled up to the apartment and got out, they were both disheveled and acting like two teenagers with hard-ons. They held hands and kissed each other madly as they walked through the thick mahogany doors.

They weren't even close to being finished with each other. That quick, hot detour in the limousine was just the beginning, and Carrie hated to admit it, but she understood now, without even a breath of jealousy, why women showed up at Trent's door at 2:00 a.m.

He was amazing.

And all hers.

The massive lobby was pretty dead except for the presence of Vivian Vannick-Smythe and her two yappy little dogs, who were both dressed to the gaudy nines, as usual.

The crystal chandelier overhead was too bright after the dim coolness of the limo. Carrie wanted to bury her head in Trent's jacket so she wouldn't be noticed and have to chat with the woman or anyone else who crossed their path tonight. She just wanted to get upstairs and be alone with Trent, have him all to herself.

And this time, *she* wanted to touch *him,* feel him in her hands, make him come apart, make his legs shake and his head spin.

Vivian stood beside the wide mahogany desk in the center of lobby, chatting with Henry Brown, the doorman. The mousy young man and the unconventional older woman were deep in conversation and it took the loud, echoing click clack of Carrie's heels against the ivory marble floors to jar them both.

"Hello, Vivian," Trent said smoothly as he and Carrie walked toward the elevator.

Vivian smiled in a panicky sort of way and muttered, "Hello, Trent," then quickly walked away from Henry, although Carrie noticed that her little dogs lingered at his feet.

Frustrated with the odd behavior of her dogs, Mrs. Vannick-Smythe gave a hard yank on their leashes before they gave up on Henry and followed the woman outside.

"What was that all about?" Carrie said as the elevator doors closed.

"Never can tell with that woman."

And that was all he was going to say on the subject, it seemed, because he'd barely touched the button for the twelfth floor before he had Carrie around the waist and pressed back against the elevator wall. His blue eyes flashed with deviousness as his knee moved between her thighs. He leaned in and he found her ear, nibbled the lobe. "I want to smell like you all night."

Ripples of hot anticipation went through Carrie's body and she grinned to herself, her eyes closing. If she had her way, Trent Tanford was never going to say those words to another woman.

His tongue flicked gently against her ear, then a soft puff of air. Her skin went up in flames and melted against him as her arms went around his neck. They made out all the way up to their floor, stumbled down the hall, barely made it into his apartment before his coat and tie were off and her dress was up around her hips.

After Trent fumbled with the key, opened the door, they pushed their way in and settled in the hall, barely hearing the phone ring.

"Don't answer it," she uttered.

He chuckled. "Are you kidding?"

Carrie dropped back against the wall as Trent dived for her, trailing hot kisses down her neck, over her collarbone. He yanked down the top of her dress, freeing her breasts.

That's when Carrie took control. She wanted him, wanted to feel his shaft in her hands, kneel at his feet and take him into her mouth, know that he was watching her suckle him just as she'd watched him with his head between her thighs in the limo.

She grabbed him around the waist and turned them both, so he was the one backed up against the wall. As somewhere in the house the phone continued to ring, Carrie grinned and started to undo Trent's belt, then his zipper. They were both breathing heavy as the machine kicked in.

"Mr. Tanford, Detective McGray here."

Carrie stilled, her fingers deep into the waistband of his boxers.

"You left your BlackBerry at the station the other night. When you come by to get it, could you stop in and see me, I have one more question about that letter, and about your—" the man paused, then "—*time* with Ms. Endicott."

When the phone clicked off, Carrie stepped back, pulled up her dress to cover her breasts. "Who's Detective McGray?"

"No one." Trent went to her, tried to kissed her, tried to get her mind back in the game, back on him, on them.

But Carrie wasn't having any of that. Her skin had grown cold in mere seconds. "Was he talking about Marie Endicott?"

Realizing that their moment of pleasure was over, Trent exhaled and said, "Yes."

Anxiety threatened to suffocate her. "That's where you were the other night? The police station."

"Carrie, you need to calm down."

"Were you called in for questioning about her death?"

"Yes—"

"But it was a suicide," she fairly shouted, panic hitting her full force.

His gaze flickered. "They're not so sure about that anymore."

"What?" She stared at him, her heart hammering painfully in her chest. "Oh my God. Are you a suspect?"

Ten

Trent stood in the hall, where not ten seconds ago he was happily making out with his wife. He didn't like the way Carrie was looking at him, accusatory and ready to believe the worst. But he was cool and calm when he spoke. "Several people in the building were called into the station to talk with police, Carrie."

"I wasn't," she said indignantly.

"Well, you didn't know her."

"And you did."

"Yes."

"You used to date her, didn't you?"

He threw his hands up. "Oh my God." He was so sick of this subject. "It was two dates. It was nothing."

But obviously Carrie didn't think so. "If it was nothing, the police wouldn't be calling here or having you come down to the station in the middle of the night." She cocked her head to the side. "What was that all about? Down at the station, eleven o'clock on a weeknight? Must've been pretty important."

Trent could feel his patience wearing thin. Why didn't he just come clean about the letter, make things easy and simple?

Maybe because nothing was ever simple when it came to women—and this woman in particular. He had a sneaking suspicion that she didn't want to believe him, whatever he said. "They had questions, Carrie. They wanted to know if I knew anything about why she might have taken her life."

"And did you?"

"No," he said emphatically.

She paused, and he thought for one brief shining moment that she was going to drop it. But her gaze searched his, looking for more. "You're not telling me everything, are you?"

He started to walk away. "I'm done here."

"Wait a minute. What about the suicide not being a suicide at all?"

"Good night, Carrie."

"Are you seriously going to walk out on this conversation?"

He whirled on her. "This isn't a conversation. This is an interrogation."

"Well, you should be used to those by now."

Anger bled from his veins. "You are…"

"What?" she urged, her green eyes flashing.

"Unbelievable. You're acting like—"

"Like what?" she interrupted. "Like a wife?"

He stared at her, his nostrils flaring. "I was going to say like a crazy person."

He saw her emotionally take a step back. She looked down, bit her lip. When she looked back up at him, he saw tears in her eyes. Her voice was raspy and tired. "Well, maybe I am crazy. Maybe I'm crazy to have thought that this could be a real marriage, where the two people in it shared stuff with each other."

Trent's gut twisted. "Like how you shared 'stuff' about your father with me? Or your mother's illness?"

His words caught her off guard, and he saw her shut down immediately. "I'm tired," she whispered, walking past him toward her room.

Trent stood there, shaking his head. "Yeah, so am I."

Carrie sat on the edge of her bed, feeling like a brat, like an ass, like a freaking two-year-old who wouldn't share her toys, but expected every other kid in the play-group to share theirs.

What the hell had just happened back there? Never in her life had she reacted that way, treated someone with such disrespect and zero tolerance.

Trent was right, she was completely nuts.

And obviously desperately in love.

Why else would she react that way? Lashing out at the man completely out of fear...

Outside her window, the lights of the city flickered under the dark sky. She had asked for the truth from him, but if she looked at herself honestly, she hadn't wanted to hear the truth at all. What she'd wanted to do was jump to the part when he confessed to something so foul she had no choice but to leave him.

She exhaled, put her head in her hands. Was that what she was doing? Using her daddy abandonment issues on him? Finding an excuse to leave him before he left her?

Outside her door, she heard the television click on, and some type of sports game blared through the surround sound speakers.

She had to right this. She had to talk to him. If she didn't, they didn't have a chance of moving beyond tonight, much less making it a year.

She grabbed her hairbrush from her purse and a pair of white underwear from her drawer and left the room.

As expected, Trent was in the living room, sprawled out on the couch, his gaze plastered to the TV. Baseball. The Yankees were playing someone, but Carrie gave the game little notice.

Her heart knocked around in her chest as she stood behind the couch. She dropped the panties over her brush, then reached over his head and waved the white underwear in front of his face.

He stilled, then looked over his shoulder at her and

said evenly, "Is that supposed to be a come-on or your perverse way of offering a truce?"

She pulled the brush back and shrugged. "Whatever gets us back into the elevator." She gave him a half smile and added, "Metaphorically speaking."

Amusement flickered in his eyes. "Have a seat."

Carrie walked around the couch. Trent turned off the game, and she sat in front of him on the coffee table.

"How about I go first?" she said.

"Okay."

"I'm sorry."

He took her hand in his and nodded. "I'm sorry, too."

The knot in her stomach eased at his quick acceptance of her apology, not to mention offering his own apology, which really wasn't something he had needed to offer at all. "That was unacceptable behavior—how I reacted to you back there. I've never spoken to anyone that way in my life."

"Wow, I feel honored," he said, humor still flickering in his gaze.

Carrie took a deep breath and tried to find a place to begin. "I was nine when my father left. I wish I could say he gave no warning, but he always warned us. Maybe he was just not into being a dad, or maybe he was just into messing with our minds, I don't know. But it was always, 'One day you won't have me to bring home a paycheck. One day you won't have me to play with or to put you to sleep or to teach you to fish or to...' well, fill in the blank. Then one day, he wasn't around."

She felt Trent squeezing her hand and it gave her the courage to keep going. "And maybe I was relieved. But I think it's made me wary of guys, and unwilling to trust them. Clearly, it has. I just didn't notice it before. There've been no long-term relationships before." She shrugged. "I always ended it before it got too serious, so it *wouldn't* get serious, you know?"

Trent nodded, smiled. "Yes. I do know."

She grinned. "Been protecting yourself, too?"

"Yes, but for a very different reason."

She didn't push him on that. It was her time to come clean. She held his gaze. "I didn't tell you about my father because honestly, I can't let myself completely trust you yet."

Trent said nothing for a moment, just looked at her. Then he lifted her hand to his mouth and kissed her cold fingers. "I understand, and I respect that."

"But I want to trust you."

"I want you to."

"I want to trust you because—" She paused. She paused because she was about to say the most important three words she'd ever said to a man, and she was afraid. But in the spirit of coming clean, she stumbled ahead. "I want to trust you because I love you."

She waited for him to react, look appalled or worse. But he didn't. He didn't look readable at all, and that freaked her out so much that when he did open his mouth to say something, she stopped him. "Please don't. Don't reply to that. I just want to put it out there by itself for now, okay?"

His eyes grew suddenly dark, yet very, very warm. He nodded, squeezed her hand again and said, "All right. We'll leave it."

"Good. Thanks."

But he added a pointed, "For now."

She nodded, breathed a sigh of relief. She just couldn't deal with his rejection right now.

He leaned forward in his seat. "I think it's my turn."

"Okay," she said with a touch of unease.

"Several months ago, I went out on a date with Marie Endicott. She was a nice woman, funny. But we had nothing in common and after the second date we both agreed there wouldn't be a third. I saw her in the building a few times and we said hello. But that was it." His voice faltered slightly on the next part. "Then the news came of her suicide. Horrible news."

He released a breath. "A few weeks ago I received an anonymous letter. Whoever sent it wanted me to wire a million dollars into an account on Grand Cayman Island or else they would expose my past indiscretions—which I later realized was my nonrelationship with Marie. Since I'd only dated her twice and had nothing to hide, I had originally dismissed the letter. I thought it was BS, someone messing with me, and I threw it away."

"Anyway, the cops called me in to question me about my relationship with Marie, see if I knew anything, and while I was there the first time, I mentioned the letter.

They told me of a similar letter that had been sent to someone in the building."

"Who?" Carrie asked, her curiosity piqued.

Trent shook his head. "They wouldn't tell me. But when I was called to come back in just recently, they showed me the letter. They wanted to know if it was the same."

"Was it?"

Trent nodded. "Pretty much, although they'd blocked out the section with the threat, so I couldn't see that part."

Carrie shook her head, thinking of people in the building. "I wonder who it was sent to." She wondered if Julia or Amanda knew anything about Marie or the letter. But she couldn't really come out and ask them, could she? This was Trent's business, and she wasn't about to share something that personal, even with her friends.

"One last thing," Trent said, capturing her attention once again. "When I was there, the captain, who's a friend of my family's, mentioned that they're starting to think that Marie's death might not be a suicide at all. But he wouldn't expound on that."

Carrie released a heavy breath. "Wow."

"Yeah."

"So, that's it?"

"That's it." He lifted her hand again, kissed her fingers again.

With a slow grin on her face, she looked him over. "No skeletons hidden in your pockets?"

He lifted his arms. "Come check my pockets for yourself."

Laughing, she went to him, sat on his lap and put her arms around his neck. "Was this our first fight?"

"Mmm-hmm." He pulled her close. "And because we had to endure such an unpleasant first fight, I think we should be rewarded with superhot first makeup—"

"Sex?" she offered, then laughed.

"Yes." He eased her off his lap, then stood. "But not here."

"What?"

"Hold on a sec." He left the room, and when he came back, he took her hand and led her out of the apartment.

"Where are we going?" she asked as they walked down the hall.

When Trent got to the elevator, he pressed the down button. "You said, 'whatever gets us back to the elevator.'" He bowed his head. "All I want to do is please you, darling."

Awareness shot through Carrie's body, heating her skin. The elevator doors opened, and as Trent ushered her inside, she laughed softly, like a naughty little girl. "But what about the residents? They won't be able to use—"

The doors had hardly closed when Trent captured her mouth.

The elevator had barely moved before Trent reached out and flicked the emergency stop button.

"But, Trent—" Carrie inhaled sharply as he pressed

her back against the elevator wall, pulled down the top of her dress, filled his hands with her breasts.

"We'll be quick," he murmured, lowering his head.

His tongue lapped at her nipple and she gasped, groaned.

"Not too quick." Every inch below her waist was aching, throbbing.

"Just long enough for you to come."

He snaked a warm hand up her dress, his fingers brushing her inner thigh. She gripped the steel railing as he found her, wet and ready for him. "Yeah…that could be pretty quick." He slipped two fingers deep inside of her. Her breath caught in her throat. "Oh, oh, my, oh, Trent, oh, g—"

Ten minutes later, mousy doorman Henry Brown had canceled the emergency call to the elevator repair company, and the building's irritated residents were finally making their way up to their respective apartments.

Carrie and Trent sitting in a tree.

K-I-S-S-I-N-G.

First comes love, then comes marriage. Then comes…

Wait a second!

First came marriage.

Laughing at her girlhood song, Carrie glanced at the clock on her laptop. It was after six. Dammit. She had a date with a very important lady tonight, and if she didn't hustle she was going to miss it.

She straightened her desk, switched off her computer and grabbed her purse. Things were going very well at her new job. She'd managed to impress everyone in her department with her efficiency and ever-present creative ideas.

Most of the staff had already left for the day, though a few workaholics still remained at their desks, glued to their computer monitors. She called out a cheery goodbye to them as she headed for the elevators.

She was so lucky. Hers was truly a dream job, and she had Trent to thank for the opportunity.

Trent. Her husband. Her lover.

She punched the *L* and sailed down toward the lobby, all the while recalling her ten minutes in heaven with him in their own building's elevator the other night.

A shiver of awareness moved through her as the doors opened. But it was quickly defeated by the sharp, oddly shaped, hundred-pound boulder she'd been carrying around in her chest ever since she'd gone completely insane and said those three words to Trent.

Outside, the manic heat of the day had barely subsided, and the delightful scent of urine and sweaty pedestrians assaulted her. She went to the curb and hailed a cab. She couldn't believe she'd told Trent she loved him. What a total idiot. At least she'd been smart enough to stop him from responding.

Not that his lack of response had stopped her from guessing at what he would have said. Trent Tanford was kind and caring and an incredible lover, but he just didn't seem like the kind of man who said "I love you" or even entertained the thought.

A cab shot to the curb and stopped with a catlike screech of the brakes. Carrie jumped in and quickly rattled off the address to the driver.

She settled back against the seat, watched the driver maneuver in the heavy traffic and continued spinning thoughts in her head. If Trent had been able to respond the other night, he probably would've said something gentlemanly and evasive like, "Thank you. I think you're amazing."

Carrie's shoulders slumped forward.

Or maybe he would've given her a wide, dimpled grin and a long speech about himself and what he wanted and didn't want in his life. How, even though he cared about her, they'd made a deal, a yearly plan, and he couldn't see past that right now....

Carrie felt light-headed. The air in the cab wasn't much better than the air outside.

It really sucked to be in love.

Or maybe it just sucked to be in love by yourself.

When the cab pulled up to her mother's building, she thanked the driver and gave him a nice healthy tip with his fare. Then she jogged up the stairs and arrived at her mother's door with an unattractive sheen of sweat on her brow.

Wanda was in the kitchen with her head in the cupboard that housed the plates and bowls. She pulled back when she heard Carrie come in. "Hello there."

"Hey." Carrie smiled, dropped her purse on the nearby hall table. "How's it going? Everything okay?"

"Everything's copacetic," Wanda announced good-naturedly, using one of her favorite new words because after a while saying "fine" and "good" to describe Rachel's doings and mood during the day got boring.

Wanda was living in now, something Carrie had wanted forever, but couldn't afford or convince her mother that she needed. Hell, Rachel wouldn't even consider Carrie being around her that often, much less a nonfamily member. But as Rachel's condition had grown worse over the past few months, Carrie had started to worry about her mother's safety from 10:00 p.m. to 6:00 a.m. Thankfully, Rachel had finally come to accept the idea of Wanda living in her home full-time, and that made Carrie feel so much better.

"So, I thought we could order some dinner tonight," Carrie said, eyeing the junk drawer where they used to keep all the take-out menus when she was a kid.

"Already been ordered," Wanda informed her, taking plates and glasses out of the cupboards and placing them on the counter. "Should be here any minute now."

"Oh, great. What did you order?"

"I didn't."

"What?" Carrie asked, confused.

Wanda looked sheepish. "Dinner has been ordered every night. It comes promptly at seven."

Carrie shook her head. "I don't understand."

Wanda paused, a knife and fork in her hand. "Mr.

Tanford set it up. He said with all I have to do around here, I shouldn't be cooking three meals a day. I told him I didn't mind, but he insisted."

Carrie couldn't believe what she was hearing. "When did he say that?"

"A few days ago. He was here for a quick visit during his lunch hour."

Again, she was completely stunned. "Trent didn't tell me he was here or about the dinners."

She shrugged. "Maybe he wanted to surprise you."

"He did."

Trent had been here? On his lunch hour?

But why hadn't he mentioned it to her?

For one brief second, she felt that familiar rush to mistrust him enter her system, but she quickly pushed it aside. Who cares why he came and if he forgot to tell her? He had been here. That was enough.

"The food comes with a server and everything," Wanda said brightly. "Oh, your mother's awake, by the way. She had a lovely bath and is resting."

"Thanks, Wanda."

Carrie walked down the hall and entered her mother's bedroom. The first thing she saw was her mother's face. She looked so young—pale, but young. Her gray hair was pulled back off her face and she looked pretty and lucid. But maybe Carrie was just seeing what she wanted to see.

"Hi, Mom."

Rachel's gaze lifted, and Carrie saw recognition. "Carrie?"

Carrie's eyes filled with tears. These moments were so few and far between lately that when they did come Carrie was filled with equal parts of thankfulness and rage.

She went to sit beside the bed. "My very nice husband has ordered the three of us dinner. Would you like to talk while we eat or watch something?"

"Carrie, dear?"

"What, Mom?"

Rachel shook her head. "I have something."

"What it is?"

"A pain."

Carrie's heart dropped. "Where? Show me."

Rachel pointed to her heart.

"How bad?" Carrie asked, fully panicked now.

"It's because your father left."

And then a different kind of panic moved in, sharing space with the sad, angry heart. "I know, Mom. It was a long time ago."

"He left because of me."

"You shouldn't be thinking about this right now." Out in the hall, the doorbell rang. "The food's here. Maybe it's that garlic bread with the chucks of roasted garlic you like so—"

Rachel grabbed Carrie's arm, squeezed until her fingers were white. "I have to think now. I have to talk about it now."

Carrie's throat ached at the sight of her mother's desperation. She didn't want her getting so upset that she had another episode like the other night, but she also understood the rush to explain. Her mother needed to say whatever she needed to say. Now. Because there might not be a later.

Carrie nodded. "Okay."

Rachel sighed, looked thankful. "I asked him to go, Carrie. You didn't know that, did you?"

"No."

"I was so tired of his threats. Every day. But most of all, the way it made you feel every time he said he was going to leave. I couldn't allow that to continue. One night, I said to him, 'Just go. Go now.'" Rachel looked up, her eyes brimming with tears. "And he did."

Carrie put her hand over her mother's and said with impassioned truthfulness, "I'm glad you did."

"But he didn't say goodbye to you," she said sadly, releasing Carrie's wrist. "I will never forgive myself for that."

"You have to forgive yourself. Just like I had to forgive myself for wishing he'd leave."

Her eyes wide, Rachel stared at her.

Carrie pushed on, glad to finally have a chance to release her own hidden guilt. "I couldn't stand it anymore, either. I prayed every night before I went to sleep that he'd leave. That morning, when I woke up to just you, I was…relieved, excited to start a new life. I missed him, don't get me wrong, but as I grew up my memories of him were far better than the reality of him actually being there. Do you understand?"

Rachel nodded, smiled, looked like her old self for a moment. "I do."

Then Wanda and the server came in with a tray full of delicious-smelling food, and Carrie silently thanked Trent for making life a little easier for them all.

They made it a foursome, insisting the server sit down and share their meal with them. Halfway through, Rachel smiled at her daughter and suggested they all watch a movie.

"Your choice, Mom," Carrie said, nibbling on a bread stick.

"To Sir With Love?"

Carrie laughed, but got up to get the DVD from the cabinet. "Listen up, everyone, just so you know what you're in for, this will be two hours of hearing my lovesick mother say how beautiful Sidney Poitier is."

Wanda grinned. "I'm up for that."

The server shrugged. "He is gorgeous."

Rachel smiled at her daughter. "Not to worry, hon, two hours go by quickly with that man on the screen."

Too quickly, Carrie thought as she dropped the disk into the player and switched on the television. In two hours, Sidney would be gone, Wanda would be on her way to bed, Carrie would be going home, and Rachel Gray might be slipping away, back inside her damaged mind once again.

Eleven

He had a wife.

She slept in his bed.

And he was okay with that.

Actually, Trent mused as he stared across the pillow at her, he was more than okay with that. He was over-the-moon about that.

The early-morning sun was crawling up the sky, inch by inch, its pale rays streaming through the windows, backlighting his beautiful bride in a haloesque glow. His sexy little angel, who had come to earth to save him from himself. And hopefully, while she was here with him he could spoil her, give her his protection and his loyalty, and offer her what was left of his heart.

She stirred, inhaled deeply.

Trent felt ready to spring. She was lying on her side, nude, hugging the sheet between her legs, and he wanted to know what her skin felt like, tasted like at 6:00 a.m. He leaned forward and kissed her softly, first her shoulder, then her upper arm.

Her eyes opened. She blinked, trying to register where she was and what was happening to her. When she saw Trent, her gaze cleared and she smiled.

"Morning."

Trent moved in closer, lying on his side, facing her, nearly nose to nose. "Hey." He brushed his nose across hers.

"Good sleep?"

"Very good. You?"

"The best." She reached up and touched his face. "Hey, my knight in Versace armor?"

He chuckled. "What?"

"Thank you."

"For what?"

She wrapped one leg around his waist and pulled him even closer. "I was at my mother's last night, and I had a lovely meal with her and Wanda—and the server."

"Uh-huh."

"Come on. The server who brought the dinner you ordered."

He chuckled. "It's nothing. She should have every comfort." And so should you, he thought, trailing a hand up her soft thigh. "Oh, I forgot to mention something about your mother."

"What?" she asked lazily.

"I went to visit her the other day, during lunch. I didn't tell you because I thought it might make you feel bad."

She came up on one elbow, alert now. "Why?"

He shrugged. "With your new job, I know you don't have the time to go over there as much as you used to, and I didn't want you to feel pressured to try and make it if I went. I'm sure you're working through lunches. Right?"

She nodded.

"I'd like to continue to visit her if you don't mind."

"Mind? Are you crazy or just—" she leaned down and kissed him "—totally amazing?" She pushed him onto his back and climbed on top of him. "Or are you both?"

"What I am," he said with a growl of need, "is very happy you're sitting on top of me."

She grinned, clearly feeling the hard and ready length of him against her bottom. "I'm going out on a huge limb here."

"Damn fine way of stroking my ego, sweetheart."

She rolled her eyes. "Big fan of double entendres, are you?"

"That one, I am." He laughed. "I mean, come on, I'm a guy." He noticed that she wasn't laughing and he asked, "You okay, sweetheart?"

"I want you, Trent."

"Good," he assured her.

"No, I mean I want you. Not for just a year." She released a breath, looked at the ceiling for a second. "God, I'm horrible at this."

Heat ripped into his gut and his heart. "You're doing just fine."

Her eyes glittered like emeralds as she stared down at him, vulnerable as an infant. "I want this, you and our marriage."

Trent stilled. He wasn't at all sure of what to say or how he felt.

"I've shocked you," she said.

"A little," he admitted.

"And you want to get out of this bed and calmly tell me that we had an agreement. And while you like me, and are attracted to me, you in no way want to—"

"Stop, Carrie. You're spinning."

She couldn't meet his eyes. "I should get in the shower."

She tried to get off him, but Trent wasn't going to let her get away. "Talk to me. Stay here and talk to me."

He held her hips, and after a moment, she met his gaze. "All right."

"As you were saying."

She released a weighty breath. "I think we're great together. I don't want to be with anyone else; I can't imagine it—ever." She swallowed nervously. "What do you think?"

"I think," he said as he reached up, curled a wedge of her hair around his fingers, "okay."

"Okay?" she repeated.

He looked into her eyes and nodded. He was, if nothing else, a man of his word.

Then he coaxed her to him and kissed her as if she was his, for more than a year, for a lifetime.

At three that afternoon, a bouquet of flowers was delivered to Carrie's cubicle, pink peonies so artfully arranged they looked like a still-life painting sitting there on her desk. She knew instantly they were from Trent, and she smiled as she opened the card.

Meet me tonight.
7 p.m.
727 5th Ave
I'll be the one holding the blue box.

Curious and unable to wait until seven, Carrie swiveled in her chair and looked up the address on Google. What was life like before the Internet, she wondered as she impatiently waited for the location to appear on the screen.

Then she saw it, where she was supposed to meet Trent tonight, and a shot of excitement went off inside of her, like fireworks against a diamond sky. It was an excitement that only a girl could truly understand.

She glanced at the time and frowned.

Four tediously long hours to go…

He saw her before she saw him, walking quickly down the street, wearing a stylish white pantsuit and black heels.

The store had just closed, and his surprise was going to be arriving at any moment. He was amazed that he could pull this off. But everything, even the famous Tiffany's store, was for rent for the right price. True, the whole thing was a bit corny and had been in done in a movie or two, but the place was also classic New York.

He watched the security guard lead Carrie through the closed steel doors. And then she was in front of him with a slightly worried smile on her lips. "Are we breaking and entering?"

He chuckled. "No. Security is outside, as you saw, and there are more of them watching upstairs. And somewhere around here there's a salesperson, but they're being discreet."

She looked around, her gaze resting on case after case of expensive jewelry. "What are we doing here?"

"Ever heard of *Breakfast at Tiffany's?*"

"Of course."

He took her hand. "Well, this is going to be Dinner at Tiffany's."

Her eyes bulged. "Are you serious?"

"As a heart attack."

Trent led her into the main room, where a dining table was set up, complete with white linens, silver flatware and more pink peonies.

Carrie stared at him. "I cannot believe that we're having dinner here. In the store. Surrounded by every precious stone and metal there is."

He nodded. "Then we have some shopping to do."

"What?" she said, shaking her head and laughing at the insanity of it all.

"I thought it was about time."

"Time for what?"

"Look at your finger."

Grinning mischievously, Carrie held up her hands and wiggled them. "Which one?"

He pointed to the ring finger on her left hand. "There's no ring on it, honey."

"Yours, either," she pointed out.

"I always thought that if I ever did get married, I'd never wear a ring."

She lifted her brows. "Interesting. And what do you think now?"

He gathered her in his arms and kissed her. "I'm thinking I want you to pick one out for me."

She smiled. "Okay."

"And I'll pick out one for you."

She smiled wider. "Okay."

Behind them, the two-person catering staff hovered, waiting to serve them. So Trent left Carrie's side, walked around the table and held out her chair for her.

She sat with a gracious thank-you to her host and put her napkin in her lap with a great flourish. Trent smiled at her. It pleased him to no end that she was enjoying herself so much.

When the waitstaff had set the meal before them, Carrie looked up, her expression a mixture of surprise and eagerness.

"Pizza?" she exclaimed.

"I thought you loved pizza."

"I do. It's perfect! This whole night is perfect."

"Pizza and Tiffany's. Classic New York."

As they ate, they talked. About work, travel, family. Up until this point, Trent had shared little about his mother and father, mostly because he didn't know all that much about them as people. But he did tell Carrie about his beloved nanny growing up and their crazy escapades in the city, and the one time they took the ferry to Staten Island and got so lost they missed the return ferry and had to spend the night at her cousin's house.

Best time of his life, he told Carrie. "Except for maybe right now."

She smiled and took another bite of her slice.

When Trent's cell phone rang, they were deep in conversation about her mother's artwork, and he let it go. But soon the beeping of a waiting text had him glancing down. "Sorry about this."

"Everything okay?" Carrie asked.

He stared at the screen. "Nothing vital. Just one of my assistants is leaving for the day."

"One of your assistants? I didn't know you had more than one."

"I have four."

"Wow. Nice promotion."

"I know it sounds crazy, but they're all vital. My workload has tripled since the promotion. Not that I'm complaining. Anyway, she stayed late to finish some paperwork I needed to have completed first thing in the morning."

"Ah. Well, it was good of her to check in. Very professional."

He heard the thin strain of unease in his wife's voice, and he dropped the phone back in his pocket and looked at her. "I wanted no interruptions tonight, but unfortunately the head of AMS doesn't get to be off duty."

"I understand," she said, her gaze flickering from him to her plate.

"It can be frustrating at times. You sure you still want to hang out with me?"

She pretended to think about it. Then she laughed and said, "Absolutely."

He reached across the table and took her hand. "I'm here with you."

It took her a second to respond, but finally, she nodded. "I know." Then she gestured around herself. "I just can't believe you did this."

"Anything for you."

She laced her fingers with his and smiled broadly.

"Are you happy, Carrie?" he asked.

"I'm with you, Tanford. That always makes me happy. Now, will you pass the red pepper flakes?"

"Oh my good Lord."

"Are you going to stare at that thing all night?"

"Don't call her a thing."

They were in bed. Trent was reading, and Carrie was staring at her ring as though it was a newborn and she wanted to memorize its face. Trent looked down his sexy black reading glasses at her. "It's a her?"

"Yes, and now you've hurt her feelings."

He snorted, took her hand in his. "You're a nut, but I love to see you so happy."

"I am and I don't ever want to be not happy again."

He examined the ring, the pretty diamond trellis band he'd picked out for her after seeing her nearly burst into tears when she spotted it behind the glass. "It's very unassuming—sorry, she's very unassuming."

"I'm not a big-rock kinda girl. This ring is me, us, perfection." She turned into him, her leg sliding across his pajama-clad thighs. It was her standard move, and she knew he loved it. "You have great taste, by the way."

He put his arm around her. "I had nothing to do with it, but thanks."

"Do you like yours?"

"I do. But I like what you had engraved on it more."

"Ah, yes." She cleared her throat and made it dramatic. *"A day, a year, forever.* Damn, I'm good." When he laughed, she looked up at him. "You haven't changed your mind about that, have you? The forever part?"

"You mean after watching you talk to your ring and call it 'she'? Surprisingly, no."

"Good man." Grinning, she reached up and slipped off his glasses. "Make love to me."

"Shh…" He was over her in seconds. "Not in front of the ring."

Carrie giggled. "She's cool. She likes to watch."

"Hmm." His mouth met hers. "Kinky."

Twelve

Trent left the police station for the third time that month, BlackBerry in hand. He nodded a silent good-bye to his attorney and stepped into his town car. It had been the same series of questions to start, with one ridiculous new one to end. McGray had asked Trent if the letter he'd received had come to his home or office, and what kind of paper both the letter and envelope were made of.

Trent had offered the man everything he could recall, but McGray seemed frustrated when he'd finally told Trent he could leave.

They were obviously no closer to solving the mystery of Marie's death.

The driver maneuvered through the heavy evening traffic. Trent had already had a full day of work, then his meeting with police, and now he was off to Pacheco restaurant. He was meeting with two long-standing advertisers and the top members of their staffs for a dinner party at the Spanish restaurant. He had wanted Carrie to come with him, but she had already offered Wanda a night off, so she was staying with her mom until pretty late.

He hated going solo to social events now.

He grinned, shook his head. What a switch.

And he really wanted her there tonight more than ever, because his father was going to be in attendance, symbolically passing the torch in front of his oldest advertisers.

But he'd see her later, in bed, and make sure she had a lovely breakfast in the morning.

God, he was such a puss.

It was five minutes to eight when they pulled up in front of the restaurant. Trent got out and headed inside.

It was lunchtime at the Park Café, and two women sat at a small table, drinking lattes and splitting an overly fattening low-fat muffin.

"Check this guy out."

A petite woman with a tight blond bun grabbed the newspaper from her dark-haired friend and thoroughly scanned the pages. "Wow. He's so hot."

"Look at that girl he's with," Dark Hair said in a severely depressed tone. "She's perfect. She's got to be

an actress or a model." She sighed. "I could never get a
guy like that."

"No normal-looking woman could get a guy like
that," Tight Bun said.

"That's because he wouldn't even notice one of us if
we walked past him."

After gulping down her coffee, Tight Bun said, "I
can't look at either one of them anymore. I have to get
to work. Do you want to go to a movie tonight?"

"As opposed to what?" Dark Hair said, grinning.
"Bungalow 8?"

Tight Bun snorted. "Yeah, right."

They both laughed, then stood up and left the Park
Café, leaving behind their empty coffee cups and the
newspaper they'd been ogling.

Carrie sipped her extra hot double cappuccino and
watched them go. She'd heard that conversation a
thousand times in her own head whenever she'd seen an
especially cute guy, an out-of-her-league guy. Hell,
she'd thought all of those things when she'd met Trent.

Thank goodness that part of her life was over, she
mused, remembering the very satisfying morning she'd
spent with her husband, followed by his sweet gesture
of serving her breakfast in bed.

Curious, Carrie reached over to their table and swiped
the paper. She turned to the entertainment section and
looked for the man and the model. When she found
them, focused her eyes on the photograph in the center
of the page, she felt the breath leave her body. There was

a picture of her husband and a beautiful blonde. The pair stood close together, Trent's arm draped around her. He seemed to be about to kiss her cheek.

The headline screamed at her:

The Pretty People Party at Pacheco

Carrie felt cold, numb as she scanned the article for her husband's name and some explanation for why he was with this woman when he was supposed to be having a dinner meeting with a bunch of old men.

Because there had to be a reason, right? He wouldn't lie to her. He wouldn't be running around with some woman when Carrie was hanging out at her sick mother's house.

She pushed back her jealousy and her quick feelings of mistrust. She wasn't going to do that anymore; she'd promised herself. There was an explanation. She just had to find it.

What she found was the article. It read:

Last night at Pacheco, AMS honcho hottie, Trent Tanford got cozy with a beautiful mystery blonde.

With her heart beating anxiously in her belly, Carrie stared at the woman. There was something about her. She looked so familiar.

Carrie squinted. She knew her.

But how? From where?

Was she a model or an actress, like those two women had suggested? Or was it…?

Then she stilled. Like a silent movie playing in her mind, she saw herself, late one night, opening the door to another one of "Trent's Troops." Carrie's shoulders dropped—her heart, too. Mystery Blonde was no longer a mystery. She was one of the women who'd come knocking on her door back in the day looking for Trent.

She tossed the paper back on the girls' table, left her coffee and croissant and walked out of the Park Café.

Why had she allowed herself to fall in love with a playboy? Why couldn't she just have left things alone? Why couldn't she have stuck to her end of the deal, the business arrangement—no sex, no love?

Dammit.

Last night when Carrie had gotten home late from her mother's house, Trent had said that his meeting had gone "well." Obviously. He had changed the subject pretty quickly after that, she recalled.

Amanda's words slithered through her mind. "Don't expect a man to change."

Back in her building, Carrie stabbed the button for the twelfth floor and tried not to think about what she and Trent had done in this elevator not one week ago.

She stalked down the hall and into her apartment. No, it was Trent's apartment. She would have to move in with her mom for now. There was no way she was staying here, with him. Not after this.

She may have been a bought wife, but she would not accept a cheating husband. One that had lied to her and promised his faithfulness.

She packed quickly, then sat down at his desk, took out a piece of paper and pen. For a moment, she wondered if she was acting rationally, if her actions and reactions were wrong, if this was about her father again.

But even her father with all his faults hadn't cheated on his wife. The facts were there. That blonde had come to Carrie's door in the middle of the night looking for Trent. And Trent had never denied that those women were his lovers.

White-hot anger ripped through her. She was through confronting him, talking things out.

She was done.

After finishing the letter and depositing it on his desk, she grabbed her things and was out the door.

He was a happily married man with a chance at a real family.

The one thing his father had done right by him.

A month ago, it had all been about gaining power and status for Trent. Now it was all about Carrie and building their future and, God help him, maybe a little Trent or Carrie Jr. if his lovely wife was up for that.

Trent walked down the hall at seven-thirty, with a take-out bag in his hand. He had no idea if Carrie liked Thai food, but he thought they could give it a try. Then maybe a movie. The last few nights had been filled with work obligations. Tonight, it would be just the two of them.

But first he had to ply her with a little wine, because he was pretty sure she had seen the daily paper. She hadn't returned any of his calls at work, which meant she was either insanely busy or freezing him out.

Not that he blamed her. He was a huge ass for not warning her. What the hell was he thinking letting his wife be blindsided by that? He'd seen that photographer, but had been too preoccupied by the advertisers and the fact that he'd forgotten some projection sheets at the office.

"Honey, I'm home."

He walked through the dark apartment, checked the bathrooms. Nothing, she wasn't around.

He frowned. Maybe she wasn't home yet. Or perhaps she had stopped by her mother's. He went to his desk and grabbed the phone. But when he saw the note with his name on it, he stopped.

As he read, shock took hold of him and held steady until he'd finished the last word. Then, as he slowly realized what Carrie had done, anger snaked into his blood and dripped from his veins. Yes, she had seen the picture, but instead of talking to him about it, she'd run. She'd run away like her damned father.

Her words the other day had meant nothing. She had no faith in him or the marriage she'd said she wanted so much. But worst of all, she hadn't had the balls to face him and tell him in person.

That he couldn't abide.

His face was a mask of rage as he crushed the note in his fist and tossed it into the trash.

Thirteen

Carrie had been living with her mother for four days when she got a letter from Trent. It was the first she'd heard from him since she'd walked out of their apartment, and out of his life.

There were some papers for her to look over, he'd written, and he was going to leave them at his office for her to pick up.

He'd also included the times of day he would be out of the office, so they wouldn't have to see each other.

Carrie's heart squeezed painfully. These had been the longest four days of her life. She missed him so badly, she ached with it. But clearly he hadn't felt the same.

She stood at the kitchen counter in her suit and stared at his note, typed up, not even handwritten.

Papers for her to look at… What were they? Separation papers? Divorce papers?

He sure wanted this over and done with in a hurry. Maybe he needed to make things less complicated for him and the blonde, she thought bitterly. Maybe the woman had already moved into his apartment, into his bed.

Suddenly, she felt as though a piano was sitting on her chest, intensifying the ache into sweeps of despair and anxiety, and grief for the loss of a wonderful friendship. But she was a stubborn person who wouldn't go crawling back to a man who didn't love her, a man who thought that a little blond candy on the side was okay.

She grabbed her purse and headed out the door to work. She'd stop by his office this afternoon, during one of his "out of the office" times. Might as well get it over with…

"Anything for lunch today?"

Trent glanced up, shook his head. "No, thanks."

Danny, the sandwich guy, didn't move. He just stood in the doorway and waited.

Trent exhaled heavily. He was in no mood for this today. "Nothing personal, Dan. I'm having lunch out."

"With your wife?"

"No," Trent muttered through a tightly clenched jaw. "Not that it's any business of yours."

"That's true."

Trent looked up, glared at the freckle-faced kid who

delivered sandwiches during the day and inhaled law books at night. "What do you want?"

"I want to ask you something."

"Ask then. I have a ton of work here."

Danny rarely walked inside Trent's office, but today he did just that, and sat down across from Trent at his desk. "If I had seemed to change into a machine overnight, a machine who never left the office, would you say something to me?"

Trent stared at him. "Yes. I would say, good for you. You understand how to make it in this city."

Danny snorted. "Maybe you would have said that before…"

"I don't have time for this," Trent snapped.

"You were happy, Trent. Happier than I've ever seen you. What the hell happened?"

Trent glared at him, really pissed off now. "It's Mr. Tanford."

Danny sighed and stood up. "All right, Mr. Tanford. I'm going. But before I do, I just want to say something." Even though Trent shook his head with annoyance, Danny continued, "When you offered to pay for my school a few years ago, my family didn't like it."

Trent scoffed. "Why the hell not?"

"They felt that only family should help family."

"Of course."

"But I told them you were like family to me, like a brother. I told them that family doesn't always come from blood."

"What's your point, brother?" Trent said with far less hostility than a moment ago.

"My point is that you may not have had the kind of family you wanted as a kid, but you can have it now."

Trent nodded. "That's a nice thought, Danny."

"She's your family."

"Stop." Trent shook his head. "Go now. I have to get back to work. I'll see you tomorrow."

When Danny left, Trent attempted to regain his train of thought, but it was impossible. Danny's words had thrown him off, made him for one second believe that he could actually have what the boy had suggested. A family. With her.

Then reality faced him head-on. He hadn't had one as a child, as a young adult, and he wouldn't have one now. Those kinds of dreams were for starry-eyed kids and Disneyland-loving adults.

The woman he'd given his heart to had thrown it back in his face.

As Trent stared at his computer screen, a thought, a question, snaked into his mind without invitation. It was a question he didn't even want to look at, because it might make him partly responsible for her leaving.

Yes, Carrie had gripped tightly to those fears of hers, but how much had Trent really tried to help alleviate them? He, too, had hidden things from her, like the meeting with the police. He hadn't laid his life bare and open for her. Was it possible that he had a few fears of his own?

He shook his head, trying to clear his thoughts, but

it was an impossible task. The idea that he might have wronged Carrie in some way, or their relationship, was now permanently embedded in his mind, right alongside an image of her face, that sweet, laughing face he knew he would never be able to forget.

The woman behind the desk asked if Carrie could wait just a moment. Carrie nodded at Trent's secretary and took a seat in the waiting area. She felt sick to her stomach. What was she doing here? she wondered miserably. Getting some papers? Something that legally called off their "deal"?

The door to the hallway was open, and Carrie could hear Trent's secretary talking to someone. Carrie turned and glanced over her shoulder. All she could see were balloons and high heels. But then, whoever was holding the bouquet of balloons handed them off to Trent's secretary, and Carrie was able to see the previous owner perfectly.

Oh my God!

The blonde from the photograph.

Carrie jumped up. Unbridled anger swirled through her, and she could hardly breathe. On unsteady legs, she walked to the door.

The blonde continued to talk to Trent's secretary. She didn't see Carrie coming. And then Carrie was in her face, seething with rage and a ruined heart.

"You," Carrie blurted out, facing the exceptionally beautiful young woman.

"Mrs. Tanford?" Trent's secretary looked worried. "If you'll just have a seat, I'll be right with you."

"Mrs. Tanford?" the blonde asked with a genuine smile. She put her hand out to Carrie. "Hi, I'm one of Mr. Tanford's assistants. I don't think we've met."

Carrie sniffed. "Oh, we've met." His assistant. Nice cover.

The woman's brows snapped together. "I'm sorry?"

"Are you? Are you sorry you ruined a marriage?"

Trent's secretary gasped, and the blonde looked shocked. "I think you have me confused with someone else."

"No, I think I remember you grabbing my husband in the newspaper."

The blonde shook her head. "No, no, no. The picture was completely misleading."

"Of course it was."

"The restaurant was very loud. Mr. Tanford was leaning in, telling me to go back to the office and get a file he'd forgotten."

Carrie snorted, shrugged. "Sure, that would seem totally logical if I didn't also remember you coming to my door in the middle of the night looking for Trent."

"That was several weeks ago, right?"

"That's right."

"I was looking for Mr. Tanford."

Carrie exhaled. This woman was as dim as a box of rocks. "I know. I just said that."

She shook her head. "No, I used to be the senior Mr.

Tanford's assistant. He couldn't find his son that night, and he sent me out looking for him. But I apologize for disturbing you. Really."

Something started to work in Carrie's chest, a heat swirling around and around like water in a toilet, warning her that perhaps she had made a huge mistake. "But the senior Mr. Tanford is retired."

Another woman came up to them, a gift in her hand. "Lauren, we have to go. Everyone's waiting."

The blonde, who Carrie now knew was Lauren, turned back to her and said, "My shower."

"Shower?" Carrie uttered weakly. "As in baby or wedding?"

"Both actually." Lauren touched Carrie's arm and explained her situation. "When Mr. Tanford retired, I was going to be out of a job. Soon-to-be married, pregnant and out of a job. Not good."

Carrie's knees threatened to buckle.

Lauren continued, "The new Mr. Tanford said he'd keep me on, and after the baby comes, too. My fiancé is still in medical school, so we don't have the greatest income right now. This company has great benefits."

If she could've given herself a superpower in that moment, she would have made herself invisible. But she was no Superwoman; she was in fact deeply flawed. She shook her head, closed her eyes for a second. "I'm such a jerk. A stupid, jealous, insecure jerk."

Trent's secretary snorted. "We've all been there, honey."

"I'm so sorry," Carrie said to Lauren.

The woman smiled. "It's okay."

"It's not, but thanks. And you can expect an enormous baby gift from me. A stroller or crib or a new house or something."

Lauren laughed. "You're funny. It's no wonder that Mr. Tanford's always trying to get home early."

Carrie felt as though she'd been stabbed. She needed to leave and quickly. She turned to Trent's secretary. "I'll be out of your hair as soon as possible. Trent left me some papers…"

The woman nodded. "They're on Mr. Tanford's desk. Do you want me to get them or—"

"I'll go myself. Thanks."

After another quick apology to Lauren, Carrie turned around and headed back into the waiting room and then into Trent's office.

She stood there for a moment, trying to get hold of herself after that debacle with Lauren.

Then she glanced around. Of course, Trent wasn't there. Yet, he was everywhere. His taste, his colors, his scent. She wanted him. So badly, she wanted him. But she knew after what she'd done and how she'd acted, she didn't deserve him.

She fingered the envelope on his desk. Her name was on it, in his handwriting. She dreaded what was inside of it. But she knew even before she opened it. Divorce papers.

She wanted to throw up. Again.

Everything was here, the year's agreement.

Oh, Trent...

He wasn't going back on anything he'd offered her. She sighed. She didn't care about that. She wouldn't accept anything more from him.

But it was what he'd included on the next page that brought tears to her eyes. Trent was going to pay for her mother's medical expenses and her care for the rest of her life.

Carrie put the envelope back down on his desk, walked out of the office and left the papers unsigned.

Fourteen

"What the hell is she playing at, Devlin? Does she want more money?" Trent sat in his lawyer's office, and stared across the desk at the man, who looked utterly nonplussed.

"She says she wants nothing from you."

"Not possible," Trent muttered darkly.

"She says she won't sign the papers unless you remove every bit of support that you've offered."

Trent cursed. "I'm not going to do that."

Devlin shrugged. "Why are you fighting this? It's every man's dream."

"This is hardly a dream, Jerry. To me, this is a damned nightmare. A week ago, I was happy. My wife was happy. She loved me. I…"

"What?" Jerry asked, hopelessly confused by his wishy-washy client.

Trent shook his head, stared out the window.

"What do you want to do, Mr. Tanford?" Devlin pressed, his hand poised over the unsigned divorce papers.

"I want to end this," Trent ground out. "This whole damn thing."

"That's what I'm trying to help you do. End your marriage."

"No, Jerry. I want to end *this*, this conversation. My marriage?" He stood up and grabbed his briefcase. "That I want back."

Hanging out on a Wednesday evening on Staten Island was a first for Carrie, but she figured she was about to embark on a good many firsts tonight and she was just planning on going for it.

She stood outside of Denino's Pizzeria Tavern waiting for Trent, nervous to her core, but knowing that what she had to say to him, what she had to propose, was good and right.

"This is an interesting place to meet."

Oh, that voice, she had missed it so much. She looked up to find him walking toward her, his gait long and purposeful. He was dressed casually in jeans and a white shirt, looking as he always looked: tall, handsome and formidable.

She tried for a light mood. "I thought you loved pizza."

His blue eyes darkened, indicating he was not in the mood for light anything. "What's up, Carrie? You didn't take the deal."

"I said I'd sign the papers."

"I don't care about the papers. What I want to know is why you wouldn't let me help you."

Her heart squeezed, and she just wanted to run to him, bury her face in his chest. "Why do you want to help me, Trent? Why not just get out without any strings?"

He shook his head. "I can't do that."

"Why not?" she said gently.

"I'm not that kind of guy."

Carrie cocked her head to one side. "Are you sure that's the reason?"

"What do you mean?" he said defensively, leaning against the exterior wall of the restaurant.

Behind them, a group of customers left the restaurant, walking off toward their cars with the scent of tomato sauce and garlic following after them.

Carrie gazed up at Trent. "Maybe you want to take care of me and my mom, keep those strings attached because you love me."

"Carrie—"

"You love me like I love you, and you really don't want this to end, but your pride is hurt, and I get that. You should be hurt. I hurt you, I panicked, and I'm so sorry—"

He pounded the wall with his fist. "You walked out on me."

"I know," she said softly. "And it was wrong and stupid, but I don't think it should end our marriage."

He looked around, gestured. "Why are we here? Staten Island."

"That story you told me about your nanny. How she brought you here on the greatest day of your life. I thought we should be here because it's the only story I know."

Anger slipped from Trent's features. "What?"

"We fell for each other right away, hot and heavy. We had a friendship, too, that's true, but we didn't go deep, Trent."

He raised a brow, and she laughed. "Yes, we had great sex, but we didn't swap stories. The way we got married was unconventional, to say the least. We didn't get our time."

"Our time for what?"

"To get to know each other. I don't know your history, your childhood, what makes you the man I love, what makes you...you." She took a step toward him, looking hopeful. "I realized that the reason I was so insecure about loving you was because I didn't have the security of knowing you—your history, your life."

"It's not a great history," he said softly.

She reached out, touched his cheek. "I don't care. It's yours and I love you."

His jaw tightened, and then he nodded. "I love you, too."

Tears pricked her eyes. She'd wanted to hear those three words from him for so long, and hearing them right now was the best present, the best reason to hope she could ever imagine.

"Good," she said, her heart racing. "Because I want to offer you a new deal."

His brow lifted. "A new deal?"

She nodded, took a deep breath, her gaze holding steady with his. "I want to offer you my love, my heart, my honesty, my commitment to this marriage, and all of my stories."

Trent reached for her then and gently pulled her into his arms. "And what do I have to give you?"

"The same," she uttered, letting her head fall against his chest.

He sighed. "I'm sorry I didn't tell you about the police and about the photographer. My whole life my parents, especially my father, seemed to jump to the conclusion that I was to blame, always to blame. I couldn't risk that with you."

"It's okay," she assured him.

"I held back. I get that." He brushed a kiss on the top of her head. "I was falling in love with you and I refused to acknowledge it."

She shook her head. "It's done. Over. Today, right here, let's start over." She lifted her head, stared up into his denim-blue eyes. "Take the deal, Tanford, and not only do we both get the history, but we get to create the future, too."

He gathered her in his arms and held her against him. "Oh my God, I love you. I was going insane without you, Carrie."

"Me, too."

"I never took my ring off. I'm such a hack."

"Then I'm a hack, too," she laughed, "because I never took my ring off, either."

He tipped her face up and kissed her, a soft, tender kiss that spoke of love and held the promise of an honest, open future. "Marry me again?"

Tears sprang to Carrie's eyes and she nodded. "Yes."

"A church wedding?"

"Yes."

He kissed her again, and this time it was raw and passion filled.

Behind them, a couple walked out of the restaurant and the woman snorted and said drily, "Get a room," before walking down the street.

Carrie and Trent broke out in laughter.

"Are you hungry?" he asked her. "Do you want some pizza?"

"I am hungry," she said, wrapping her arms around his waist once more, breathing in the scent of him. "For pizza, for you, for our life together, and for those slightly disturbing stories of you as a bad little boy."

He grinned. Oh, those dimples. "Why don't we start with the pizza, then work our way down that list, okay?"

"Absolutely," she said, curling into him as they walked into Denino's, ready to begin again, starting with a little pizza pie, and a night that was truly classic New York.

* * * * *

PRINCE OF MIDTOWN

JENNIFER LEWIS

Jennifer Lewis has been dreaming up stories for as long as she can remember and is thrilled to be able to share them with readers. She has lived on both sides of the Atlantic and she worked in media and the arts before growing bold enough to put pen to paper. Jennifer is happily settled in New York with her family and she would love to hear from readers at jen@jen-lewis.com.

Dear Reader,

I grew up surrounded by old hand-coloured editions of fairy tales that had belonged to my mother and her mother and probably her mother, too. When my editors asked me to write this story for the PARK AVENUE SCANDALS series, I jumped at the chance to create a prince from an exotic faraway country.

While some of the story takes place in the New York City area where I live with my own handsome prince, I had a great time inventing Prince Sebastian's homeland of Caspia. I think everyone should have a chance to create a country. What would you like to see in yours? Mine has warm sunny weather (with no humidity!), calm blue seas, rugged terrain for hiking, striking classical architecture and delicious Mediterranean food.

By the time I'd finished writing, I was sure the ancient and picturesque nation of Caspia could be found on a map somewhere between Italy and Greece. I was also ready to book a trip there as soon as possible.

I hope you enjoy your journey to Caspia with Sebastian and Tessa.

Jennifer Lewis

To the editors at Desire who've encouraged me
and supported my books, including senior editor
Melissa Jeglinski, my first editor Demetria Lucas
and my current editor Diana Ventimiglia.
Big thanks to the people who read this book
while I was writing it, including Amanda, Anne,
Anne-Marie, Betty, Carol, Cynthia, Leeanne,
Marie and Mel, and my agent Andrea. Once
again I am indebted to Amanda and Carol
for their business expertise.

One

"You can't leave."

Sebastian Stone, Crown Prince of Caspia, spoke with such authority and conviction that for a moment Tessa Banks actually believed him.

Her boss's hard, handsome features seemed taut with stronger emotion than usual. He shoved a hand through his black hair and rose from the wide antique desk in his Midtown Manhattan office.

Tessa's stomach contracted with anxiety—and with the infuriating heat of arousal he always stirred in her.

Hang tough. This is your life.

She took a deep breath. "I've been your personal assistant for almost five years. I appreciate the freedom and responsibility you've entrusted me with, but it's time for me to move on."

"Move on?" He blew out an exasperated breath. "This

is not a gypsy caravan. It's a business. I'm counting on you to help me sort out this mess that's been dumped in my lap."

Tessa resisted the urge to point out that Caspia Designs might well have more in common with a gypsy caravan than an actual business. The conglomerate of luxury brands was colorful, extravagant and weighted with tradition. A crystal ball might reveal more lucid information than accounting ledgers that could only be described as "creative."

It was obvious, however, that her boss was not in a joking mood.

He strode across the office and grabbed the pile of papers from his in-box. "Please schedule a meeting tomorrow morning with Reed Wellington. I wish to consult him about my plans for Caspia Designs." He paused and flicked through the mail, a frown on his majestic brow. "And you must find me a new house sitter."

What? Did he plan to simply ignore her resignation?

Tessa's skin prickled with a combination of fury and desperation as she stood in speechless silence.

Her boss shook his head as he studied one paper. Accounts receivable, probably. It wasn't a pretty sight.

She wished she wasn't leaving at a time when Sebastian needed help pulling Caspia Designs together. He'd been handed the reins of the once-prestigious company by his father, the king, only to discover it was in a shambles.

But if this was how little concern he showed for *her* needs, she should be glad to leave him in the lurch.

Things must be serious, though. For one thing, he was wearing a suit. Usually his broad chest bore the insignia of whatever luxury brand he'd most recently convinced to open a boutique in his beloved Caspia. Fendi, Prada, Gucci—if there was a T-shirt with the logo on it, Sebastian cheerfully wore it to celebrate the new partnership.

Today fine gray wool draped his powerful physique. She should heave a sigh of relief that at least she didn't have to tear her gaze from his impressive biceps.

Right now she was too damn angry to care.

She laid her company PDA on the desk. "I'm moving to California in two weeks. If you prefer, I can leave immediately."

Sebastian muttered a curse, but still didn't look up. He flipped over a page of the report she'd put together and traced a column of numbers with a sturdy finger.

Tessa blinked, struggling to keep her breathing under control.

After all this time she was another office fixture, like the Aeron chair, the platinum penholder or the rack of servers. A simple, functional object without a will of its own.

"Goodbye." Her voice shook as she took a step toward the door. She had to climb over one of the cardboard crates of dusty papers that had consumed most of this last month, including three solid weekends. She'd given enough of her life in service to the Crown of Caspia.

"Where are you going?"

Sebastian's voice rattled the antique floor-to-ceiling windows that flooded the nineteenth-century brownstone with light.

"If you'd cared enough to listen, you'd know I'm leaving for California!" She'd never raised her voice to him before.

Sebastian put the file on the leather surface of the desk. "Tessa, you can't be serious?"

"Why not?" She wished her voice didn't sound so whiny and uncertain.

"Because I *need* you."

Spoken in his deep voice, the words echoed through her.

She steadied herself with a hand on the door frame.

If only he did need *her,* not just a faceless assistant who took care of everything so efficiently that she rendered herself invisible.

But he didn't. He had celebutantes and supermodels and starlets from Hollywood to Bollywood hurling themselves at him every minute of the day.

She should know. She fielded their calls.

"Tessa." He stepped toward her, skillfully negotiating an open box of papers. "You do realize I'd be lost without you."

His eyes fixed on hers with penetrating intensity. Large, dark and slightly almond shaped, those eyes had the power to make her do almost anything.

Her toes curled inside her shoes.

He's just saying it to stop you from leaving him in the lurch.

Still…

She lifted her chin. "I'm turning thirty in a month." She hesitated. Her personal life wasn't his business.

"What does that have to do with anything?"

Typical. Why would he care that she wanted a husband, children, a real life?

No need to mention that, she told herself. Better to leave with a shred of dignity. "It's time for a change."

"Tessa." He crossed his arms and stared at her. "If you were dissatisfied with your position in any way, you should have come to me immediately. Is it your job title? Your salary? We'll change them right now."

"It's neither of those things."

She hesitated, anxious not to reveal that *he* was part of the reason she needed to leave.

Sebastian Stone, christened The Prince of Midtown by the New York tabloids who tracked his every bold move, was a constant reminder of everything she was missing.

Especially since he barely knew she was alive.

"I feel as if I'm stuck in a rut. My life is slipping through my fingers…" Could she come up with anything that wasn't a soggy cliché?

"And California is the golden land of opportunity?"

"I know it isn't, but I need to shake things up." She shrank from his forceful black gaze and paced across the room. Her heart hammered beneath her designer dress.

"What's the job you've been offered?"

She shoved her hair behind her ear. "I don't have a job lined up yet. I'm sure I can find one when I get there."

"Then why California? You're not running off after some man, are you?"

Tessa froze. Her stomach lurched. "There is someone, yes."

Sebastian hesitated. An unfamiliar sensation crept over him. "I didn't know you were seeing someone."

"Well." Tessa blinked. "You're my boss."

"But we're friends, too, are we not? You could have told me you were being swept off your feet and were preparing to run away and desert me."

"You've been in Caspia for the last three months. I haven't seen you."

True.

"And it's not as if he's asked me to marry him or anything, so there wasn't that much to tell." She shoved a hand into her hair. Long, golden hair. Rumpled, as if she'd been running her fingers through it all day.

Unexpected desire mingled with the irritation in his blood. "So he's asked you to move clear across the country for him, but he's not even proposed to you?"

Her high-boned cheeks colored. "No. It's not like that."

"Who is this man?"

Tessa blew out a breath. "His name's Patrick Ramsay. He's a lawyer." She picked up a paperweight off the desk and held it poised in her elegant fingers. "We've been seeing each other for a few months. He's joining a practice in L.A. and, two days ago, he asked me if I'd like to move there with him."

"And you said yes?" Disbelief and indignation made him splutter.

She spun on her long, slender legs and strode across the room. "I told him I had to think about it. Now I've thought about it." She kept her face turned away from him. "And I've decided it's just the change I need."

"You're wrong." He'd never been so sure of anything.

She turned to face him, her green eyes wide. "I feel bad leaving, especially now that you've taken over Caspia Designs. I know there's a lot of work to do. But what if this is my one chance?"

Her voice rose to a high note that tugged at something in his chest. How could such a beautiful and talented woman be willing to throw her whole life away on a gamble?

"The name Patrick Ramsay rings a bell." An alarm bell.

"He's quite well known. He represented Elaina Ivanovic in her divorce from her husband Igor."

Sebastian's hackles shot up. "The *divorce* lawyer?" He'd seen that smarmy hustler on TV. Patrick Ramsay didn't know the meaning of the term *low blow*.

She nodded, jerked her imploring gaze from him and started across the far end of the room. "He's very nice, really. Busy, as you'd expect, but kind and thoughtful and— Oh!"

She tripped on an open box and sprawled forward. Adrenaline surged through Sebastian and he leaped across the room. "Are you hurt?"

"No! I'm fine. How silly of me." She blushed charmingly as he helped her up, her hand hot inside his.

On her feet, she pushed her hair back. "It's my fault for leaving these boxes everywhere. I'll stack them against the wall before I go."

"You'll do no such thing." He still held her hand. He didn't want to let go of it. To let go of Tessa.

She was the best assistant he'd ever had. Since he now spent most of his time in Europe, he needed someone he could count on to show up for work even with no one else there. Tessa had proven herself a sharp-minded self-starter and—until now—as steadfast as the rocks in the ancient harbor at Caspia.

He trusted her with everything, from his personal affairs to the embarrassing state of Caspia Designs's financials.

She tried to pull her hand back. He held it fast.

"Tessa, you are indispensable to me. What can I say that will make you stay?"

Her gaze skittered over his face and he sensed the swell of her emotion. Her muscles tensed, as if she wanted to say something but couldn't form the words.

Why had he never noticed how mobile and expressive her mouth was? Or that her skin had an iridescent sheen, like a haze of gold dust?

In that moment of contemplation she jerked back and tugged her hand from his grasp. Cool air assaulted his palm.

She turned and strode away, her slim body held stiff. "I don't want anything."

"I do."

The words fell from his lips before he'd formulated the thoughts to go along with them.

It pained him to see her pacing the floor like a nervous colt, ready to gallop off to disaster.

She belonged here, with him.

His own conviction surprised him. Was some primal masculine jealousy aroused by the thought of her with another man?

Possibly.

She bent over a box filled with hanging files. Her back strained under the weight as she tried to lift it.

"Put that down." He marched over, hefted the box off the floor and shoved it against the wall. The exertion felt good. Then he heaved another into position next to it. He glanced at Tessa. "I don't want you injuring yourself."

A brow shot up and her green eyes flashed. "I may be skinny, but I'm strong."

She picked up a box, dumped it next to his, then dusted her hands and placed them on her hips. Which had the unfortunate effect of drawing his attention to the hourglass waist hidden inside her simple gray dress.

Desire heated his blood.

"You know you're only making it more impossible for me to let you go." He smiled.

She flashed back a defiant grin. Then it faded. "I can't stay."

Her pulse fluttered at her neck and he resisted a sudden, fierce urge to press his lips to the quivering, warm skin.

"I'm afraid I can't let you go."

She let out a sharp laugh. "You can't *let* me? Off with her head? Those days are over, even if you are a prince."

He laughed. "A beheading does sound counterproductive. But I do insist you give the ancient, sovereign nation of Caspia at least the customary two weeks' notice." A plan blossomed in his mind. "You must come to Caspia with me. Immediately."

"Oh."

A tiny fire lit inside her eyes. Good.

"I need you to arrange an immediate meeting of the principals of Caspia Designs. The chief executives of each of the subsidiary brands *must* be there, no matter what it takes to bring them."

He watched for her reaction. The prospect of cajoling pleasure-seeking European plutocrats into attending to actual business might make some people quit on the spot.

But not Tessa. A glow of appreciation filled him as she simply nodded.

"To be honest, when I took the job, I hoped it would involve some travel. I'd be glad to come to Caspia before I go."

Had he truly never taken her to Caspia before? Surely he'd remember the vision of all that golden hair being tossed by the sea breeze. He'd grown to think of travel as a tiresome necessity. He clapped his hands together. "We'll fly tomorrow in my private plane. Arrange for a 2:00 p.m. departure."

Energy surged through him as his plan took shape. This trip would take Tessa's mind off that divorce-mongering cad who wanted to steal her away from him.

Not that his interest in her was personal, of course. He took both business and pleasure very seriously, which meant keeping them strictly separate.

But the charms of Caspia—combined with some judicious charm on his part—would soon make Tessa realize she'd been crazy to ever think of leaving.

Two

Relief surged through Sebastian as he grasped his old friend's hand in a warm handshake. Reed Wellington was the kind of man you wanted on your side in a crisis. His clear blue eyes never reflected a hint of worry.

"Sebastian, I'm sorry I couldn't make the snowboarding trip to Kilimanjaro, but Elizabeth thought it sounded, well, crazy."

Sebastian laughed. "I guess that's the problem with being married. You wind up stuck with someone who truly cares about you."

"Yes. And you have to stop hurling yourself off mountaintops." His eyes crinkled into a smile. "When are you going to get married, eh?"

"Never. Or when I meet the right woman. Whichever comes first." He got this question a lot.

"No one can accuse you of not trying your best to bed every eligible woman in the world."

"Just doing my royal duty."

"Seriously, isn't there a lot of pressure on you to sire the next heir to the throne of Caspia?"

"I try not to think about that. Besides, we Caspians often live to be over a hundred and my father's barely sixty."

"All that goats' milk yogurt, huh?"

"Food of the gods."

They shared a chuckle but Sebastian couldn't help thinking Reed's laugh was a little too hearty. Forced, even. And what was it with married people trying to shove eternal bondage down your throat?

"You're here about Caspia Designs?" Reed gestured for him to sit in the leather chair opposite the wide walnut desk. The room was decorated like the headquarters of an eighteenth-century shipping magnate.

Sebastian eased himself into the chair. "I am. I'm in dire need of your business expertise. I'm afraid the company is in worse financial shape than I'd suspected."

Reed's expression changed to one of concern. "How so?"

"Until I took over the reins a year ago, Caspia Designs was overseen by Deon Maridis, an old and close friend of my father's. He's a good man, but the company's profits went into a slow slide under his watch."

Sebastian fought an urge to loosen his collar. "Last year the company actually lost money."

"What?" Reed sat up. "I confess luxury brands are not my area of expertise, and I can imagine the company is mature and not growing much, but Caspia Designs owns some of the most renowned luxury brands in the world. Aria cars, Bugaretti Jewels, LeVerge Champagne, Carriage

Leathers…Why, I bought my wife one of their bags last Christmas and it nearly bankrupted me." He laughed for a second, then frowned. "How can they be losing money?"

Sebastian leaned forward. "Our brands have been known as the best of the best since the 1920s when the company went public, but many of them have barely changed since. Production methods are outdated and inefficient, and there's been little effort to attract new customers. There are now a host of luxury jewelers, vintners and the like, and most of them have better distribution and marketing than the ones owned by Caspia Designs. I want to shake up the companies and get them operating like a real business. I also plan to market the goods to a younger audience."

"Sounds as if you need to do some rebranding. Like Burberry and Mini Cooper."

"Exactly."

Reed tilted his head and smiled. "Sort of like you've been doing with Caspia."

Sebastian couldn't help a swell of pride. "It's true. Ten years ago, Caspia had virtually no foreign investors, no tourism, little business beyond those that had existed for hundreds of years."

Reed raised an eyebrow. "Now you have hotels and luxury boutiques and restaurants for tourists to spend their money in. And you accomplished it almost single-handedly over the last ten years."

"My assistant, Tessa, must get some of the credit." Her green eyes flashed in his mind. "She's an organizational genius."

"You're lucky to have her."

"Don't I know it." Sebastian's fist clenched. How could

she plan to abandon him at a time like this? "And we'll be working hard to make Caspia Designs a good investment for all our shareholders."

"I don't doubt you'll succeed."

"I intend to, but I'm used to building from scratch, not fixing something that's broken. I need your advice on how to turn the individual companies around, and fast."

"Hmm." Reed tapped his gold pen on his blotter. "If I were you, I'd start by scheduling a meeting with the President and CEO—or their equivalents—of each company within Caspia Designs. Get them all together and read them the riot act."

"I've already asked Tessa to schedule a meeting."

"Excellent. At that meeting, challenge them to come up with ten ways to immediately increase market share and profitability in their own company." He gave Sebastian a series of examples of companies who'd effected a similar change by bringing in experienced managers or reinventing their product for modern markets. "You could hire a consulting firm to investigate and give you additional ideas."

"I prefer to solve our problems internally. These are all businesses with quality products. They've been resting on their laurels, and it's time to shake them up."

"I can see them shaking already. You can do anything you set your mind to. Even snowboarding down Kilimanjaro." He leaned back with a wistful smile.

Sebastian's chest filled with regret that his friend had missed the experience. "You should have been there."

Reed looked away, picked up a pen and tapped it on his blotter. "Yes. Well. I have other commitments now." A muscle twitched at his temple. His blue gaze seemed less bright than usual.

"How is Elizabeth? I haven't seen her in a long time. Is she still your secret weapon on the doubles court, as well as the love of your life?"

Reed's eyes crinkled. "She sure is. We'll have to get together for a game sometime with you and whoever your current mixed-doubles partner is."

Sebastian shrugged. "I'm playing singles at the moment. Got business to take care of."

"Even if we don't see you on the courts, you must come to our anniversary party."

"What is it, three years?"

"Five." Reed's jaw stiffened.

Not the most reassuring indication of marital bliss.

"That's great." He leaned over the desk and slapped Reed on the arm. Tried to sound enthusiastic. "Just let me know where to show up. And you know the two of you have an open invitation to visit Caspia again whenever you like."

"I'll take you up on that soon. Right now I'm in the throes of starting a new company. It's sucking up even more of my free time than all that partying we used to do when we were younger."

"Who says I've stopped?" Sebastian raised a brow.

"You always did have impressive stamina. One day you'll meet a woman you actually want to stay home with."

"So they tell me, but I don't plan to wave the white flag of surrender anytime soon."

The doorman pulled open the door and Sebastian stepped into the lobby of his building. Vivian Vannick-Smythe's two fluffy white dogs stopped scratching at the priceless Oriental rug and turned to growl at him.

If that woman led him around on a string all day, he wouldn't be in a good mood, either. Sebastian shot the dogs a sympathetic glance.

"Prince Sebastian!" Vivian turned to him with a winning smile. Or had too much plastic surgery left her expression permanently fixed like that?

"Hello, Vivian."

"How lovely to see you here. I noticed you haven't been around much lately."

"I've been in Caspia."

"Ahh." Her dogs lunged at his pant leg, yowling and snapping at the end of their embroidered leashes. "I read about those nasty storms in the Mediterranean. I do hope Caspia didn't suffer too much damage."

"There were some losses to the olive crops, but happily no one was hurt."

"What a relief. Backward countries do seem to suffer the most from these things."

Sebastian's hackles shot up. "Caspia is in no way backward. If you were to visit…" *Perish the thought.* "You'd find a thriving, modern country on the brink of becoming one of the prime luxury tourist destinations in the world."

"How charmingly passionate you are about your homeland."

Sebastian glanced up to see if the elevator was coming. *Yes, thank God.*

The doors opened and Vivian's paisley skirt swirled about her ankles as she walked in. Her dogs yapped around Sebastian's ankles, loud in the enclosed space.

"Hold the elevator!" A deep voice rang across the marbled lobby.

Sebastian looked up to see Gage Lattimer diving past the doorman.

Vivian's dogs diverted their hostile intentions to him. Fortunately for Sebastian, Vivian followed suit.

"Why, Gage, our man of mystery. I was just chatting with Prince Sebastian." She shone that fixed smile on him. "He should be a role model to you. He does live up to his clean-cut image."

Clean-cut? Sebastian resisted the urge to test his chin for stubble. He'd been called a lot of things, but clean-cut wasn't one of them. Maybe she meant the suit?

He shot a puzzled look at Gage.

"Are you implying something?" Gage raised an eyebrow at Vivian.

"Moi?" She forced a laugh. "Of course not. I believe people's personal affairs should be kept private."

Gage shook his head.

An awkward silence thickened in the air. Well, not exactly silence, what with all the growling.

Sebastian's muscles unwound a bit when the elevator reached his floor. He held the door open for Vivian to exit, her leashed demons scampering ahead of her.

Unfortunately they lived on the same floor.

Happily the walls were thick.

Her dogs wiggled with excitement as she fumbled in her purse for her key. They actually looked sort of adorable for once and he couldn't resist crouching to pet one of the fluffy fur balls.

It turned and snapped at him, almost catching his finger.

Never mind.

Sebastian's apartment had a neglected air. His former house sitter, Carrie Gray, hadn't left his employ to marry that long ago, but already stacks of unopened mail tilted precariously on the hall table. He picked an envelope off the top and ripped it open.

"You are cordially invited to celebrate the landmark status of our building."

He snorted.

Yes, 721 Park Avenue was a beautiful building, but it probably wasn't much over a hundred years old. Parts of the royal palace in Caspia were rumored to be five thousand years old.

That was a landmark.

He flung the envelope back on the pile and lifted his foot to step over the bag he'd dropped in the foyer the night before. He'd gone straight from the plane to the office to an all-night party and hadn't had time to unpack. It was inconvenient having no one to do it for him.

But the bag wasn't there.

Did he hear voices?

He did. Female voices.

Interesting. Especially since he hadn't brought anyone home last night.

Anticipation pricked through him as he walked down the marble-floored hallway toward the living room.

A familiar mane of blond hair cascaded over the back of an uncomfortable eighteenth-century chair. "Tessa."

She jumped. "Oh, Your Highness, I didn't hear you come in."

"Your Highness?" He lifted a brow.

"I'm interviewing candidates for your new house sitter." She indicated a red-haired girl seated opposite her.

He smiled at them both. He always could count on Tessa to handle everything.

* * *

Tessa excused herself for a moment and hurried after Sebastian. "I unpacked your bag. I'm not sure if I did it right. Let me show you where I put things."

She rambled on, suddenly feeling like an intruder in his private space. His house sitter used to handle the apartment, so she rarely came here. She was embarrassed that she still hadn't had time to tackle his mail. "I didn't mean to surprise you. I just thought it would be a good idea to interview the house sitters here so they'd have an idea of what the job entails. The antiques and all. You can tell a lot about someone by the way they treat your home."

"Good thinking."

She rushed along the hallway. Why was she so anxious? Perhaps because she was also secretly interviewing for her own replacement.

"The agency had three girls ready this morning, and I didn't want to wait, or to interrupt you at Reed's. How did the meeting go?"

"Great. I wanted to get his advice on how to bring Caspia Designs into the twenty-first century." He glanced at her. "Or even the twentieth."

His mischievous grin made her heart beat faster.

"You'll turn the company around fast."

"With your help." He shot her a dark look. "Starting with this trip to Caspia."

She swallowed. Even poring over the inadequate and whimsical financial reports of Caspia Designs had made her fall a little bit in love with the country. It seemed a land ruled by passion rather than politics. Exuberance rather than economics.

Much like its devastatingly handsome prince.

Tessa bit her lip. Already she'd reconsidered her plan to leave. Sebastian paid her well and treated her kindly. Her parents told her she was mad to quit a job with such excellent benefits.

But she'd spent most of her adult life working with the rich and famous, first at a PR firm and now here. She was sick of glitz and glamour. She'd trade it in a heartbeat for the simple happiness her parents still shared after nearly fifty years of marriage.

For some reason being tall and blond attracted the biggest jerk in every room she entered. She'd had enough of being arm-candy for movers and shakers who weren't interested in anything beyond a night of sex.

Normal "regular guy" types *never* asked her out. Patrick was the best thing to happen to her in a long time. Yes, he was a high-profile lawyer, but he was down-to-earth and practical. He called when he said he would. He took her out on dates—when he had the time—and treated her with respect.

Something she'd begun to worry would never happen.

In his large, uncluttered bedroom, Sebastian removed his jacket and started to unbutton his shirt. Tessa dragged her eyes away. "I hung your pants and shirts in the closet. And I put your…underwear in the drawer."

Her cheeks heated. Handling his boxers had felt way too personal.

"You didn't have to do that." His fingers continued down his buttons. He tugged his shirt out of his pants to undo the bottom ones and she fought an urge to run for the door.

But she didn't want him to know that watching him undress affected her. He was probably used to undressing in front of…staff. It meant nothing to him.

She meant nothing to him.

For years she'd been telling herself her silly attraction to her boss would fade over time. She'd fall for someone else.

But other men seemed pale and uninteresting compared to Sebastian.

Except Patrick, of course. He was thoughtful. Nice. Considerate.

He wasn't quite ready for fatherhood yet, but maybe once his big case was over and they settled into a comfortable house in a nice quiet neighborhood with trees and grass and…

Uh-oh. Sebastian's long fingers undid the button on his pants.

She headed for the door. "I put your toiletries in the bathroom. Well, your toothbrush. I didn't see anything else."

"I don't need anything else."

"I'll get back to my interview." Her voice was high and squeaky. She heard the swish of his pants sliding over his long, muscled legs.

"Did Dior Homme send the T-shirts?"

"Um. Yes. I put them…" She'd have to go back into the bedroom to find the shelf. Squinting to avoid the vision of a seminaked Sebastian, she hurried to the closet.

"Here, on the middle shelf." The fresh pile of shirts commemorated the deal he'd brokered to open a Dior boutique in the row of luxury stores along the harbor in Caspia. She picked up a large black T-shirt with a geometric design and held it toward him while keeping her eyes averted.

She could smell his scent. Soap and skin. A hint of sweat.

How could that get her blood pumping? He was just a *guy,* for crying out loud. Patrick smelled much nicer, of that woodsy cologne he wore. Which, actually, she hated. But she could buy him another.

"Tessa."

She turned without thinking. At the exact moment he lifted the T-shirt over his head and flexed all the muscles of his wide, bronzed chest.

Her knees buckled and she struggled to stay upright.

Not a problem. She didn't like big muscles anyway. Too brutish.

She preferred men who were…cerebral.

"What do you think?" He indicated the T-shirt freshly pulled over his thick pecs.

"Nice design." Her voice came out weird and flat. A light dusting of black hair roughened his hard, bare thighs below the T-shirt hem.

"Yeah. I like this new line. Did you take some for your-self?"

"I don't wear extra large."

"You could wear them in bed." His low voice tickled her ears.

Tessa's eyes widened. Her face heated. Sebastian was thinking about her in bed?

Oh. Get over yourself.

If anyone knew that women like to sleep in oversize T-shirts, it was Sebastian. He'd seen a lot of women in bed.

"Sure. I'll grab a couple."

"Great." He shot her a white-toothed smile.

That set her on alert. Why was he smiling at her for no reason?

Because he wants to keep you around as his serf, organizing his files and answering his phone, dummy.

"I'll go finish the interview."

"I appreciate it. I'm going out to grab something to eat. You want anything from the café?"

"I'm fine. Thanks for asking."

Again, the niceness. Very suspicious.

Sebastian strode across the room, legs still bare. He slid a hand under his T-shirt to scratch his rock-hard belly while he contemplated his impressive collection of jeans.

Tessa managed to rasp, "See you later," as she rushed out the door.

The Park Café was the closest eatery, so Sebastian went there often when he was in town. He'd spent several weeks in New York in the spring and had hand-trained one of the young servers to make the perfect cup of coffee—or at least the closest possible approximation available in this part of the world.

His heart sank as he entered the bright space of the café to a sea of new faces. Then he spotted Reed and Elizabeth Wellington sitting at one of the café tables. He waved and tried to catch their eye, but they were deep in conversation.

"What can I get you?" asked the perky young server.

"I'd like a pastrami on rye with Russian dressing and nothing else. And a seven-shot espresso."

She vanished, her expressionless face imparting confidence. What a relief not to be peppered with questions about lettuce and tomatoes and mayo.

His synapses tingled in anticipation of a welcome jolt of caffeine.

He glanced over at his friends' table. Reed leaned forward, talking in hushed tones, while his wife looked strangely tight-lipped. Were they arguing?

The server returned with seven tiny china cups of espresso. *Here we go again.* "In one cup, please."

She picked up a paper cup and began to pour them in.

"They'll be too cool. Could you use china and heat it again?" He kept his voice pleasant.

"Milk and sugar?"

"No milk, no sugar, no cinnamon, no froth, no chocolate curls. Just the coffee."

His sandwich appeared, loaded with unwanted vegetables.

Sebastian rubbed a hand over his face.

He'd be home in Caspia soon.

"I don't think you do!" A raised voice caught his attention and he turned to see Reed, who'd stood suddenly, scraping his chair back on the tile floor.

Elizabeth looked panic-stricken. "Please, Reed…" he heard her say, before the server plunked his big mug of espresso on the counter.

He swiped his credit card and turned in time to see Reed striding out of the restaurant, a black expression clouding his chiseled features.

Alarmed, Sebastian glanced at Elizabeth, who stared after her husband with a stunned look on her face.

Sebastian snatched his cup and plate off the counter and hurried to the table. He sat without waiting for an invitation.

His gut twisted when he saw her eyes brimming with unshed tears. "Elizabeth, what's wrong?"

He reached for her hand but she snatched it up and

dabbed at her eyes with the napkin. "Nothing! Nothing at all. I'm fine." A sob belied her words. "Allergies. They're terrible at this time of year." She drew in a sharp breath. "How are you, Sebastian?"

"Once I've had this coffee, I'll be okay." He took a bracing sip. Elizabeth was obviously in distress and it pained him not to be able to help her. "Can I get you something? Some chocolate?"

She laughed. "Chocolate usually does help, doesn't it?" She glanced toward the door. "But not today. I have to run, I have an appointment." Hands shaking, she gathered her handbag and a large shopping bag. "I'm sorry I don't have more time to chat. I've—" Her voice caught.

Something was very wrong.

"I understand. Another time." The platitudes felt hollow and useless, but she clearly didn't want to talk.

He rose from his chair and kissed her cheek. Cold as ice. "And, Elizabeth, if you ever need anything, anything at all, don't hesitate to call me."

She nodded and hurried away.

How odd. She and Reed always seemed like the perfect couple. Their wedding had been the social event of the season, the bride radiant, her handsome groom the toast of the city for months. Sebastian had even found himself contemplating the joys of marriage—for a week or two.

Luckily it had worn off.

Five years later and here they were: arguments, tension, tears.

Marriage did not look like fun.

Three

Sebastian brimmed with anticipation as he marched across the tarmac toward the plane. "Tessa!"

At the sound of his voice, she looked up and smiled. "Hello, Sebastian."

She stood at the bottom of the movable stairs, fiddling with the strap on her bag. The wind molded her thin dress to her body in a way that made his blood pressure jump a notch.

Her legs were endless. Slender and shapely. The kind of legs that could wrap around you and hold you in a vise of pleasure.

Not that he had any intention of seducing his assistant into bed.

Even he had his limits.

At least he thought he did.

"Don't be nervous. Our pilot is very experienced. Have you met Sven?"

"Yes, he introduced himself. I'm more excited than nervous. I actually love to fly. It's fun seeing the world from above."

"I do agree." A smile settled over his face as he took her elbow and led her up the stairs.

Sebastian refused to discuss work during the flight. He wanted Tessa to relax and enjoy herself. To banish any thoughts that she was bored and ready to "move on."

Any "moving on" would be accomplished in his comfortably appointed jet. "Champagne?" He lifted a bottle out of the fridge.

Tessa's eyes widened. "It's only two o'clock."

"That means it's eight in Caspia. They always say to pack and dress for your destination, so why not drink for it, too?"

He popped the cork.

Tessa bit her lip. "Okay. You're the boss."

"Exactly. You'd better do as I say." He handed her the glass. "Here's to your maiden voyage to Caspia." He clinked his glass against hers.

Excitement sparkled in her big, green eyes. "I've never left the country before."

"You're kidding?"

"Nope. I flew around a bit on business for my first job, but mostly to L.A. I've never been to Europe."

"Not even to visit friends?" Sebastian found this hard to believe. He knew quite a few people who went to boarding school with Tessa and they were as likely to be found on the ski slopes of Gstaad or the beaches of Provence as in their Wall Street watering holes.

Tessa put her champagne glass on the table. "I went to St. Peter's on a scholarship." She raised her eyes to meet his at the mention of the highbrow prep school. "I'm not really one of them."

"One of who?"

"You know, the jet set, or whatever you want to call it."

She looked so anxious that he managed to suppress the smile tugging at his lips. "Um, Tessa, I hate to be the one to break this to you, but you're sitting in a jet right now, waiting to take off."

She swatted his idea away with a movement of her graceful hands. "You know what I mean. This is part of my job."

Sebastian slammed his glass down next to hers. "I don't want to hear anything more about any *job*. You are vital to the economic growth of the nation of Caspia. You have a *career* with us."

He'd make it a personal challenge to make sure she stayed. He did enjoy a challenge. The curse of a competitive nature.

"Buckle up." Sven's voice came over the radio. Sebastian watched as Tessa fastened her buckle over her slim hips. Her long fingers were magnificent. He could imagine them dancing over the strings of a Caspian harp.

Or over the muscles of his belly. And lower. Between his thighs…

He shifted in his seat. "Sven, let's take the temperature down a couple of degrees."

Tessa looked sideways at him. "Do we have to hold on to our glasses?"

"Can't hurt." Sebastian swept hers up and handed it to her. Their fingers brushed for an electric moment. He sipped the dry Blanc de Noirs, but the sparkle of the bubbles only increased an intriguing sense of anticipation that crackled through him.

Tessa peered out the window as the plane lifted over the ocean, her long neck craned forward. "Goodness, New York really is a bunch of islands, isn't it? Wow, what a beach. The breakers look awesome from up here. And I can see a fishing boat! I never think of people fishing near the city. And look at all those swimming pools on Long Island. Don't these people know there's an ocean right there?"

Her eyes shone, dazzled with sights he'd long ceased to notice.

Sebastian laughed.

Caspia with Tessa was going to be fun.

Tessa couldn't help feeling a little sad as their plane approached their final destination in the dead of night.

All across Europe, towns and cities had glittered amongst vast swathes of dark countryside. Snowcapped mountain ranges shimmered in the faint glow of the moon.

That same moon reflected off calm ocean water as the plane banked on approach to the airport in Caspia. Giddy from champagne and from chatting with Sebastian about everything under the sun, she couldn't imagine getting any sleep before morning.

The plane landed on the runway with barely a bump. Sebastian peered out the window. "My driver is waiting. We'll be at the palace in ten minutes."

The palace.

Tessa's skin grew tight as terror crept over her.

An actual palace with a real king and queen living in it.

She glanced sideways at Sebastian. He was stretching, which had the unfortunate effect of pulling his black T-shirt tight over the granite-hard expanse of his chest.

She jerked her eyes away. In addition to being a royal prince, he was her boss, for crying out loud.

Her heart hammered as the pilot opened the door and ushered them down the steps. Sebastian gestured for her to go first, so she stepped out into the dark night.

A cool breeze rushed her face, rich with the smell of the sea.

"Home sweet home." Sebastian drew in a hearty lungful. "I find it harder and harder to leave and each time I return, I'm more grateful than ever."

"I guess that's good, since you couldn't really leave anyway, could you?" How odd to grow up with the obligation of being a monarch some day. To have no choice in who or what you could become.

"No one truly leaves Caspia. Even when you depart, you'll always carry a piece of her with you."

His voice echoed with such gravitas that she glanced back to see if he was joking.

Apparently not.

He stared straight ahead, his strong features highlighted in the airport floodlights. "Dmitri!" He waved at the uniformed chauffeur standing in front of a long, black limousine. "I'd like you to meet Tessa, my right-hand woman."

Dmitri nodded. Sebastian's odd introduction gave her a little surge of pride. She wouldn't mind being the right hand on so sturdy and capable a body.

The limo drove them swiftly to the palace, where people materialized out of the darkness to carry their bags.

A lamp-lit passage led to a cool atrium with a trickling fountain. Two young men rushed forward to ply them with damp towels and glasses of cool water.

Flustered, Tessa watched Sebastian as he wiped his face vigorously with the towel. She didn't want to smear the plush, white cotton with her makeup so she used it to pat her neck.

The water had a deliciously sweet taste, and she finished the whole glass in one draft. As soon as she was done, a man with a jug refilled it.

"Thanks," she murmured, before sipping again.

So this is what it was like to be waited on hand and foot. Kind of weird, but she could see how you'd get used to it. She tried hard not to giggle.

Just nerves.

"I'll walk Tessa to her room," Sebastian declared. Her skin tingled as he slipped his warm, strong arm inside hers in a proprietary gesture that made her blush.

It was all so strange. Mosaics glittered under her feet. Stone pillars flanked the wide hallway. They walked through the silent palace, the darkness of night softened only by light from wall sconces.

At the end of another long hallway, Sebastian led her through an open pair of double doors into the most glorious room she'd ever seen.

A vast bed filled the center of the huge chamber. Silk curtains billowed from a central point in the ceiling and cascaded down to form a luxurious canopy. The bed itself was lush with patterned pillows and soft-looking covers.

If there were a pea under that mattress, it wouldn't bother her one bit.

"I hope you'll be comfortable. You can ring this bell if you need anything." He pointed to a tiny golden bell, resting on a magnificent gold-inlaid dressing table. "Or call me on my cell." He yawned. "I need some shut-eye."

He closed the door behind him as he left.

In a panic, Tessa realized she didn't have her bag. She rushed to the door, then the open closet caught her eye.

Her clothes hung inside it.

She inhaled, and walked over. Yes, they were really her clothes, with her unpacked duffel bag placed neatly on the floor of the closet.

She swallowed and lifted her nightgown from a hanger. She'd splurged on a gauzy white cotton gown, trimmed with lace, that seemed appropriate for sleeping in a palace.

In front of the magnificent silk-draped bed, however, her nightgown looked more suitable for a milkmaid.

She changed, washed her face at the polished brass basin in the bathroom and brushed out her hair.

She stood for a moment at one of the long windows, holding the heavy drape back. Pale moonlight poured onto the floor at her feet, making the mosaic sparkle.

She climbed onto the cloudlike softness of the high bed, under the layered canopy.

She really should call Patrick in New York. She'd promised to let him know she arrived safely. He'd insisted on knowing every detail of her itinerary so he could get in touch with her at any time.

He was just like that. Caring.

But surely he wouldn't mind if she called first thing in the morning?

It was nearly nine when Tessa finally awoke and peered at her watch in the curtained gloom. She could hear noise outside the windows, the distant honking of car horns, the mutter of conversations, even a clatter of hooves.

She sprang off the bed and hurried to the window. Bright golden sunshine streamed in as she parted the curtains.

Wow.

The room had a magnificent view over the city. White-washed buildings clung to the hillsides, their simple, organic shapes suggesting that they'd been there almost as long as the land itself.

The procession of crisp, white walls descended gradually toward a wide bay. Long seawalls created from massive stone blocks encompassed the harbor like two welcoming arms, the sea within them as calm as a pond.

The whole effect was like something out of an ancient myth. She half expected to see Helen of Troy sail into the harbor on a trireme rowed by a hundred oarsmen.

But modern life intruded cheerfully on the ancient splendor. Cars wound up and down the hill toward the harbor. Laughter and the strains of a Madonna hit mingled with the song of birds that fluttered back and forth between tall cypress trees.

Her cell chimed and vibrated on the dresser. She rushed to grab it. Patrick.

"Hi."

"I've been worried sick. I even checked the airline flight data to see if there were reports of an accident. Why didn't you call?"

"Oh, we got here so late and I was tired. It's sweet of you to worry, but really, I'm fine."

"Do you have your own room?"

She laughed. "No, I'm in the harem with all the king's wives." He didn't laugh back. "Of course I have my own room, silly. And it's so beautiful. But I'm not sure my blow-dryer will work here."

"Do be careful of the voltage. You never know what to expect with foreign wiring. I am worried about you being all alone in a foreign country."

"I'm not alone. I'm with Sebastian."

"I know."

When she finally got Patrick off the phone with assurances that she had not been killed in a midair collision or sold into slavery, she had a quick shower. As she suspected, her dryer was a useless lump of plastic and metal since the wall outlet was a different shape than her plug. She towel dried her hair as best she could and was putting moisturizer on her face when she heard a knock on the door.

She almost dropped the bottle. "Come in?" The uncertainty in her own voice made her even more nervous.

The door flung open. Sebastian stood silhouetted against the bright corridor. "I trust you slept well."

His soft voice wrapped around her like the warm morning breeze.

"I did." She pushed back a hank of her still-damp hair. "I can't get over how lovely it is here."

He smiled. "You've seen nothing yet. Come, eat." He held out his arm for her to take it. He wore a collarless white linen shirt. Tailored black pants added to the impression of casual elegance.

Not that she cared what her boss wore.

Tessa walked across the room, the skirt of her pale green dress swishing around her legs, then matched his long stride down the colonnaded hallway.

He directed her into another wide, bright chamber. Floor-to-ceiling frescoes depicted a magnificent procession of men and horses, pennants flying.

Tessa tugged her gaze from the art and focused on the other people in the room. A middle-aged man and woman sat at one end of a long, white stone table.

"Mama, this is Tessa, my New York assistant."

The woman rose from her carved chair, tall and graceful, her silver hair pulled back into a chignon. She held out a heavily ringed hand and Tessa hurried forward to shake it.

"It's an honor," murmured Tessa, attempting a curtsey. This was *The Queen*.

"And this is my dad."

Tessa shook his offered hand. "It's a pleasure to meet you, Your Majesty."

Maybe he heard her voice shake, but the king patted her hand gently and looked at her with the kindest eyes she'd ever seen. "The pleasure is all mine, my dear."

He also had silver hair, with patches of black above his ears that indicated it must once have been as dark as Sebastian's.

"What'd the cook rustle up for us this morning?" Sebastian reached forward and grabbed a rasher of bacon, then popped it in his mouth. "Mmm." He pulled out a chair for Tessa, directly opposite the queen. She slid into it as gracefully as she could.

A plate materialized in front of her immediately, borne by a silent servant.

"Do help yourself, dear," the queen said in perfect, British-accented English. "If you don't see anything you like, we can have something prepared."

"Oh, that won't be necessary, it all looks marvelous."

Tessa had no appetite whatsoever in the presence of three crowned heads—including Sebastian. She'd never paid much attention to his being a prince before, perhaps because the whole concept of royalty seemed rather alien back in the States. Amidst the splendor of the royal palace, however, it was impossible to forget.

Sebastian offered her various dishes, and she took a small amount of each. Eggs scrambled with herbs, freshly baked rolls covered in fragrant sesame seeds, crispy bacon and spicy sausages, fresh peaches and plums, sliced and laid in an interwoven pattern, and a dish of creamy yogurt with sweet, golden honey.

"Tessa, what part of the States are you from?" The queen's question had a tone of mild interrogation.

"Connecticut."

"A lovely state. Are you near Greenwich?"

"Yes, very close." In geography. In lifestyle, though, a million miles.

Tessa hated saying where she was from. Wealthy and privileged people immediately assumed she was one of them. It was embarrassing for everyone when they eventually found out she wasn't.

That's when she learned who her real friends were.

She had to give Sebastian credit. He hadn't blinked when she told him she was a scholarship student.

But why would he care? She was just his employee.

"And what does your father do, dear?" The queen lifted an elegantly arched brow.

Jeez. Was she back in high school? Rich people could be very predictable. "He's retired now."

She sipped her juice. Partly to prevent her tongue from saying, *He's a retired school custodian. Yes, you heard right, he cleaned the school. Not quite what you were expecting, was it?*

The queen's tight smile did nothing to soothe her churning stomach. Suddenly she wished she was back home, under the covers in her familiar apartment.

Still, she attempted to act normal and make polite conversation during the meal, instead of gazing around the room and gawking at her companions.

It wasn't easy.

When the king and queen left the room together, it was all she could do not to sag in her chair in relief.

"More yogurt?" Sebastian lifted the ornate golden urn that looked as though it had been passed down at least ten generations.

"No, thanks. I really should get to work. Would you please show me where the files are? I want to dig out what we'll need for the meeting."

"Absolutely not." He rose in a swift motion. "We have far more important things to do."

"Like what?"

"You must see our country. More coffee?"

"No, thanks, I'm fine. I might blast off if I drink more of that stuff."

"Good, right?"

She couldn't resist smiling in response to his enthusiastic grin. "Fantastic." Her toes tingled at the idea of exploring the world she'd glimpsed from her window. "Could we go see the harbor?"

"Of course." Sebastian rose from his chair and held out his hand for her to take it.

He never did that at the office.

Tessa slid her fingers into his strong hand, and let him pull her from her chair. He didn't move out of the way as she stood, so she found herself dangerously close to his muscled chest. His warm, male scent of sunshine and spice.

Her skin prickled at his nearness.

Why didn't he move?

His dark eyes drifted over her pale green dress. "You look lovely today, Tessa."

"Thanks." She swallowed.

He never usually noticed what she was wearing.

He hadn't let go of her hand, either. Her palm heated against his.

What was he up to?

Four

"Your hair is wavy." Sebastian's gaze followed the undulating mass of hair that she'd tied back with a clasp before breakfast.

Tessa's hand sprang self-consciously to her head. At least it was nearly dry. "My dryer didn't fit the outlet."

Sebastian reached behind her head, his arm almost brushing her cheek in a swift movement that made her gasp. With thumb and finger he unsnapped her hair clip and removed it. Her hair tumbled down her back.

His eyes shone with appreciation. "You should always wear it like this." He pocketed her clip. "Why do women scorch the natural beauty out of their hair?"

"It looks neater blow-dried straight."

"I disagree." He reached into her hair.

Tessa fought the urge to protest. This was totally unprofessional! He stroked her hair. Heat rippled in her belly and she swallowed the desire to purr like a contented cat.

She gulped for air. Had he forgotten she had a boyfriend? "Where are we heading?"

"The harbor. I'll phone ahead and have my boat prepared."

He withdrew his hand from her hair and reached into his pocket for his cell.

Oh, how the other half lived.

Tessa expected a chauffeured limousine—especially since that's how Sebastian generally moved around New York.

But no. They left the palace on foot, through an arched doorway that took them out onto one of the winding cobbled streets flanked with whitewashed buildings.

She was even more astonished when Sebastian stopped to greet ordinary citizens. He seemed to know everyone on a first-name basis, and inquired after their families and their businesses like an old friend.

Weirder still, Tessa found she could understand snatches of conversation, although she'd never had the need to learn the Caspian language.

After a few introductions, she made a halting attempt to greet an elderly man in Caspian.

Sebastian rewarded her efforts with a broad grin. "You speak like a native."

"No, I don't! But I'm having fun trying. How come so many of the words sound familiar?"

"Did you study Latin in school?"

"I went to St. Peter's." She chuckled. "You know the snootiest prep school on the East Coast made everyone take Latin."

"That's why you understand us. Caspians speak a dialect of Latin that's changed little since the time of the

Roman Empire. Add a vowel at the end of a few words, and you're speaking Caspian. Some words haven't changed at all. *Te amo,* for example, still means *I love you.*"

Mischief sparkled in his eyes.

Tessa ignored the rush of heat to her chest. He was toying with her! What a nerve. Just because she'd handed in her notice he thought he could let loose and flirt with her before she quit?

Te amo. Yeah. Right. As if she was dumb enough to join the cohorts of women notched on his bedpost. Maybe he thought it would be fun to make her fall in love with him—then dump her—as punishment for quitting her job and leaving him in the lurch.

Sebastian had a reputation for treating seduction as a sport. His little black book—little BlackBerry, rather—must have a thousand names in it. She knew about all those starlets and models and fashion designers, not to mention tennis star Andrea Raditz and soccer champion Leah Mannion. Oh, yes, and half his graduating class at Brown University. And let's not even get into all those British girls he'd romanced during his years at Eton.

Loving Sebastian was a game with a very crowded playing field, and she had no intention of joining in.

When they reached the end of a row of stuccoed buildings, Tessa stood facing the magnificent bay she'd seen from her room.

The sea breeze cooled her, and the salt air mingled with the sharp scent of lemons piled high on a nearby market stall.

"This scene looks as if it hasn't changed in two thousand years."

"It probably hasn't, at least on the surface. The wireless

Internet is pretty recent." He flashed a sly smile. "No one's sure who first built this harbor. It's been here for all of recorded history."

They walked toward the water. Almost turquoise in the shallow bay, it lapped against ancient blocks of stone worn smooth by the passage of a million feet.

A long painted boat bobbed a few feet offshore, and Sebastian waved to the man seated in its prow. He punted the boat alongside the quay, and lashed it to a giant iron ring.

The boatman was young and handsome. Tessa found herself held on both sides by gorgeous Caspian men as she stepped down into the rocking, red interior.

Sebastian jumped in after her. He landed so lightly on his feet, the boat barely twitched. "Feels good to be back on the water. A true Caspian gets edgy on dry land for too long."

He settled back into a red velvet banquette that spanned the width of the boat. "Give us the full tour, Dino. Tessa has never been to our country before."

"That is deprivation, indeed," said Dino, in unaccented English.

"*Ita vero,*" agreed Tessa in Latin.

Sebastian grinned. "Show-off."

Tessa raised an eyebrow. "Yeah, and?"

He leaned back on the seat and once again wove his long fingers into the thick, loose mass of her untamed hair. "I like a woman who's not afraid to show what she's made of," he whispered.

Dino tactfully kept his eyes on the harbor wall as they rowed toward it.

Tessa's blood heated with a mix of excitement and

confusion. Her nipples rose to meet the delicate chiffon of her summery dress, and she became instantly aware that they were likely visible, since the strappy design didn't allow for a bra.

"What impressive stonework," she exclaimed, to draw Sebastian's eyes away. The last thing she needed was for him to think she was aroused. "How did they get it here?"

"Historians speculate that they floated the huge carved blocks out there on wooden rafts. They also talk about a giant golden statue that used to guard the entrance to the harbor."

"What happened to it?"

"Some people think it's buried under the sand out there. A team of archaeologists once tried to find it, but they couldn't. With new sonar technologies, though, it might be worth another look."

"Could be an interesting tourist attraction."

"Exactly."

Attracting people to Caspia was a passion of Sebastian's. Now that she was here, she could see why. "How come there hasn't been much tourism until now? It's so incredibly beautiful."

The sun sparkled on the clear, shallow water. She could see the clean sandy floor below. A boat loaded with fresh-caught fish chugged by, heading for the quay.

"For so long, we had no hotels, no advertising, an obscure language that no one speaks." He glanced at her, sun dancing in his dark eyes. "Much as it pains me, I suspect the average person still isn't even aware Caspia exists."

He turned to stare at a white-sailed yacht cruising nearby. "Tessa, does that man look familiar?"

She squinted against the high sun and looked at a tall, tanned man with salt-and-pepper hair in a yellow polo shirt. She recognized his face from the TV news. "It looks like Senator Kendrick. What would he be doing here?"

Sebastian grabbed a pair of binoculars out of a compartment under the seat. "I thought so. He used to live in my building." He leaned over the side of the boat. "Michael! Charmaine!"

He spoke rapidly in Caspian to the boatman, who steered in their direction. Within minutes, Sebastian was helping Tessa up the ladder into the Kendricks' yacht.

Sebastian kissed them on both cheeks and introduced her. Nervous, she babbled that she was his assistant visiting from New York.

"I can't believe you came to Caspia without letting me know," Sebastian chided gently.

"We didn't really plan our visit," Mrs. Kendrick explained. "Michael decided to surprise me with a whirlwind tour of the Mediterranean to celebrate our thirtieth wedding anniversary."

Thirty years? Tessa hoped she looked that good ten years from now. Charmaine Kendrick's short, blond hair swept back to reveal an alert face. Her rose-colored shorts showed off fit, tanned legs.

"And naturally we couldn't sail right past Caspia," cut in the senator. "Not after you've sung its praises to us so often."

"You can see I wasn't exaggerating." Sebastian had his arm around both of them. "I'll be deeply offended if you won't join us at the palace for lunch."

Mrs. Kendrick brightened at this suggestion, but her husband quashed it with the explanation that they had a strict itinerary to stick to.

"Twenty ports in twenty days." Charmaine laughed. "We're expected in Piraeus tomorrow morning."

"What can I show you of Caspia while you're here? The ancient market? The early Christian frescoes? The Ottoman mosque?"

Tessa's ears pricked up. She silently voted for the frescoes.

Mrs. Kendrick shielded her eyes from the sun with a manicured hand. "Oh, my goodness, does that sign say Dolce & Gabbana?"

"It does." Sebastian grinned. "And that's BCBG Max Azria right next to it. How about some shopping?"

The senator clapped Sebastian on the back. "Charmaine never says no to shopping."

"Well, dear, we do have a lot of functions to go to. And I didn't realize it would still be so warm at this time of year."

"And scanty evening wear is something *I* never say no to." Senator Kendrick's tanned face eased into a grin.

The senator begged off going ashore with them and asked Tessa to keep him company while Sebastian took Mrs. Kendrick to the stores in his gondola.

Tessa didn't mind. She'd rather sit on a yacht and watch the water than shop any day. And if she remembered right, Senator Kendrick was a keen supporter of spending for education, a cause she held dear.

He guided her to the front of the yacht, where two padded seats looked out over the prow. She eased herself in next to him.

"So, you're Stone's assistant?"

"Yes." She turned to Kendrick with a smile. "I'm here to organize a meeting."

"Working for royalty must be rather bizarre for a girl used to American democracy." He puffed his athletic chest inside his lemon polo shirt.

"It was a bit strange at first, but I don't think much about it. The people of Caspia seem very content with their royal family."

"I don't suppose they have much choice." Senator Kendrick leaned in. His grin gave her a close-up of his blazing white teeth. There was something weird about his skin. Smooth and shiny, it looked like the skin of someone who'd had dermabrasion to erase wrinkles.

She looked over to the quay, where Sebastian was helping Mrs. Kendrick out onto the stone sidewalk that flanked the row of luxury boutiques.

"You're a quiet one, aren't you?"

"I guess I'm just dazzled by the view."

His pale blue eyes fixed on hers. "I'm rather dazzled by it myself."

Something about the way he stared at her made Tessa's stomach tighten.

"Too much foreign food and foreign scenery makes me pine for a little taste of home." He leaned in so close that his freckled arm brushed against hers. Her hairs stood on end.

She forced a laugh. "You're craving corn dogs and apple pie?"

"Something like that. I bet you're tired of being hit on by swarthy Mediterranean men."

"Not at all. The Caspians I've met have been very polite and charming."

"Carrying a torch for your prince, are you?" Senator Kendrick's salt-and-pepper eyebrow lifted.

"What?"

"I suppose all silly young girls fill their heads with fantasies of crowns and coronets. An American senator has a good deal more power than a tin-pot monarch."

"I imagine that's a matter of opinion."

Her stomach knotted. It would be tough to swim for shore in the long dress. She'd lost sight of Sebastian, too. He'd gone into one of the shops.

She decided to redirect the conversation. "What do you think about mandatory school testing? Do you think it ensures an even playing field, or do you think it makes teachers gear lessons too much toward the tests?"

Senator Kendrick threw his head back and guffawed with laughter. "I came here to get away from all that claptrap and political bull. Now I'm sailing on a boat with a beautiful blonde and she wants to bend my ear about education? I feel as if I'm back in New York."

The disgust in his voice made her eyes widen. She thought she caught a whiff of something on his breath, too. Whiskey?

She gathered her skirt about her knees and groped for a good excuse to leave the intimate seating.

"Where do you think you're going?"

"I'd like to take a walk on the deck."

"It's a small yacht. There's barely room to take three steps." His pale eyes narrowed. He leaned over her and trapped her with his arm by placing his hand on the armrest on the far side of her. "I can think of some far more interesting things to do."

He's going to kiss me.

The thought rushed Tessa's brain as his pursed lips rushed her mouth.

Instinct kicked in. Since she couldn't pull back, she whipped forward and smashed him in the nose with her forehead. She was on her feet and back on the deck in seconds. A young male sailor knelt nearby, winding some rope.

Senator Kendrick appeared around the sail, rubbing his nose. He glared at her. "Don't get the wrong idea."

"Don't worry, I didn't." She stood with her hands on her hips.

Now that her adrenaline was flowing she'd like him to try that again. She'd enjoy pitching him into the drink.

Maybe he read her mind, because he disappeared down some stairs into the belly of the boat.

She dusted her hands, which felt oddly satisfying. Hopefully her forehead wouldn't bruise. What a jerk! Did he think she'd *want* to kiss him?

She suspected he didn't spare a thought for what she wanted. She was a nobody. An assistant. A pretty, empty-headed bimbo to toy with.

The disturbing part was that she didn't want to tell Sebastian. He was obviously pleased to have important American visitors come to his country and she didn't want to spoil it for him.

It seemed an eternity before Sebastian finally appeared, his gondola laden with shiny bags from the boutiques.

Sebastian was all smiles as he helped Charmaine Kendrick back onto the boat. Tessa's heart squeezed with pity for the woman married to such a—

Now, now. She was the assistant to a prince. Nice girls didn't use words like that.

The senator—and she used the word loosely—must have been watching from below, because he came on the deck as soon as they arrived. He marched right past Tessa without looking at her.

"Did you buy some beautiful things, my dear?" He kissed his wife's cheek. "You know I want you to have everything your heart desires."

To make up for your cheating louse of a husband. Tessa could barely keep a straight face. Just the sight of the man made her flesh crawl.

"Tessa." Sebastian's voice in her ear made her jump. "Are you okay?" He murmured it low.

"Sure. I'm fine." Her attempt at bright and breezy came out rather stiff.

Sebastian shot a glance at the senator, who was "oohing" over some shimmery red number his wife pulled from a striped bag. "Seriously, you don't look yourself." His dark eyes filled with concern as he looked at her again.

Her stomach tangled. Should she tell him?

For all she knew her revelation might start an international incident. And she didn't want anything else to spoil this beautiful day. She was pretty sure the senator would turn tail and run as soon as she and the prince left the boat.

"I guess I don't have my sea legs yet." She glanced at the mirror-calm water of the harbor and swallowed.

"In that case, we must get you back on solid ground."

Senator Kendrick clapped a jovial hand on Sebastian's shoulder. Was his nose looking a tad swollen? "As I said, we've got a full itinerary. Our captain informed me that we must set sail before noon or we'll never make Piraeus in time."

He shot an icy glance at Tessa. She lifted her chin.

Yes. Definitely swollen. And a black eye seemed to be starting on the left side, too. Hah! Maybe he'd think twice before assaulting someone next time.

Sebastian kissed Charmaine on the cheek and made her promise to come back. Tessa was relieved she wouldn't be here when they did. She managed a curt goodbye to the man who'd spoiled her perfect morning.

Back in the gondola, with Sebastian's big, protective presence beside her, she shivered with relief.

"Enough boating for you." He leaned over the side and trailed his fingers in the water. "Warm. Want to take a dip?"

"Right here?" Panic crept over her. "I don't have a swimsuit with me."

"You didn't bring one at all?"

"No. I came here to study the files and help with the meeting, remember?"

"Oh, yes. That." He seemed to have genuinely forgotten. His eyes brightened. "We must find you a suit immediately."

He murmured instructions to the boatman. Spoken fast, the language was much harder to understand. She did catch the word *Valentino*.

"I don't need a Valentino swimsuit," she protested. "Is there an ordinary clothes store where I could find a suit?"

"What's wrong with Valentino?" He raised a brow.

"It's outrageously expensive, that's what."

Being a prince clearly made you lose touch with reality. Which probably didn't much matter if you were a prince.

She, however, had to save for the down payment on the apartment she'd be renting in LA. Patrick hadn't yet mentioned cohabiting and she'd decided it would be tacky and pushy to suggest it.

They could work up to that.

She wouldn't tell Patrick about the senator, either. He'd probably think she'd been dressed too provocatively or something.

"Beautiful things are always expensive. It's the way of the world." Sebastian eased his broad shoulders against the velvet seat.

"No, they're not." She sat up. "Usually things that cost nothing are the most beautiful." She looked up to where the sun illuminated the rocky peaks that stood sentinel over the town. "Does the blue sky cost money? The clear water? The fresh air?"

She paused. Perhaps there were cleanup crews constantly at work scrubbing and whitewashing Caspia.

"The sun in your golden hair."

Sebastian's low voice caught her off guard.

"What?"

"Beautiful." His eyes were narrowed, seductive.

Heat swelled in her chest, then morphed into a clench of anxiety. Was she inadvertently sending out some signal that she was interested or available?

She crossed her arms over her chest. "For all you know it costs a fortune to get my hair this color."

"Does it?" He looked curious.

She laughed again. "No. It's naturally a dark, mousy blond."

"It's perfect. And the Caspian sun admires it as much as I."

For a second she thought he was going to weave his fingers into her hair again. Her body braced in a mixture of terror and anticipation.

The boat bumped gently against the quay.

The boatman lashed the long boat to a metal ring set in the giant stones.

Tessa gathered her long dress and climbed out of the yawing boat with as much dignity as possible. The ancient stone buildings stood shoulder to shoulder along a stone walkway, inlaid with mosaic. She noticed small, tasteful signs above some of the doorways. "Chanel, Ferragamo, Armani."

"All the stores we've been working with."

He linked his arm though hers. She had to admit that his strong arm felt wonderfully supportive after what she'd just been through with a man she once respected. Sebastian would never take advantage of a vulnerable woman.

Not unless she wanted him to.

Now that she'd seen the Kendricks' white yacht leave through the harbor mouth, she started to relax, caressed by gentle sea breezes and the bright sun.

Inside Valentino, Sebastian addressed the fawning male clerk. "We'd like to see some swimsuits."

"Bikini or one-piece?"

"Bikini," Sebastian said firmly, before she'd managed to get her mouth open. The clerk hadn't even glanced at her. She wasn't sure he was even aware of her standing there, next to His Royal Highness.

"That's the one." Sebastian pointed to a greenish suit, four microscopic triangles held together by gold rings.

Tessa tilted her head. "Are you sure that's not a pair of earrings?"

Sebastian chuckled. "Try it on. If it doesn't fit the rest of you, we'll hang it from your ears."

Reluctant, she took the hanger and followed the clerk into a changing room. Thick carpet greeted her feet as she slipped off her sandals behind a heavy curtain. Was she supposed to go out and show Sebastian the bikini?

There was no mirror in the curtained cubicle, so she had to creep out into the main dressing room to confront her almost-naked body in a wall of mirrors.

She approached the mirror carefully, expecting an eyeful of skinny-and-pale.

"Very nice."

Sebastian's deep voice made her jump. She spun around to see him standing by the entrance to the dressing rooms, arms crossed and a smile of appreciation sneaking across his arrogant mouth.

"I could use a tan."

"Then the sooner we get out in the sun, the better." His smile became a broad grin. He held out his arm. "Let's go."

She laughed. "I have to get dressed again. And pay. This scrap of fabric is probably two hundred dollars."

He smiled wryly. "I've already paid. Here's the matching sarong." He handed her a shimmering piece of green-and-gold fabric.

Their hands brushed as she took it from him. A swift touch that made her heart beat faster.

For all she knew it was actually five hundred dollars and the sarong twice as much.

She sucked in a breath.

Eek. This was all a bit much.

It wasn't appropriate to let her boss dress her up like a Barbie doll. Especially when she was practically engaged to someone else.

Thoughts of Patrick seemed rather out of place here in Caspia. He didn't like hot sun and he'd be bored on the water. When they'd gone sailing out of Westport with one of his clients, he'd kept flipping on his PDA to check stock quotes.

Very practical. Sensible. The kind of person who'd make a responsible husband and father. So she'd better make sure she kept Patrick—and her own future— foremost in her mind.

Five

White liveried servants brought Tessa and Sebastian a lunch of handmade delicacies on the private palace dock. Hidden from the world by carved stone walls, they sipped fresh lemonade with sprigs of fragrant mint while seawater lapped at the sun-bleached quay. Bright flowers bloomed in ornate urns, their leaves occasionally ruffled by the warm breeze.

Tessa wriggled, trying not to get too comfortable on the soft lounge chair. She wore the bikini. She could hardly refuse when he'd sunk so much money into it.

"I really should call the attendees for the meeting."

"Not yet. You need heliotherapy." Sebastian picked up the hem of his shirt and pulled it over his head in a quick motion.

She jerked her gaze away from the sight of his bronzed washboard abs.

"Helio-what?" She fixed her attention on a seagull, then quickly became dizzy as it turned in tight circles, scanning the water for its lunch.

Sebastian was stretching. She could tell without looking.

Her nerve endings could see him. All the tiny invisible blond hairs all over her. Her nipples must be looking, too, because they buzzed like pressed doorbells.

"Heliotherapy. Sunlight as a curative. Practiced in Caspia since the time of Hippocrates."

She couldn't manage to avert her eyes as he eased back into his chair, settling his broad shoulders into the soft fabric.

A narrow cyclone of black hair started between his well-developed pecs, twisted down the center of his rock-hard stomach, then disappeared below the button of his black trunks.

"I thought…" Her voice was a hoarse whisper. She cleared her throat. "I thought the sun gave you skin cancer."

Sebastian snorted. "Caspians have the longest lifespan of any people on earth." He lifted his arms behind his head, and his impressive biceps bulged.

Tessa blinked.

"Well, you have pretty dark skin." All over. At least the parts she could see. She tried not to think about the others.

"So did you last summer. Have you been living under a rock this year?"

She couldn't help laughing. "I have, lately. The rock of Caspia Designs and its gritty financials."

Sebastian turned his head and assaulted her with one of his penetrating stares. "And that is exactly why I won't have you scurrying off to bury yourself again."

His eyes grazed her face, then wandered over her neck.

"You need sun, good food, fresh air and laughter. Then you won't want to run away to California in search of things that can be found right where you are now."

He settled his head back with a smile of satisfaction and closed his eyes.

He'd noticed her tan last summer?

She'd managed a large group plot in a local community garden, which kept her outdoors digging, weeding and watering at least an hour a day.

She'd had a great time, too. Hadn't spent one single evening sighing over her lack of husband prospects or her ticking biological clock.

This year she hadn't the time or energy for the garden. So she'd also missed out on the companionship, sunshine, fresh air and fresh food that came along with the experience.

Instead she'd been telling herself things would get better once she left New York and started over.

Maybe Sebastian had a point.

A self-protective urge to argue with him tickled her vocal cords. But he looked so peaceful and contented lying there in the sun. She didn't want to be snotty and point out that the older citizens of Caspia were pretty leathery looking.

Besides, she liked leather.

Still, sunblock would be a good idea. She fished the bottle from her bag and started to rub it on her exposed belly.

"Let me help."

She glanced up to see Sebastian's winning smile again. The one that made her so suspicious of his motives.

She fought the urge to laugh. "That's okay, I've got it covered."

"Not yet, you haven't. I'll do your back." He took the bottle from her in a firm swipe. "Turn around."

She turned, swinging her legs to the other side of the lounger. "Are you this commanding with people who aren't your employees?"

"I prefer to think of myself as straightforward."

His hands settled on her shoulders.

One way to be straightforward.

Breath rushed out of her lungs at the sensation of his broad fingertips, moist with lotion, rubbing her skin. He smoothed the sunblock over the nape of her neck, feathering it over her vertebrae with little thumb motions. She curled her toes, trying to fight the warm pool of arousal spreading in her abdomen.

His broad palms swirled lotion over her shoulder blades, kneading her muscle at the same time. It was hard to ignore the sensation of release spreading through her.

Then his fingers slid under the scanty string of her bikini. She gasped. For some reason the gesture seemed shockingly intimate.

"Hold still. I need more lotion." His voice was unusually gruff. She felt quite naked as he pulled his hands from her body.

She heard him rubbing the sunblock between his hands to warm it, and her skin tingled in anticipation of his touch.

Ooh. Right there in the sensitive spots on either side of her waist. She tried not to wriggle. Or giggle.

His fingers slid around to rub it over her belly button. She should protest that she could do that herself, but she'd lost the power of speech.

Probably because in reaching forward to rub her front, Sebastian had moved so close that she could smell his stirring male scent.

"Relax," he commanded. "Why are you tightening up?"

Um, because my boss is rubbing my bare flesh with his fingers?

She managed to clear her throat. "Guess I'm over-worked. Must be my demanding boss."

"I'll have a word with him."

She could hear the smile in his voice.

He pushed his fingers into the tight muscle on either side of her spine, causing her to arch her back and let go a tiny moan of pleasure.

"Ah, yes."

"What?" she croaked.

"I can see the problem."

"What problem?" Ohhhh. His thumbs settled into the dimples above her bikini bottom. That felt...wicked.

"You need to let go of *all* tension."

"I think I'm pretty close."

"No. Your muscles are still working to hold you up-right." His palms rubbed the sides of her waist. There wasn't even a hint of lotion left on them. Ripples of sensation skittered over her.

"Let me guess, you want me to lie down."

"No."

He didn't stop kneading the muscles behind her hips. She craned her neck around to read his expression.

His dark eyes flashed mischief. "I want you to float."

Sebastian lifted her off her chair before she could draw breath to protest. He held her in his arms, and for a second she thought he was going to heave her right into the water lapping against the stone quay.

Instead he marched to the edge, and jumped.

She let out a piercing scream as they plummeted through the air for a split second before splashing into the water. Tessa managed to close her mouth before they plunged below the blue-green surface into the silent world below.

Eyes shut tight and Sebastian's strong arms still tight around her, she surfaced, gasping for breath. "What the—"

"Now relax."

"Relax? You've half drowned me!" She struggled, trying to get free of his arms.

She looked up at his face as he brushed a strand of hair off her cheek. His expression was serious, his touch deft and careful.

Then their eyes met and her stomach did a weird leaping thing.

Being held close against his warm, wet chest felt anything but safe.

He trod water, holding them both up. His powerful legs created a swell, while his embrace seemed effortless, and strangely soothing.

"Let your legs float. I won't let go. I promise."

His deep voice tickled her wet ear.

She fought the ripple of pleasure it summoned. "Why would I believe you after you already dunked me?"

"The Caspian royal family never breaks a promise. Our motto is Honor Omnia Vincit."

"Honor conquers all, huh?"

"Engraved on my heart."

He flexed a brawny bicep in her face. There, scrolled into the pattern winding over his arm, were the words he'd spoken.

She tried to brush off the sensations sneaking through her. "I've got news for you. Your heart isn't really on your sleeve. It's an expression."

Sebastian's mouth creased into a smile. "Maybe I should dunk you." He dipped her a couple of inches.

Her stomach tightened, then softened when he brought her gently back to the surface. Water played over her stomach, echoing the ripple of arousal inside it. "It's a beautiful tattoo. Does every man in the family get one?"

Sebastian glanced down at it. The pattern of stylized leaves traced the swell of his muscles to ring his upper arm just below the shoulder. "I've had it so long I forget it's there. But no, it's not traditional." His eyes sparkled with humor. "My mom almost died when she saw it. I got it when I was sixteen after I went to an Eric Clapton concert in London with some friends."

Tessa laughed. "That's such a…regular guy thing to do."

"Who says I'm not a regular guy, as well as a prince?" He raised a brow.

Somehow that stopped her in her tracks. Not that she was making any tracks, since Sebastian still held her fast in his arms and her feet bobbed near the surface of the water. Royal trappings aside, Sebastian *was* just a guy. With a mind and heart and feelings. Like everyone else.

Like her.

She ignored the funny sensation in her gut. "It's lucky I was always strapped for cash as a teen or I might have the New York Knicks emblazoned on me somewhere. What made you decide to get the family motto?"

Sebastian looked at the scrolled words. "Caspia and its people are my team. I might have occasionally cheered for, say, Manchester United, but my heart is always in Caspia, and as you've observed, I wanted to wear it on my sleeve. Still do."

His eyes shone with a mix of passion and humor that made her heart squeeze.

How had their relationship gone overnight from five years of formal and professional relations to half-naked conversations and underwater encounters?

In some ways it was her wildest fantasy come true. The man she'd admired and mooned over for so long was actually teasing and flirting with her. It was hard not to be flattered.

And excited.

Sebastian adjusted his grip, sliding his strong arms under her. "Let your head rest. Let go. The water will carry you."

"I think you're doing most of the work."

"I wouldn't call it work." His deep voice had a playful tone.

But what was he playing at? They both knew this flirtation couldn't go anywhere. Not anywhere sensible, at least.

She shot him a challenging glance. "Me, either. I have phone calls to make."

"First you must heal and recover. Hydrotherapy has been recognized for thousands of years as a powerful curative." He shifted one of the hands supporting her torso and splashed a few drops of water on her hot skin.

She swallowed hard, trying to crush the sensations swelling inside her. "You should open a spa. Ancient healing therapies seem to be a specialty of yours."

"Excellent idea. Why didn't I think of that? See how valuable you are to me?"

"Oh, stop it."

"Stop what?" His expression was all innocence.

"Buttering me up so I'll stay and work for you."

Or do whatever else it is that you have in mind.

"Can you blame me?"

"Well, no. I am efficient and organized." She raised a brow. "And I do my best to present a professional appearance. Though that seems to have fallen by the wayside today…" She glanced at her bare stomach. Drops of seawater sparkled on skin that had already started to tan. A result of Sebastian's unthorough sunblock application.

What was he doing with his fingers? The pads of his fingertips played her waist like a piano, dancing over her until her insides hummed like vibrating strings.

Her nipples poked against the fabric of her scanty top. Heat and moisture gathered between her thighs, making her glad her bikini bottom was already damp.

Sebastian lowered his head so that his breath heated her ear. "As you point out, you are perfect. Which is exactly why you can't leave. I won't let you."

She shivered, the force of his words sinking in.

I don't want to leave.

She writhed slightly, trying to regain control of her body. The sensations swimming through her were startling and unfamiliar. Warm water swirled around her while the breeze tickled her bare skin above it. Sebastian's powerful hands held her crushed against his muscled chest. His musky scent wound through the salty tang in the air, threatening to overwhelm her senses.

Suddenly she was panting, gasping for breath, struggling against the firm hold of Sebastian's arms and the ache of her unwelcome arousal. "I have to stand!" She shoved against him with her elbow.

"It's too deep."

Flailing in the water, she started to panic. Frantic kicking had freed her from Sebastian, but now, head reeling and body throbbing, she couldn't seem to remember how to swim.

"It's okay, Tessa, I won't let you sink." Sebastian took her hand and tugged her gently to the stone dock. He didn't try to grab or control her, just guided her through the water. She grabbed a metal ring and clung to it.

She blew out a sharp blast of air. "I'm sorry. I guess it was all too much. I'm not cut out to be relaxed. It freaks me out."

Sebastian's look of concern eased into a grin. "You're a real New Yorker. You'd rather resist than relax."

"I'm from Connecticut," she protested.

"Same thing."

"No, it isn't."

"See, you want to fight me already."

"I do not!" She shifted her grip on the ring. How had this man managed to so thoroughly unhinge her?

"Oh, yeah?" He shoved his hand in the water and splashed her. Hard.

She splashed back and kicked with her feet, showering him completely with water until he ducked below the surface.

He rose up, laughing. "See what I mean?"

She shoved another wave of water at him. Damn. He was right. She felt better already.

She could even stare right at his handsome face with the water streaming over its hard lines and feel…almost normal.

"Do you surrender?" she challenged.

"Caspians never surrender."

"Honor Omnia Vincit, and all that." Her eyes wandered to the tattoo circling his thick bicep.

"Exactly. And since I am a man of honor, I'll help you out of the water. I think we've both had enough hydrotherapy for one afternoon." His black hair hung in his eyes, dripping with water.

He looked very unroyal.

And devastatingly handsome.

"It's okay. I can swim. I grew up in a coastal town. In *Connecticut*." She dodged his offered hand and darted around him, diving under and pulling hard for the stone steps twenty feet along the dock.

As she climbed out of the water she sensed his eyes on her. She adjusted her scanty bikini, not that it made much difference. His steady dark gaze threatened to evaporate the water right off her.

This was *so* wrong.

A strange noise pierced the air. It took her a full five seconds to realize it was her cell phone. She dived for it, dragging her sarong over her bare legs.

Patrick. His work number. He'd called three times this morning just to "see how she was."

How could she talk to him now, while her inside pulsed with desire for another man?

Guilt speared through her as she pushed the button to send him straight to voice mail.

"*Now* can we see the files? I'm kind of a workaholic, so I get neurotic if I'm not allowed to work."

"You are working. You are my assistant and you are assisting me in enjoying my day." His arrogant expression dared her to argue.

She fought the urge to laugh. Obnoxious jerk!

And he was right, too, which made it worse.

She sucked in a deep breath and tried to compose herself. All she had to do was survive her two weeks' notice without doing anything stupid, then she could get on with the rest of her life.

"Do you have jeans?" His question yanked her back to the present.

"Yes."

"Great."

He shrugged his white linen shirt back on, right over his wet skin. It clung to his ripped chest in a very disturbing way. She was still attempting to tear her gaze from the sight when he looked up. "What are you waiting for?"

"What am I supposed to be doing?"

"Getting your jeans."

"Oh."

Sebastian looked at her as if she'd lost a cog or two. He was right. Of course, it was all his fault.

"I'll, uh, be right back." She strode into the palace, hoping she could find her way to her room.

In the wide, colonnaded hallway she passed the queen, who was talking at top speed on a cell phone. Despite her damp and seminaked appearance, Tessa prepared her brightest smile. Her Royal Majesty glanced up but didn't make any acknowledgment.

Ouch.

What did she expect? She was Sebastian's assistant, not a visiting princess. *Get over yourself already.*

Six

Sebastian drove through the gates that kept the rest of Caspia outside the palace walls. He negotiated his Land Rover through the narrow cobbled streets with expert ease, pausing for an occasional chat through the window.

"I think it's really nice that the royal family is so intimate with the people," Tessa remarked. She thought, too, that Sebastian seemed more relaxed here than in New York. There he often looked tense and rushed.

"Ha. It drives my mother crazy. She prefers to maintain a majestic distance. But my dad and I like people too much. We couldn't be cool and distant if we tried."

He leaned out the window to beckon a flower seller, then exchanged one of Caspia's large, colorful banknotes for a ribbon-tied bunch of pink, bell-shaped flowers.

He handed it to Tessa.

Now he was giving her flowers?

"Smell them."

She wanted to laugh. Typical of Sebastian to buy her flowers then order her to smell them.

She buried her nose in the soft petals. "Mmm. They smell like honey."

"Our Caspian honey smells like these flowers. It's the most delicious honey in the world."

"Of course it is." She grinned. "Is there anything in Caspia that isn't the best in the world?"

Sebastian turned to her—while continuing to speed along a windy, narrow stretch of road—and gave her an incredulous look. "You've spent a day here. Surely you know the answer to that already." He faced front again and she loosened her grip on the door handle. "We're headed for the place where these flowers grow, in the cool and shady crevices of our mountains."

"Let me guess, they're the most beautiful mountains in the world?"

Sebastian stared straight ahead as he drove. "You're catching on."

The Land Rover climbed toward the sky, bumping along a narrow, unpaved track. Grasses and wildflowers grew sparser as they rose through the rugged terrain, past the occasional grazing goat.

When it seemed as if surely they'd scrape the roof of the car on the hovering white clouds, he screeched to a stop in a cloud of dust.

"Jump out."

She did. And it was quite a jump, onto loose shale. She skidded then got her footing on the desolate crag they'd ascended. She was about to make a crack along the lines

of "where's the royal pavilion?" when she looked up and
the view made words shrivel on her tongue.

The land descended right from her toes in a sweeping
cascade of rock, grass and flowers still brilliant in the
dusk. A wide plain of grazed meadows punctuated the
dramatic slope, then the land descended again to the city,
where the red clay roofs of the ancient buildings hugged
the hillside as it ringed the harbor.

"We're two thousand feet above sea level."

The ocean, far below, crinkled and twinkled in the setting sun. She could make out the dots of bright colored
fishing boats returning to the harbor, and others setting out
for the night's catch.

Smoke rose from chimneys, no doubt rich with the
aroma of Caspian dinners being cooked.

The lowering sun just touched the wide, dark sea, a
bright orb that bathed land and water in transparent golden
light.

It was so beautiful Tessa could hardly breathe.

"Now you've truly seen Caspia. This is our whole
nation."

Sebastian's deep voice drew her gaze from the view. His
pride and emotion were written plainly on the strong features of his face.

He stared at her. His gaze heated her face, but she
couldn't find words to cut through a new tension that
thickened the air.

He reached out and again he played with her hair. She
couldn't move. Her synapses crackled as excitement rushed
through her.

The golden light burnished Sebastian's complexion to
a warm bronze, making him more handsome than ever—

like a prince from an ancient myth, here to rescue her from the humdrum reality of life and transport her to…

Somewhere like this.

"She must have looked like you." His words were almost a whisper. His fingers roamed in her hair as his gaze wandered over her face and neck.

"Who?" She tried to ignore the hum of arousal vibrating through her.

"The golden statue."

"The one that used to stand in the harbor?" Tessa squinted at him. She expected to see his face crease into a laugh, but it didn't.

"Yes." He tilted his head and gazed into her eyes. "The ancient statue of Andara that used to watch over our bay. The guardian of the people of Caspia."

He paused and his eyes narrowed. "Now that I see you here, with your bright hair streaming in the breeze and the sun on your golden skin, I can picture her perfectly."

Embarrassed, Tessa pushed a stray hair off her face. She could feel heat rising to color her cheeks. "I'm glad sunset in Caspia suits me, but I'm just Tessa from Connecticut. Trust me on this."

His eyes held hers, unblinking. "Tessa from Connecticut, you are the most beautiful woman I've ever seen."

He spoke with such conviction that the breath crept out of her lungs.

Then a shard of good sense peeked through the sudden fog of desire: *This is Sebastian Stone, world famous seducer.*

"You're not bad yourself, in the right light." She tried to laugh, but no sound came out.

She stood transfixed by the hot gaze of his dark eyes. Something in her said "run!" but she didn't move a muscle.

Then he stepped forward and pressed his lips to hers in a swift motion that almost buckled her knees.

His hard torso brushed her breasts, tightened her nipples into peaks. He gathered her into his arms, his strong hands covering her back as he pulled her closer.

Gentle at first, his kiss deepened, becoming forceful, intense. A current of heat seared her as his tongue touched hers.

His rough cheek against her own sun-heated face roused her senses. He smelled like sun and earth and salt air—not the things you'd expect a prince to smell like—but magic, and she couldn't help but respond.

Her arms slid around his waist, against the hard muscle of his back. He groaned as his pelvis bumped against hers. The rough denim of his jeans chafed her. She wanted to slide his jeans down over his powerful thighs and…

Tessa! The shocking thought tugged her out of the haze of raw, pulsing lust that deprived her of her common sense.

What were they doing?

Well…right now Sebastian was devouring her neck, his mouth hungry and unforgiving, his teeth scraping deliciously against the ultrasensitive area behind her ear.

And she was moaning… Or would that sound be better described as whimpering?

Stop!

The word formed in her brain, then dissipated into a fog of desire as Sebastian took her mouth again in a hot, un-relenting kiss.

She didn't want to stop. Not at all. The sensations pouring through her like thick honey made her want to beg for more.

So what if he was her boss?

If he was a prince?

If he only wanted her for one hot, raw, ravenous night?

She shivered, her desire for him almost too much to bear.

Her fingers clawed at his shirt, then reached under it to touch his hot, hard muscle. She ground her hips against his and he responded, molding himself to her.

Her breasts crushed against his chest, her nipples thick with sensation as he hiked up her shirt and slid his hand over her bare back.

Then Sebastian unbuttoned her shirt. Slowly, carefully, his big fingers handled the buttons with gentle care. He eased it down her arms.

Her own breaths were ragged and unsteady in the quiet dusk. She saw the last copper rays of the sun as it sank behind the sea, taking with it the heat and bustle of the day.

And leaving the rich, thick darkness of the night.

Through her bra Sebastian laved her nipple with his tongue. Sharp sensation skidded over her and she almost lost her footing. His quick hands and strong arms soon righted her. He held her steady, tight, as he lowered his mouth and sucked—hard—on her other nipple.

The rough gesture aroused her to the point of agony.

"Come." He took her hand.

His thick arm supported her across a patch of slippery shale and up the side of a rocky ledge.

He stepped through a narrow opening between two boulders and gestured for her to follow.

Tessa's legs shook under the weight of unfamiliar feelings and sensations, as she stepped through the rocky opening. Behind the rocks lay a flat patch of hilltop, lit only by a slim, crescent moon.

Soft, thick grass tickled the sides of her feet above her sandals.

High rocks hid them from everyone and everything but the slender moon. Sebastian pulled her close and she shivered as he wrapped his powerful arms around her and held her tight.

Being wrapped in Sebastian was perfect.

Too perfect.

"Um, what are we doing?"

"Right now, I'd say we're hugging." He nuzzled her neck.

Shimmers of sensation danced along her shoulder and cascaded over her torso.

Her unclothed torso. Her shirt was out there on the rock face, somewhere.

"And now…we're kissing." The end of the last word blurred as his lips settled over hers.

His tongue danced with hers, making her insides twist and untwist in a pulse of excitement.

Her breasts met the night air as her bra came unhooked. "And now I'm undressing you," he murmured, pulling back just enough to get the words out.

He slid her bra over her arms, his fingers gentle, his eyes hungry.

"Beautiful."

His words caressed her along with his touch.

She did feel beautiful right now. Couldn't help it, with Sebastian's warm, dark gaze heating her blood.

She lifted his shirt over his head, which took some help, as it didn't seem anxious to leave his thick muscles.

His torso shone like pewter in the scant moonlight, that line of dark hair twisting down into his jeans.

Jeans that bulged with arousal.

Tessa breathed out slowly, trying to keep a clear head as she unbuttoned the snap at his waist. He was hard as the rock they stood on. She reached in and took him in her hand, enjoying the force of his arousal, kissing him, breathing in the rich, male scent of him.

"Tessa." His throaty voice caressed her ear like a summer breeze.

She heard the snap of her own jeans, but barely felt them slide over her thighs and down her legs. Her whole body sang with so much sensation.

Sebastian rubbed his thumbs over her nipples, which stood to attention. Her belly shuddered as he pressed his thick erection into her soft flesh.

His thigh pressed between hers, rough denim against her bare skin. He grasped her backside and pulled her closer, higher, pressing her breasts against his chest and crushing her mouth to his until she thought she'd catch fire.

"Take them off," she breathed. Indelicate in her desperation, she shoved and pushed at the stiff fabric of his jeans. "Lie down."

She thought she saw the gleam of his grin in the dark as Sebastian lowered himself into the cool, soft grass. She tugged his jeans and he sprang free, then she pulled them down over his legs.

Wow.

Sebastian's muscled, athlete's body looked like an ancient statue come to life. And why wouldn't it? He was descended from the warriors and champions of the ancient world. The tribal tattoo on his arm only added to the effect.

His fierce arousal heated her blood as he rolled a

condom over it. She climbed over him, hungry for his hardness inside her.

Her hair brushed his chest as she took him deep. Her moan pierced the silent night air and made her open her eyes for a split second.

She saw darkness. Silence. The stars.

And Sebastian.

She couldn't stop now even if she wanted to.

Shivering with the force of her need, she rocked, drawing him deeper into her pulsing core.

Urgency kicked into a fierce rhythm, and she wasn't sure how much longer she could last without blasting out into the stars. Then Sebastian reversed their positions in a deft move that left him on top and her down in the soft grass.

She writhed under him, enjoying the contrast of his hot, hard body and the cool, yielding ground. Sebastian's hands roamed over her skin, squeezing and enjoying her body. He sucked her breasts and the skin of her neck until she cried out.

Deep inside her, his erection danced, stirring sensations she'd never experienced before. Never even imagined.

She couldn't stop moving, wriggling under him, pressing herself to him and shifting her hips against his, testing and enjoying each new wrinkle of pleasure and the fresh ache of raw passion.

Kissing was clearly Sebastian's first language. His kisses came in unending variety—soft and teasing, wicked and sly, rough and hungry; or slow, controlled and throbbing with reined-in desire.

Strange, new feelings built inside her, consuming her, taking her over like an invasion.

She exploded into climax totally without warning, pealing out a sharp scream that rang over the nation of Caspia, followed by a series of hard gasps as sensation racked her body.

Her nails clawed into Sebastian as his own climax shook him. Then he lowered himself to her, heavy and breathless. He pushed his hands into her hair, holding her, and he pressed his rough cheek to hers.

Emotion swelled inside Tessa. Sebastian was so passionate in every other part of his life, should she be surprised that his lovemaking reflected his nature?

Stars danced in front of her eyes and she wasn't sure if they formed part of distant solar systems or were the creations of her own bedazzled brain.

Sebastian eased himself off her and lay on the ground beside her, his arm wrapped around her chest.

She felt…protected. Cherished.

Not loved, though.

Even now she didn't delude herself, even for a split second, that Sebastian Stone, Crown Prince of Caspia, could love her.

Which was fine. Because she had…

Ohmigod. Patrick!

She tried to sit up, but Sebastian's arm was too heavy on her chest.

She'd just cheated on the man she planned to— potentially—spend the rest of her life with.

Horror descended over her like a bucket of cold water. She hadn't even thought of him. Hadn't cared at all about him.

His message was still flashing, unheard, on her cell phone.

She sank back into the grass, head pounding.

"You okay?" Sebastian's deep voice stirred a fresh pulse of arousal.

"Sure. Fine." She swallowed. "Great."

She spotted a torn condom packet lying in the grass. She'd been too carried away to think of practical things. She was on the pill—at Patrick's insistence—but Sebastian didn't know that. It was thoughtful of him to remember protection.

Naturally the notorious Prince of Midtown carried a ready supply wherever he went. Perhaps he'd planned this.

Tension tightened her muscles.

Sebastian propped himself on one elbow. Her resistance ebbed as he stroked her cheek with his thumb. "I like a woman who knows how to give orders."

Her eyes met his. Humor sparkled in his dark gaze.

"Orders? What do you mean?"

Sebastian laughed. "I guess you were so caught up in the moment, you don't remember commanding me to strip and lie down."

He brushed a kiss over her lips. They parted, as heat rushed through her, embarrassment mingling with unavoidable desire.

She bit her lip. "Did I really? I'm so sorry."

"Don't be." Sebastian's wide mouth turned up at the corners. "I loved it." He growled and nipped at her neck. "Why shouldn't you ask for what you want? That's the best way to get it."

He licked her lips and pressed his mouth over hers in a hot, raunchy kiss.

She couldn't resist twisting to crush her body against his, flesh against flesh, enjoying the heat and hard masculinity of him.

He pulled back for a moment to look at her. "Too many people drift through life, afraid to ask for what they want. Afraid to figure it out, even. I'm glad you're not like that, Tessa."

I'm not?

She blinked and shoved a hand through her hair—which was no doubt tangled and filled with bits of grass. "I'm not so sure I do know what I want."

She wanted change, for sure. A shake-up. New surroundings. New possibilities.

And here she was, naked in the arms of a royal prince, on a foreign mountaintop.

Apparently she'd succeeded. Though this was not exactly what she'd had in mind.

Sebastian brushed his lips over her forehead. "You knew exactly what you wanted a few minutes ago. And I suspect that a few minutes from now you'll have some more strong ideas on the subject."

His suggestive tone tugged at a knot of need deep inside her. His mouth followed the cord of arousal down her torso, sucking her breasts, feathering butterfly kisses on her stomach, until his head was buried between her legs, kissing and licking her into an alternate dimension.

"Don't stop!" Her hips bucked at the sensations roused by his lips and tongue. "Faster, harder."

Sebastian responded instantly to her rasped requests, driving her deeper and deeper into a dark oasis of pleasure that blotted out the moon and stars.

Then he was inside her again, turning her mind and body inside out in explosions of rapture and sheer, earth-shaking pleasure.

This time they came together. A perfectly orchestrated

explosion, controlled yet devastating, that left them clinging to each other, sweaty, ecstatic and gasping for breath.

Even when blood started to return to her brain, Tessa was unable to summon a lick of embarrassment.

Sebastian lay fast asleep, his face buried in her hair, hugging her like his favorite teddy.

And weirdly enough it felt totally natural and comfortable.

Although his princely upbringing had created a sense of entitlement that could make him seem brash or arrogant, Sebastian was an affectionate and giving person. Something obviously appreciated by the citizens of Caspia, his vast crowd of friends, and the hordes of beautiful women who flung themselves at him daily.

The same could not exactly be said for Patrick. He was nice, but in a shy, reserved, New England kind of way. You could call him standoffish.

No one would ever call Sebastian standoffish. If he had a standoff with anyone, it would be a colorful occasion worthy of a tabloid front page.

There were a few of those in the media file.

He lived every day, every hour, with passion.

He even slept with passion. She smiled as she saw the blissful expression on his handsome face, the rapid movements of his eyes under his closed eyelids.

Is he dreaming about me?

She cursed herself for the thought, but went back to it anyway. Maybe he was picturing her, all in gold, standing guard over the Caspian harbor.

Two hundred feet tall.

Telling him to get his clothes off. Now!

She chuckled. The subtle movement made Sebastian snuggle closer.

Oh, dear.

This was all a little too wonderful. She had that nasty sensation right before you rip off a Band-Aid.

The next part is going to hurt.

Seven

Sebastian woke Tessa with gentle kisses. He made love to her one more toe-curling time before they tugged their clothes on and drove back down the mountain, just in time to beat the dawn.

Tessa wished she could disappear as they steered past the palace guards at 5:00 a.m.

No prizes for guessing what we've been up to, she mentally told them.

Sebastian didn't seem the slightest bit put out.

Of course, he probably brought disheveled but satisfied women back to the palace at dawn quite often.

He did show some circumspection in guiding her through the halls. That was nice. She didn't want to run into either of their royal majesties until she'd managed to get the leaves out of her hair.

Then he kissed her good-night, with a provocative thrust of his tongue.

Oh, boy.

Tessa collapsed onto her bed in a puddle of dreamy lust.

"Good morning, Tessa." The queen looked up from a large newspaper, printed in French. "You look a bit flushed. Are you feverish?"

Tessa gulped. "I'm fine. Maybe I got a bit too much sunlight yesterday."

Or moonlight…

After only a few hours sleep she eased herself into her seat and spooned some yogurt and honey into a bowl. Once again she'd come to the table with shower-damp hair.

Sebastian whistled as he helped himself to a heaping portion of some kind of Caspian fish stew. For breakfast.

Tessa wanted to kick him under the table and tell him to look less exuberant. He was going to give the game away.

Perhaps he just didn't care?

He chatted with his father about fishing reports and a construction project in the hills, and regaled Tessa with tidbits and statistics about Caspia's economy.

Sebastian could be quite grumpy in the morning, especially before the vat of coffee—with the consistency of used motor oil—he needed to get his systems going.

Today he was downright bubbly even before his first sip. The king's bright eyes twinkled with good humor as Sebastian described the previous day's tour of Caspia. She could see where Sebastian got his natural joie de vivre.

His looks clearly came from his mother, a severe beauty with bone structure sharp as a deadly weapon. She chatted politely with Tessa, asking innocuous questions about her college studies and her life in New York, but she didn't have the warmth of the Stone men, and Tessa was glad when she swept off to some assignation.

Sebastian's father leaned back in his chair. She could swear he was giving her a once-over. It would be disconcerting if not for his good-natured expression. "Do you ride, Tessa?"

She hesitated. *Ride what? A bike?*

Sebastian took a swig of coffee. "He means a horse."

"Oh. Yes, actually I do."

Sebastian looked surprised. "I thought you were from the city."

"I learned in school. To be honest, I haven't ridden since then. So maybe I've forgotten how."

"Impossible." Sebastian rose and dropped his napkin on the table. "Gio, tell the stables to prepare Alto and Magna for us immediately."

Tessa's mouth dropped open. Her adrenaline surged. Was it fear of making an ass of herself on a horse she couldn't control? Or a rush of excitement at the prospect of riding a horse again after all these years?

Sebastian pulled out her chair as she stood. "Do you have riding clothes?"

She shot him a look that said *You're kidding, right?* Then remembering the king was watching, she said, "I'm afraid not."

Sebastian suppressed a snort of laughter at her attempted change of demeanor. "Don't worry. We'll find you some."

He whipped out his cell and murmured something in Caspian. When he hung up, he was beaming. "Caspia is never more beautiful than from the back of a horse."

* * *

Sebastian loved to gallop across the open grassy meadows that belted the middle of Caspia, between the high mountains and the city. It was even better with Tessa galloping like a gale at sea in front of him, her golden hair whipping about her shoulders.

It was all he could do to keep up, and his mount was usually the more spirited of the two.

Tessa Banks was something else.

"You learned how to ride at St. Peter's?"

She turned her horse in a fast circle and came up beside him. "Yup. I got a job grooming the other students' horses and the instructor was nice enough to give me some lessons."

Her white cotton shirt was damp with perspiration, and Sebastian admired the view of her dark bra underneath. He raised his gaze, not wanting to harden painfully against the pommel of his saddle.

"And soon I was exercising the horses, as well as grooming them." Her face shone in the midday sun, her color heightened by exertion.

He could swear on his life that he'd never seen a more beautiful sight.

Tonight she would glitter amongst the crowd at the benefit ball. He'd be the envy of every man in the room.

She patted her horse's neck. "This does beat filing."

He took a minute to process her words.

Oh, yes. She was his assistant.

He'd forgotten about that.

Still, no reason he couldn't escort her to the ball. She was his guest here, in addition to being an employee.

Awkward that he'd slept with her. He usually had strict

rules about that sort of thing, drummed into him with stern warnings by his mother, and gentler and more practical admonitions from his father.

So far, he'd kept the house rules.

But there was something about Tessa that made rules seem foolish and irrelevant.

"We must choose your gown." He let his eyes drift over her long, muscled body as it flowed with the horse's supple back.

"Gown? For what?"

"Tonight's ball for Harvest of Health. It's one of my mother's favorite charities. She's invited all the crowned heads of Europe."

Tessa eyes widened.

"It'll be fun. They're not all over seventy. You'll enjoy the dancing."

Tessa slowed her horse to a trot. Sebastian's own mount was so fired up it took Sebastian a moment to rein him in and trot back to her.

"I don't think I should, Sebastian." Her lovely face looked troubled. "Last night was…wonderful, but I don't want people to talk about me."

"Of course you do. If no one's talking about you, it means you're not having enough fun."

She laughed. "I'd rather live the kind of life that doesn't make the headlines."

Sebastian stiffened, which made his horse jump. By the time he had it going forward again instead of sideways, Tessa was walking along on her horse, looking ahead, as if he wasn't even there.

Why did it bother him that she didn't want the kind of life he led?

He was hardly planning to marry her.

His horse gave another leap sideways.

He turned him in a circle and stroked his neck.

Well, he wasn't.

From the corner of his eye he saw Tessa lean forward to brush a fly from her horse's mane. Like all her movements, the gesture was as elegant as a ballerina's arabesque.

A thick sensation crept across his chest, tightening it. He shook it loose with a jovial chuckle. "I probably should feel guilty about depriving Caspia Designs of your capable hands."

"But let me guess, you don't." She turned to him, her lovely face lit with a grin.

"Not in the least. Race you!"

He surged forward. Maybe exertion would burn off some of the adrenaline surging in his blood.

Alone in a palace hallway, Tessa tried to walk with as much dignity as possible. Her dress, picked out that afternoon at one of Caspia's chichi boutiques, clung to her body like sea spray. The fabric, beaded with a million tiny jade-colored beads, swung as she walked, shimmering with every movement.

Sebastian had talked her into it. At least wearing a dress this heavy probably counted as weight-bearing exercise.

Not that she needed any after galloping all over the countryside with Sebastian, then indulging in an afternoon of Sebastian-funded power shopping to "support the local economy."

Speaking of Sebastian, where was he?

From the cool solitude of the colonnaded hallway, Tessa

could hear a hum of voices, clinking glasses and tinkling laughter. With each step she took the din grew louder.

The ball.

Her stomach turned over.

She'd never been to a ball.

Although she went to a school where balls were a fairly common form of vacation pastime, she couldn't remember ever being invited to one.

No doubt her classmates—with that inimitable prep-school-bred radar that can distinguish "one of us" from "one of them"—had known better than to ask her. Thus avoiding all kinds of embarrassment of her not having the right clothes to wear, or the correct etiquette.

She'd managed to dodge the gaffes she was about to make right now.

"You look breathtaking."

Sebastian's voice in her ear was low and thick with admiration.

"Thanks," she managed.

"I've been waiting for you. I thought you might not want to walk in there alone."

His thoughtfulness warmed and soothed her anxious heart. "You're so right." She smiled. "I'm trying to walk without getting tangled in my dress."

His dark gaze swept along her legs. "I can see how that could be a problem. Your legs are very long."

"They used to call me Knitting Needles."

Did she have to tell him that?

One dark brow lifted. "Because your legs are so long?"

Her face heated. "Yes, and my mom was always knitting. She brought it with her everywhere. She used to knit through all my basketball games."

Shut your trap and stop babbling!

Sebastian's curious gaze deepened. "You played basketball?"

"What else would I do with a body like this?" She gestured at her too-long-and-tall physique, accidentally grazing her knuckles on the green beads.

The mellow hum of music and a hundred conversations swelled as they neared the large atrium where the party was taking place. She walked along the receiving line, shaking hands with the king and queen, despite the fact that she'd had breakfast with them that morning, then a liveried servant announced her name to the crowd.

These people loved ceremony.

"Sebastian, dahling!" An older woman with about a kilo of diamonds hanging from her neck stalked forward on spindly legs. "How lovely to see you. I can't believe we missed each other at Philip's shindig last month."

Sebastian murmured pleasantries.

Tessa's frontal lobes buzzed with the realization that Philip's shindig was that big party in Monaco during which Sebastian was photographed with no less than twelve different wealthy beauties.

The guy from the clipping service had even joked that Sebastian made every minute count.

"And this is Tessa Banks."

Tessa glanced at him, expecting him to add "my assistant." But he didn't.

The woman looked at her expectantly for a moment, then held out her bejeweled hand.

Tessa shook it.

"Charmed, my dear."

"Oh, me, too!" She swallowed. *Did she have no social graces whatsoever?* "It's a lovely night."

She could almost hear Sebastian laughing. But he had the decency to make it silent laughter.

He slid his arm around her back and drew her away. She tried not to get distracted by the warmth of his hard muscle, which was obvious even through his austere dark suit.

"She's harmless," he muttered. "Which is more than I can say for this one. Hello, Faris."

Tessa's shoulders tightened. She recognized the name. Faris Maridis was a frequent and impatient caller when Sebastian was in New York. He always took her calls.

A tall, black-haired woman in a dark blue dress swept toward Sebastian. She grabbed him by the shoulders and planted extravagant kisses on each tanned cheek, leaving moues of red lipstick.

Tessa fought the urge to whip out a tissue and wipe them off.

"You're so wicked, Sebastian darling! Why haven't you taken me out on the *Mirabella* yet?"

His new yacht. She'd seen the paparazzi pictures.

"I've been busy with the lovely Tessa." He gestured to her. Faris whipped around. She gave Tessa a glare that raised goose bumps, then morphed into a big, toothy smile.

"Tessa? I don't believe we've met. Oh, wait! You're Sebastian's little 'girl Friday,' aren't you?"

Tessa blinked. People didn't usually call you "little" when you were nearly 5'10".

"She's my right-hand woman." Sebastian clearly relished the description. As he said it, his arm slid protectively around her waist.

She softened under her bead-encrusted dress.

Faris's sharp dark eyes darted to Sebastian's gesture, then back up to Tessa. They narrowed. "Is this your first time in Caspia, Tessa?"

"Yes. Sebastian's been kind enough to show me almost every inch of it."

"Has he now?" She shot an icy smile at him. "Sebastian is always so *thorough* when he entertains guests." She tilted her head. Her black hair was slicked into a chignon pierced by a single black hairstick. "Especially female guests." She winked at him.

Tessa flushed. It didn't help that Sebastian squeezed her bottom gently at that exact moment. Her nipples tightened and heat gathered between her hips.

She struggled to keep a straight face.

What if someone saw?

"Faris is one of my *oldest* friends." Sebastian stared at her. "That's why she feels free to be so shockingly rude to me."

Faris looked startled and let out a hollow laugh. "Oh, Sebastian, you are too much. Shall we ride tomorrow?"

"I think the horses could use a day of rest after what Tessa and I put them through today." He smiled and squeezed Tessa again.

She tried not to fall off her spiky heels.

Faris's red lips pressed together. "Daddy said you're calling a meeting about Caspia Designs."

Sebastian stiffened. "Yes. Tessa's arranged a gathering of the board for next Tuesday."

"Daddy's rather bored playing golf every day. The firm was always sort of a pet project for him."

"I can tell," murmured Sebastian through gritted teeth. "It's time to take Caspia Designs in a new direction."

Faris raised a slim brow. "Don't forget, Daddy is your father's oldest friend."

That explains a lot. Tessa had wondered why the firm had been allowed to stagnate under incompetent management for so long. Uncollected debts, dwindling markets, exorbitant costs leading to tiny profits on even the most expensive items.

She jumped as the band struck up a fast-paced new tune and people started leaping around as if they had fire ants in their pants.

"Come." Sebastian grabbed her hand and pulled Tessa into the fray. "It's our national dance. You'll like it."

She wasn't sure if his last words were conviction based on personal knowledge of her, or a royal command. She decided to assume the latter.

Sebastian grabbed her hand and whirled her around, then they took off across the floor at a galloping pace in a kind of whirling polka.

Blasts of trumpet and the rolling thunder of drums filled the air with a steamroller of sound. Colors and lights flashed before her eyes as they whipped around the room. Sebastian's strong arms and capable guidance swept her into the dance as if she knew it.

By the time the trumpets subsided to a farewell hum, she was gasping for air and dying to do it again.

"See, I told you." Sebastian pushed a stray strand of hair behind her shoulder. His own black hair remained slicked into place. His stern features betrayed no emotion.

But something new and different sparkled in his dark eyes. She couldn't help a rush of excitement as he stared at her.

"That was fun."

The music slowed to a lilting dance number. Tessa wondered if they'd exit the floor. She should probably dash to the bathroom and make sure her makeup wasn't streaming down her face.

But Sebastian pulled her into his arms. "Don't even think of running off."

Tessa laughed. Partly to distract herself from the rather overwhelming sensation of being pulled close to Sebastian's broad chest.

His black suit had an unusual design, a sleek jacket with no lapels and a Nehru collar. Smooth black pants with no crease. Hip and modern, rather than classic and traditional.

The Caspian royal family apparently preferred clean designer lines to gold brocade and rows of medals.

But no amount of well-cut cloth could hide the brawny muscularity of Sebastian's athletic body.

The scent of him, musky and enticing, enveloped her as he held her close, swaying to the music.

"Where were we before we got so rudely interrupted?" His low voice tickled her neck. "Oh, yes. Basketball. High school or college?"

"Both. I got a scholarship to St. Peter's and another one to college. It's the only reason I was able to go to either of them."

"Your family isn't well-off?"

"Not like that. My dad had the same job for forty years. He made a living but not enough to send me to the ritziest school in New England."

"What did he do?"

"Custodial director. That's what he always called himself." She looked right at Sebastian. "At the high school."

His eyebrows lowered slightly in an expression of confusion. "Custodial director. Is that…? I mean, did he…?"

"Clean the school? Yes." It came out a little sharper than she'd intended. But she'd had this discussion before and it usually ended in raucous laughter and raised eyebrows and her never being treated quite the same again.

Which was fine. Better to know who will treat you fairly and with respect, and who won't.

She looked at him, ready to see laughter and derision in his eyes.

Instead she saw something very different.

Admiration.

She sucked in a breath and dragged her attention to the dancers behind her.

"I'm impressed." His deep voice tickled her ear. "Not only can you play basketball competitively, but you managed to negotiate the social jungle of two of the world's most exclusive schools."

"Oh, I don't know that I so much negotiated it as made my own way through with a hatchet." She raised an eyebrow.

He laughed. "I'd have liked to see that."

"It wasn't pretty."

"I guess that depends on your aesthetic." His dark eyes roamed over her face, and her skin heated under his appreciative gaze.

"I bet you fit right in with all those children of CEOs and foreign dignitaries." He tilted his head, stared right into her eyes. "You look like an aristocrat. An American princess."

Tessa burst out laughing. "What does an American princess look like?"

Sebastian's lips twitched as he tried to keep from smiling. "Majestic."

"Well, I guess you're an experienced judge so I'll have to take your word for it."

It was so easy to forget that Sebastian was one of the fabled Crowned Heads of Europe.

You'd expect a monarch—even a future one—to be starched and stodgy. To have clothes tailor-made on Jermyn Street, not in a Milan design atelier.

In his leisure time you'd expect him to wear an earth-toned Harris tweed jacket, not a black Dolce & Gabbana T-shirt that clung to his rippling muscles.

On the other hand, you might well expect a future king to spend his time traveling the world, dancing and yachting and riding and skiing and seducing beautiful women from every nation.

In that sense, Sebastian was every bit a traditional prince.

And she'd better not forget it.

Sebastian couldn't take his eyes off Tessa's lithe body as it moved beneath the subtle sparkle of her dress.

He couldn't take his hands off her, either.

Electricity crackled between them as he held her close in a slow dance hours later. He felt hot and he wished he could peel some clothes off.

But he was too well trained in Royal Dignity for that.

And there'd be plenty of time for peeling clothes off later. In fact, he was making very detailed plans to extract Tessa's gorgeous glowing body—inch by inch—from her slinky gown.

Desire surged in his blood as she smiled at him. Such a warm and open smile. So different from the calculated simpering he'd grown used to.

"Your mom is staring at us." Tessa leaned in.

He could smell the scent of her. Rich and sweet, like honeyed baklava. "Do you think she's upset you're spending so much time dancing with your assistant?" Concern troubled her green eyes.

"No." He leaned in and couldn't resist planting a soft kiss on her ear. "Perhaps she's transfixed by your ravishing beauty."

Tessa blinked.

"Have I embarrassed you?" he said softly.

"Yes." She flashed a glance at him. "I was taught to beware flatterers."

"Wise advice. But many women would be upset if no one stared at them."

Faris, for example. She lived for the spotlight. He kept hoping its bright light would attract a suitor she couldn't resist, so she'd stop trying to sink her manicured talons into him.

His mother had assured him that Faris was "waiting for him."

That was going to be a long wait.

"What are you smiling at?" Tessa smiled, too. He eased closer. Her high heels made her almost his height, and they danced pressed to each other from cheek to hip. Their feet barely moved, though other guests swirled around them to the music.

His blood pulsed in time with the drumbeat. He had to work hard to keep his hands from creeping down to enjoy the curve of her pert bottom.

Her back called to his fingertips, bare in her low-cut dress.

Tessa's cool fingers crept over his shirt collar and roamed into his hair.

He pulled her closer still. Her hips swayed against his,

rhythmic, hypnotic. When he glanced down, her eyes had closed. Her lovely face shone with a rapt expression.

A thick sensation built inside Sebastian's chest. A thicker one started to pound between his legs.

She'd forgotten everyone else in the room. Given herself to the music, their dance.

To him.

Sebastian laid a soft kiss on her neck and she writhed against him.

Her sensual movements surprised him.

Had she forgotten they were surrounded by a thousand people?

Decades of stern training kept him on high alert at all times. Ready to represent the nation of Caspia in everything he did.

But now even he was beginning to lose his firm grip on protocol and etiquette.

Tessa's fingers wound around his neck, pulling his face to hers.

Then their lips met in a cool, fresh kiss.

She tasted like mint. Sharp, spicy and bracing.

Her cool tongue challenged his to a duel, and he couldn't help but spar and parry with it, claiming her mouth in a kiss that deepened with each beat of the music.

The beaded fabric of her dress stirred his senses as he ran his hands over her curves, imagining the feel of the smooth skin beneath.

Hard inside his tailored pants, he suppressed a groan as her soft, wet tongue licked his lips.

He wanted her.

Now.

"Tessa." He growled the word more than spoke it. His

blood had departed his brain for more primal regions of his body.

She didn't respond except to clutch him closer.

Her fingers now ran over his suit jacket, plucking at the stiff fabric.

He fought the urge to peel it off.

"Tessa." He breathed it, trying to arch away from her, his arousal so intense it hurt.

"Sebastian," she rasped, her body pressed to his, still swaying and swinging to the music.

Then she gasped and sprang back.

She staggered back a few feet, crashing into an older couple. The gray-haired old fellow was almost bent double under the weight of his ceremonial medals and he pitched to one side.

"Oh, goodness." She grabbed his arm and righted him. "I'm so sorry!" She glanced at Sebastian, her eyes wide.

She patted her hair, as if it was wild and windblown. A pink flush spread over her cheeks, contrasting prettily with the cool green of her dress.

Sebastian had never seen a more enticing vision.

"Let's go somewhere quiet," he told her.

Her eyes widened. "But we can't. *You* can't." She glanced out at the crowd of dancers swirling around them.

"Oh, yes, I can." Resolve, and painful longing, thickened his voice.

"But it's your family's party. Your parents will be upset if you… They'll think I'm some kind of…" Her blush deepened.

"I don't care what they think. You'd better come with me now, or I'll have the palace guards arrest you and bring you to me."

He saw his own excitement reflected right back at him in sparkling green.

"Gee. I've never been arrested by palace guards before. I might like it."

"Don't tempt me."

"I think I already did."

Her bright gaze dropped to the unseemly bulge beneath his pants.

His erection throbbed.

"If you don't come with me right now, you're in danger of high treason."

Her mouth formed a provocative O.

"It's a capital offense."

She tilted her head and narrowed her bright eyes. "Have a lot of women sacrificed their lives defending their virtue?"

"Not a single one."

His eyes roamed hungrily over the glittering green of her dress, shimmering under the lights like a mermaid's lithe tail.

He couldn't wait. He reached out and grabbed her arm. Her skin felt hot against his palm. The ache in his groin intensified as he pulled her close and wrapped his arm around her waist.

She stiffened, but he didn't loosen his grip. There was no way he'd let her get away now.

He knew she wanted him every bit as much as he wanted her.

Eight

"Where on earth is Sebastian going with that young woman?" Rania, Queen of Caspia, leaned toward her husband. Even her favorite Vivaldi made her head ache tonight.

"I can't say, dear."

"You may not want to say, but I think we both have a pretty good idea. When is that boy going to grow up?"

"Sebastian is thirty-four years old. I think most people would say he is grown up."

Ugh! Her husband could be so obtuse. He simply stood there, staring out over the crowds. All their friends and the crowned heads of every remaining monarchy in Europe gathered under this roof tonight.

While their only son crept off to go get naked with…a servant.

She shivered.

"She's his assistant, for God's sake!"

"Lovely girl."

Her husband's silver hair still curled elegantly around his majestic head. He had the same proud profile and easy good humor that had driven her half-wild as an impressionable girl.

These days he sometimes drove her completely mad.

"Have you forgotten that our son is the future king of Caspia?"

"I am aware of that."

"He should be courting women of his own stature. Girls of noble blood."

"I'm sure Sebastian will choose an excellent wife."

"Sure, are you? What makes you so sure? Lately I don't feel sure of anything."

She fanned herself with a linen cocktail napkin. Another of those awful hot flashes, come to remind her of her own mortality and that the future lay with the next generation.

Which Sebastian might be creating right now with his own office assistant.

She fanned harder.

Her husband turned to her.

Oh, dear. His *stern* look.

"Rania, darling. Sebastian is high-spirited, yes. But he is Caspian to the core. He loves our country and its people with all his soul. He'll rise to the task of devoting his life to them as their king. Why shouldn't he have some fun before he assumes the weighty mantle of responsibility?"

"Oh. Did you miss out on all that fun by marrying me too young?"

"Rania." He pressed a soft kiss behind her ear.

Her knees still buckled slightly when he did that. Her heart softened toward her warm and trusting husband.

"Sweetheart, I'm just worried, that's all. Wouldn't it be better for everyone if he was safely settled down with a nice girl like Faris?"

"Faris is a lot of things. Nice isn't one of them."

Her husband stared out again at the crowds, his expression rigid.

"Darling, Faris is the daughter of your oldest friend. What on earth would Deon say if he heard you?"

"I don't intend for him to hear me, but I don't intend to encourage my son to be a martyr to Faris Maridis, either."

"But they've known each other almost since birth. After our own, her family is the most prominent and oldest in Caspia. She's beautiful. Surely you'll admit that?"

"Yes. No question. She is beautiful. And I pity the poor sod who gets dazzled into marrying her."

"But what if Sebastian does choose someone like his own secretary? Stubborn as he is, he's quite capable of it." She fanned herself again, feeling breathless and faint. "Not only is she American, she's not even from money. Sebastian admitted it himself."

Her husband raised an eyebrow. "You asked him?"

"Well, yes. Why not?"

Her husband burst into a guffaw of laughter.

Rania frowned. Very briefly. Then she reassumed her habitual public expression of beatific contentment.

It wasn't easy being queen.

The French champagne tasted bitter and foul to Faris. *Right in front of everyone!*

Pawing at each other like teenagers. That girl with her head thrown back, eyes closed, swaying in his arms.

Disgusting.

And Sebastian grappling her like a rugby opponent. Without a thought for all their friends and family in attendance.

Anger and humiliation clawed at her gut.

She'd laughed off his dalliances with starlets and socialites. Those fluffy girls were no match for Sebastian Stone. She was invariably gratified when he appeared in the papers with a different girl-of-the-moment the following week.

She really shouldn't concern herself over this scrawny American girl who filed his papers for a living.

Faris adjusted her beautiful midnight-colored dress over her creamy décolletage.

Tessa Banks was a nobody. A member of staff.

So why had Sebastian clung to her as though she held the secret to eternal life?

He'd stared at her. Stroked her.

Kissed her.

She'd never seen that look of distracted preoccupation on his face before.

Faris touched her hair to make sure her chignon was still perfect. You never knew when someone would snap a picture.

Sebastian was *hers*.

They'd both known that since birth. Their mothers had joked about their future marriage from the time they fought over rattles on a blanket spread in the palace gardens.

It was fate.

Destiny.

She would one day be Queen Faris of Caspia.

She didn't mind waiting. She'd waited thirty-four years, for crying out loud! Lucky thing she didn't look a day over twenty-five. But people were starting to talk. It was time for the marriage to happen.

She was determined to extract a proposal from him this year.

By any means necessary.

The sound of the party faded as Sebastian led Tessa down a long corridor. Her heels clacked on the stone floor as she tried to keep up with his swift steps.

"In here." He tugged her into a darkened room and closed the door. Tessa tried to catch her breath. She couldn't see a thing. Electricity crackled in the air between her and Sebastian, heightened by their lightning escape from the party.

A light bloomed under Sebastian's hand. An oil lamp, set into a recess in the wall.

"We don't use electric light in here. Too many precious items that might fade."

"Where are we?" She still couldn't see much in the pulsing gloom of the lamp. A sultry scent, like sandalwood, hung faint in the air.

"This is the oldest part of the palace. The walls here are six-feet thick. No one will hear us."

Desire thickened his voice.

Tessa's face heated and her breasts tingled beneath her dress.

He lit another oil lamp, illuminating a low seating area in a corner of the room. Gold thread shone in the lush fabrics and brocade dangled from thick pillows.

Sebastian took her hand, his skin hot on hers. "Are you tired from dancing?" He stroked her cheek with his thumb.

"Not at all." Excitement hummed in her blood. Her voice sounded breathless. "You?"

He answered her with a hot, hard kiss that stole the last

of her senses. His hands roamed over her dress, over her breasts, her backside, her thighs, with rough and lusty movements quite unlike his restraint at the party.

His eyes were so dark they appeared black, bottomless and brimming with desire.

For a moment she thought he might rip off her couture dress in one swift movement. But he turned her gently, his hands at her waist. He undid the hooks and eyes along the back of her dress with skilled fingers. Even if the expense meant nothing to him, Sebastian appreciated the artistry and hard work that went into designer originals. The heavy, beaded fabric slid over her like a lover's caress.

"You were beautiful in the dress, but without it…" He exhaled softly.

His fingers sparked trails of shimmering excitement. He unhooked her bra and carefully removed it. A slight breeze through a high window stung her nipples to tight awareness.

She tried not to wobble as he layered kisses along her spine. Kneeling behind her, he tugged her skimpy silk panties down over her legs, until she wore nothing but her strappy high heels.

He stood and she turned to face him. The look on his face transfixed her. Raw lust, yes, but something deeper and more powerful shone in his eyes and hardened his strong features.

Desire echoed through her like a crack of thunder. He'd shed his jacket and she'd been reaching up to unbutton his shirt, but suddenly her hands fell lower, and they both struggled with the fly of his pants, shoved them down and rolled on the condom.

He entered her slowly, cupping her buttocks as she pressed the length of her body against his. Aroused almost to boiling point, she gripped him as he thrust his hard length into her.

Against her back, the cool stone of an ancient column felt heavenly. It held her upright as Sebastian devoured her mouth and drove into her body with forceful thrusts.

The pent-up taut desire that had built like a fire while they danced could no longer be contained. Tremors rippled between them as their bellies clashed. Sebastian's rough kisses only strengthened her agonizing craving to draw him closer. To become one, even for a moment.

The mere touch of his lips unleashed a starburst of bright light and color in front of her eyes. The teasing scratch of his nails set her skin shivering and tingling.

She bucked against him, taking him deeper, clawing at the fabric of his shirt.

Sebastian thrust harder, taking her further on the journey out of her body and mind and into an alternate dimension of fierce, pounding desire that made her blood thunder in her veins.

The world dissolved—along with all barriers between them—as they exploded into orgasm. The rush was so intense that Tessa lost consciousness for a split second before she crashed back to life in Sebastian's strong arms.

Bittersweet relief rang through her as the tension slipped from her body and she held on to her lover for dear life.

Sebastian released a groan in her ear. His shirt was bunched up over the thick muscles of his chest, forgotten in their urgency. Tessa's arms were fast under it, wrapped around his hot, perspiring skin.

His heady male scent stole over her senses, making her want to bury her face in his neck and drink him in.

"Much better," he murmured, holding her tight.

She wanted to laugh, but she knew exactly how he felt. "Me, too." Still, her legs were shaking. "Maybe we should sit down before we fall down."

"Good idea." He eased out of her carefully and she shivered, already craving him inside her again.

Worse yet, he disappeared into the shadows, leaving her naked against the cool stone pillar.

He returned with a long sweep of silk fabric. "Lift your arms."

She obeyed. He wrapped the material, purple with a gold border, around her with practiced movements, then secured it at her shoulder with a gold pin. The fine silk fell to the floor, billowing slightly in the breeze.

"I feel like I've stepped into a myth."

"Maybe you have." His deep voice rippled through the air like smoke.

She gasped as Sebastian swept her right off her spike-heeled feet and into his arms. He marched across the room and laid her gently on soft cushions in the sitting area.

A bowl of fragrant oil smoldered over a tiny candle, filling the room with its seductive scent.

"Champagne?"

Sebastian had stripped off his crumpled shirt and his bronzed torso gleamed in the scant light.

"Um, sure."

He moved to a wall behind her, and drew out a bottle.

"What is this room used for?" She still couldn't make out much in the dark.

"It's the antechamber behind the throne room. Guests are sometimes entertained here during official functions."

"Ah. That explains the champagne." She took the offered glass, bubbles sparkling in the warm glow from the candle. "And you keep silk robes on hand in case anyone spills Bollinger on their clothes?"

Sebastian smiled slowly. "The robe you're wearing is from our national collection. It was created by royal weavers who once did nothing but create cloth for the family."

"Oh, goodness." Tessa's skin shrank from the priceless history draped over it. "I'm not sure I should be wearing it. I'm kind of sweaty."

Sebastian shrugged. "What's the use of keeping something that cannot be worn? The weavers put their heart and skill into creating the finest fabrics known to mankind. I'm sure they'd rather their efforts caress a beautiful woman glowing with the heat of passion, than sit in a trunk waiting for moths to find them."

Glowing. Okay, that worked. "The silk is as soft as fleece. Was it made recently?"

Sebastian made a wry expression. "No, I'm afraid royal weavers went the way of the royal soothsayers. The events of the twentieth century encroached on Caspia as they did every corner of Europe. It's a miracle that we still have our treasures. The crown jewels are kept locked in the vault here, too. Would you like to see them?"

Tessa's eyebrows shot up. "Sure, I'd love to." She started to get up.

"Wait here. I'll bring them to you."

The mysterious gleam in his eye made her stomach flutter. Or was that an aftershock from her orgasm? She sipped her champagne and fanned herself, which made the incense flame flicker.

Sebastian returned with a large box of dark wood, intricately carved with figures. His thick arms strained under its weight.

"Goodness, what's in there? Gold bricks?"

He chuckled and studied her face, her neck.

She heated under his regard.

He lifted the lid, reached into the box and plucked out something shiny. "This one."

Something sparkled in the dim light, but she couldn't make out details.

Sebastian reached over her shoulders and laid cool, heavy metal on her collarbones. He fastened it behind her neck.

"Beautiful."

"It's a necklace?" She touched it with her fingers. The metal was heavily ornamented, encrusted with jewels. Carnelian maybe? It was hard to tell in the darkness. "What are these?"

"Rubies."

She sucked in a breath. "And the necklace is gold?"

"Twenty-four karat."

"Isn't pure gold very soft?"

"Yes, that's why it must be saved for special occasions." He looked right into her eyes. "Like tonight."

That fluttering sensation again.

Sebastian pulled out another gem-encrusted treasure. "Hold out your right wrist."

He fastened the linked bracelet, heavy as a manacle and almost as tight, around her wrist. "You're slim, like the ancient people. It fits you perfectly." He caressed her wrist with his thumb.

"How old are these pieces?"

"They date back at least to the time of the Byzantine Empire, but they may be centuries, even millennia older. Caspia was sacked in 550 A.D. during the reign of Justinian. The library was burned and all records destroyed. Our history up to that point is as much legend as fact."

He plucked out a slim ring of gold, like a headband. He turned it so the single gem was at the front, then settled it on her forehead.

Like a crown.

Tessa felt her face heat. As much from Sebastian's serious expression as from the weird situation.

Never in her wildest dreams had she imagined she'd wind up sitting in the Caspian Palace, dressed as a royal princess. Suddenly she felt like a chimp decked out for a tea party.

"Why so jumpy?"

"It's just weird, that's all. I don't feel right in these things."

Sebastian took her hand and pulled her gently to her feet. "Nonsense." He took a couple of steps back. She stood there, swaying in her heels, as his eyes roamed over her, searing her flesh right through the thin silk. "These jewels are flattered by your beauty." His voice rumbled, echoing slightly off the stone walls. "As if they were made for you."

Sebastian couldn't take his eyes off her.

His golden goddess, tall and regal, her striking features chiseled by the chiaroscuro of candlelight. The draping silk displayed her magnificent body to perfection and the heavy majesty of the gold pieces enhanced her natural proud stance.

He couldn't think. Could barely breathe.

"It's just me. Tessa." Her green eyes were wary.

"I know. That's why I can't stop staring."

"It must be kind of bizarre seeing your royal jewels on a regular person. I'd better take them off."

"No!" The word flew out. "I love to see you in them. Partly because you are 'a regular person' as you call it. I love that about you. You're not jaded and bored with the pleasures of life, like so many women I meet."

"I guess that's because I haven't had the opportunity to burn out yet. A few more grand balls, a hundred more boat trips in the harbor, a thousand gallops across the country-side and I might be yawning behind my champagne glass, too." Her eyes sparkled.

"Never."

"How do you know?"

"I'm a good judge of character."

She lifted her chin. "I did get bored with being your assistant."

He couldn't help smiling. "I don't blame you. It was a boring job."

"I'm afraid I'm better at riding than at typing corre-spondence."

"Most emphatically."

Her eyes widened.

"I didn't mean that your correspondence is lacking," he turned to add. "Just that you're being wasted on it. You're meant for so much more than sitting at a desk, talking on the phone."

"Like what?" She crossed her arms over her chest, the provocative and unladylike gesture a sharp and delicious contrast with the traditional attire.

He loved it.

You are meant to be my queen.

His brain threw out the words. He blinked, swallowed and cleared his throat. "Let's sleep in my bed," he rasped.

Her eyes widened.

"There's a secret passage. No one will see us." He knew Tessa would prefer to keep it a secret and he wanted to preserve her modesty.

He scooped up the box. "We'll take these with us. I think I need to see them all on you."

She laughed. "I won't argue. A girl doesn't get dressed up in ancient treasures every day."

He gathered their clothes, and with his arm around her waist, he led her through the low, arched doorway in the thick walls, and along the dark, cold passage that led from the old palace to the relatively modern fourteenth-century wing.

On the dark silk sheets of his bed, he dressed her in deep blue lapis, the gold-flecked stone mystical in the candlelight against her golden skin.

Then emeralds. The heavy collar circled her slender neck and brought out the vivid green of her eyes.

Magic.

The familiar environment of his bedroom—the room he had slept in since birth and which he would one day share with his wife—seemed transformed by her presence.

True, he had invited girls to try on the royal collection before. This particular seduction technique was surefire. He'd recommend it to anyone with a priceless collection of ancient treasures and a beautiful but hesitant woman.

Right now, he was the one being seduced. Not by the sight of hammered gold or precious jewels, but by the splendid woman wearing them.

"You're spoiling me, Sebastian. What if I wake up tomorrow and just don't feel like myself without emeralds on?"

"There's an easy cure for that. Emeralds."

"Being a prince definitely makes you lose touch with reality."

"I'm in touch with reality," he protested. Mostly he wanted to touch her breasts, high and enticing. Or her thighs, sleek, long and gleaming in the warm light.

"There won't be any emeralds in my life once I go home."

He frowned. Go home? Why on earth was she thinking about that now? The prospect wrenched at his gut.

"There will always be emeralds in your life," he growled. "Your eyes."

Her sweet laughter tickled his ears. "You're sweeping me off my feet and it's not a nice thing to do. I have a regular life to go back to. I think Caspia has ruined me for everywhere else."

"You're falling in love with our country?"

She startled a little when he said the *L* word.

Truth be told, he did, too.

She recovered quickly. "How could I not? Everything about it is perfect. The sea, the sky, the mountains, the lovely people."

"The dust, the flies, roaming goats, the smell of raw fish." He narrowed his eyes and tried not to smile.

Her eyes shone. "Exactly. They're all perfect."

His chest tightened as a rush of feeling flowed through him. He did love everything about his country. Even the things others might criticize. Now Tessa felt the same?

Perfect.

She'd better not be thinking about going back to Phil or Paul or whatever his name was. Throwing her life away in a gamble for some elusive happy-ever-after.

He'd cure her of him.

By the time he was done with her tonight, she wouldn't be able to think about anyone. She'd be too exhausted, satiated and suffused with pleasure to remember her own name.

He'd make sure of it.

Desire shivered through him. He wanted her naked again, with nothing between them. The jewels ornamented her beauty, but didn't enhance it.

Tessa was most beautiful as simply herself.

He unhooked the heavy emerald necklace and pressed a warm kiss to her lips.

Her tongue sneaked into his mouth as she kissed him back with passion. Forgotten, the strings of green gems slid between her lush, high breasts and got lost somewhere down in the sheets.

Sebastian got lost somewhere in her lips, in the soft embrace of her arms and the rich sweet scent of her.

When he made love to her again, he didn't think about charming her or cajoling her or trying to win her over.

He couldn't think about anything. His heart was too full with emotions he couldn't name.

His heart?

His friends teased him for being heartless, but Sebastian always laughed it off. He wasn't heartless. In fact, he was very affectionate and caring.

Just on a short-term basis.

But tonight…

Tessa's head lay on the pillow next to him, her golden lashes lowered in sweet sleep, her hair flung back from her lovely face.

He drew in a long, sharp breath, which didn't ease the strange fullness in his chest.

He had a heart, all right. And he was in serious danger of losing it.

Nine

Tessa didn't show up at breakfast.

Not to worry, Sebastian told himself. She was a big girl and he wasn't her shadow.

Sebastian sat at the table and helped himself to some eggs. His dad was immersed in the London *Times* and his mom was already gabbing on the phone about some charity luncheon.

He yawned and reached for the silver tray with his mail. He tried to forget the groaning stack of unread correspondence in his New York apartment. A couple of party invitations. A postcard from his pal Ravi, trekking in Nepal. He slit open a slim ivory envelope with his silver opener.

He saw black letters, printed so neatly a machine could have done it.

You are the future King of Caspia.
Your children will rule Caspia one day.
Do not insult our nation and take a foreign bride.
Especially one who is of low birth.

There was a long gap on the paper.
Then the words.

Like Tessa Banks.

Sebastian's empty stomach growled, as much with rage as hunger. Who *dared* to insult Tessa in this way?

He lifted the coffeepot from its open-flame burner and placed the crumpled sheet directly on the flames. It withered into a leaf, then turned to ash.

His mother looked up. "What on earth are you doing, dear?"

"Destroying trash."

"You could have asked Theo for a wastepaper basket."

"Yes." He ripped off a hunk of fresh bread. He was used to petty jealousies and trumped-up scandals. Gossipmongers looking for drama.

They came with the territory of monarchy.

Already the note drifted from his mind like the burned-out embers.

In the spacious palace offices, Tessa spread her notes and contact information out on an antique desk. She planned to call all the meeting attendees to confirm their arrival times and remind them what was expected of them

She'd even dressed in a smart beige pantsuit. She was here on business, and intended to remind people of that fact. Lately she'd noticed the staff giving her sideways looks in the hallways. No doubt they wondered what she was up to, gallivanting all over Caspia with their prince when she was here to arrange a meeting and organize some files.

Whatever they were thinking, she'd prove them wrong.

Well, not *wrong,* exactly. It was a bit late for that.

She pushed her hair out of her eyes and blew out a breath.

She'd succumbed to Sebastian's charms like so many other women before her.

She probably never stood a chance. Everything about Sebastian was intoxicating. His energy and spirit, his warmth and passion, his kindness and—

Hello, you have a job to do.

Tessa flipped through the numbers in her PDA and was about to dial the first.

Then she hesitated. She suddenly remembered the way Sebastian had looked at her last night, as she sat on his magnificent bed, decked out in his country's royal splendor.

The memory took her breath away. His eyes, dark and wide and so full of…love.

Impossible?

Suddenly hot, she lifted her hair off her neck. It was hard to think. Thoughts of Sebastian consumed her mind and tormented her body.

She couldn't forget his rough yet gentle hands on her body, his rousing kisses, or the lovemaking that left her gasping and shivering with ecstasy.

Then there were his intimate conversation, his genial smiles and encouraging caresses.

Of course, he was warm and enthusiastic with everyone. Sebastian never met a person, or an animal, he didn't like. She'd even seen him give a friendly and encouraging pat to an olive tree.

She couldn't help smiling as her chest filled with affection for him.

They'd worked together for nearly five years and their relationship had always been professional. Cordial. Polite.

Suddenly it was so different.

He'd danced with her in front of hundreds of guests at the ball. Held her and kissed her as if she was his…girlfriend. Was she totally delusional in imagining it as a possibility?

Her PDA screen had gone blank. *Hey, you're here to work.* She snapped herself to attention and punched the button to make the first call. It would be embarrassing if no one showed up for the meeting.

Still, she wondered if Sebastian was already looking for her. Maybe even heading toward her right now.

Her fingers and toes tingled with delicious anticipation.

Once the first round of phone calls was made, the sun was high in the sky. She decided to step out onto the terrace outside the offices and enjoy the view of the harbor and some heliotheraphy while she typed the agenda from her notes.

She stepped over the threshold, put her laptop on a carved, stone table and stretched.

Then she noticed someone watching her.

A tall, slim woman. Standing on the far side of the long terrace, in the opposite direction from the harbor.

"Ms. Banks." The woman's voice rang out across the stone tiles.

"Hello?" Tessa squinted in the sun. It wasn't the queen, but she looked vaguely familiar.

Faris. The woman from last night with the blue dress and the snotty remarks. What was she doing here?

Faris marched toward her, heels clicking on the stone tiles. A long white dress draped over her slender yet voluptuous body.

"I imagine you're busy arranging all the details of your little meeting."

Tessa's back stiffened. "It's a pretty big meeting. Thirty principals."

Faris waved an elegant hand. A tinkly laugh grated on Tessa's ears. "How tiresome to put it all together. I do admire you working girls. I'd never be able to keep up a fake smile while wading through all that drudgery."

"Hardly drudgery here on this lovely terrace. I couldn't be happier." Tessa forced a bright smile. Her hand itched to slap Faris's expertly made-up cheek, but she managed to resist.

"It must be marvelous to be content with so little. But I suppose you get used to it." Faris glanced out at the horizon, as if deep in philosophical contemplation. "I imagine the difficult part will be going back to the rat race once you've become used to living in a palace."

"I suspect I'll manage." Tessa arranged her papers on the table. She tried not to think about how hard it really would be to return to the dreary world of subway platforms and electric bills.

There wasn't going to be any liberating move to California now. By sleeping with Sebastian she'd slammed the door on that possible future.

Unease tightened her muscles, along with guilt that she'd cheated on Patrick and fear of what lay ahead of her now. She wasn't really foolish enough to think that she had a future with Sebastian.

Was she?

"Sebastian's such a charmer, isn't he?" Faris stood over her, casting a long shadow across Tessa's notes. "Let me guess. He gave you his famous 'royal treatment.'"

Tessa frowned. "Sebastian has been very gracious."

Faris tilted her head. "Which did he choose first? The gold diadem or the emerald necklace?" A smile played about her perfectly shaped mouth.

Tessa's own mouth dropped open.

"Oh, come on. Just between us girls. Those rubies are heavy, aren't they?"

"I—I don't know what you're talking about." She swallowed hard.

Faris narrowed her dark eyes. "Did you think you were special?" She pouted. "Oh. Sebastian can be quite wicked. Don't take it personally, though. He doesn't mean to break your heart, he just can't help it."

Her laugh rattled in the air. "And you shouldn't feel bad, either. Half the women of Europe have worn those jewels with stars in their eyes, myself included."

Tessa was seeing stars in front of her eyes right now. Her desire to slap Faris was morphing into a desire to get face-to-face with Sebastian and—

She sucked in a deep breath. "I hate to be so…bourgeois, but I'm afraid I have work to do."

Faris smiled. "Of course you do. I just thought I should warn you. That's all. As a *friend*."

The final word dripped with malice.

Tessa's good cheer plummeted with each farewell click of Faris's sharp heels.

She sagged into the cushioned wrought iron chair. The bright sun and the glare of white buildings and blue sea hurt her eyes.

How naive could she be?

Did she really think Sebastian dressed her up like a queen because he wanted to make her *his* queen?

It was a little fun foreplay for him.

A practiced seduction technique.

Not that he needed to seduce her. She'd been ready to rip his clothes off on the dance floor.

Besides, they'd already made love—no, scratch that, they'd had sex—before he started weighing her down with jewels.

She drew in a ragged breath. She had nothing to be ashamed of. She hadn't begged to get decked out like a Homerian goddess. It was all his idea.

And he had enjoyed it.

Even now her heart swelled as she remembered the caress of his dark eyes. Of his big, gentle hands.

Her PDA vibrated and she picked it up.

The number on the screen made her heart thud.

She inhaled and composed herself. "Hi, Sebastian. How are you?"

"That depends on how you are." His low, seductive voice tickled her ear.

"I'm fine."

"Theo told me you had breakfast early so you could get to work."

"Yes. I had to call the meeting attendees. Make sure they're coming." She could barely get the words out. "I'm about to type the agenda."

"Can you fit me into your agenda today?" His tone

was warm and flirtatious. She couldn't help a stirring of excitement in her chest.

Then the image of Faris, mocking her about the jewels, cooled her blood. "You're the boss."

"Oh, yeah. I forgot about that. Want to go for a ride?"

"I can't. I haven't even started the agenda yet and the meeting is tomorrow. Let me get it typed up so you can look at it. This afternoon I'll print and collate the copies."

"I'm sure someone else could do all that."

"It's my job."

"Magna misses you."

"Who?"

"Your horse. She told me this morning."

"Oh, stop." She couldn't resist chuckling. "She's probably plotting her revenge."

"I'm plotting my revenge. I can't believe you beat me to the top of the crag last time. I've got a reputation to defend."

Tessa's blood heated with the thought of racing up the mountainside on the athletic and bighearted mare.

The prospect of another carefree, exhilarating day with Sebastian.

But it wouldn't be the same. Not now that she knew the magical night they'd shared had been a standard offering from his well-worn repertoire.

Her heart clenched. "I wish I could, but there's so little time left that I need to focus and get this done. I've goofed off enough already."

"It doesn't count as goofing off when it's on the boss's orders."

He sounded so cheerful. He obviously thought he had her thoroughly under his spell.

Which was true, until a few minutes ago.

She actually owed a debt of gratitude to the mean-spirited Faris.

"I should command you to cease and desist all tiresome administrative activities."

"I'm not in the mood to be commanded."

"I might be."

Oh, why could she picture his mischievous grin so clearly? Her chest hurt with trying to fight off emotion.

"Seriously, I *want* to get this done." At least then she would have actually accomplished something here in Caspia other than being Sebastian's Playmate-of-the-Week.

"Okay, okay. But don't miss lunch or I'll have the royal guard hunt you down. One o'clock in the dining room."

"Sure." She hung up.

She could make it through another lunch. Another dinner even. She could smile and be polite and hold her chin up.

The meeting was tomorrow and after that she could begin the heartbreaking process of leaving behind the most wonderful days of her life.

Of trying to forget Sebastian.

"Tessa!" Sebastian rose to greet her as she entered the dining room on trembling legs. She hadn't seen Sebastian's parents—aka the king and queen—since her embarrassing display at the ball the previous night.

"Good afternoon," she said with what she hoped was an obsequious nod.

"Come sit here next to Mama." Sebastian indicated an empty chair. His mother looked every bit as surprised and not-delighted as Tessa. What was he trying to pull?

She did like the way he still called his mother "Mama." It was kind of cute.

For a womanizing jerk.

Sebastian held out the chair next to his mother for Tessa then returned to his seat on the other side of her. His father sat farther down the table, perusing a newspaper folded open to the crossword puzzle.

The prickly and poised Queen of Caspia surveyed Tessa down the length of her elegant nose. "How are preparations for the meeting coming?"

Tessa opened her mouth to reply, but Sebastian cut her off.

"She doesn't want to talk about that boring stuff. Didn't she look radiant at the dance last night?"

His dark eyes shone with the same admiration she dimly remembered from— Oh, my gosh. It was only this morning he'd layered soft, wet kisses over her neck and breasts.

"Yes. That was a pretty dress, dear. From one of your new boutiques?" She managed her entire response without glancing at Tessa.

Sebastian shot Tessa a warm smile. He didn't seem to notice she wasn't glowing back. A young man in a white uniform served her bread and salads, and she tried to eat a bite or two. But it was hard.

Last night had been so magical. So special and so perfect.

And now here was Sebastian right in front of her. Brawny arms revealed by the rolled-up sleeves of his white linen shirt, and his sun-bronzed face creased in a cheery grin.

He was exactly the same person he'd been yesterday. The easygoing royal playboy who dated a different girl every week.

It was she who had changed.

Her throat dried as she realized the full extent of the problem.

She'd fallen in love with him.

"…haven't forgotten the Sons of the Garter benefit tonight, have you?" Sebastian's mother leaned forward.

Sebastian frowned. "Oh, that again? I thought I just survived the last one."

"These men are our nation's heroes. Some of them fought in World War II."

"I think *all* of them fought in World War II. There can't be a man under eighty in the Order of the Garter."

"All the more reason to pay your respects and celebrate their achievements. It's part of your royal duty."

She underscored the last two words with a slight growl that made Tessa jump in her chair.

"I know, and I do appreciate their sacrifices." Sebastian looked at Tessa and leaned forward. "These men have some amazing stories to tell. Wait till you hear Leo Kahn talk about the time he—"

"Tessa won't be there." The queen's lips were so tight the words barely came out. "The event is for gentlemen only."

Sebastian shot an apologetic glance at Tessa. She resisted the urge to sag in her chair with relief. She couldn't imagine spending another night at his side, pretending to be cheerful and gregarious when her heart was crushed and bleeding inside her.

"Besides, I imagine Tessa will be busy with preparations for the meeting. It's not fair to divert members of staff from their duties for your own entertainment."

She shot a piercing glance at Tessa and then punctuated it with an icy smile that froze Tessa's already shrunken stomach.

Sebastian waved a dismissive hand. "Tessa's never been to Caspia before. She represents our country every day in the business we do. It's essential that she become familiar with our nation."

The queen stabbed a piece of tomato, then glared at Sebastian with narrowed eyes. "There's such a thing as being *too* familiar."

"Too familiar?" The king's gruff voice chimed in. "Impossible. The whole world should know our nation like an intimate friend." His twinkly smile eased the tension in Tessa's gut. "Which aspects of our country have you enjoyed so far, my dear?"

Your son.

Tessa swallowed hard. "Sebastian was kind enough to take me for a ride in the mountains. I can't say I've ever had a more wonderful experience in my life." Her voice cracked a bit on the last sentence, and she looked down at her plate.

"Ah, the mountains. Said like a true Caspian. People praise our calm water and our classical buildings, but a Caspian knows the mountains are the bones of our country and our source of strength. They've protected us from invasion for hundreds of years. I like nothing better than a ride in the mountains, myself." The king leaned toward her, a look of genuine warmth on his face.

Tessa shrank back. He wouldn't be so friendly if he knew what she'd been doing with his only son last night. If he knew that she, Tessa Banks, secretary—nobody—

had entertained mad and delusional thoughts that Sebastian might actually care for her.

That right now she was rendered speechless by unfamiliar and painful feelings for him.

"Tessa—" the queen's voice cut into her thoughts "—are all the attendees for the meeting confirmed?"

She cleared her throat and tried to sound calm. "All except one. Pierre de Rochefauld of Château D'Arc winery has been hard to reach."

"Filthy stuff, anyway." The queen spoke to Sebastian. "Loaded with sulfites. Their Bordeaux gave me a frightful migraine last time I drank it."

"Everything gives you a migraine lately, Mama. You should stick to our Caspian grappa." Sebastian took her hand and squeezed it. Tessa was surprised to see the Queen of Mean pat her son's face affectionately.

Maybe she wasn't made entirely of Caspian marble.

Queen Rania's steely gaze returned to spear Tessa. "So all is ready for the meeting?"

"Not quite. I still need to make copies of the agenda, and I have some research to do in the files."

"We mustn't keep you." The queen raised her brows as she attacked another slice of tomato.

"You're right. I must get back to work." Tessa sprang from her chair, glad of the chance to escape.

"I'll come with you." Sebastian was up and halfway around the table before he'd finished speaking.

"Sebastian! You promised you'd take me to the new Ferragamo boutique this afternoon."

Sebastian leaned over his mother and kissed her on the cheek. "Mama, you've been to every Ferragamo boutique in the world. I'm sure you can handle it by yourself."

The queen pouted and shot a glance at her husband. Tessa scurried from the room, heart pounding, with Sebastian behind her like a shadow.

"Don't mind Mama. She's not always such an old battle-ax," he whispered, as they hurried along an empty corridor. "She's going through the change of life and it's making her cranky."

Tessa didn't think hormones were involved. More likely Queen Rania felt it beneath her dignity to eat lunch with her son's whore-of-the-moment.

But Sebastian's apologetic expression, combined with the intimate family confession, tugged at something inside her.

Then she remembered Faris's words: *He doesn't mean to break your heart. He just can't help it.*

And apparently she just couldn't help having her heart broken. How could she not fall for Sebastian? She'd been carrying a secret torch for him for years. Now that she'd gotten to know him even better, now that they'd shared joyful adventures and breathtaking intimacies… It should be no surprise she was done for.

She hurried along the corridor. "You should take your mom shopping. I have a lot to do."

"I'll help you with your work." His hand on her arm made her start. She pulled back carefully, ignoring the heat left by his palm.

"There's nothing at all challenging to it. I just need to locate some missing audits. Things that didn't make it to New York for whatever reason. We never received the files on Château D'Arc."

"And now you can't get in touch with the company principal?"

"No. He's the owner, too. He inherited the wine business along with the family estate. I've been meaning to follow up more aggressively, but I haven't had time." She shot him an accusatory look.

"Hmm. I'll call him from the offices."

"That might be a good idea, actually. His assistant keeps making strange excuses. I get a weird feeling he's actually there when I call. He'd come to the phone for you."

"Royalty has its privileges." Sebastian winked.

Tessa smiled, then it withered on her lips as she remembered all the privileges he'd taken with her last night. It probably didn't even cross his mind that a night like that could haunt her forever.

He'd probably already started to forget it. He'd think no more of her than Senator Kendrick would have if she'd let him kiss her because he was a senator. Wealthy and powerful men had no need to consider the feelings of others.

By next week, Sebastian would be flirting and laughing with someone else.

"What's the matter?"

"Nothing." Her breathing had become audible. The thought of Sebastian with another woman was a knife to her gut.

Which was ridiculous, because of course she would see him with other women. Unless she steered clear of every glossy magazine and skipped over the social pages of the New York papers for the rest of her life.

She picked up her pace. Did these corridors go on forever? There must be miles of them inside this palace.

Sebastian hovered so close behind her she could almost feel his body heat in the still air.

When they reached the office, she thrust her Rolodex

at him, where it sat flipped open to Pierre de Rochefauld's office number at Château D'Arc. He whipped out his phone and she rushed off to the file room that was down some stairs on the far side of the office.

She heard Sebastian greeting someone in French as she pushed deeper into the long, tunnel-like room. Thick walls rose into an arch over her head. This room must have been some kind of storage cellar in the old days. The newest paperwork was in a long metal filing cabinet in the office itself. Down here, the older papers were kept in wooden crates stacked side by side on ancient wood shelves.

Where could the Château D'Arc stuff be? There were a few token papers in the recent files, but no sign of the audits, or any hard financial data. Maybe they got buried in with the old papers?

"Tessa." Sebastian appeared in the arched doorway. He stepped down into the cramped space, and her body tingled with the urge to step toward him—and an equal but opposite urge to run for her life. His dark eyes shone in the dim light from a single, uncovered bulb. "You were right. He was there. Prickly guy, but he says he's coming to the meeting."

"Thanks for making the call." She moved her fingers through a box of files, and avoided looking at him. "I appreciate it."

He walked through the room, moved up behind her and settled his hands on her waist. He pulled her close until her backside touched the crotch of his pants. "All work and no play makes Tessa—"

"Useful." She tried to wriggle away, but his hands held her fast. "I came here to work and I'm totally embarrassed by how little I've done. I'm sure your mom isn't the only one who's noticed."

He rubbed one hand over her tummy. His broad palm heated her skin right through her smart suit. "Come on, Tessa. Let's go up on the mountain. We'll ride and then we'll…" He leaned into her and feathered a soft kiss— with warm tongue—on her neck right below her ear.

Her legs wobbled and her nipples tightened under her blouse. "I can't," she rasped. "I have to find the files." She couldn't do that again. Have the most breathtaking ride of her life, then make love to Sebastian under the sky.

Not now that she loved him. It would hurt too much. She'd start crying or begging or something.

She had no idea what she'd do. She'd never been in love before.

And already it hurt more than all the songs and poems had warned her.

"I don't want to." It was the truth.

"Why?" He stopped layering breathy kisses on her neck.

"I want to do my job for the same reasons you're going to that ceremonial dinner tonight. It's your duty, and doing it gives you a sense of satisfaction."

"Oh, Tessa." He rubbed his hands over her blouse, over her breasts and belly, then down along her thighs. "You're driving me crazy. I want you. *Now.*"

She could feel his erection hard against her backside. Feel herself growing hot and slick against him. Her face heated with the desire to kiss him. To strip his clothes off right here in the dim and dusty file room. To rub her hands over his rough thighs, and lave his hard muscle with her tongue.

Uh-oh.

This was the crazy part of her talking. The part that got her in way over her head and was now about to wrap her in a cement overcoat if she didn't save herself.

"Sebastian." She writhed against him, struggling to free herself, but only getting more aroused and dangerously unhinged in the process. Already he had her shirt untucked and his fingers roved over her bra. "Please stop."

His hand stilled. He must have noticed the pleading tone in her voice. "Last night was fun, but...not now."

"Last night was more than fun." Desire thickened his voice.

So true. Right now it was a disaster. She'd fallen in love with her boss.

For whom she was just another playful pastime.

He picked up her hair and laid it gently behind her shoulders. "I understand." He kissed her bared cheekbone. "Truly, I do. There is joy that comes with fulfilling responsibilities, and pain that comes from shirking them."

"Yes." She flipped through some files, pretending she was actually getting back to work.

He backed away. Already she felt his absence like raw skin under a freshly picked scab. "You're one in a million, Tessa."

His footsteps retreated behind her and she sank against the wooden box in front of her, heart pounding and tears rising in her throat.

One in a million, indeed. Perhaps she should feel honored to be included among the many beautiful women Sebastian had bedded.

But she didn't. She felt devastated.

Ten

Sebastian strode along the east corridor, whistling despite his uncomfortable erection. It would go away. Eventually.

Then tonight, after the Sons of the Garter dinner, he'd go to Tessa's room and they'd make love all night long.

Love. He rolled the word over his tongue, silently tasting it.

Yes. He liked it. What he felt for Tessa was totally unlike anything he'd experienced before. His heart flapped in his chest on grand eagle wings and he longed to shout his feelings from the parapets. He should laugh at himself for being so thoroughly smitten with her.

But why not? Her beauty was just the beginning. Tessa Banks was also smart, practical and determined. Energetic and enthusiastic. He loved when her green eyes sparkled with mischief. She was cheeky and fun.

An arched opening at the end of the corridor framed a

view of the harbor. He stopped and watched a fine sailboat enter through the harbor mouth.

And Tessa understood about duty.

She was the kind of woman who'd accept that she was marrying a country, as well as a man. With her by his side, he could feel himself at last transformed into a man steady and strong enough to lead his people.

And to be her husband.

"Sebastian!" A low female voice rang along the stone corridor.

Faris.

His erection withered. Sebastian managed to grunt a greeting. Her father was his dad's oldest and dearest back-gammon and fishing buddy.

Shame he was also the man who'd watched Caspia Designs slide downhill over the past decade.

"Hello, my darling." Faris gathered his face in her horrible soft hands and pressed her rubbery lips to his cheek.

"What are you doing here?"

"Daddy's playing boules with your father. I came along to keep him company. I'm so glad I ran into you as I'm gasping for some sea air. You can take me out on the *Mirabella*."

"Plenty of sea air here on the balcony." He gestured to the view of the harbor.

"Oh, don't be a big grouch. Though I don't blame you for being a bit on edge after the way your secretary behaved last night."

"What are you talking about?" he growled.

"Pawing you like a rock groupie in front of everyone. So vulgar and embarrassing. But what can you expect? American girls aren't raised with any sense of propriety."

Sebastian's blood pumped with force. If Faris Maridis were a man, she'd be out cold on the hard stone by now.

"Don't you ever…" His voice was so low he could hardly hear it. "*Ever*…speak of Tessa Banks that way again." He stared right into Faris's soulless, kohl-lined eyes. "I am delighted to be the happy recipient of her affections. You are the one with no sense of propriety, insulting my guest in my own home."

Faris's long neck stiffened. "So that's how it is. Well, I'm sure you'll come to your senses sooner or later."

Sebastian battled the urge to hurl some choice insults after her, or order her off the property. But he was too well schooled in the art of diplomacy. Their families had been close allies and friends for hundreds of years and this insult was a tiny mosquito sting in the grand scheme of things.

He turned back to enjoy the view of the harbor as Faris's heels rang a brisk retreat down the corridor. His muscles stung with the urge to move, to run or fight…or make love. But he'd prove to Tessa that he could respect her wishes and keep his hands off her.

He struck out for the stables. Maybe a ride in the mountains would cool his blood.

But it didn't. Sebastian and a lathered Alto spun in agitated circles on the mountaintop, neither able to settle enough to enjoy the view. Even the ocean below seemed to heave with discontent, the sun glittering off restless peaks outside the harbor.

That night his frustration increased when the rounds of formal speeches by the Sons of the Garter continued until 2:00 a.m. Too late to disturb his lovely Tessa.

He spent an uncomfortable night aching for the soft embrace of her affectionate arms. And dreaming of the morning sunlight in her bright eyes.

"Tessa!" Sebastian's voice ricocheted off the stone columns and floors and bounced along the grand corridor.

Tessa's heart surged. But she clung tighter to the sheaf of meeting agendas in her arms. She refused to let her excitement show on her face. "Good morning, Sebastian."

He strode toward her, grabbed her and kissed her on the cheek. His lips stirred a flush of heat that spread across her face.

How could he kiss her here in front of everyone? Three of the distinguished meeting attendees stood within ten feet of her. Did he want the world to know he'd slept with his own assistant?

Maybe he didn't care. Perhaps his reputation as a playboy was a badge of pride.

"How was the Sons of the Garter dinner?" She tried to sound brisk and cheerful.

"Long." Mischief shone in his dark eyes. "Especially when there was somewhere else I'd much rather be." His steady gaze goaded the heat to her chest.

To her poor, beleaguered heart.

She sucked in a deep breath and tried to shove away the emotions barreling through her.

She'd waited for him, fear alternating with hope. *One more night, just to remember.*

Then hope turned back to fear as the hours stretched on and he still didn't come.

Maybe he's hooked up with Faris. Yes, she'd had that thought. And why not? Sebastian was anything but a faithful, one-woman man. She'd be a fool to imagine he was pining for her, too.

What did it matter why he didn't come? If he was too busy. He wasn't hers to pine for.

A gray-haired man in an expensive tweed jacket approached Tessa and she handed him an agenda with a wide smile. She wondered which of the Caspia Designs bigwigs he was.

Sebastian greeted him warmly and they spoke in French.

She didn't understand a word. And why would she? This wasn't her world. Yes, she'd been to the right school, but she'd never moved in these circles where everyone spoke five languages and was old and dear friends with everyone else.

When she realized Sebastian was introducing her, she made an effort to nod and smile. All the while wishing she could run away to hide and lick the wounds that were already so deep they'd take years to stop bleeding.

How could I have been stupid enough to let myself fall in love with him?

Tessa seemed preoccupied and Sebastian couldn't blame her. His own adrenaline ran high as he entered the meeting, flanked by the president of Carriage Leathers and the CEO of Bugaretti Fine Jewelry. The opportunity to turn these fine old companies around and increase their profitability was invigorating.

He began the meeting by inviting the business owners and executives to think outside their well-polished boxes of tradition and habit. When would Tessa make an entrance? Sergei, his father's secretary, was taking the minutes, presumably because some of the principals would be speaking in languages Tessa didn't know.

Still, he expected her to sit in. The inner workings of Caspia Designs were her business, too. Especially now that he was sketching plans to invite her into partnership of a far more permanent kind.

Lunch took place right there in the conference room—colloquially known as the War Room for its role in shaping Caspian history. Still no sign of Tessa.

While the participants drank coffee, Sebastian asked Sergei where she was. The older man glanced about the room, as if Tessa might pop out from behind a gilded column, then shrugged. Strangely anxious, Sebastian slipped out of the room and down the hall to the offices.

His spirits lifted when he saw her packing papers into the cardboard crates used to transport them to New York.

"Tessa." He said her name with a satisfied smile.

But when she looked up, her face was white, her cheeks hollow. Her magical green eyes glazed with unshed tears.

He rushed forward and took her in his arms. "What's the matter?"

"Nothing." She bit her quivering lip.

"Nonsense. Tell me." Urgency made his tone curt. "Please."

"I'm leaving as soon as the meeting is over."

Sebastian waved his hand dismissively. "Don't be ridiculous."

Her big, glittering eyes fixed on his. "I'm not."

"Tessa." He spoke her name like a chant that soothed him. He rubbed his thumb over her chin. Her lip no longer quivered and he wanted to kiss her soft mouth. "After what we've shared, I know you're not still thinking about running off to California with Paul or Peter or whatever his name is."

She trembled in his arms. "I have to go. I'm sorry I can't

fulfill my two weeks' notice but I'm sure you understand why it would not be appropriate for me to work for you any longer…under the circumstances."

The last three words were spoken in a hushed whisper.

"Sebastian! Where are you?" A masculine shout made him jerk his head around. His dad.

"I'm in the file room." He didn't release Tessa from his arms.

His dad called from the doorway. "Sergei's been looking for you. We're all ready to resume the meeting."

"I'll be right there."

Tessa's long golden lashes hid her eyes. "You must go."

"We'll talk after the meeting." He squeezed her arms. He wanted to fold her in his embrace and hold her tight.

"I won't be here." Resolve shimmered in her soft voice.

Panic seized his heart. "You can't leave."

"I must go." He could see her hands were shaking.

"That's impossible." Surely he could prevent this. His ancestors would simply have forbidden her to leave.

But those days were over. Tessa was an independent-minded American—one of the many things he loved about her.

"Sebastian!" The king's voice reverberated off the stone walls. "We're all waiting."

Tessa's fingers pushed against his chest. "Sebastian, *please* go back to the meeting."

He looked deeply into her eyes. She understood about duty. She wouldn't really leave.

He'd asked her to stay and he could always count on Tessa.

He kissed her cool cheek, and released her from his arms. Then he walked away, with unease crawling over his skin.

Back in the meeting, he couldn't settle. The din of the room hurt his ears. Raised voices bounced off the marble columns and the mosaic floors. How could Tessa even think of leaving? Couldn't she see that he needed her?

He dragged his focus back to the agenda, typed by Tessa's elegant fingers. He had a meeting to lead and a company to save, and he was brought up to accept that his duty to his country must come before all other concerns.

At the end of the meeting, Sebastian rose and pushed past the meeting attendees heading for the doorway. He rushed to the office, his heart in his mouth.

But it was empty, except for the neatly stacked crates in the center of the room.

In the hallway he collared Paulo, the footman. "Where's Tessa?"

"I do not know."

"Find her!"

An ugly sensation gripped his gut. Where could she be? He marched along the hallways to her bedroom. He flung open the door, to find Anis changing the bedsheets. "Where's Tessa?"

"I think she left for the airport." The shy maid looked apologetic.

Paulo rushed into the room. "She left for the airport in a car forty minutes ago."

"Dammit!" Sebastian's shout ricocheted off the frescoed ceiling. How could she do this to him? "Get the rear gates open. Now!"

Already he raced along the passages to the garage. He could take his Land Rover through the orchards behind the palace and cut across the fields to the airport.

His father held out his arms for him as he pelted down

the main hallway. "Sebastian, where are you running to? The guests await you at the reception."

"Tessa's gone." He didn't even try to hide the panic in his voice.

"I know, son." His father grasped his arms. "Your mother arranged a private plane for her. It left five minutes ago."

"But why?"

"One cannot always understand the ways of women, my son."

"I must go after her."

"In a plane, to catch her in the skies? It's not possible."

"But I…" He didn't know what to do. This was the first time in his life that a woman had outright rejected him.

Pain seared his heart.

I love her.

He didn't say it though. Even in his distressed state he wasn't ready to confess to loving a woman who didn't love him back. He didn't wish to bring shame on the crown of Caspia.

"Duty comes first, son."

"I know, Papa, but…" Words failed him.

His father patted his cheek. "Come, eat and drink. Some things are meant to be, and some are not. Everything will look brighter in the morning."

Sebastian stumbled after him, his heart hollow with disbelief. His arms ached with the longing to hug her.

Would he never hold Tessa again?

"Sebastian, darling!" He stiffened as Faris's silvery tones rang out behind him. "Wait, sweetheart, my dress is so tight I can't walk fast. And Daddy has a walking stick, remember?"

Sebastian heard the tap of wood on stone and turned around. He didn't want to insult Faris's father. Deon Maridis had been in the meeting, and gracefully endured a harsh critique of his methods of management. Sebastian thanked the older man for his participation and help, and managed a civil greeting to Faris.

A fever of longing and despair racked his body. It was hard to talk, to be polite, when all he wanted to do was follow Tessa.

To the ends of the earth if necessary.

Faris held her father's arm tightly. She knew her family's close relationship with Sebastian's was her trump card where her prince was concerned. Sooner or later he'd see sense and realize he had to marry her.

She intended to make it sooner.

The brief conversation with her father had given her some excellent ideas.

"Sebastian, you seem awfully distracted."

"Long meeting," he grumbled.

"I think you need an evening of delicious relaxation. Perhaps a soak in the warm waters off your private dock, by candlelight? A massage with scented oils?" She waved her fingers in the air, to suggest the delicate motions she'd make on his skin.

Sebastian glanced at her hands and gave her a look of dismay.

Faris faltered. Perhaps her nails were a bit long for massage. Though honestly, she wouldn't mind shredding his flesh to ribbons the way he'd humiliated her the other night at the ball.

But at least one tiresome problem was out of the way.

She'd passed "it" in her car on the way here, and one of the palace servants had confirmed her suspicions. "I hear your assistant went back to New York in a hurry. Did she get tired of Caspia?"

"No," growled Sebastian. He looked away, tension tightening his features.

"Perhaps Caspia grew tired of her?" she purred. Quite likely Sebastian had already tired of boinking his secretary.

Sebastian's eyes flashed. "Why don't you mind your own business?"

They both glanced at her father. Mercifully he was rather deaf, but even he looked up. Sebastian nodded to him, then strode off so fast Faris didn't have a prayer of trying to catch him in her fitted dress.

What had gotten into him?

She knew exactly what had gotten into him.

She frowned, then wiped the unflattering expression away. No sense getting wrinkles over some trampy American chit.

Somehow, Tessa Banks had managed to worm her way into Sebastian's affections. And she, Faris Maridis, future Queen of Caspia, was going to flush her out.

With extreme prejudice.

Eleven

Sebastian woke up and again the hollow sense of loss hit him.

Repeated phone calls to the New York office had gone unanswered. Her cell phone was turned off.

Tessa was AWOL.

Not that he had the power to give her leave to go anywhere, now that she'd quit. He'd instructed that her last paycheck include a substantial bonus. He wanted to prove to her he didn't hold a personal grudge.

And he wanted her back.

His cell rang on the dressing table. He rubbed his face and rolled out of bed, then wearily picked it up.

"Sebastian." His father's voice made him sit up. "There's an article in the papers. Come to the dining room immediately."

Adrenaline snaked through his gut. "What's it about?"

"Just come. Now."

Sebastian pulled on pants and a shirt and slipped his feet into shoes. Could it be about Tessa?

Bad news?

He strode along the empty hallways to the dining room.

Could she be hurt? In trouble? Caught up in something she was afraid to tell him about? That would explain her strange behavior.

If that sleazy lawyer Patrick Ramsay were involved, he'd tear him limb from—

"Mama, Papa, what's the matter?" Their stricken faces stopped him dead in the doorway.

His father tapped the paper in front of him. "The participants of the meeting were sworn to secrecy, were they not?"

Sebastian strode into the room. "Yes. They all signed a confidentiality agreement."

"Then how do you explain *this*?" He pointed to an article near the bottom of the page.

Sebastian grabbed the paper and scanned it.

Caspia Designs Mired in Debt and Mismanagement.

He sucked in a breath as he read. The article was brief. A single column, laying bare the company's recent stagnation and the sliding profits of its component parts. It mentioned large debts recently incurred by Château D'Arc wineries. And the final paragraph outlined a problem that Sebastian had never mentioned outside the meeting—not even to Reed—that the company was plagued by decades of uncollectible accounts, amounting to a potential write-off of more than three million dollars.

He could barely focus on the tiny words.

"Tessa Banks uncovered all those debts, didn't she?" Sebastian's mother took a sip of her coffee.

"There wasn't much to uncover. They were sitting right there in the books. Deon Maridis had been letting accounts receivable slide for years."

His father leaned forward. "Deon saw them as debts from personal friends. Good people who'd pay eventually."

"But they won't, will they?" asked his mom.

"Some of our oldest customers aren't as rich as they used to be." The king sighed and leaned back in his chair. "They rested on their laurels too long just like Caspia Designs. That didn't stop them buying jewels and champagne they couldn't afford, though."

"What would happen if you tried to collect through professionals?" His mom lifted her coffee cup.

Sebastian and his dad stared at her in horror. The king almost rose from his chair. "Shame our friends with lawsuits and public humiliation? Never. I'd pay their debts myself first."

The queen's eyebrows rose. "I hope that won't be necessary."

Sebastian put the paper on the table. "These debts won't matter in the long run. We'll write them off and get the businesses humming the way they should be. Profits will be back up within the year."

His dad clapped his hands together. "Thank heaven we've got Sebastian in on the game to shake things up."

"This article will cause the stock to move, though." Sebastian glanced back at the paper. "And it won't be going up." He whipped his PDA out of his pocket and pulled up his ticker symbols.

An ancient tribal curse fell from his lips.

His father tapped the paper. "Who could have let this leak out? I'd stake my life on the good faith of our principals."

"Pierre de Rochefauld was rather evasive." Sebastian remembered the dismal accounting ledgers Tessa had unearthed on the ancient and unprofitable Château D'Arc wineries. "And he wasn't happy when I read him the riot act for getting his winery into debt this year to pay for repairs to his château."

"But would he want his own debts publicized in an international paper?" His father shook his head. "I think not."

His mother waved her hand dismissively. "I agree with your father. They were all such charming gentlemen. Even the girl from Carriage Leathers was delightful."

"She's not a girl, Mama. She's at least your age."

His mother narrowed her eyes. "What are you implying, Sebastian?"

Sebastian rubbed his temples.

"I know you're fond of Tessa Banks…" His father's soft tone made him look up. "But what do we really know about her?"

Tessa pulled another long strip of packing tape and ripped it off with a loud rasp. She'd well and truly mucked up her life. Now she had to move on whether she wanted to or not.

She'd given notice on her apartment before she left for Caspia and it was already rented for the following month. She had to be out by the end of the day or lose her deposit.

She smoothed the tape over the flaps holding a box shut. Lucky thing she had so little stuff. She could stow it in her parents' basement until she figured out a game plan.

Which was a challenge, since the first thing she'd done when she got back was tell Patrick she wasn't moving to California with him.

Heat crept up her neck in shame at how she'd betrayed him. Cheated on him after only a couple of days in Sebastian's company. She deserved everything that fell on her now.

She hadn't told Patrick what really happened. Just that she'd had a "change of heart." She hadn't even had the guts to tell him face-to-face.

Oddly he'd sounded almost relieved. Maybe he somehow knew she was an unreliable and untrustworthy partner.

And her job at Caspia Designs was history. Even if Sebastian did want to keep her on—she was an efficient and experienced worker, after all—she'd rather be honorably dead than sit there typing his memos while fielding phone calls from his newest girl-of-the-week.

She slumped for a moment and rested her forehead on the cool cardboard of the packing carton. She cut herself some slack by acknowledging she'd had no chance. He was Sebastian. She was doomed the moment he decided to flirt with her.

Her heart still squeezed when she remembered the warmth and passion she'd seen in his dark eyes. Of course it had just been lust, but…

"Oh, dammit all to hell!" She pounded her fist on the box. It would have been so much easier to get on with the rest of her life if she hadn't royally screwed up this part.

No pun intended.

He hadn't called. What had she expected? Besides, she'd mailed her cell phone back to the office. She didn't want him thinking she'd try to sneak any "free perks" on account of their intimacy.

Her door was ajar in a vain attempt to create a cross breeze in her top-floor apartment, and she heard footsteps on the stairs. Tessa frowned. The Man-With-Van wasn't due for another hour. Besides, she hadn't buzzed anyone up, and her neighbors were all at work. "Who's there?"

She sprang to her feet as the door swung open.

"What's the matter?" Sebastian materialized in the doorway.

Her mouth fell open.

"I heard you cry out. Are you okay?" He looked around, taking in all the boxes. The ugly mess that was her upended life.

"Um, sure. I'm fine." She cringed that he'd heard her curse.

Her heart pounded. He'd come after her. Did this mean…?

Hope faded as she looked at him. Tension tightened his hard features and knotted the muscles under his dark gray T-shirt.

An awkward silence thickened the air.

"Are you responsible for the leak to the *Wall Street Journal?*" His black gaze bore into her.

Tessa shrank back. "What? I don't know what you're talking about."

Sebastian's eyes narrowed. "Apart from the principals at the meeting, who all signed a confidentiality agreement, you are the only person who was privy to the most recent financial details. Even the auditors haven't seen them yet."

"And you think I leaked them to the press? I would never do that." Horror soaked through her. He thought she was capable of that kind of betrayal?

She swallowed hard and forced back sharp tears.

Obviously their kisses, their caresses had meant less than nothing to him.

And they'd meant *so much* to her.

He glanced around her apartment. "Moving, I see."

"Yes." She could barely get the word out. She needed him out of here *now,* before she started bawling. "I didn't leak the information and I have packing to do. Could you please leave?"

Her voice quavered on the last word, dangerously close to a sob. Sebastian's expression softened for a moment, then closed over again. Hard and rigid.

He backed toward the door, perhaps unwilling to take his eyes off her because he didn't know what she'd try next.

She held herself steady, lifted her chin. Dared him to believe what he wanted about her.

His unrelenting gaze made her knees tremble, as it always had. But this time a claw of sadness gripped her heart.

He turned and left the room.

Tessa sagged, barely able to stay on her feet as she watched him head for the stairs.

She knew it was just a fling. A stupid fling. A mistake.

Her carefully planned future with Patrick might not have been filled with sweaty nights of passion, but it could have brought the joys of children and family life. That was a dream that might have actually come true.

But now? She'd chucked it all away to fall madly in love with a man who thought so little of her that he believed she'd betray him and his company.

A loud, ugly sob flew from her mouth.

Did he think she was out for revenge?

Perhaps she should want revenge for how he'd seduced her. She felt so broken now. Something had been taken from her, something she never knew she had until Sebastian found it deep in her.

The capacity for sheer joy.

Now that she'd lain in Sebastian's arms, her body intertwined with his hard muscle, her mind and soul aloft with bliss, she'd never be happy with an ordinary "relationship" again.

Sebastian crashed down the stairs, his heart racing.

He had a hard time thinking straight after he saw those boxes. Tessa was packing to move to California, exactly as she'd planned.

He'd planned to greet her warmly, win her back. Until he saw that she'd already moved on. Left him behind, part of her old life.

He hadn't meant to rudely accuse her, but the pain of seeing her preparing for her new life without him had cut him to the quick and made fresh, poisonous doubts spring into his mind.

She'd denied leaking the information, but she'd seemed tense, strung out...*afraid.*

Like someone who'd done something they shouldn't have.

He thumped his hand on the metal railing and cursed the hot wave of desire that had crashed through him at the sight of her face. Of her long, lean body encased in faded jeans and a skimpy white tank top.

His chest ached, too. He'd climbed the stairs on a crest of anticipation and adrenaline, footsteps springing with hope and excitement at the prospect of seeing Tessa again.

But those emerald eyes had greeted him with suspicion.

With hostility.

An ugly curse flew from his lips as he bolted out into the hot, late-September-afternoon sun of the Brooklyn street. His limo was parked up the block and he stalked over to it in the foulest mood of his life.

How could he have been so wrong about her? He'd dreamed of making her his future queen. Of sharing his life with her.

Was she angry he'd forced her to stay when she wanted to go to California? Was she upset that he'd seduced her?

He slammed the limo door and fell against the seat. "Back to Park Avenue." His driver had the tact not to turn around or inquire after his activities.

Sebastian clenched his fists as regret soaked through him. He'd coaxed Tessa into bed while she was an employee and he had authority over her. And when he knew that she was involved with another man.

Maybe she had good reason to be angry.

He could have handled things differently.

No, he couldn't. He'd been completely besotted by her. Common sense didn't stand a chance when he saw the Caspian sun dance in her golden hair and heard her laughter mingle with birdsong high on the mountaintop.

He held his head in his hands.

Tessa was still leaving for California with another man.

Sebastian's first experience with total rejection hurt like a crushing blow to his chest. His natural instinct was to fight back, to slay his opponent and emerge victorious in the tradition of his ancestors.

But he was wise enough to know that no true victory came from sheer force.

The phone was ringing as he shoved open the door to his apartment at 721 Park Avenue. He walked right past the phone on the foyer table, slammed into the kitchen and poured himself a glass of water, waiting for the machine to pick up.

Incessantly it rang, pounding his aching brain. The machine must be full. That happened sometimes when there was no one around to check it. Now he needed a new house sitter *and* a new assistant. Was there no one he could depend on?

He marched back into the foyer, picked up the receiver and barked, "What?"

"Sebastian, darling."

Faris. He narrowly resisted the urge to slam the phone down. It was probably she who had filled the machine, though, so he might as well find out what she wanted and get her out of his hair.

"I heard how your former assistant leaked proprietary information to the *Wall Street Journal*. I'm just sick about it! You think you know people, but you can't trust anyone these days. It's so hard to find good staff."

Sebastian's tongue twitched with words that might have flown off it if he weren't so used to representing his nation in everything he said and did.

"We don't know who leaked the information." He hated Faris gloating over Tessa's betrayal. It fomented something ugly and painful in his gut.

"Oh, come on, darling! I know you had a bit of a soft spot for her, but really. They probably threw some money at her and she blabbed it all."

"I hardly think the *Wall Street Journal* is offering cash for tip-offs."

"All those proprietary details. Shocking! I do hope she doesn't spill any other more *personal* information to the press." Her smarmy tone made his back stiffen.

"Tessa would never do that." His voice rumbled with conviction that he truly felt.

"Still defending her? Oh, sweetheart, I'd better fly out there and kiss you all better."

"Please don't." He ended the call, his flesh crawling at the prospect of Faris's lip-gloss-drenched kisses.

Something still gnawed at him.

And it wasn't anything as transient as lust.

It was doubt.

Could Tessa really have leaked company information? He couldn't truly accept the idea. Defending her came as naturally as breathing.

Probably because he was such a sucker for her.

He slammed the phone into its cradle on the hall table, which caused a cascade amongst the mail piled there. Envelopes, cards and junk mail slid down onto the parquet floor.

He bent to grab a handful of it, and something caught his eye.

An envelope. A slim beige rectangle. Nothing strange about it, except that it looked eerily familiar.

He slit it open with his thumb.

Black ink crawled over the pages like a drunken spider. "Sebastian darling, I…" He crumpled it and was about to throw it on the floor when that gnawing sensation in his gut turned into sharp claws.

He unfolded the paper with the same revulsion he'd felt at the dining table in Caspia when he opened an identical envelope with an identical piece of paper inside it.

Different writing. Same person.

He let the paper and his hand fall to the table and he leaned on it for a moment. Faris had written him that sleazy, threatening note telling him not to marry a foreign bride and insulting Tessa by name.

That truly surprised him. He wouldn't have thought even Faris capable of something quite so vulgar.

What else might she try?

The spore of suspicion mushroomed in his brain. Her father was in the meeting about Caspia Designs. Faris could easily have teased some details about the company out of him.

Another thought soaked into his cortex. The article had very specific information about Château D'Arc and its disastrous recent debts. No doubt the reason Pierre de Rochefauld had been so reluctant to show his face at the meeting.

But Tessa didn't know about the new debts. They didn't come up until late in the afternoon.

After she'd already left.

A fierce surge of adrenaline stung Sebastian's muscles. He was going to the offices of the *Wall Street Journal* right now to find out the source of this information.

As he strode through the lobby of his building, mind racing, he almost knocked right into his neighbor Amanda Crawford. The lively event planner was tall, blond and beautiful.

But she wasn't Tessa.

He managed a friendly greeting and a kiss on the cheek.

She gave him a faux-stern look. "I don't think I ever got your RSVP for our party celebrating the landmark status of this old heap." She gestured around the glittering marbled space of the lobby.

"Oh, yeah." He grimaced. "Sorry, my mail is a disaster as I haven't been here much. Carrie quit and I don't have a new house sitter yet. I saw the invite in the mess, though. I'll be sure to come if I'm in the country."

Amanda leaned into him, her gray eyes twinkling with mischief. "Lucky thing you're so lovable, Sebastian. You already missed the party. But never mind about that, you've also missed the juiciest gossip of the decade while you were away. The police seem to think that Marie Endicott's death was a homicide."

Sebastian froze. "You're kidding." Marie was the younger sister of his friend Drew from boarding school. He'd known her as a cute, curly-haired pest, then later as a successful woman with her own real-estate firm. She'd lived in the building for a while, until one day she jumped off the roof. An apparent suicide.

Amanda grabbed his arm. "Not kidding. Apparently there are tapes of the incident. From security cameras on the roof. I guess they prevent burglars sneaking in from adjoining buildings or something. But the tapes have gone missing."

Sebastian's chest tightened. "That's terrible. Who would kill Marie?"

"That's what everyone wants to know. Bizarre, isn't it?" Her conspiratorial whisper chilled his blood.

How did such terrible things happen? His heart went out to her brother and parents. "I hope they catch whoever did it. Let me know if there's anything I can do to help."

"It's shocking how many crimes go unsolved in this city." Amanda shook her head.

He bid her goodbye, cursing the harm cruel people inflict on others.

I know one crime that won't go unsolved.

Sebastian wasn't leaving the newspaper offices until he uncovered the source of the leak.

Twelve

Sebastian flew out of the *Wall Street Journal* offices on a wave of excitement.

A staffer told him the story was put together at the European office in Brussels, where one of Sebastian's oldest friends worked as an editor. Sebastian got his friend on the phone, he'd talked to the reporter, and within minutes he had all the information he needed. He didn't even have to ask them to reveal their source.

Faris had leaked the information.

Keeping calm, Sebastian offered a story on how he intended to turn the companies around within the year. He talked to a New York reporter for more than an hour about Caspia Designs and its challenges and prospects for the future, until Sebastian excused himself on the pretext of urgent business.

Very urgent business.

He jumped into his waiting limo and slammed the door. "Tessa's apartment in Brooklyn, and hurry!"

Tessa had nothing to do with the story. The reporter confirmed that he had never heard of her.

Sebastian's heart threatened to beat right out of his chest as he thought of the way he'd cruelly accused her and refused to take her word for her innocence. He wouldn't be able to eat or sleep until he'd offered her his most profound apologies.

But she wasn't there.

Repeated ringing on the doorbell followed by calling up to the open windows brought one of her neighbors to the door. The bearded young man explained that she'd moved out, with all her belongings, about two hours earlier.

She'd left no forwarding address.

Cursing, Sebastian figured he'd earned the humiliation of tracking her down at Patrick Ramsay's. It didn't take long to find out where the divorce-lawyer-to-the-stars kept his private office, and Sebastian pulled up in front of the midtown brownstone intent on a dignified and gentlemanly exchange.

As he climbed out of the car, the man in question appeared at the top of the wide stairs, wearing a gray pin-striped suit and carrying a furled umbrella.

Sebastian squared his shoulders. "I'd like to see Tessa."

Pale eyes squinted at him. "Who are you?"

"Sebastian Stone. I'm her…" His heart yearned to say "I'm her lover" but he held himself in check. "I'm her former employer."

"Oh, right. The *prince*." His tone of derision caused Sebastian's hackles to rise.

Still, this was the man Tessa had chosen. He held himself steady. "May I speak with her, please?"

"You may speak with whomever you like. You won't find her here, though."

"Where is she?"

"Hell if I know. I got a Dear John phone call a few days ago. Just as well, as I've been offered a big new case here in New York and won't be able to make the move we'd discussed. I assume she told you that we were—"

"Yes." Sebastian cut him off before he could use any unpleasant descriptive phrases. A ray of hope flashed through him as the lawyer's words sank into his brain. "She broke off with you?"

"Yes. Ironic, really, since a week ago she was hinting about marriage and all that jazz. Hardly my cup of tea when I spend all day rending asunder what the good Lord has joined together." He laughed.

Sebastian clenched his fists. "Where do you think she went?"

"No idea. For all I know, she went to California without me."

Panic flashed through Sebastian.

"I doubt it, though," Patrick continued. "She didn't know anyone there and she's not the type to jump off a precipice." He leaned toward Sebastian. "She's a sweet girl. You will give her job back if she asks, won't you?"

"Yes," Sebastian rasped, slightly revising his opinion of Ramsay.

But I hope to give her so much more.

He headed to where his limo idled in an illegal parking space. As they drove back to Park Avenue, he tried to rack his mind for someone who might know where Tessa would be. Maybe if he combed through the Rolodex she'd recently reorganized for him, he'd come up with something.

He'd left her on the brink of tears, devastated that he thought her a traitor to the company.

He'd assumed her behavior sprang from guilt. Now he was sure—so sure—that it came from the pain of seeing his lack of faith in her.

He crashed through the doors of 721 Park Avenue with such force that the women waiting for the elevator swung around to see what all the commotion was. Carrie and Julia.

Carrie waved. "Hi, Sebastian." His former house sitter looked radiant with happiness. She still lived in the building with her husband, Trent Tanford. Sebastian held Trent personally responsible for his own overloaded answering machine and teetering stacks of mail.

Still, he didn't begrudge Carrie her happiness. He kissed her on both cheeks. "Marriage appears to be treating you well."

"It is. And we're getting married again." She blushed.

"Already? To whom?" He raised an eyebrow and tried not to grin.

"Each other, of course. But our last wedding was kind of…rushed. This time we're going to make it perfect." Her eyes sparkled. "You will come, won't you?"

"I can never resist a wedding." Sebastian did enjoy weddings, with their promise of a bright future and children and the continuation of life's cycle. All Caspians loved weddings.

His heart squeezed.

If he could just find Tessa and convince her to marry him.

"Do you notice something different about Julia?"

"What?" Carrie's words tugged him back to the present. He scanned Julia. He'd heard that the former resident of his building had married Wall Street whiz Max Rolland a couple of months ago. She'd moved into his place just a block or so away. Julia looked lovely as always, her blue eyes shining and her skin glowing with good health. Perhaps a little plumper than usual, but he wasn't idiotic enough to say that.

Julia laughed. "I'm pregnant, Sebastian. Five months, in fact, so don't worry about noticing my expanded girth."

"Congratulations." He kissed her on both cheeks, and again for luck. His heart tugged again. "Your baby will bring you and Max so much joy."

Joy he wanted to share with Tessa.

Pain sent a surge of adrenaline spearing through him. He grabbed Carrie's arm. "Carrie, you and Tessa were friends, weren't you?"

"Sure. What's up?"

"I must find her. She quit her job and now she's moved out of her apartment. She left no forwarding address and I…" Words failed him as he scanned her face, hoping she could help.

Understanding dawned in Carrie's sharp and compassionate eyes. "I think she said something about going to her parents' house in Connecticut until she finds a new place. They live in Stamford. I have the address upstairs. Come on up and I'll give it to you."

Sebastian drove his own car to Stamford. He didn't want a driver idling nearby, glancing at his watch. Even his Alfa Romeo seemed wound-up and jumpy, and the traffic on I-95 ratcheted his blood pressure higher as the day stretched into late afternoon.

What if she wasn't there? He'd thought about calling but decided not to. If he were Tessa, he'd slam the phone down on himself.

What he had to say could only be said face-to-face.

He hated GPS, but as he drove into the labyrinth of the old coastal city he turned it on and punched in her address. Neat brick pseudo mansions lined clean, quiet streets. Already he found himself scanning the sidewalks for signs of Tessa.

He turned again, onto a sloping street of older wooden houses, and again into a street of modest homes facing a weedy basketball court.

Sebastian snapped to attention. Basketball. Could this be her old neighborhood? There were people on the streets and he was tempted to stop and ask about Tessa, but the GPS told him to keep driving, so he pushed onward.

It finally brought him to a stop in front of a tiny, mint-green cottage, surrounded by a chain-link fence. A huge oak tree towered over the tiny structure, shading out all possibility of grass in the postage-stamp-sized lot.

Tessa grew up here? When she'd said she came from a modest background, he'd imagined an ordinary suburban home with a grassy yard and a large dog. And a garden shed the size of this house.

But as he stepped out of the car and rounded the oak tree he saw a familiar slender form, bent at the waist, her tempting backside jutting toward him.

Joy surged through him. "Tessa."

She glanced up, startled. She held a paintbrush between her teeth, and quickly removed it as she registered his presence. A can of red paint sat on the sidewalk. She unbent herself to reveal a half-painted metal mailbox.

Then she went back to painting it.

She didn't say anything at all.

Sebastian approached her, his heart so full it could burst. "Tessa, I'm here to offer my most humble apologies. I know you didn't leak the story and I should never have accused you. I'm sorry from the bottom of my heart."

She didn't look up. He thought for a second that her hand trembled, but it kept moving, making strokes of red paint over the battered metal of the mailbox.

An emotional outpouring of Caspian words flooded his brain, but he forced himself to slow down and think in English.

"Faris leaked the story. I suspect she did it to come between you and me."

Her hand paused in its brushing motion, muscles tight. "It really doesn't matter who leaked the story." She stared at the mailbox. "I don't even care if you believe it was me. It won't make any difference in the long run. You'll turn the company around and everything will be fine."

Her voice was flat. Lifeless. Her hair was pulled back in a ponytail and loose strands fell to cover her face, hiding her from him. The air had cooled and she wore a gray sweatshirt, but he could still see the tension in her neck and shoulders.

Was she afraid to turn and look at him?

Pain jerked through him and he stepped forward and grabbed her arm holding the brush.

She felt warm and alive, and already sweet relief cascaded through him. *He'd found her.*

When she glanced up, her wide green eyes brimmed

with tears. Distress shadowed her lovely features and her usual glow had dimmed almost out of existence.

His chest constricted. "I'm so, so sorry." The words fell from his lips. Almost meaningless. They weren't the words he wanted to say. That he needed to say.

"You're on my mind day and night. My flesh aches for you and my heart craves you close." His voice trembled as hope and longing overflowed.

She blinked, startled. Two fat sparkling tears rolled from her beautiful eyes.

He reached up and brushed one away with his thumb. He inhaled deeply.

This was no time for caution or royal dignity.

"I love you, Tessa, and I can't live without you."

Tessa blinked rapidly, trying to clear her eyes. She couldn't see through the mist of tears and she wanted to make sure she was really awake and right here on the planet earth. She barely believed this scene could exist outside of her imagination.

Sebastian's face hovered inches in front of hers, his forehead creased with concern and his dark, expressive eyes fixed on hers.

I love you.

Surely she hadn't heard those words. But they echoed in her ears, off the great oak tree, off the faded aluminum siding of the house behind her.

Her stunned silence seemed to encourage him. He took her hand in his. The warmth of his touch was like a shot of adrenaline to her heart, which kicked inside her chest.

Painful.

He raised her hands and kissed her knuckles. Which,

she noticed with embarrassment, were smeared with red paint.

"Each day without you has shown me how much I want you in my life. How much I need you." His intense, dark gaze stole her breath. "I know you ended your relationship with Patrick and I...I beg you to come home with me. I want you by my side, every day, for the rest of my life."

Tessa's mind swam as shivers of amazement skittered over her flesh. *Could he really mean it?*

The sound of a car horn a block away yanked her back to the present. To the tiny front yard with its chipped mailbox. The ordinary street with its motley collection of the least-valuable real estate in Stamford.

She gestured around her. "Sebastian, this is where I come from. I'm not royal, or aristocratic, or any of the things you'd need in a...partner."

She didn't say the word *wife*. He hadn't asked her to marry him.

"Where you come from doesn't matter. I come from Caspia and I'm in love with an American woman. Nothing is more natural than two people falling in love. You and I are meant to be together. I know it in my soul."

He squeezed her hands and the truth of his words echoed in her heart.

The screech of hinges made her glance up to see her mother in the doorway of the house.

"What's going on out here, dear?" Her mom came out of the doorway and down the single step.

Tessa tugged her hands and Sebastian released them. "Um, Mom, this is Sebastian Stone. He's my...boss." Her face heated. "My former boss."

Sebastian strode forward, past the paint can and up the

cracked front walk. He looked huge in the minuscule front yard. He also towered over her tiny, gray-haired mom, who pulled her sweater about her to ward off a sudden September chill.

He held out his hand. "Mrs. Banks, it's an honor to meet you."

"Sebastian Stone...the prince?"

He bowed slightly. "At your service, madam."

"Well." Her mom smiled, a flush lighting her smooth cheeks. "Tessa has told us a lot about you. She had a lovely time visiting your country and I told her she was silly to leave her good job."

Tessa swallowed.

"I think she was absolutely right to quit." Sebastian's voice rang out in the quiet neighborhood.

Tessa froze.

"I've been wasting her talents on filing and office duties, when she's capable of so much more."

He took her mother's hand in both of his. "Mrs. Banks, did you ever think of moving to a warmer, more cheerful climate?"

Her mom hesitated, looking confused, then turned back into the house. "Harry, come here, dear."

Tessa shoved a hand through her hair, which wasn't a good idea since it was in a ponytail and her hand had paint on it. Her heart thudded so loud she was sure they could hear it. What on earth was Sebastian doing?

Her father shuffled forward, using a walker because of his advanced osteoarthritis. He hesitated at the step, and Tessa moved to help him down, but Sebastian beat her to it, offering his strong arm for support.

Her mom patted her dad's arm. "Harry, it's Tessa's

boss. The prince." She hissed the last word as if it was some kind of hint.

"Pleased to meet you, young man."

Tessa smiled as her dad's rich, self-confident voice echoed in the air. He wasn't intimidated by anything, least of all royalty. He and Sebastian shook hands. "My daughter tells me you have a beautiful country."

"Caspia is indeed the loveliest place on earth. I think you'd like it very much if you were to visit."

"I don't doubt it. We're dreading another winter. I can feel its teeth already. We're trying to figure out how to move to Florida." Her father laughed.

"Caspia is warm and dry year-round, and we treasure people of mature years for their wisdom and experience."

Tessa's eyes widened.

"We have the highest life expectancy of any country on earth, so you can tell we take good care of our older citizens. If you were to move to Caspia for your golden years, you would find the climate salubrious and the people most friendly and welcoming."

"It does sound pleasant." Her father smiled and glanced at Tessa, obviously as perplexed as she was. "We'd better leave you two young people to your business, right, dear?" He winked at her mother.

Tessa gulped. She stayed rooted in place while her dad shuffled back inside with her mother fussing over him.

Once the door was closed, she put her hands on her hips. "What's going on?"

Sebastian marched back toward her and took her hands again. Excitement sparkled in his eyes. "If you're moving to Caspia, your parents must come, too."

"What are you talking about?"

He looked amused. "I'm proposing to you, of course."

Proposing what, exactly? Her heart beat so fast and hard she couldn't speak. Which was fine, as she had no idea what to say.

Sebastian pulled a ring off his little finger.

Tessa gulped. *Was he—?*

He eased himself down so that one knee rested on the concrete pavers of the front walk.

Blood rushed to her brain and she found herself gasping for breath.

Sebastian bent his head for a moment, then looked up at her. "Tessa, I wish to spend the rest of my life by your side. I've been waiting all my life for you. I know you're the woman who was born to be my queen one day."

Her legs grew shaky. *Queen?*

"I promise to be a caring and faithful husband and a loving father to our children."

Children? Her heart squeezed.

"I wish for you to have the happy life you were prepared to move to an unknown city for, except I wish to share it with you in Caspia."

Tears gathered in her eyes again. She couldn't help it. It was too perfect, too wonderful.

Sebastian cleared his throat. He looked into her eyes with a gaze so filled with emotion that it stole her breath. "Tessa Banks, will you be my wife?"

The words, thick with feeling, shuddered through her and shook her to her core.

But no response came to her lips.

It was too good to be true. It couldn't be real.

She shook her head, trying to scatter the thoughts that crowded her like gulls at a beach picnic.

Sebastian took her hand, and for a moment she thought he was going to force the ring onto her trembling fingers.

But he didn't. He squeezed her hand gently and rubbed her palm with his thumb. Then he stood and closed his warm, strong arms around her shaking shoulders.

"I love you, Tessa. Maybe I'm coming on too strong and trying to rush you too much. It's okay if you're not ready to agree right now. Being a queen is not something everyone aspires to."

Queen? She'd forgotten about that part. Of course she couldn't marry him. He'd come to his senses and realize what a horrible mistake he'd made soon enough.

"I can't be a queen." Her voice sounded high and thin as she admitted her failing. "I know I sound like one of your crowd because I went to St. Peter's, but deep inside I'll always be Tessa Banks, from right here."

The lowering sun threw unflattering harsh shadows over the less-than-elegant surroundings. A group of kids on their way home from school called out to them, whistling and laughing.

Sebastian resisted her attempt to pull away and tugged her closer. "I know you will always be Tessa Banks, from right here." His eyes shone. "That's one of the many things I love about you. You're down-to-earth and practical and you don't expect to have life handed to you on a silver platter. You're warm and funny and brave and beautiful, and I love you exactly as you are." He stroked her cheek, making her skin hum. "We'll share a good life together."

Oh, dear. Tears filled her eyes again. The worst part was that she believed him. She could so easily picture a full and happy life with Sebastian: nights in his embrace, days in the beautiful Caspian countryside, children running along the palace corridors, breakfast in the royal dining room…

With the king and queen.

That splash of cold reality snapped her back to her senses. "Sebastian, I'm sure you would be a fantastic husband and father, but there are a lot of people who'd be very unhappy to see us married. Your mother, for example."

Sebastian pressed his face into her neck, which sent a rush of heat flooding through her. "Don't worry about my mother. She can be silly and snobbish sometimes, but it's just the way she was brought up. She's a good person at heart. I know you won't believe me now, but I think the two of you will be close friends one day."

Tessa wanted to laugh. He spoke of the future, so certain it would happen. Her doubts were irrelevant.

How could you not love that kind of confidence?

"My father adores you." He nuzzled her gently. "He offered his full approval of any intentions I had toward you."

Tessa jerked back. "You told him you had intentions toward me?"

"No, but I guess it was written all over my face and he wanted to let me know it was okay."

"I guess that was before you all decided that I leaked the story." She narrowed her eyes.

"No, it was after." He grinned. "I guess that's when Dad knew I was really serious about you. I didn't believe the leak could be you until I came to your apartment and found you packing up—to move away with another man, I thought—and you were so nervous and evasive. I didn't know what to think, except that I was losing you."

Tessa let out something between a laugh and a sob. "I couldn't stand to be near you in case you found out how crazy I am about you. I was so humiliated by being in love with you when I thought I was just another notch on your royal bedpost."

Sebastian threw his head back and laughed. "You do love me, too! I knew it."

She cocked her head. "No one could accuse you of lacking self-assurance."

"True, true. But I must assure you that those notches on my bedpost date back to an entirely different generation. Somewhere around the late sixteenth century, we think." His eyes glittered with mischief.

"I guess that's a liability of hanging on to used furniture."

His mouth fought a smile. "Caspians are practical people. We're satisfied with the best of everything and we don't give it up easily." He pulled back a little. His dark eyes looked at her steadily. "I know you fell in love with Caspia, as well as with me."

"You make me sound so promiscuous." She tried to laugh, but his serious gaze demanded a real answer. "Yes, I did. I'd never dreamed such a magical place could exist. I confess I've missed Caspia almost as much as I've missed you."

"Your parents would be happy there."

Her chest tightened. How typical of Sebastian to make plans for everyone. "It was thoughtful of you to consider them."

"I'm Caspian. Family is the foundation of our culture." His gaze softened. "And I wish for you and I to create the next generation together."

It was lucky Sebastian held her tight, or she might have collapsed into a swoon and cracked her skull on the concrete. Too many dreams coming true all at once could be dangerous for a girl.

"Your role as queen will not always be easy, since being a monarch does come with responsibilities, but I know you're resourceful enough to handle your role with grace and ease."

She bit her lip. Put like that, as a *job,* even being queen did seem…doable. She was nothing if not a hard worker. She blew out a long, shaky breath.

"Let's try this again." Sebastian loosened his hold on her, and lifted the hand holding the ring. "Tessa Banks, will you be my wife?"

She stared at the ring, a gold hoop scrolled with vines. "Yes." She stared into his dark eyes. Passion shone there, and love, and the promise of the joy they could share. "Yes. I will."

He slid the ring onto her ring finger. Her skin tingled as the cool metal settled into place. The ring was far too big, but somehow it felt exactly right.

Sebastian gathered her in his arms and kissed her with a desperate urgency that echoed her own. Desire and hope crackled through her with electric force.

She clung to him, to his sturdy strength, as the fear and hurt and sadness that had hounded her home from Caspia wafted away on the late-afternoon breeze.

She'd hoped for a loving husband to create a family with. Little did she know she'd been working with him for nearly five years.

She knew Sebastian so well that of course she loved him. She'd dreamed of touching him, of kissing him, of being held in his arms, but she'd never dared to dream of sharing her life with him.

Her dreams and reality had crashed into each other with explosive force, lighting up a future brighter than anything she could have imagined.

Sebastian's tongue sent shivers of excitement chasing through her. Resisting the urge to writhe against him, she opened her eyes. "Hey, I have a reputation to protect in this neighborhood."

"You're not allowed to kiss your husband?"

She stared at him. "When you put it that way, I guess it's okay."

His lips settled back over hers as his powerful arms held her close. Warmth and pleasure suffused her whole body, until she floated on a cloud of joy.

She still felt like Tessa Banks, from right here.

Except that now she was the happiest woman on earth.

* * * * *

Have Your Say

You've just finished your book.
So what did you think?

We'd love to hear your thoughts on our
'Have your say' online panel
www.millsandboon.co.uk/haveyoursay

- 🌹 Easy to use
- 🌹 Short questionnaire
- 🌹 Chance to win Mills & Boon® goodies

Visit us Online

Tell us what you thought of this book now at
www.millsandboon.co.uk/haveyoursay

YOUR_SA